Harlequin Man of the Month Collection

Passionate, honorable…and a little arrogant—these men are always sexy and completely irresistible.

Whether heading an international empire, saving a family's legacy or leading a kingdom, our heroes live life with undeniable passion. And within the pages of this special collection they meet their match in beautiful, intelligent and determined women who are up to the challenge of winning the hearts of these formidable men!

Wherever you find them—at the office, on an island or in the bedroom—these heroes are sure to seduce, because above all else they know that love is the greatest goal.

If you enjoy these two classic Man of the Month stories, be sure to check out more books featuring strong, captivating heroes from the Harlequin Desire line.

USA TODAY Bestselling Author

Katherine Garbera
and

New York Times Bestselling Author

Elizabeth Bevarly

AN IRRESISTIBLE TEMPTATION

HARLEQUIN® MAN OF THE MONTH

Recycling programs
for this product may
not exist in your area.

ISBN-13: 978-0-373-60106-6

An Irresistible Temptation

Copyright © 2015 by Harlequin Books S.A.

The publisher acknowledges the copyright holders
of the individual works as follows:

Master of Fortune
Copyright © 2010 by Katherine Garbera

The Temptation of Rory Monahan
Copyright © 2001 by Elizabeth Bevarly

This edition published by arrangement with Harlequin Books S.A.

For questions and comments about the quality of this book,
please contact us at CustomerService@Harlequin.com.

Printed in U.S.A.

CONTENTS

MASTER OF FORTUNE
Katherine Garbera

This book is dedicated to Rob, Courtney, Lucas, Josh and Tabby for making our summer in England so much fun and for putting up with me saying "just one more photo!!"

Acknowledgments

I'd like to thank my good friend Kenny Howes for answering my questions about the music industry; Kenny has been rocking out for as long as I've known him. Any mistakes in this book are my own.

I'd also like to thank Krista Stroever for all of her hard work on editing this manuscript. Also a quick shout-out to my friends who always have my back: Nancy and Mary Louise—you guys rock!

Prologue

"Why are we here?" Henry Devonshire asked. He sat in the boardroom of the Everest Group in downtown London. A nice view of the Thames was visible through the plate-glass windows.

"Malcolm has prepared a message for you."

"Why should we listen to this?" Henry faced the lawyer across the polished boardroom table.

"I think you'll find your father's—"

"Malcolm. Don't call him my father."

The Everest Group had always been Malcolm Devonshire's life. Of course, now that he'd turned seventy, it was no surprise that the old man had gotten in touch with him and his half brothers. He probably wanted to make sure that his life's work didn't end with his own death.

Geoff was the eldest of the three of them. Henry

couldn't really say much about the other men. He didn't know either of his half brothers any better than he did their biological father. Geoff's very aristocratic English-looking nose betrayed his place in the current royal family.

"Mr. Devonshire is dying," Edmond Strom said. "He wants the legacy he worked so hard to create to live on in each of you."

Edmond was Malcolm's…butler, Henry thought. Or maybe man of affairs would be more apt.

"He didn't create the legacy for us," Steven said. He was the youngest.

"Well, he has an offer for the three of you now," Edmond said.

Henry had actually met his father's lawyer and personal assistant more times than he had his father. Edmond had been the one to deliver Christmas and birthday presents when he'd been younger.

"If you would all please sit down and allow me to explain," Edmond said.

Henry took a seat at the end of the conference table. He had been a rugby player and a pretty good one to boot, but that had never gotten him the one thing he'd really craved—Malcolm's acknowledgment of him. He couldn't explain it any better than that. His own father had never recognized any of Henry's accomplishments. So he had stopped looking for it and gone his own way.

Which didn't explain why he was here now. Maybe it was simple curiosity about the old man.

Edmond passed three file folders across the table, one to each of them. Henry flipped his open and saw the letter his father had written to the three of them.

Geoff, Henry and Steven;

I have been diagnosed with terminal brain cancer. I've exhausted every avenue to try to prolong my life and have now come to believe I only have six months left.

None of you owe me allegiance, but I hope that the company that brought me into contact with your mothers will continue to prosper and grow under your leadership.

Each of you will control one of the divisions. You will be judged on the profit you make in your segment. Whoever shows the best acumen for running their segment will be appointed CEO and Chairman of The Everest Group.

Geoff—Everest Airlines. His time as an RAF pilot and traveling the globe will serve him well.

Henry—Everest Records. I expect him to sign the music groups he's already helped make their way up the charts.

Steven—Everest Mega Stores. Hopefully his genius for knowing what the retail public wants will not fail him.

Edmond will monitor your progress and make reports to me. I would have come to speak with you today, but my doctors have confined me to my bed.

I have one caveat. You must all avoid scandal and focus on running your segment or the deal is off, regardless of profit. The one mistake I made in my life was letting my personal life distract me from my business. I hope the three of you can

benefit from my mistakes and I trust you will accept this challenge.

Yours,

Malcolm Devonshire

Henry shook his head. The old man had just said
he considered their births a mistake. Henry had no
idea how Geoff and Steven would feel about that, but
it ticked him off. "I'm not interested."

"Before you turn down Malcolm's offer, you should
know that if any of you opt out, the money that was put
in trust for your mothers and for each of you will be for-
feit upon his death. The company would retain it all."

"I don't need his money," Geoff said.

Henry didn't either, but his mother might. She and
her second husband had two sons they were raising.
Though Gordon made a decent wage as head coach for
the London Irish, they could always use a little extra,
especially since they'd have to pay for university for
those boys.

"May we have a moment to discuss this alone?" Steven asked.

Edmond nodded and left the room. As soon as the
door closed behind Edmond, Steven stood up.

"I think we should do it," Steven said.

"I'm not so sure," Geoff said. "He shouldn't put any
stipulations on his will. If he wants to leave us something, so be it."

"But this affects our mums," Henry said, siding with
Steven as he gave this more thought. Malcolm had broken off all contact with his mum once she was pregnant. That had always bothered him. He'd like to give
her something of Malcolm's…the thing that Malcolm

had prized more than any of the actual living people who'd been in his life.

"It does affect them," Geoff said, leaning back in his chair as he thought it over. "I see your point. If you two are in then I'll do it, as well. I don't need his approval or his money."

"Me, either."

"So we're all in?" Henry asked.

"I am," Geoff said.

"I think he owes our mothers something on top of child support. And the chance to turn a bigger profit than he did? Now *that's* something I can't resist."

Chapter 1

Astrid Taylor had started working for the Everest Group exactly one week ago, and her job as it had been described to her had sounded…like a glorified nanny but it paid well and that was all that mattered right now. She was to be an assistant to one of Malcolm Devonshire's sons.

Her experience as an executive assistant for legendary record producer Mo Rollins had ensured she'd get the job with Everest Records. She was glad they hadn't asked too many questions about her dismissal from her last job.

"Hello, Ms. Taylor, I'm Henry Devonshire."

"Hello, Mr. Devonshire. I'm happy to make your acquaintance."

Henry held his hand out to her and she shook it. He had big blunt hands with neatly trimmed square nails.

His square-jawed face sported a nose that looked as though it may have been broken more than once. Only fitting since he'd been a first-class rugby player until an injury sidelined him. He was still lean and athletic looking.

"I need you in my office in five minutes," he told her. "Bring everything you have on Everest Group Records. Financials, groups we have signed, groups we should drop."

"Yes, sir, Mr. Devonshire," she said.

He paused on the threshold before entering his inner office and smiled at her. "Call me Henry."

She nodded. Dang it, he had a perfect smile. The kind that left her feeling utterly gob smacked. Which was ridiculous. She'd read the reports in the tabloids and gossip magazines—he was a player. One with a different girl every night, she reminded herself.

"Please, call me Astrid," she said.

He nodded. "Have you been working here long?"

"Only a week. I was hired to work specifically with you."

"Good, then you won't be torn about who is in charge," he said.

"No, sir, you're the boss," she quipped.

"Indeed I am."

She started pulling together the reports he'd asked for. Since her career-ending affair at her last place of employment, she'd made a promise to herself to be utterly professional this time. She had always liked men and, to be honest, knew she flirted more than she should, but it was her way.

She watched him walk away. Flirting in the office was a bad idea, but he was charming. It wasn't as if

Henry Devonshire was going to make a real pass at her. His social circles contained supermodels. But she'd always had a weakness for blue eyes and a charming smile. It didn't hurt matters that she'd had a little crush on Henry Devonshire when he'd been introduced as the starting flanker for the London Irish ten years ago.

So she was ready for Henry's requests. She had everything in a folder on her desktop and printed off the information for him. She also copied the file onto their shared server.

Her phone rang. Glancing down at the multiline unit, she saw that Henry was still on his extension.

"Everest Records, Henry Devonshire's office," Astrid said.

"We need to talk."

It was her old boss and former lover, Daniel Martin. Daniel was a bit like Simon Cowell, a record executive who turned everything he touched to gold. But when the gold lost its luster, Daniel moved on. Something Astrid had experienced firsthand.

"I don't think we have anything left to say." The last thing she wanted was to talk to Daniel.

"Henry Devonshire might feel differently. Meet me downstairs in that park area between City Hall and Tower Bridge in ten minutes."

"I can't. My boss needs me."

"He won't be your boss for long if you don't speak to me. I think we both know that. I'm not asking for too much of your time, just a few minutes."

"Fine," Astrid said, aware that Daniel could ruin her chances at Everest records with just a vaguely worded comment about her past job performance.

She wasn't sure exactly what Daniel wanted—their

relationship had ended so badly. Maybe he wanted to make amends now that she was back in the music industry. At least she could hope.

She sent Henry an instant message telling him she'd be right back and set her phones to go to voice mail. Five minutes later she was walking through the green area on the banks of the Thames. Lots of office workers were sitting outside on the smoke breaks.

Astrid hurried past them looking for Daniel. She saw his honey-blond hair first. The weather was cloudy and wet today and a little chilly, and Daniel was wearing his favorite Ralph Lauren trench coat with the collar turned up.

Despite the fact that she was over him, she couldn't help but notice that he looked good. Women were watching him, and Astrid saw the disappointment on more than one girl's face when he turned toward her. In the past she'd relished the envious stares of other women. Now she knew that they had nothing to be envious of. With Daniel Martin the charm was only surface deep.

"Astrid."

"Hi, Daniel. I don't have a lot of time. What did you want to see me about?"

"What do you think you are doing working for Everest Records?"

"They hired me. I needed a job since I'm not independently wealthy," Astrid said.

"Don't be glib."

"I'm not trying to be. What are you really attempting to say?"

"That if you poach any of my clients...I will ruin you."

She shook her head. How could not know her at all?

"I'd never do that. I'm not trying to get ahead by using someone else."

"Just be warned. If you come anywhere near my clients, I will call Henry Devonshire and tell him everything that the tabloids didn't uncover about our affair."

With that, he turned on his heel and walked away from her. She just watched him leave, wondering how in the world she was going to protect herself from Daniel.

Hurrying back to the Everest Group skyscraper, she took the elevator up to her floor, not talking to anyone along the way.

She stopped in the doorway leading to Henry's office. "May I come in?"

He was on the phone, so gestured for her to enter. She came in and placed the files he'd asked for on the corner of his desk.

"That sounds good. I'll be there tonight at nine," Henry said. "Two. There will be two of us."

He hung up the phone and looked up at her. "Have a seat, Astrid."

"Yes, sir."

"Thank you for the material you prepared. Before we dive into work, tell me a little about yourself."

"What do you want to know?" she asked. Somehow, blurting out her entire past history didn't seem prudent. And she'd learned that if she didn't ask for specifics on questions like that one she ended up revealing things she could have kept hidden.

She was hoping that working at Everest Records would be the buffer she needed between her past and her future. A job that would keep her so busy she'd stop worrying about would-haves and could-haves and learn to live again.

"For starters, why are you working at the Everest Group?" he asked, leaning back in his chair and crossing his arms over his chest. The tight black sweater he wore pulled against the bulging muscles in his biceps. Clearly the man worked out, she thought.

"They hired me," she said. After her talk with Daniel, she was afraid to say too much.

He laughed. "So it's just a wage to you?"

She shrugged. "It's a bit more. I really like music and being part of your team sounded like a lot of fun. A chance to see if we can find the next big thing…" She shrugged. "I've always thought of myself as a trendsetter, so now I have a chance to see if I am."

At one time she'd thought she might become a record producer. She understood the job and the hard work that went into it, but she'd figured out that she didn't have the attitude needed to make it there. She couldn't be passionate about the artists she promoted and then walk away from them when their sales started to tank. She liked to think she had integrity.

"That makes working for me easier, I think. I'm going to need you to be more my personal assistant than my secretary. You will be available 24/7. We won't be keeping regular office hours, because I mean to make this division of Everest Group into the most profitable. Do you have any objections?"

"None, sir. I was told that this job would be demanding," she said. She looked forward to it. She needed a demanding job to sink her teeth into. She needed the work to keep her so busy she never had time to think about her failed personal life.

He nodded and gave her that little half smile of his. "Normally we won't be in this office. I'd like to work out of my home in Bromley or my apartment here in London. We will mainly be listening to music acts at night."

"That's fine, sir." To be honest, she didn't need a lot of sleep.

"Good, now down to business. I need you to set up a file to keep information from several talent scouts. I am also sending you an e-mail with the people who work for me," he said.

She nodded and made notes as he continued to set out the terms of the job. Despite the fact that the papers made him out as a playboy, it seemed Henry had cultivated a network he could use for business.

"Is there anything else?"

"Yes. I've been pretty good at picking acts when I hear them at clubs, but I like a second opinion."

She nodded. "Why do you think that is?"

"Probably since I'm the typical person that most of these labels are targeting. I am young, social and know the scene." He nodded. "I think that has given me a good ear for trends. What about you, Astrid?"

"I love music." When she'd first moved to London she had been in the thick of the nightlife. Her sister Bethann and she had shared a flat and worked menial jobs and went clubbing with friends most nights. But then Bethann had become a legal assistant and gotten engaged and her social life had changed. "Part of the reason I was hired was because I'd been a personal assistant to Daniel Martin."

"What are you into?" he asked. "What kind of music do you like?"

"Something with soul," she said.

"Sounds…"

"Retro?"

"No, interesting."

She left his office and tried to concentrate on the job ahead but she had enjoyed Henry—way too much for a boss. And he *was* her boss, something that she had to remember because she wasn't interested in starting over again with a broken heart and an empty bank account.

Henry watched Astrid leave. His new PA was cute and funny and a bit cheeky. Having her in his office and on his team was going to make this job much more enjoyable.

Despite the fact that many people believed him to be nothing more than a celebrity sportscaster and philanthropist, Henry did have a serious side. He certainly played hard, but few people knew he worked even harder.

It was a lesson he'd learned from his stepfather, Gordon Ferguson. He'd first met Gordon when he was eight years old. Two years before his mum and Gordon married. Gordon was the head coach for the London Irish now but back then he had been one of the assistants. He'd helped Henry hone his rugby skills and made him into one of the best team captains of his generation.

Henry's office was on the top floor of the Everest Group building. It was situated in a corner with a nice view of the London Eye across the Thames. He glanced around the nicely appointed office, feeling a bit uncomfortable. He knew he couldn't work in a place as boxed in and sterile as this one.

He needed to get out of here. But first he wanted to know a little more about his assistant and about the task he'd taken on.

At first, when he'd heard Malcolm's offer, he didn't care if he won the challenge or not, but now that he was here, his competitive instincts were rising to the fore. He liked to win. There was a reason he'd been named as RFU Player of the Year. He liked being the best. He hungered for it.

He skimmed the reports that Astrid had prepared, making notes and trying not to remember how long Astrid's legs had appeared under that short skirt she'd had on. And her smile…her mouth was full and tempting, and more than once when she'd been sitting there he'd wondered what her lips would taste like under his. Her mouth was wide, her lips plump, everything about her was irresistible.

Office romances weren't a good idea, but he knew himself and he was attracted to his assistant. He decided he wouldn't act on that attraction unless she showed some sign of interest in him. He needed her to win this challenge and to be honest, winning was more important than starting an affair.

"Henry?"

Astrid was standing in the doorway; her short curly hair brushed her cheeks. He really did like the slim-fitting skirt she wore—it was plaid and her black knee-high boots made her look tall. The plain black sweater clung to her breasts, and he realized he was staring when she cleared her throat.

"Yes, Astrid?"

"I need to pop down to legal to get Steph's offer details in to legal. You mind if I let my phone go unanswered?"

"No, not at all. That was quick." He was definitely going to like the perks that came with working in a large company. Being able to delegate tasks and have them done quickly—that was something he'd needed for a while.

Henry had been producing on his own in between handling his own endorsement deals for athletic shoes and soft drinks. He'd also hosted a kids' sports TV show that had run for two seasons. He liked the perks that went along with being a celebrity, but hadn't relished having to do so much of the legwork himself.

She smiled at him. "I aim to please."

"You've accomplished that," he said.

She left and he turned his chair so that he was facing the windows instead of watching the empty doorway. He'd always been a bit of a loner and that had suited him but having someone work for him...she was like his butler, he thought.

Yeah, right. He'd never ogled Hammond's legs. Yet he had to remember that Astrid did work for him. His own mother's affair with her record producer had led to the end of her singing career and his birth. He wondered sometimes if she ever resented that, but she'd never said.

He brushed that thought away. This was a new century. Attitudes were different than they had been in the '70s. But he still didn't want to make Astrid feel uncomfortable in the office with him.

At the same time he knew that he wasn't going to be able to resist pulling Astrid into his arms before too long and finding out how good that sassy mouth of hers tasted under his.

His phone rang and he reached for it. "Devonshire here."

"Henry? This is your mum."

He loved how she always identified herself even

though he could never mistake her for anyone else. "Hello, Mum. What's up?"

"I need a favor," Tiffany Malone-Ferguson said. "Do you know anyone at Channel Four?"

He knew a few people there. And he was afraid that this was going to be another attempt for his mother to regain the limelight. When pop stars and celebrities from the '70s and '80s had started turning up on game-style shows on Channel Four, his mum went mad. She'd said that she could return to the spotlight now that his half brothers were older.

"I have talked to everyone I know over there more than once."

"Will you try again? Gordon suggested I start a show like that American show *The Bachelor*, but for rugby players. I know the lifestyle and I could definitely help arrange suitable girls. Not those tart scrummies that always pop up in the tabloids."

This idea wasn't half-bad. He made a few notes and asked her more questions about her idea. "I'll see what I can do."

"You're the best, Henry. Love you."

"Love you too, Mum," he said, disconnecting the call.

He held his mobile loosely in his hand for another minute until someone cleared their throat and he glanced up to see Astrid standing in his doorway.

"Yes?"

"I need your signature on these forms. The runner from talent scout Roger McMillan dropped this demo off with a note that they are playing tonight. And I'm going to need you to give me a little more information on Steph," she said, holding a sheaf of papers toward him.

He gestured for her to come in.

"Also the head of legal wants a meeting with you to discuss contract procedures. I know you said we'd be working out of your Bromley office, but the management staff have enquired about setting up meetings with you. Do you want me to direct them to your home office?"

He leaned back in his chair. "No. I think we'd better establish a day in the office each week for meetings. I have six direct reports, right?"

"Yes, sir."

"Have them all scheduled for tomorrow," he said. He'd learned the hard way at rugby that if he didn't go for his goals he'd never achieve them. And teamwork was paramount to winning.

"Astrid, bring me the personnel files on all of the staff. After I've reviewed them, you can schedule the meetings. Does anyone have anything that's pressing?"

"Just legal and accounting. You need to be added to the signature authority card before you can sign this contract."

"Do you have that form?" he asked.

"It's at the bottom of your stack. I'll walk it down to accounting once you sign it."

He pulled the paper out of the stack and signed it. There were a few other housekeeping-type forms for him to sign. Astrid had prepared them with his name and flagged the places where he was supposed to sign.

"Thank you, Astrid," he said, handing them back to her. "You're a very efficient assistant. I'm sure Daniel was devastated to lose you."

She flushed and looked away, but didn't respond. "You're welcome, sir. Was there anything else before I go?"

He stared at her mouth for a minute, knowing his obsession with her lips was going to get him into big trouble. All he really wanted was to taste them.

Chapter 2

Astrid hoped that Henry never called Daniel to find out why she left her last job. Despite how close she and Daniel had become during their affair she knew he wouldn't give her a good reference. Hell, he'd said as much earlier.

At the end...there'd been all those sick days.... Daniel hadn't been very understanding. She wrapped an arm around her own waist as she struggled for a moment to keep the past where it belonged.

Astrid spent the rest of the day trying to stay focused on her job. But Henry seemed to need her in his office a lot as he got acclimated. And she found herself entranced just the tiniest bit.

He was smart and funny. Yet even innocent flirtations in the office were dangerous. Hadn't she learned that the hard way?

She walked down to the legal office and left the paperwork that Henry had signed with the proper legal secretary.

Henry's office was empty when she returned to her desk; she'd poked her head in his office to see if he needed anything. She'd listened to a few songs that Steph Cordo had sang…and that she'd heard on the morning talk radio.

She downloaded the song on iTunes and added them to her playlist. One thing she'd learned working with Daniel was to be very familiar with the artists and groups that label was pursuing. So Steph was the first of many new artists she'd be listening to. It would help give her a feel for what Henry liked, too.

Henry entered the office a few minutes later with three other men, none of whom she knew. He directed the men into his office.

"Hold my calls," Henry said.

"Certainly, sir. May I speak to you for a moment?" she asked.

"What's up?"

"These men aren't on your calendar…. Do you not want me to make your appointments?"

"Oh, of course I do. I'm just not used to having an assistant," Henry said.

She nodded. "Do you need anything for the next thirty minutes?"

"That's pretty specific," Henry said.

"Sorry about that. I'd like to go for lunch. My sister just rang and said she could meet me," Astrid clarified.

"Go on then. I'll be in this meeting for at least that long."

"Do you want me to bring you back something?"

"No. I'm meeting my…half brothers. That still sounds strange to me when I say it."

"I'd heard you all were getting together lately."

"Heard where?"

"Um…well, I read about it in *Hello!*" Astrid refused to be apologetic about it. *Hello!* and other celebrity magazines were a resource for people in their industry. Daniel used to have her keep clippings of their artists so they could track their popularity.

"Gossip rags?"

She arched one eyebrow at him. "Where else would I hear about your meeting them? We don't exactly run in the same circles."

He rubbed the back of his neck. "I know the feeling. They aren't my crowd either."

"No, celebrities and footballers are more your speed," she said. "I guess that's how you have your finger on the pulse of what's next."

"Maybe. I think it's more a feel for what the public is hungry for."

He had a point. "I think you're a very savvy man."

"I am," he said. "Before you head to lunch, will you call Marcus Wills for me? I'm supposed to have drinks with him, but I don't think I'll have time between meeting with the other Devonshire heirs."

"Not a problem. Do you have his number handy? I haven't merged your contents file with mine yet," she said.

"I'll IM it to you."

"Great. I'll take care of it."

He nodded and walked away, and she couldn't help but admire his butt. He stopped in the doorway and glanced back over his shoulder. She blushed when he gave her a knowing smile.

"I guess you still work out even though you don't play anymore," she said.

"Didn't *Hello!* magazine have the scoop on my gym membership?" he asked.

She shook her head. "No, they didn't. I'm hoping to make a little on the side by selling them the exclusive story."

He threw his head back and laughed. And Astrid couldn't help chuckling along with him. He *was* fun and after the heartache she'd endured for the past year of her life she needed that.

"You'll do, Astrid."

She winked at him. "I know I will."

Henry went into his office, and Astrid made the call he'd asked her to before leaving to meet her sister, Bethann.

Bethann was sitting in the sun on one of the benches that lined the walkway along the Thames—the exact spot Astrid had met Daniel earlier. This part of London was newer and lined with glass-and-steel buildings, but across the river was the old Tower of London. Her sister looked up as she approached and waved.

Astrid hugged her sister as soon as she was close enough.

"How is the new job going?" Bethann asked.

"It's good. I think working for Henry is going to be just what I need. He's focused on signing new acts."

Bethann handed her a sandwich. "Be careful. The last job nearly ruined you."

She shook her head. It didn't matter that they were

both grown woman; Bethann still thought of her as her baby sister who needed looking after.

"I am very aware of that. I just meant…never mind."

Bethann reached over and put her arm around Astrid's shoulders. "I love you, sweetie. I don't want to see you hurt again."

"I won't be," Astrid said. She'd made up her mind when Daniel had fired her that she wouldn't be used again. Not by any man. But that didn't mean she couldn't enjoy working for Henry.

Considering he, Geoff and Steve all had the same father, they didn't really have that much in common. If he had to guess why, he'd say it came down to their mothers: three very different women.

Malcolm had played fast and loose with all of their mothers. The paparazzi had photographed him leaving all of their residences, and Henry knew from things his mother had said that seeing Malcolm with his other lovers had slowly crushed her.

Tiffany had gone through a total confidence change in the six months leading up to his birth. No longer the brassy Irish singer who had melted men's hearts, she'd turned distrustful of compliments and started to doubt her own abilities as a singer.

The paps still dogged her even after she'd broken things off with Malcolm. But in later years she'd found happiness with Gordon—a kind of love, she told Henry when he'd asked her about it, that she'd never found with Malcolm. She'd said that her love with Malcolm had burned hot and fast but that Gordon was a slow burn. Henry hadn't understood that as a teenage boy, but as a man he was starting to.

He was very aware the paparazzi were probably having a field day seeing the three brothers together now, which was why they'd chosen to meet at The Athenaeum Club instead of a pub. He'd learned as a youngster that ignoring them and going about his life was the only way to be happy.

And happiness was one of his chief concerns. He saw Geoff sitting on a high stool at a table in the back of the establishment and nodded to acknowledge him.

Henry was stopped several times by fans from his playing days as he walked through the club. Henry exchanged a few words with every one of them. Shook their hands and signed napkins and scraps of paper. His stepfather had always said that players should remember without the fans they'd be back on their local pitch playing for fun instead of money.

And his fans had made him very wealthy.

Geoff was on the phone, seated at the back of the club. So Henry took his time. Everyone always wanted to know whom he favored in the 6 Nations game—a tournament held between the first nations to play each other in rugby. Originally it had been England vs. Scotland, but over time had grown to include Ireland, Wales, France and Italy, as well. And it went without saying that Henry always favored the home team.

As he approached Geoff, the other man motioned he'd be another minute, so Henry detoured to the bar and ordered a beer. He wasn't too keen on this get-to-know-you meeting, but both Steven and Geoff had outvoted him, so to speak.

He brought his drink back to the table where Geoff was as the other man disconnected his call. Geoff stood and shook his hand.

"Where's Steven?"

"His secretary called and said he'd be running late today."

"I can't stay long. I've got things to take care of before I hit the clubs tonight. How'd you like your first day?"

Geoff arched one eyebrow at him. "Probably as well as you did. The airline is a well-oiled machine, and I think we should be able to show a large profit during the terms of the will."

Henry realized that Geoff expected to win. Probably by order of his birth he should inherit the entire Everest Group but Henry wasn't ready to back down and give up the fight. It would take signing just one phenomenal group for his segment to outperform Geoff's airline. And Henry was damned determined to make sure he found it.

"How's the record label?"

"Good. It's in good shape and I have the right people in place."

"I always heard you were a team player," Geoff said.

"It's served me well all my life," Henry said.

"Good to hear it."

Henry had heard that Steven and Geoff were both loners. Steven's mother was a twin. And, according to the media, very close to her extended family.

His mobile beeped and he glanced down to see that a text from Astrid had arrived. He skimmed it and turned his attention back to his Guinness. He and Geoff talked about sports and Henry noticed that the other man was uncomfortable with him.

Geoff had grown up in the spotlight as part of the royal family. Henry wondered if being around a rugby man such as himself was what bothered Geoff. Though rugby was a ruffian sport, it had always been played by those of the middle and upper classes.

"Do you see your mum much?"

"Every Sunday for brunch," Henry said. His mother had done her best by him. Making sure that he grew up in comfortable surroundings with the family she'd created for them. Being left by Malcolm Devonshire hadn't put her off her dreams of family.

"That's good. My cousin Suzanne is a huge fan...."

"Does she want an autograph or a chance to meet her?" Henry said. His mum was just that, his mum, but he was very aware that to other people she was a pop star. And despite the fact that she hadn't had a hit in fifteen years, she was still very popular. And when he'd been in secondary school, all of his mates had listened to her records. Tiffany couldn't walk down the street without being recognized.

Geoff laughed. "She'd settle for an autograph."

"Send me her name and I'll get Mum to autograph a picture for her."

"Thanks. If there's ever anything I can do for you."

"I'll keep it in mind."

Steven showed up a few minutes later. "A girl is at the front desk asking for you, Henry."

"A girl?"

"Astrid something. I told them I'd let you know."

"Thanks. I guess that means I need to go."

"Do you?" Geoff asked. "Who is she?"

"My new assistant, Astrid Taylor."

Steven signaled the butler and ordered a drink. Geoff rubbed the back of his neck.

"Did she used to work for Daniel Martin?"

"Yes, I believe she did. Why?"

"I recall reading something in the business journal about it. She sued them because they didn't give her adequate exit benefits. Just be careful."

"I always am," Henry said. "I know a lot about building a winning team."

"I'll say. Do you have time for another drink before you go meet her?" Steven said as his drink arrived.

Henry wasn't sure and being indecisive didn't sit well with him. He shook his head. "I better not. We have a couple of meetings tonight. I appreciate the information Geoff. I'll keep my eyes open."

Geoff laughed. "I sound like my sisters passing gossip."

"You have sisters?" Steven asked.

Henry had to laugh at that. They'd been linked... well their *names* had since their birth, but they were virtual strangers.

"I have two younger brothers," Henry said.

"I'm an only child." Steven took a sip of his drink. "But we can talk about siblings later."

"I'm not sure I trust Malcolm not to throw something else at one of us," Geoff said.

"I agree. I'm surprised even being faced with his mortality has made him contact us," Henry said.

"Too right," Geoff added.

"I don't give a damn about his legacy," Steven said. "I'm in this for the money and the challenge."

Henry laughed at the way Steven said that. This man was someone who just said what he wanted, to hell with the consequences.

"I see your point."

"Good...on that note, I think you should know that

I've been contacted by a magazine…Fashion Quarterly—"

"Isn't that a woman's magazine?" Henry asked. His mum loved the magazine and read it cover to cover each month.

"Yes, it is. The editor-in-chief needed a favor from me and I helped her out in exchange for a promise to run some articles on us in her magazine."

"On us?" Geoff asked. "Everything I do has to go through the Royal Press Office."

"It's on our mums, actually since it's a woman's mag but they will mention our business units and do a bit of a showcase on each one as well," Steven said.

"My mum will love that," Henry said.

"I'm not so sure about this," Geoff said.

"Just talk to her," Steven said. "We need the publicity and this is a nice angle."

"I'm in. You don't need to convince me," Henry said, glancing at his watch. "Is there anything else we need to discuss?"

"I like your idea of using the airlines to promote the album covers," Geoff said. "So I'll be calling you tomorrow or the next day to get a team together to move that idea forward."

"I'll look forward to your call," Henry said. "Steven, I've got a few ideas for using the Everest Mega Store to promote my newer artists. Do you have time to meet with me this week?"

"I do. Shoot me over an e-mail with your availability and we will make it work," Steven said. "I have to go to New York to check out our North American operation."

"Indeed," Henry said. "So we're doing this again next week?"

"Yes. I think a weekly check-in is a good idea," Steven said.

Henry left his half brothers and walked slowly through the club. He didn't worry about Malcolm because that man was a stranger to him just like Steven and Geoff, and he was the type of man who didn't worry about the future. He'd take care of what he needed to.

And right now that involved finding out a little more about Astrid and her past employer.

He spotted her standing at the coat check. She was talking on her mobile and turned around as he came down the stairs. She waved at him and smiled.

He smiled back, thinking that talking to his assistant was going to be very enjoyable.

Astrid hung up the phone as Henry joined her. He looked good in his trendy casual clothing. He wore gray trousers and a button-down shirt left open at the collar with a navy blue sport coat that made his eyes seem brighter. He smiled at her as he approached, and she just stood there for a minute not saying anything.

It didn't help that he was one of the rugby players she'd had an insane crush on when she was a teenager, which made it harder for her to see him as her boss now that they weren't in the office.

"Hello, Astrid. What did you need me for?"

"A signature. Without one your staff isn't going to get paid," she said. They all got paid monthly, so missing a pay period could put a lot of the staff in a bind. And since she'd only just started at Everest Records she didn't have the relationships needed to finesse the payroll clerks into giving her an extra day.

She handed him the papers and he signed them with a flourish. His signature had style just like the man.

Oh, for God's sake, she thought. She was developing a crush on him. On her boss! This had to stop.

"Thanks."

"No problem. Are you going back to the office now?"

"No. I have a runner waiting for this packet. I'm supposed to meet you in fifteen minutes and I'd never make it on time."

"No, you wouldn't. Did you eat yet?" he asked.

She shook her head. There hadn't been time. She handed the packet to the runner she'd brought with her, and he took it and left.

"Want to grab a bite?" Henry asked. "I'm hungry."

"Sounds good."

He led the way out of the club. "Do you have a car?"

"No. I take the underground mostly. Congestion charges and parking are outrageous," she said.

"That they are. There's a congestion charge around my neighborhood. I have to pay to drive home." Traffic was a major problem in some London areas, so a charge had been introduced to ease traffic flow during certain hours.

"Not many days," she said. "I hear you get home in the wee hours of the morning."

He chuckled. "That's true. But if I kept respectable hours I'd have to pay."

"You do now with the job," she said.

"That's true," he said. "What about you?"

"What do you mean?" she asked.

"Is this job keeping you respectable?"

She had no idea what Henry was after with his questions. The valet brought his car around and after she was seated in the Ferrari Enzo, Henry put the car in gear. He drove with confidence and skill, negotiating the traffic with ease. She couldn't help but admire the way that he drove. She was beginning to believe there was little that Henry didn't do well.

"Of course it is."

"Did your last job, working for Mo Rollins's group, do the same?"

She had a sinking feeling that he'd checked her employment record. Had he found out about her affair? Bethann had suggested to her before she'd taken this job at Everest Records that she should work in another industry, but the record industry was all she knew.

"I took that job really seriously, Henry. I was a good employee and supported Daniel in every way I could."

"But he still let you go," Henry said.

"I had a health issue," she said. This was a nightmare, she thought. When she'd been in the throes of her affair with Daniel it had never occurred to her that someday she'd be answering questions about why she no longer worked for him.

Henry braked to a stop as they neared Kensington High Street. She knew he planned to check out Roof Gardens, the eclectic nightclub owned by Richard Branson, tonight.

"Babylon okay for dinner?" he asked.

"Yes." She'd never eaten at the trendy high-priced restaurant before. When she'd been with Daniel, even when they'd been dating, they had tended to stay more to economical places. Daniel only spent money on his clients.

Henry pulled up to the valet stand and got out. Astrid climbed out on her side and wished for a moment she'd taken time to dress a bit differently for her day. She was already realizing that Henry was different. That didn't mean he would treat her better than Daniel had. This was a job, she thought. *Nothing more*. The measure of the man she worked for was better than her previous boss. And she knew she was going to have to change and probably grow a bit to keep up with him. She shifted the strap of her large shoulder bag and hurried around to the sidewalk so she was next to him.

There were a few paps—paparazzi—who took some photos of Henry. She stepped back so he could be photographed alone. He posed and talked to the photographers and signed a few autographs before reaching for her hand and drawing her up the path to the entrance.

She knew that Henry hadn't finished questioning her about her past and Daniel. She also decided if she played her cards right, she could keep him off the topic tonight.

"Does that happen to you often?" she asked when they checked their coats downstairs.

He smiled ruefully. "Yes. I'm used to it, though. My mum says that it's part of our life being in the spotlight. I grew up around it. I don't court them, but if they want a photo I give them one."

"Isn't it intrusive?" she asked.

He stopped and pulled her toward a quiet corner. "It's my life. I don't think about it. When I was a player, I didn't like them because they were a distraction and some of the other players would let the paps keep them from concentrating on the game. But now, they are what keeps my lifestyle going forward," he said.

"You're a very smart man," she said, coming to the conclusion that the showman, the charming playboy that he projected to the world was just one of the many facets of the whole man.

"Indeed. So that's why I'm not going to let you distract me from the fact that you still haven't told me everything about your last employer."

Chapter 3

Astrid tossed her head to the side and gave him a look that told him he was going to have to be subtler if he wanted to find out about her past. He nodded and took her arm leading her to the maître d' stand. They were seated shortly at an intimate table for two that had a nice view. He realized he didn't want to look at anyone but Astrid.

She was a mass of contradictions and she fascinated him.

"I think the London music scene is really hot right now. So many little local acts are making it big, not just here but in the States."

"But are they ready for it?" Henry asked.

"I'm not sure they are. You've grown up in the spotlight and you know how different it is from the paps in the States. I think that some of the groups aren't really ready to handle the fame that they achieve so quickly. And the American market can be fickle."

"Yes, they can. I've been trying to caution Steph that making it big there will mean a meteoric rise, but it could be followed by quite a crash."

"It's good that you've taken the time to talk to her. I can help with that, as well. I listened to her music earlier today and the demo that Roger dropped off. I also think I know some venues that will suit the style of music you're looking for."

"And what kind is that?"

"Something with a hook, of course, that is catchy and that people will remember. But I think you're also looking for music that has some heart to it."

He nodded. She did indeed know what he was looking for. That made him uncomfortable. He liked to play at being an easygoing guy that everyone knew and who in turn knew everyone, but in reality he kept himself distant. The only woman he could really claim to know well was his mother. And she was, by anyone's definition, eccentric.

But Astrid was different. She was calm and quiet at times. Like now.

"How long did you work for the Mo Rollins Group and Daniel Martin?" he asked. Mo Rollins was a legendary producer who had established his own label after leaving Sony-BMG. Daniel was one of his up and coming protégés.

"Only eighteen months, but I had worked as one of the assistants to Mo's executive assistant for more than three years before that."

"Did you like it?" he asked. It made no sense that she'd leave that job and then come work for him. If she wanted to work in the music industry, then the job had been ideally suited for her. Henry told himself that he wasn't asking her because he was curious about the woman. He needed to know about her past because she was part of his team and he needed to know every nuance of his team if they were going to be a success.

"I loved it," she said, putting down her wineglass. She leaned across the table and put her hand over his. She had neatly painted nails and her hand was very soft against the back of his. Being a rugby player he'd always had calloused or bruised hands, but hers were soft and cool.

"I know you want to understand why I left such a high-profile job. There's a lot to it…. It was a highly personal health issue and I just don't—" She broke off, tears filling her eyes.

Henry turned his hand over under hers and held hers loosely in his grip. He understood about secrets and personal issues. He could hold off for now, but before too long he would know *all* of Astrid Taylor's secrets. HR had screened her and wouldn't have hired her if there was anything untoward in her past.

"Very well. Tonight you are going to meet Steph Cordo. Part of your role will be to act as an assistant to my stable of artists until they hire their own people," Henry said.

"Right. I've done that type of work before. I can handle that."

"I know you can handle it, Astrid. You're very adept at doing what needs to be done," he said.

She flushed. "My sister says it's a gift."

"Really? Why?"

"Um…I was always a bit of a suck up when we were

younger. But being nice does open doors," she said with a wry little grin.

"Indeed."

Henry noticed he was still holding her hand. He stroked his thumb over her knuckles and watched her face. She flushed again and then pulled her hand back. She licked her lips, which were wide and full. Her mouth moved and he knew she was saying something, but for the life of him he couldn't concentrate on her words.

All he could do was watch them move. Stare at her white teeth and very pink lips and wonder how her mouth would feel under his.

"Henry?"

"Hmm?"

"The waiter asked if we wanted dessert," she said.

"Sorry, mate. I'm good. Would you like something, Astrid?"

She shook her head.

He asked for the check and Astrid excused herself to go to the ladies' room. It was odd that the old man had decided to get in touch with him now, but Henry thought that the job at Everest was going to be a fun challenge.

He'd long since stopped thinking of Malcolm as any type of relation. The man had sent gifts at birthdays and Christmases over the years, but Henry didn't really know him. He'd always been a sort of Dr. Who character that came in and out of his life with no real notice.

But Henry felt the need to know more about him now. Malcolm held the key to any future success his team would have because of the will. His BlackBerry rang and he glanced at the screen. Henry had a firm policy of not talking on his cell phone when he was out with another person.

Alonzo, one of the men he paid for tips on new bands, sent a text message that he had a group that Henry should check out playing later in the evening at a club a few blocks from where they were. Henry noted it.

He wasn't one for letting any leads slip by him. Maybe that was why he hadn't had a problem transitioning from rugby player to entrepreneur back when he'd first retired.

He glanced up as Astrid was walking toward him and simply watched her. She moved like many women did when they knew a man was watching. Her hips swayed languidly with each step and her arms moved by her sides.

"You're staring at me, boss man."

"You're a very pretty girl, Astrid."

She tipped her head to the side. "Thanks, I think."

"You think?"

"Is it a genuine compliment, or are you just buttering me up for some nasty assignment?" she asked.

He shook his head as he stood. He put his hand on the small of her back and directed her out of the restaurant. He knew she didn't need his hand on her to figure out which way to go, but he wanted to touch her. There was something…almost irresistible about her.

"It was genuine. If I ask you to do a task you find distasteful it won't be hidden in between something pleasant."

She paused and glanced back at him. He stopped, and their faces were very close together. "Promise?"

"I promise," he said. Before he could say anything

else, a flashbulb blinded him. He turned to face the cameraman, but the person was retreating.

They met Roger McMillan, a friend of Henry's, at the first club they entered. The place was crowded, as was to be expected, but they were immediately ushered to a VIP area cordoned off by velvet ropes.

Roger shook her hand and said something to her, but she couldn't hear him over the music. She nodded and would have excused herself but Henry grabbed her hand and led them to a table in the back.

It was a little quieter and Roger introduced himself again.

"Astrid Taylor," she said.

"She's my assistant. You will be calling her every morning by ten with any new groups you've identified."

"Got it. There's not much going on here tonight. But the deejay has a tip for us on a hot new group. Once he takes a break, he's going to come and meet us."

"Sounds good," Henry said.

"I'm going to make the rounds, see if there are any artists here tonight that you should meet," Roger said.

He excused himself and left the table. Astrid realized that Henry wasn't going to ease into his new job but had already hit the ground running. Unlike Daniel, he knew how to delegate. Henry wasn't all about himself.

"Why are you watching me like that?" he asked.

"You aren't going to follow Roger or send me after him?"

"Why should I? He knows what's expected of him and he's never let me down."

She shook her head. "That kind of attitude is different."

Henry nodded. "Everything I need to know about life I learned on a rugby pitch."

"Truly?"

"Indeed. The first thing I learned is that if you don't trust your teammates then you don't trust yourself. You can't be everywhere. So you must surround yourself with like-minded people."

"So many people in this business are…elbows out. You know, always trying to shove themselves to the front of the line. When I worked for Daniel and Mo Rollins there was always a list of calls to be made just to make sure that people were doing what they were supposed to do."

Henry leaned in closer. "Is that one of the reasons why you left?"

"No. It isn't," Astrid said.

Henry put his arm around her shoulder and drew her back against the banquette. "I can't be successful until I know every member of my team—their strengths and their weaknesses."

"I don't have any weaknesses from my past that you need to worry about, Henry. I'm telling you everything you need to know about me."

Henry stroked one finger down the side of her face and she shivered. She wanted to rebuild her life and she couldn't do that if she was lusting after him.

"Let me be the judge of that," he said.

It took just those few words to convince her that he wasn't the easygoing guy he wanted the world to think he was. Henry Devonshire was a man used to getting his way. And right now that meant he was going to try to uncover her secrets.

Her secrets.

She had so many. And she knew there was no way in hell that she was going to trust Henry Devonshire with them. Men had let her down. Not her dad. No, her pop was a stand-up sort of guy. But the men—man—she'd met since she'd left home... Daniel Martin had broken her ability to trust. He had shown her that not all men rewarded her trust in them.

"Not just yet," she said.

He nodded and sank back into his own chair. "You don't trust me."

"I don't know you," she said. That was one lesson she had learned. Not everyone she met had the same feelings of loyalty toward their friends that she did. And until she really had Henry's measure as a man, she wasn't about to trust him.

When she'd first started her affair with Daniel, she'd known it was risky to be involved with her boss, but the thrill of falling in love with someone as dynamic as Daniel had offset that. More than that, she'd also had her belief that Daniel was falling for her. And that made the risk more manageable—only after she found herself dumped by Daniel and pregnant with his child did she realize that her sense of loyalty was different than his.

"Point conceded," Henry said. "What do you think of this deejay?"

"He's okay," she said. "His sound is very funky and modern, but there's nothing to make him stand out from any of the other clubs."

"I agree. He's just one of the crowd, but he does have a good ear. We're looking for artists who can stand out in the crowd whether they are loved or hated, as long as they are noticed. I'm going to chat with him and see if he has any tips for me."

It was twenty minutes later when they left for a club in Notting Hill. Cherry Jam had a New York City feel to it. She saw two mates from her old clubbing days, and Henry nodded her off as he was dragged into a rugby conversation with Stan Stubbing, a sports reporter for the *Guardian*.

Molly and Maggie Jones were sisters who were only eleven months apart. Maggie, the older of the two, was actually Astrid's age.

"Astrid! What are you doing here?"

"Working! I'm here to check out the bands."

"I thought you'd stopped working for that record producer," Molly said.

Astrid swallowed. She had become used to the questions about her leaving Mo's organization, but she'd never really figured out a good answer. "I just started a new job with Everest Records."

"Which explains why you are here with Henry Devonshire. He is one cute guy."

"He's my boss," Astrid said.

"He can still be cute," Maggie pointed out.

"True. What are you drinking?" she asked her friends.

"Pomegranate martini. Want one?"

"I'd love one," Astrid said.

Molly went to the bar to get her one, and she and Maggie looked for a place to sit but the club was packed and the long, low tables were all full.

She glanced at the VIP area, where Henry had a table with Roger and a woman who looked familiar. He waved her over as soon he glanced up.

"Go on," Maggie said.

"You can come with me. Henry won't mind."

"All right then. Here's Molly with your drink," Maggie said.

Henry was seated at the head of the U-shaped booth and Roger sat on one side. Astrid slid in next to the woman, Molly followed her and Maggie sat next to Roger.

"Astrid, this is Steph Cordo. Steph, this is my assistant Astrid."

Astrid shook the other woman's hand. She was older than Astrid expected her to be. Most pop singers seemed to be sixteen these days, but Steph was at least twenty-five. Her eyes said she'd experienced a lot of life.

"Nice to meet you."

"You, as well," Steph said.

"These are my friends Maggie and Molly Jones," she said to the table.

Once everyone was introduced, Roger and Henry went back to discussing the music business and Astrid turned to Steph.

"Tomorrow we're going to have a lot for you to do. Did Henry mention that to you?"

"Yes. He also said you'd be setting up an appearance at the Everest Mega Store."

"I will? I mean, of course I will. We can talk about that tomorrow. When is the best time to reach you?"

"Anytime except the afternoon. That's when I sleep."

Maggie laughed. "I wish I had that schedule."

Steph flushed a little. "I've always been a night owl, and my mum's a nurse. She used to work the overnight shift when I was growing up.... I guess I developed the habit early of staying up to talk to her."

"My dad worked nights for a while before he bought

his own cabs. We used to have breakfast every morning before school," Astrid said.

Her dad had been a cab driver while she was growing up. He still owned a cab but had hired another man to drive it when his health had started to fail. Her mum had been a stay-at-home mum while she and Bethann were in primary school, then she'd gone back to teaching.

"Me, too. My mates were always having dinner with their folks, but for us it was breakfast."

"Us, too. When my dad got sick, that was the one tradition we kept to even when he was in hospital— Bethann and I would make sure we stopped by at breakfast time."

"What was your dad in hospital for?"

"Diabetes," Astrid said. "He's had it for most of his life, but he hates to eat right."

"My mum would have given him hell if he'd been one of her clients. She is adamant that you can't neglect your health, and I've picked up a few of her healthy habits," Steph said.

"Me, too. I think because my dad's health has always been so bad I'm really aware of what I'm eating and the effect it has on my body. I don't want to end up like him if I can help it."

"Is he bad?" Steph asked.

"Wheelchair bound," Astrid said.

"How has your family handled that?"

"My sister and I take turns going down and helping our mum out. And we paid to have parts of the house converted so he could use his wheelchair in it. The hallways were so small."

"I know what you mean. My mum is always saying this country is behind the times with awareness for the disabled."

"The thing is, if my dad had been better about eating right he might not have needed the wheelchair. I didn't mean to say that he could have helped it—"

"I know what you mean," Steph said. "You just want to prevent that from happening to you if at all possible."

"Exactly. I just want to live a normal life."

"I've always been baffled by the words *normal schedule*. No one really has one. But I think we find 'normal' for ourselves," Steph said.

"Is Astrid keeping you entertained?" Henry asked.

"Very much. I like her. She's not like the other people who I've talked to in this industry."

"In what way?" Henry asked.

"She's real people," Steph said.

Astrid smiled and realized that she could be friends with this woman. Something she'd sort of picked up from Steph's chart-topping song "My World."

"It's going to be nice working with you," Astrid said.

"I think so, too," Steph said.

The conversation drifted in another direction and Steph turned to talk to Henry. Astrid chatted a bit with Maggie before the other woman and her sister had to leave. She watched them go, regretting that she'd shut herself off from her old life when she'd lost her last job. Being pregnant and having the complications she'd had had put an end to her nightlife. And then the scandal and rumors about her firing and her relationship with Daniel had made her want to hide.

And she had, by retreating to her home and not talking to friends.

The need to run and hide from everyone meant that

she'd been missing out on a part of herself. She vowed never to do that again.

"Sorry, Astrid, but could you let me out?" Steph asked.

"Certainly." Astrid scooted out of the booth until Steph left and then sat back down.

"Pretty good evening so far. I think you have convinced Steph to sign with Everest Records. She was afraid that we'd be all corporate and not 'get' her music."

"Of course we won't be. I like her. I wasn't trying to convince her of anything."

"I know, that's why it worked. I think you are going to be an asset to my team," Henry said.

Astrid smiled and felt a flush that came with knowing she'd done a good job. That was it, she told herself. It had nothing to do with the fact that Henry had leaned in close to her and had his arm around her shoulder.

"I want to hit one more club before calling it a night," Henry said. "You up for that?"

She thought about her after-Daniel routine—evening television programs followed by a cup of chamomile tea and bed by eleven. For the first time since she'd lost her baby she felt alive. Really alive.

"Yes, I am."

"Good. Let's go," Henry said.

They talked a little more about what he wanted on their way to the next club, and Astrid was careful to listen to what he said. Throughout the rest of the evening he didn't push anymore to find out why she'd left Mo Rollins's organization, and she was glad of it.

She knew, though, that it was a temporary reprieve. Henry was going to get the answers to his questions.

He was simply biding his time and letting her get to the point where she was finally comfortable.

She thought she'd have weeks to get to the point where she'd casually mention Daniel and the fact that over the eighteen months she worked for him their relationship had progressed from professional to personal, but that all changed when they left their third club of the evening and she stepped out into the night air and nearly collided with a tall, broad-shouldered man.

"Sorry," she said, glancing up into eyes that were very familiar.

"Astrid? What are you doing here?" Daniel asked.

"Working," she said.

"For me," Henry said, stepping behind her and putting his arm on her elbow as he drew her away from Daniel.

Chapter 4

Henry didn't like the way the other man was looking at Astrid. It was more than the way an ex-boss should. Over the course of the day he'd started thinking of her as his. Not in a sexual way...well, not completely in a sexual way. And he could tell from the frozen expression on her face that this man wasn't a friend of hers.

"Henry Devonshire," Henry said, offering his hand to the man.

"Daniel Martin."

Suddenly a lot of things fell into place. Astrid's old boss was more than her boss. No wonder she'd been reluctant to talk about him.

"I've heard a lot about you."

"You, as well. Steph Cordo was quite a coup for you. A lot of producers are envious they didn't get the drop on you."

Henry smiled affably. His time in the spotlight taught him how to conceal what he really felt about others. And he didn't like the brash American Daniel. He rubbed Henry the wrong way.

"Henry's got an eye for talent."

"Let's hope he can also spot the slackers," Daniel said.

Astrid flinched and drew her handbag closer to her body. "I've always known how to build winning teams. There's our car. Good evening, Daniel."

Daniel nodded, and Henry led Astrid to the valet stand where his car waited. She was eerily silent for someone he'd come to expect to be sassy and spunky. Was the cheeky girl he'd come to know just a façade, and was this introspective woman the real Astrid?

"Daniel was the reason you left your last job," Henry said.

"It was attendance, like my record stated. I know that Daniel wouldn't have given me a recommendation."

"He didn't."

"Figures."

"How long were the two of you involved?" Henry asked.

"Why do you think we were?"

Henry gave her a shrewd look. "Ex-lovers make everyone react differently than ex-bosses. So…how long were you two involved?"

"Too long," Astrid said. "I…I'm not normally like that. I really thought that Daniel was a different man."

Henry sensed that about Astrid. She was funny and outgoing, but he had noticed earlier in the evening that she kept a barrier between herself and others. He'd recognized that trait mainly because he always did the same.

"Do you want to talk about it?" Henry asked.

She shook her head and clenched her hands tightly on her lap. He knew that she was trying to control her reaction to seeing her ex-lover.

Henry said nothing, just kept driving. He didn't know where Astrid lived, and he didn't want to interrupt her in the middle of whatever she was going to say.

"I always thought… Well, that hardly matters. Where are we going now?" she asked.

"Home. But I'll need your address."

"You can drop me at the nearest Underground."

"No, I can't. They've stopped running at this hour."

She glanced at her watch and then shook her head again. "You're right. I live in Woking."

He put her address into his Sat Nav system and then followed the directions of Mr. T's voice. As he expected, Astrid laughed a little the first time the recorded voice told him to "turn around, fool."

"I can't believe you have that rude voice on your Sat Nav."

"It's Mr. T. That's his persona—big tough guy."

"I don't get it. But then Americans are very different, aren't they?"

"Some. They don't get rugby, which makes no sense at all to me."

She smiled again, and he felt good for having made her smile. "I guess they are just daft."

"Must be. Do you follow rugby?" he asked.

"Some," she said, blushing the slightest bit. He could only see the rise in color as he braked to a stop for the traffic light. "I used to when I was younger."

"Which teams?"

"England, of course, in the 6 Nations."

"Have you been to any games?" he asked.

"A few. I used to be really into going to the games at Madejski Stadium to watch the London Irish play."

"Why'd you stop?" he asked. His old team was still a contender.

"My dad got too sick to go. And it was always something I did with him."

"Your family must be very close," he said.

"Why do you say that?" she asked.

"You had lunch with your sister, went to games with your dad."

She shrugged. Something he noticed she did a lot when she was evading answering a question. "I suppose we are. What about you? Your mum is Tiffany Malone. That had to be exciting."

"She's still my mum," he said. "We're quite close, actually. She loves being a mum and smothers my brothers and I with her mothering."

Astrid smiled again. "Are you a bit of a mummy's lad?"

"What do you think?"

She tipped her head to the side as she studied him and, having lightened her mood, he felt as if he was seeing the return of Astrid. Not that tight-lipped stranger whom Daniel Martin had evoked.

"I think you are a man who knows very much what he wants and probably doesn't look to anyone for approval."

He nodded. "Damn straight. Now which place is yours?"

She pointed to a modern block of flats and he pulled into the parking lot. She reached for her door as he turned off the car. He got out and met her as she exited the car. It had started to drizzle on the drive, and the rain made her hair curl.

She stared up at him for a minute, chewing on her lower lip. "Thank you for the ride home. And for…well for being so nice about everything. You made seeing Daniel again bearable for me."

"You're welcome," he said. He cupped her elbow and led her to the entrance of the building.

"Well, good night, then," she said.

"Good night, Astrid," he said. But instead of doing the smart thing and letting her enter her building, he touched the side of her face and lowered his head to kiss her.

Astrid leaned up into Henry's kiss. He didn't put his arm around her, but kept one hand on her face. His lips rubbed lightly over hers, and she stood on tiptoe to get closer to him. His lips were soft and provoked a slow burn.

The reaction of his mouth on hers sent tingles down her body and she opened her mouth on a sigh. She tasted the minty crispness of his breath before his tongue brushed over hers. Forgetting everything, she felt only his mouth on hers.

The hand on her face slid to the nape of her neck, and he held her firmly as he took complete control of their kiss.

She couldn't think.

She didn't want to. She'd watched Henry all day and night wondering what it would be like to be in his embrace, and now she knew. It was intense.

He smelled earthy and masculine. His cologne was expensive and crisp—she suspected it was custom-blended just for him. She closed her eyes to focus her senses in the experience.

He pulled back, and she opened her eyes to see him staring down at her. He said nothing but rubbed his thumb over her bottom lip and then stepped away from her.

"Good night, then," he said.

She watched him walk back to his car and realized she was still standing there like a ninny. She unlocked the lobby door to her flat building and walked in without looking back at him.

Danger loomed—real danger of falling for Henry Devonshire. A man who would never see her any differently than Daniel had. How could he? His mother was a pop star, his father was a billionaire entrepreneur and she was the daughter of a schoolteacher and a taxi driver.

When was she going to learn?

Why did she have a weakness for men who were...

"Not good for me," she said out loud.

She kicked off her shoes as she entered and dropped her keys on the kitchen counter. It took her fifteen minutes to get ready for bed, but once she was there she couldn't sleep. She just kept reliving, not the encounter with Daniel, which she'd expected, but the kiss with Henry.

She'd never been kissed like that before. It had been too intense. Her vows to herself about not getting involved with men she worked with melted away.

She drifted off to sleep and woke early for work. She dressed in an ultraprofessional suit that she'd worn to her interview with Malcolm Devonshire's assistant Edmond. That suit was her armor when she needed to be professional. Bethann called, but Astrid let it go to voice mail because Bethann could always tell when something was going on in Astrid's life. Her older sister had known her affair with Daniel had gone wrong just from the way Astrid had said hello.

The train was busy, but that was normal for the morning. She knew she was going to have to figure out an alternate way to handle her commute once she started going out at night with Henry. She tried to fill her mind with to-do lists and other meaningless tasks, but the one thought that kept circling around was what would happen when she saw Henry.

How was he going to treat her today?

Her mobile rang again and she hit the quiet button. The part of the train she was on was a quiet zone, so she couldn't talk to Bethann even if she wanted to. A minute later she received an instant message on her Smartphone. They each had a BlackBerry so could use the Messenger on that.

Bethann: Stop ignoring my calls.

Astrid: I'm on the train, Bethann. I can't talk just now.

Bethann: Where were you last night?

Astrid: Working.

Bethann: I left you a voice mail at home…I'm worried about you. I think you should have taken a job in my office.

Astrid hadn't even seriously considered working with

her sister at the law office where Bethann was a solicitor. She loved Bethann, but the other woman was demanding and very bossy. If they worked together, Astrid was afraid she'd lose it and say something that would hurt her sister's feelings.

Astrid: I like working in the music industry. My stop's next. Daniel contacted me and threatened to tell Henry awful things about me.

Bethann: I'm going to contact his office today. We filed a wrongful termination.

Astrid: I know but the fact that I settled makes it seem like there was something untoward between us.

Bethann: There was.

Astrid: Stop being a cow about that. I need you to just tell me everything's going to be okay and the one mistake I made falling for that man isn't going to ruin the rest of my life.

Bethann: Love, don't say things like that. You are on a better track now. Sorry for being bossy.

Astrid: No problem. Sorry for getting all emotional.

Bethann: Have a good day, sis.

Astrid: You too. TTYL.

She entered her office to find three e-mails from

Henry, the last one saying he'd be in the office later this morning.

She stashed her handbag and started to work. Tried to get into the flow of the office. There were a couple of coworkers that she'd started being friendly with in the kitchen area where the coffeepot was kept, but this morning she kept to herself. Stayed at her desk and just worked.

She had made mistakes with Daniel. At first their relationship had been like this one with Henry, and now she was afraid of repeating those same mistakes. She refused to let that happen.

Just because they spent every eight hours together in the office and then most evenings together didn't mean they were growing closer. She had to remember he'd been happy last night because she'd helped convince Steph to sign with Everest Records.

Daniel had been happy with her too, and then she'd started to fall for him. Or rather let him seduce her. She couldn't make that mistake again. Henry was her boss and unless she wanted to go back to Farnham with her tail tucked between her legs she needed to make this job work.

She wasn't going to have that fairy tale happily-ever-after with Henry even if he was different from Daniel. She had to remember that she wasn't like other women—not anymore—and she didn't have the option of being a wife and mother to fall back on. For her it was a career or nothing.

She needed to keep to her vow. She needed to remember that if she had to leave *this* job, her only option might be working for her sister.

She didn't want to have to start over yet again. The

only way she was going to keep this job was to be firm with herself and focus on doing the best she could.

She almost believed herself that she could do it, she could keep her vow—until Henry walked through the door.

"Morning, Astrid. Have you got any messages for me?"

She looked up into his bright blue eyes and forgot what he'd asked. All she could remember was the way his shoulders had felt under her hands last night. The softness of those firm lips of his against hers. And the way he'd twisted his fingers in the back of her hair.

"Astrid?"

"Yes, Henry."

"Messages?" he asked.

She handed him the messages and realized she'd done it again. Allowed her crush to interfere with her professional career.

Henry had taken one look at the button-down suit that Astrid had on and realized that kissing her last night had been a mistake. He knew he had to retreat. Had to give her room to regain the confidence she'd had the day before. He should have known that a woman who'd been badly burned by an office affair wouldn't want to jump into another one with her new boss.

But the moonlight had been too entrancing.... Hell, the moonlight had absolutely nothing to do with why he had kissed her. It had been Astrid—her lips, her body and her sexy smile that had tempted him. That and the fact that he didn't like that Daniel Martin had touched her. That the other man had at one time claimed Astrid as his own.

He was first and foremost a competitor. The need to win had been burned into the fabric of his being at a very young age. His mother had often blamed Malcolm for the fact that he was so competitive, but she was just as aggressive when it came to her career.

There was a rap on his door.

"Come in."

"Sir, I mean, Henry. Davis from accounting is here to see you."

"Close the door, Astrid," Henry said.

She stepped inside and closed the door behind her. "Yes?"

"Does he have an appointment?"

"No. But he says its urgent. You do have ten minutes if you wanted to see him. Just a reminder—Steph Cordo is due here in twenty minutes and I know you want to be available then."

He smiled to himself. She was very efficient and the best assistant he'd ever had. Okay, the only one, but she was still good.

"Thank you. When Steph gets here, escort her to the conference room. We'll bring in everyone she needs to talk to. Also, Steven will be stopping by toward the end of the hour with her."

"Steven?"

"My half brother. We are going to set up an in-store performance for Steph at the Everest Mega Store located in Leicester Square."

"Sounds good. Do you want me to interrupt if Davis isn't out of here in ten minutes?"

"That'd be great."

She turned to leave, and though he was trying to

keep his mind on business, he couldn't help but notice the way her slim-fitting skirt hugged the curves of her backside.

"Henry?"

She paused in the doorway. "After Steph's appointment, I'd like five minutes of your time."

"What for?"

"We can speak later. I don't want to mess up your schedule."

"Davis can wait. Tell him I'll have time tomorrow morning and then come back in here."

"Really—"

"I've made my mind up."

She left without another word. It was good to be the boss. Since he'd earned the top spot on the team and here at the office, he got things his way. Something that Henry freely admitted he liked.

She reentered his office less than a minute later, closing the door behind her, but remaining in the doorway.

"Sit down."

She did.

"What's on your mind?"

"Last night."

"What about it?"

She took a deep breath and looked him straight in the eye. His respect for her rose a notch.

"I like you, Henry. But this job…I'm aware that this is probably my last chance to make a go at the music industry. And I don't want to mess this up."

"Why would last night have anything to do with that?" he asked. "I'm not your last boss. If I kiss you, I'm not going to fire you."

She glanced down at her lap where her fingers were tightly laced together. "I wasn't fired due to our affair. Daniel kept me on after things ended. I don't want you to get the wrong impression of Daniel."

Henry didn't like her defending the other man. That reaction made little sense to him so he ignored the source. "Why then?"

"I was sick. And I did take a lot of time off from work. That was what made him sack me."

"Did you find it difficult to work with him after your affair ended?" he asked. Then realized he was prying into very personal areas. He could work with Astrid, kiss her and whatnot, without knowing any of the details of her past. Except he wanted to know more.

"No. It was something else entirely. But I like you and I really like this job. I don't want to make another decision based on lust and end up regretting it."

Henry leaned back in his chair. "So you lust after me?"

"Henry, please, I'm trying to be serious."

"Sorry, Astrid, but you brought up sex and I'm a guy. That means my mind is going to automatically shut down."

She smiled. "You are more than some sex-crazed maniac. That's why I'm talking to you. I know you want to beat your half brothers and I think we have a chance of doing that, but only if we both concentrate on business."

"This is all in my best interest?" Henry asked.

"Well, it's not going to be bad for me, either," she admitted.

His respect for Astrid rose even more. And he realized she wasn't the kind of woman he'd always been attracted to. She was so forthright. She wasn't just out for herself and what she could get.

That was more refreshing than he would have imagined.

"I just want us both to be successful," she said.

He stood up and walked around to the front of his desk, leaning back against it so that he faced her. "Thank you, Astrid. I will do my best to keep my baser instincts in check, but I'm not sure I'll be successful."

"I'm going to keep dressing in my ultraprofessional suits," she said.

He laughed. It wasn't the clothing or her sexy body that was making him want her, though they definitely played a part. It was the woman she was, but he doubted telling her would help either of them.

It was a late night almost three weeks into her tenure at Everest Records. She'd been on the phone with a number of radio stations throughout the U.K. and Europe to make sure that everyone had received the packages she'd sent out about Steph.

Henry had been out doing his nightly club thing, and she was sitting in the office by herself.

"Another late night?"

She looked up to see him standing in the doorway. "My boss can be a slave driver." She smiled.

"Really? I thought I was easing up a bit. Giving you room to grow and all that."

"Is that what you are trying to do?"

"I think so. You said that you wanted a career in music so I've been introducing you to all the departments—A & R, marketing."

"It has been smashing," she said.

"Truly?"

"Well, it's different than what I did for Daniel. I mean, for him I was just his assistant, but you are giving me my own responsibilities. I'm enjoying it."

Henry nodded. "Good. Then maybe you can start to relax here at the office."

"I already have," she said. It surprised her. She'd kept her guard up and tried not to see Henry as anything other than her boss. But he was a stand-up guy behind the celebrity profile. She fielded a dozen questions a day from magazines and newspaper reporters about where he was going to be. Some of the information she leaked because Henry wanted some extra coverage for a group or for his friends.

"Good," he said again, leaving her to go into his office. She just sat there and tried not to think too much about the fact that he was treating her like an employee and he hadn't tried to kiss her once since that night at her flat. Which was perfect, really, since she wasn't interested in him as a man. At least that's what she kept telling herself.

Astrid borrowed her sister's car for the evening and left it parked near Waterloo Station so she could have Henry drop her off there if she needed to. She didn't want to risk having him at her flat again. They were hitting another string of clubs tonight. It had been four weeks since she'd talked to him in his office. For the most part he kept his hands to himself. But his gaze often lingered on her lips or her figure.

And she found herself wishing she'd kept her mouth shut. She wanted to feel his arms around her. Each night in her dreams she relived that brief kiss he'd given her at her door. She wasn't going to allow herself to pine for him, but a part of her—the part that she sometimes thought would never come to her senses—longed for Henry.

She took the Underground to Covent Garden and walked to Bungalow 8. The exclusive club had been known to turn away even celebs, so she was a little intimidated to approach the bouncer.

"Can I help you?"

"I'm meeting Henry Devonshire," she said. "I'm Astrid Taylor."

"Of course, Ms. Taylor. He asked that you join him in the VIP area. The hostess will direct you once you are inside."

The electronica music pulsed through her body as she followed the hostess to the VIP area. She should be getting used to so many late nights, but she wasn't. And when she approached Henry's table, she noticed that it was full of people. She'd realized quickly that part of Henry's charm was his easygoing manner.

No wonder the bouncer had simply let her in. She was probably one of fifteen people who'd used Henry's name to get in the door tonight.

He looked up when she approached and gave her a half smile. He gestured for her to have a seat at the end of his table and she sat down next to a man she'd seen on TV and Lonnie from their office. She chatted with the TV guy—"call me Alan"—until he left with a group of three women. Henry waved her down to a seat next to him.

"Have you been listening to this group?"

"Hard not to," she said. Since the music even in the

VIP section was blaringly loud, it made conversation impossible.

"What do you think of it?"

She turned her head toward the sound and closed her eyes. One of the first things she'd realized about good music was that it had the power to entrance a person. Make someone forget about the problems of everyday life. The band didn't spark that feeling.

"It's nice."

"But not great," Henry said.

"Exactly. They are a good band and I bet they'd do well for one album, but I don't think they have the kind of sound that would sustain a lasting career," she said.

"Good. I like your instincts."

"Thanks," she said.

"The next band is the one that Roger recommended to me. I think you'll like them."

"Why?" she asked. She wanted to know what Henry thought she'd like and why. Did he really know her? It had only been a few weeks, though she'd come to know him pretty well since they'd spent so much time together.

"Because they have a nice sound with a pop groove but there's something retro about their lyrics. They talk about real emotions, which I've noticed you like as I've been listening to the tapes of the bands you want me to sign."

"I noticed you noticing," she said. Over the past two weeks he had paid a lot of attention to her at work, asking her opinions on bands, giving her decision-making power on booking groups for radio tours and whatnot. Mostly he's treated her like a respected peer, and that was all she'd needed.

"Good. I wanted you to see that I'm not like Daniel," Henry said.

"Why?" she asked.

"Because I'm going to kiss you again, Astrid, and this time I don't want you to run."

She felt foolish when he said it like that. But then she was human, she thought. And resisting temptation, especially the type that he offered, was too hard.

"I'm not going to make another foolish mistake," she said, not sure if she meant the words for Henry or for herself.

"Good," he said. He reached under the table and took her hand in his. His big hand completely engulfed hers. They announced the band XSU. Sounded like some American university band and the guys looked the part.

In their denim jeans and faded vintage T-shirts they looked as though they were meant to be singing to university crowds instead of this very upscale and trendy club in London.

They introduced their first song and the music was… sex-disco. A pulsing beat that made her want to get up and dance. She was tapping her feet and noticed that Henry was moving to the beat, as well. The dance floor, which had been crowded before now, seemed to be a single solid wave of dancing bodies.

Henry used his grip on her hand to tug her to her feet. They were in the middle of the swaying crowd. Henry's body brushed hers often as they danced, each brush reminding her that she'd done a poor job of keeping the distance she'd wanted between them.

She tried to be stiff, tried to keep a part of herself locked away but it was impossible. She wanted Henry.

And this music reminded her that life was meant to be lived, not hidden away from.

She stopped thinking she had to be professional and just relaxed, allowing herself to just be herself. And that moment changed her. She looked into Henry's impossibly blue eyes and saw more than she'd thought to see.

In taking the measure of the man, she knew that no matter what happened between them, she'd never regret the time they spent together.

Chapter 5

Something had changed in Astrid when XSU had started playing. She seemed to sparkle with life as she moved on the dance floor, and Henry wanted to be the only one who basked in that glow.

He kept one hand on her hip as they danced. Her body brushed against his, teasing him with each rhythmic move she made. He wanted more than those fleeting touches. He wanted her breasts pressed solidly against his chest, his hands holding her hips and that tempting mouth of hers under his.

The music stopped, but he scarcely noticed. The crowd applauded, and in the back of his mind Henry realized that he'd found the first group he'd sign to the Everest Records label, and he'd use a similar path to the one he developed with Steph Cordo. But he'd also found something else, he thought.

Astrid watched him with those big brown eyes of hers, and he leaned in and kissed her. He didn't think about consequences or warnings. Didn't think about winning or business. Just thought that this woman was temptation incarnate and he was tired of denying himself.

He lingered over her mouth. The last three weeks had been too long as far as his body was concerned. Blood flowed heavier through his veins. Her hands came to his shoulders, anchoring her as she rose on tiptoe to deepen their kiss.

The crowd swayed around them as the band moved on to the next song, but Henry felt the world narrow until he and Astrid were alone.

She tasted tangy and sweet and of something that was uniquely Astrid. There was an energy between them, and when he lifted his head she tunneled her fingers into the hair at the nape of his neck and brought their mouths together again.

She sighed as he kissed her. "I've been dying for your kiss."

He took her hand and led her off the dance floor. "Have you?"

She nodded.

"I'm tired of pretending that I don't want you, but that doesn't mean I think this is right. You already guessed that my relationship with Daniel complicated my last job. I can't afford to let that happen again."

"What can I say to change your mind?" Henry asked.

"I'm not sure. I just…I'm not saying I don't want you, just that I'm not sure it's wise for me to get involved with you, Henry."

"We will figure it out," Henry said. "I want to go talk to the band. Want to come with me?"

She nodded.

He held on to her hand and he no longer felt that she was just his assistant. Now he knew she was his. And he liked that. He needed to make love to her before he'd really feel she was his.

The band had a small group of women hanging around them as he approached. Henry used his celebrity to get closer to the band. He approached the black-shirted bouncer protecting the backstage area, who was turning away scantily clad women and overzealous fans.

"I'm Henry Devonshire, and I'd like to speak to the band."

"Henry Devonshire. I saw you score a converted try in the last minute of the London-Irish game—your last one."

"That was a great game. Stan got that penalty and I thought we were going to lose."

"But you didn't. You were brilliant."

"Thanks," Henry said. "I'd appreciate it if you'd let us back to see that band."

"Sure thing, mate." The bouncer stepped aside and let them through.

"Henry Devonshire," he said as he approached the lead singer.

"Angus McNeil," the young man said, shaking Henry's hand.

"I like the sound of your group."

"Thanks, man. We've been experimenting with a lot of different influences and I'm not sure we have it right yet."

"I'd like to talk to you a little more about that. I'm in

charge of Everest Records now," Henry said. "Do you guys have a manager?"

"Yes. B&B Management."

"I've never heard of them," Henry said. He glanced over at Astrid to see if she were familiar with the company, but she shook her head.

"It's actually my older brother and one of his mates," Angus said a little sheepishly. "No one wanted to talk to us unless we had a big deal going. So Bryan went to the library and got a few books.... Ah, man, you don't want to hear all that, do you?"

"Yes, we do, Angus," Astrid said, stepping forward. "At Everest Groups, we like to know everything about the artists we sign."

"That's why we are here," Henry said. "Do you have another set or can you guys come with me to talk?"

The other band members had wandered over to their group and milled about exchanging glances. Henry decided he should step away and let them talk.

"Here's my card. I'm going to be out in the club for another hour or so. If you have time to talk tonight, great, if not, no problem. Call tomorrow and we will set up something."

He led Astrid back to the VIP area, but he was restless and didn't want to sit and wait. He ordered drinks for both of them and Astrid put her hand on his.

"I can feel the energy crackling around you. What are you thinking about?"

Henry didn't like to share his most intimate thoughts so he kept silent until he realized that Astrid would give him the distraction he needed. "That you still haven't told me your secrets."

"Well, that will have to wait for another time. A noisy nightclub is no place for an intimate conversation."

"I disagree. This is the perfect place. There's a feel of anonymity to being here. The background noise keeps others from hearing."

She tipped her head to the side and then leaned forward so that their noses almost touched. "It wouldn't keep you from hearing."

He arched one eyebrow at her. "Good. Tell me your secrets, Astrid."

She shook her head. "Not unless you tell me yours. Not the stuff I can read in *Hello!,* but the real Henry's secrets. Why are you so restless right now?"

Henry didn't want to share that with her. He was reluctant to let anyone know about the impulses that had always driven him—the need for immediacy in every area of his life.

Astrid was still almost high on her new sense of self. She had always let the men in her life...well, Daniel, set the tone and the pace of their relationship. And she knew if she was going to have any chance at making any kind of relationship with Henry work, she needed to change.

Instead of focusing on hiding her own secrets, she wanted to know about his. What had shaped Henry into the man he was today?

He wrapped his arm around her shoulder and drew her closer to him. "I'm not restless, love. I want to be alone with you so we can finish what we started on the dance floor."

She shivered as he spoke straight into her ear. The

warmth of his breath against her neck sent electric pulses flooding through her body. She wanted him, too.

And that scared her. Lust she could deal with but this was more than lust. She liked Henry. Liked the man who was more than his press bio. And she was afraid to trust that gut-deep feeling about Henry. She thought he was different, but there was no guarantee any relationship between the two of them was going to last more than a few months.

"What's that look for?" he asked her.

"I'm scared that I'm in over my head," she said in a moment of candor. She might regret it later, but if she'd learned anything it was not to pull her punches. There was no "safe-route" in any relationship.

"My first year as a professional rugby player I was constantly terrified. My stepdad was the coach and I knew that if I screwed up, he'd come down on me. And I played from a place of fear for the first three games, before one of the guys said to me, 'I heard you were good, but now it looks like that was all bullshit.'"

"That wasn't very nice."

Henry shrugged. "I was giving in to the pressure from every avenue, so I made a decision that I was going to play for myself. Not for Gordon or for the crowd. Just for myself."

"Did that work?" Astrid asked.

"Yes, it did. My playing started improving and eventually I was made captain."

"Good job," she said.

"I used that same theory off the pitch. I live my life on my terms."

"I'm trying to do the same, but there is always a fear—"

"Stop worrying, Astrid."

He glanced over her shoulder and stood to greet someone else—a tall dark-haired young man whose shaggy hair reached his shoulders.

"I'm Bryan Monroe. I represent XSU."

"Glad to meet you. This is Astrid, my assistant. Would you like to sit down and join us for a drink?"

"Love to."

Astrid sank back into her seat and just observed Henry doing his thing. People came and went from his table, which was the norm for Henry, but he kept his attention on everyone. He always had a glass of seltzer water on the table in front of him. She'd quickly realized that her boss didn't drink on these long nights out. And he had a work ethic that would put anyone to shame.

Daniel had often used other people to make things happen. She had observed him leaving clubs early with groupies while his underlings stayed and talked details. Every minute she spent with Henry made her like him a little more.

She started to get tired and fought to keep from yawning at about two in the morning. She signaled to Henry that she was going to leave.

"Wait for me," he said to her.

Thirty minutes later, they walked out of the club together. "I think we're going to get XSU."

"Definitely. Bryan sounded very encouraging. I'll follow up with him first thing tomorrow."

"I'll give you a ride home," Henry said.

"Not necessary. I drove Bethann's car today."

"Why?"

"I didn't want to take advantage of you. I appreciate the fact that you are always giving me a ride but it seemed important to have my own way home."

"Why is that?" he asked.

"Because I always want to invite you up to my place and that's not a good idea, is it?"

Astrid didn't regret her candor. They both knew the attraction between them was growing. There was nothing they could do about it.

"I think inviting me up is a fine idea. Why haven't you?"

"Because you're my boss, Henry," she said. The night breeze was cool and a little crisp as she tipped her head back to stare up at the stars.

"Why is your name Henry?"

He laughed a soft sound. "It was my mum's dad's name. What about you, Astrid?"

"My mother got it from a book. Bethann was named after my mum's mum and me...I get a name from a book," she said.

"What book?"

"*Pippi Longstocking.* The author was Astrid Lindgren. My mum said she wanted me to have that passion for life that Pippi always had."

Astrid looked back over at Henry to find him watching her with that unreadable expression of his. She was talking too much, she knew, but she was tired. Physically of course, because her body had yet to adjust to the night owl hours, but also tired of keeping parts of herself from Henry. She wanted him to know the woman she was. Wanted him to look at her and see the real woman.

"I like that. Your mum sounds like she knew what she was doing when she named you," Henry said.

Astrid wasn't certain about that. A part of her had

always felt as though she had to live a larger life than her sister. Bethann was driven and always made the right choices. She had achieved more and accomplished great things, as opposed to Astrid, who was always starting over.

"I'm not so sure. But I do like where I am right now," she said.

Henry grabbed her hand, linking their fingers together as they walked down the street to where he'd parked his car.

"Have you ever thought about what you'd name your children?"

Astrid felt a sting of tears at his question. And turned away from him.

"Astrid?"

She shook her head. "Probably after my parents. You?"

"I've always thought I'd name a son after Jonny Wilkinson, the great rugby player."

"Better hope your wife likes the sport," she said. She tried to keep her tone light, but she knew that children was never going to be an easy topic for her…. How had they taken this track?

Henry didn't want to talk about kids; he'd never really thought much about them other than when his mum had given birth to his two younger half brothers. But there was a tone in Astrid's voice that made him believe he should pursue this line. There was something more to the way she had answered his throwaway question.

"What are your parents' names?" he asked.

"Spencer and Mary," she said. "I really don't want

to talk about this. I'm not even sure how we ended up on this topic."

He unlocked the passenger door of his car and helped her inside. He walked around to the driver's side and sat behind the wheel for a minute before starting it.

"My mum contemplated naming me Mick after Mick Jagger, but in the end she said she wanted to name me after the man who always loved her."

"That's sweet," Astrid said. She had to wonder how hard it was on Henry growing up the way he had. "Why did you play rugby? Wouldn't it have been easier for you to try to be a musician?"

Then she covered her mouth with one hand as a thought occurred to her. "Or can't you sing?"

"I can sing," Henry said. "Not very well, but I can sing."

"So why not music?"

"I'm a stubborn cuss," he said, starting the car. "I didn't want anyone to say I had anything given to me. I started playing rugby when I was eight. I'd already grown up in the glare of my mum's spotlight and the infamous circumstances surrounding my birth…. If I achieved anything I wanted it to be on my own terms."

He pulled out and started driving toward Astrid's car. "Where are you parked?"

"Near Waterloo," she said, giving him directions to the location.

"You were very wise to make that choice so young," she said. "Bethann is like that. She's a solicitor. Always knew she wanted to be one."

"What about you?"

"I always knew I wanted to live in London," she said

with a little laugh. "I love the excitement of the city and being so close to everything."

"Why don't you live in town?"

"Well, Woking was all I could afford on my own and all my mates are married now. Anyways, that's why I have a flat in Woking."

"I meant how did you find your way to the music industry?" Henry pulled into the car park where she'd left her car.

"My car's in the second level," she said. "I took a job out of university as a receptionist. It was with Mo Rollins Group, and I just sort of worked my way up. The funny thing is the longer I worked there the more at home I felt.

"It's that green Ford Fusion."

He pulled up behind the car and she gathered her bag to get out. But he wasn't ready to say good-night just yet.

"And now you're working for me. Still like this industry?" he asked.

"After a night like tonight? You bet. I loved the raw sound of XSU and once you sign them it'll be exciting to watch their transformation into a solid band."

"I agree. I had thought of being a sports agent or a recruiter."

"Why didn't you? I remember that telly show you had a few years ago that featured child protégés of the sports world."

"You do? Did you watch it?" he asked.

"Sometimes," she admitted. "How did you get into doing that?"

"My mum knows all kinds of people in the entertainment industry and after my injury she started putting me in touch with them."

"She sounds like she's very helpful."

Henry laughed. "She's a meddler. I told her I was going to live off my investments and just party all the time. That motivated her to use every contact she had to get me in touch with someone who could put me to work."

"And she got her way, didn't she?"

"Yes, she did. So I had the show, and I was talking to my own agent from when I was with the London Irish, but it was a frustrating job and I didn't really enjoy it."

"Is that when you turned to music?"

"Yes. I had the contacts in this world," Henry said.

"And it gives you something in common with your mum."

"Yes, it does. Want to come back to my place for a nightcap?"

"Um...what?"

"I don't want this night to end. I don't think you do either," he said.

She hesitated and then sighed. "No, I don't want it to end. But I have a busy day tomorrow."

"I know your boss."

"Yeah, that's what I'm afraid of. It's hard to balance working together with a personal relationship."

"Is it? Everest Group has no policy against fraternization, so your job isn't in jeopardy at all."

"Will that still be true if I say I want to go home?" she asked.

"Of course it will be. I think you know me better than that," Henry said. "And if you don't, then going home is definitely what you should do."

She bit her lower lip. "I'm sorry."

"It's fine. I guess I'll see you at work tomorrow."

"Yeah," she said, climbing out of the car. He watched her walk to her vehicle, and she opened the door, tossing her purse inside before looking back at him.

"Do you really want to pursue a relationship with me?" she asked.

He nodded. He couldn't get her out of his mind and he was tired of trying. He was going to have Astrid Taylor if for no other reason than they might be able to work without the tension of wondering what they'd be like together.

"I'm going to be honest with you, Henry. I'm not sure sleeping with you is in my best interest."

"Well, when you put it that way, I'm not either," Henry said. He reached out and tugged on one of her curls. He didn't want her to say no to him, but he knew that she had a lot more at stake than he did. He was trying to go slowly with her, but he was used to just reaching out and taking what he wanted.

And damn the consequences.

"Come to my country home this weekend," he said. "We can ride horses and play rugby and get to know each other."

She shook her head. "I already have plans."

"Then invite me along," he said. A shy man never got what he wanted.

"It's with my family.... Still want to come?"

"Yes. What's the occasion?"

"My sister's birthday. My mum's having a dinner party for her."

Henry realized that Astrid thought she had taken a

risk by inviting him. And he wasn't about to pass it up. "I'd love to."

"Good. I'll see you at work tomorrow, Henry. Thanks for the lift."

"You're welcome. Drive safely, Astrid."

She got in her car, and he backed up to let her leave in front of him. She was completely unlike any other woman he'd ever met and he was beginning to understand that was part of what attracted him to her.

Chapter 6

Astrid had had second, third and fourth thoughts about inviting Henry to her parents' house for Bethann's birthday, but she'd asked and he'd accepted, so there was no turning back now.

Henry hadn't been in the office the past two days so she hadn't seen him since she'd invited him. He'd sent her a text message the night before, asking what time to pick her up. Now she was standing in front of the mirror in her bedroom wishing that she'd turn into someone else. Someone who knew what she was doing with her life instead of a woman who just bumped along.

The bell rang and she sighed.

She walked through the flat and opened the door to find Henry standing there. He wore a striped button-down shirt with an open collar and a pair of dark trousers. He hadn't shaved but the light beard on his jaw made him look even sexier than he normally did.

"Come in," she said, stepping back so he could enter. "I have to grab my bag and then I'll be ready to go."

"Take your time," he said.

She went down the short hall to her bedroom and gathered her stuff as quickly as she could. When she came back Henry stood in front of the wall where she'd hung her family pictures.

"Is this Bethann?"

"Yes. When she passed her A levels. That's my parents' place, as well."

"Everyone looks happy," he said.

"We generally are," she said. She'd taken that happiness for granted. Thought that because she had a sunny outlook, her life would follow that path. But experience had taught her otherwise.

"Ready then?"

"Yes," he said, walking toward her. But instead of continuing on to the door, he stopped and pulled her into his arms.

He kissed her, and she shut her eyes, savoring that moment of closeness. A moment that passed all too quickly as Henry ended the kiss and then put his hand on the small of her back to lead her to the front door. He waited while she double-checked her lock and then they went downstairs.

A neighbor whose name she didn't know snapped a photo of them and then asked to have his picture taken with Henry. This was his life, she thought as she snapped a photo and then returned the camera.

Henry's mobile rang when they were in the car and on the A. He glanced at the caller ID.

"It's my mum. I have to take it."

"No problem," she said.

He put the phone on speaker. "Hello."

"Hi, Henry, it's Mum. Have you had a chance to talk to your friends about the television idea?"

"Yes. They are taking the idea up the chain of command. I think we will hear something soon."

"That's good. What are you doing today?"

"A birthday party for a friend," Henry said.

Astrid liked the respect and affection in his voice as he spoke to his mother. It was clear that their relationship was a close one. She continued to listen in on their conversation until he hung up.

"Sorry about that," he said.

"It's fine. She dotes on you, doesn't she?"

"Too much I think. But for a long time it was just the two of us, and she's never stopped taking care of me."

"That's really sweet. When did she remarry? I think you said you had some half brothers."

Henry talked and drove, weaving effortlessly through the traffic. His car had a powerful engine, and he drove fast but not recklessly. There was that sense of controlled power that she was continuously aware of with him.

"She married Gordon when I was nine. I'd started playing rugby and he was at a tourney we went to. They met there. My mum…she's vivacious. Everyone is entranced by her when they meet her."

"Much like her son," Astrid said.

"I don't know about that. I don't think I'd look nearly as good in her hats," he said very seriously.

"Are you having me on?"

He laughed. "I am. I got a lot of things from my mum."

His Sat Nav with the Mr. T voice directed him off the

motorway and toward her childhood home. She started
worrying about how her parents would be with Henry.

They thought nothing of delving into someone's past.
And Henry…he certainly had had an interesting one.
He parked on the street in front of the house, and she
reached over to stop him from getting out.

"Yes?"

"Listen, everyone is going to be curious about you.
Don't take it personally. They are just that way."

"It's fine. I'm hoping maybe they'll answer a few
questions for me."

"What about?"

"You. I've been waiting for you to tell me your secrets, and I think meeting your family will show me
another side of you."

Astrid shook her head. She wasn't ready to tell him
all the details of her relationship with Daniel. That she'd
gotten pregnant and lost the baby—and her life and her
dreams had changed. "I'm nothing special, Henry. I'm
just like any other girl from Surrey."

She reached for the handle of the door, but Henry
stopped her this time. "You're not like anyone else in
the world, Astrid."

There was something in his blue eyes that made her
want to believe him. But she was afraid to trust. Afraid
to believe in anything that this man had to say. Yet at the
same time she was afraid that those barriers wouldn't
be enough to protect her. Because no matter what she
tried to tell herself, she knew that she was starting to
trust him.

That was why she'd invited him here today and why
she let him take her hand in his as they walked up to

the front door. Bethann answered the door and Astrid realized her older sister wasn't too pleased with her, or her choice of date.

Henry took his a pint of Guinness outside to the deck, where he stood next to Astrid's dad, Spencer. Spence had a thick Cockney accent and a tattoo of a dancing girl on his forearm that he'd picked up while he'd been in the Royal Marines in Japan. He was affable, but a quiet man who was confined to a wheelchair due to complications from diabetes.

He recognized Henry from his playing days, but had immediately confessed that he preferred football to rugby. The conversation was pleasant enough until Astrid's sister Bethann came to join them.

"Can I have a word?" Bethann asked.

"Sure," Henry said.

"Walk with me down to the summerhouse," she said.

It was easy to see that this woman was a solicitor. Astrid was by no means a passive woman, but Bethann was every inch the protective older sister.

When they got to the summerhouse, Bethann took a seat on the red cushion and gestured for him to do the same.

"You look like you're about to bring me up on charges," he said.

"Don't make fun. I'm sorry if you think I'm out of line, but I can't just let you go without saying something."

"Saying what?" he asked.

"My sister isn't someone you should toy with. She has a family who cares about her, and I think you should know that my practice specializes in women's rights."

Henry felt a swell of compassion for Bethann. Clearly she was at least a little aware of the situation with Astrid's previous employer, and Henry could tell that she was struggling to protect her little sister.

"I am so informed. I have no intention of harming your sister, Bethann. I am attracted to her, and if she decided she wants more from me, then there is nothing you can say that will stop me."

"All men say that."

"Even your husband? Did he make a promise to you and break it?" he asked.

He'd met Percy Montrose, Bethann's husband, briefly before the other man had left to run to Tesco for more ice.

"Especially him," she said. "But when he messes up he fixes it. And I want to know if Henry Devonshire is the kind of man who will do the same."

"Is there really anything I can say that would convince you that I'm an upstanding man? You seem to have your mind made up about me."

"I don't. I'm sorry if it seemed that way. It's just—listen, I love my sister and I don't want to see her stuck—"

Henry put his hand on Bethann's shoulder. "Me, either."

She looked at him, her level stare probing and then she sighed. "Okay."

"Henry?" Astrid called.

"In here," he said.

"Percy's back and we are ready to eat," Astrid said.

"Great," Bethann said, stepping around them and heading up toward the house.

"What did she want?"

"Just to make sure I wasn't going to hurt you," Henry

said. "Whatever happened with Daniel…there was more than the ending of an affair, wasn't there?"

"I can't…I don't want to talk about that right now, okay?"

Henry saw the distress he'd caused her with his question. It was the second time he'd seen the sheen of tears in her eyes.

"Let's go up to the house," he said, letting his pursuit lie for the moment.

She put her arm through his as they walked up to the patio, where her mother had set the table. It was a beautiful day, the kind that they'd learned to relish in England since it was so often cloudy or rainy.

But today the weather was nice. Percy was a likable fellow who had a dry wit. He had no problems teasing everyone at the table including Henry. Astrid clearly liked her brother-in-law and flirted in an innocent way with the man.

"Are you a football man like Spencer?" he asked Percy.

"Not at all. In fact, Spencer used to be a big London Irish fan."

"Used to be?"

"Don't get around as good as I used to, so I miss a lot of games. Watching it on the telly isn't the same," Spencer said, shifting his wheelchair to intercept the conversation.

"No, it's not. Are you managing well with the wheelchair today?"

"Listen to your doctor," Spencer said by way of answer. "I didn't and look where it got me. I'm afraid I'm a bit stubborn. May have passed that trait on to Astrid."

"I have to say I think you have. She definitely knows her own mind," Henry said.

"That she does," Spencer agreed. "But we did love those games. You know my girls tried to get me to a few once I was in this damned chair but it was too much work and it broke my heart seeing them so exhausted from everything that I told them we weren't going anymore."

"Yes, he used to take both of the girls to the games when they were little. I believe that Astrid even had a poster hanging on her side of the bedroom.... Which player was that?" Percy asked.

Astrid flushed and Bethann swatted at her husband. "Enough out of you."

"You had a poster on your wall?" Henry asked.

"It was of you," she said. Everyone at the table was laughing.

"She had a huge crush on you when you first joined the team," Mary said.

"Mum!" Astrid was flushed with color. And for once she was at a loss for words. Here, with the people who knew her best, there were no barriers like the ones she usually kept up.

"Well, Bethann had a crush on Ronan Keating, and she was an adult then."

"He's cute," Bethann said.

"He looks nothing like me," Percy said.

"I am allowed to like men who don't look like you," Bethann said.

"No, you're not," Percy said with a grin.

The conversation continued on in the same vein and Astrid leaned over to him. "Who's your secret crush?"

"Umm...I don't believe I ever had one."

"No Victoria Beckham posters on your wall?"

He shook his head. He had never been much into lusting after unattainable women. He preferred to focus his attention on real women.

"Come on, whom do you like?" Percy said.

Henry reached under the table and took Astrid's hand in his. "Astrid."

"Oh, ho," Percy said. "Trying to show me up?"

"Is it working?" Henry asked.

"Yes!" Bethann said. She smiled at Henry, and he knew that her fears had been placated for the time being.

The afternoon at her parents' had spilled over into evening, and it was after ten when Henry and she pulled into the parking area at her flat. Henry had been a good sport all day.

"Thank you," she said, caught in a peaceful glow. She kept her head resting on the back of the seat and just turned it to look at him.

"For what?" he asked.

He'd left the car running and the music playing softly in the background. An American group—the Dave Matthews Band—"Pay for What You Get." It was a pay-it-forward type song that made her realize that no matter where a person was in life, everyone paid the cost for their actions. It was a song about karma, and today she felt hers was good.

Today she'd seen that Henry *was* the type of man she'd thought he was. He blended easily with her family, even though she knew he probably could have bought and sold them many times over. He had fit in, something that Daniel never had. In fact he'd never even met her family, although they'd dated for over a year.

"For putting up with my family," she said.

"I like your family. It took me a bit to realize your dad was having me on with liking football."

Astrid smiled. "He's like that. It's a harmless thing."

"I know. I like him. He reminds me of my stepdad."

"In what way?"

"The way he is with you and your sister. The love he has for your mum. I can tell that family is important to Spencer and it is to Gordon, as well."

"Really? I'm going to tell him. My dad will get a kick out of that."

"Is the wheelchair why you stopped going to the rugby matches?" Henry asked.

"Yes," she said. "It's hard for him to get around and the seats we typically had weren't easy to get to."

They'd tried to go a couple of games but it really had been a struggle. She had noticed that her father got angry at himself for not having the abilities he used to.

"I have a box at Madejski stadium. Do you think your folks would like to join us at a game?"

"I know they would," she said. "Would you really invite them? It's meant for corporate socializing, isn't it?"

"I can use it for whatever I want," Henry said. "I'm the boss."

"You like saying that, don't you?"

"Yes, I do. I'm a leader."

"Always?"

"Yes, except for when I first started playing, I've always been the one in control. The one making sure everyone else got to where they needed to go."

He was good at it. She suspected it was simply his affability that made most people unaware of the core of steel in him. Subtly events and people were moved where he wanted them to be.

Even her?

She told herself she was the one woman who saw him and who knew the truth about the man behind his BBC Channel Four exposé profile. But she wasn't entirely sure.

It hadn't taken her too long to realize that Henry was really good at keeping the spotlight off himself. He had secrets, same as she did, but he kept them hidden.

"Invite me up," he said.

"I was thinking about it."

"Good. I'll get your door."

He was out of the car and around to her side in minutes. She liked that he took the time to open her door for her. It was old-fashioned but a sign of respect.

"I didn't invite you up," she said, feeling more like herself when he reached for her hand to help her out of the car.

"I know. But you're going to."

She just laughed. He was all things to everyone. Today she'd seen how easily he could charm her taxi-driver father, her solicitor sister and her brother-in-law. "Promise me this is real."

He looked down at her. "What do you mean?"

She took a deep breath. Was she being too needy? Or reading things into this—into him? Was she making him into the man she wanted him to be? "Are you pretending to be what I need you to be?"

"Why would I? I'm not playing games with you," he said.

She wanted to believe. She truly did. She would

make herself crazy if she tried to examine every move he made.

She led the way up to her flat, surprised at how not-weird it felt to have Henry in her place. She took off her shoes because her feet ached after wearing heels all day.

"Would you like something to drink?"

"Coffee would be great," he said.

She went into the kitchen to make it. When she came back out, Henry was thumbing through the stack of CDs that she had in her living room. "I have too many, I keep saying I'm going to get organized…."

"I'm the same way. I like your taste."

"Do you now?"

"Indeed. Do you mind if I put on some music?"

"No, go ahead. I have some biscuits if you'd like something with your coffee," she said.

"I'd love some. I have a bit of a sweet tooth."

"I've noticed."

"Have you?"

"That little jar of sweets on the end of my desk. I must have refilled it at least three times a week since we started working together."

"You've found me out," he said.

"I have. And I intend to know all about you before much longer," she said. Better to know his secrets than let him find out hers. She left him at her CD player and went to pour the coffee for them. She brought it into her sitting room on a tray that had been her grandmother's.

Henry was leaning back on the settee with his eyes closed. She had switched on her iPod with its Bose docking station, and some old-time jazz played in the background. Louis Armstrong with Ella Fitzgerald singing. The playlist was mellow and eclectic.

She sat down next to Henry and he put his arm around her shoulders and drew her close to his side. After a few minutes he tipped her head up. His mouth moved over hers with surety, and this time there was nothing light or short about his kiss.

Chapter 7

"Dance with me," Henry said. He stood up and drew her to her feet and into his arms.

She wrapped her arms around his waist and rested her head against his chest as the song changed, and the sweet mellow sounds of Alan Jackson filled the room. The country music singer had a way of making Astrid cry whenever she listened to his singing, but she really liked the raw emotionality of his music.

As they swayed, Henry sang quietly along with the music, his deep voice finding the countermelody to Alan Jackson's. And despite what he'd said earlier about not really having any musical talent, she could tell that he did.

She tipped her head to say something to him, but his mouth captured her words, and he kissed her deeply while he moved their bodies in time to the song.

He bit her lower lip lightly as he pulled back. Nibbling kisses trailed against her jaw until his tongue brushed at the spot just under her ear.

"This is what I wanted to do to you when we were in the club on Wednesday. Pull you into my arms and run my hands down your back."

She shivered, loving the intimate sound of the words spoken right into her ear. "Why didn't you?"

"There were too many people around. I didn't think you'd welcome a photo in *Ok!* of the two of us."

"No, I wouldn't have." She'd had enough of tabloids to last a lifetime.

His hands found the back of her skirt and drew it up her legs. She felt his hand on the back of her thigh as the music changed to Bonnie Raitt, burning in the fire of love. A fire built in her with the brush of his hands against her. His hips moved in time with the music. His erection brushing against her lower stomach and the music combined with Henry's touch seduced away her fears and worries until she was nothing but a bundle of need and want.

And all of it was centered on Henry Devonshire.

She unbuttoned his shirt so she could rub her hands over his chest. He had a light matting of hair and she liked the way it felt against her fingers. She ran her hands over his pecs and then slowly traced her way down his stomach.

His mouth on hers was hot and real. The sting of his five-o'clock stubble against her skin excited her. He found the zipper in the side seam of her dress and lowered it and before the next song came on the stereo, she was down to her ice-blue panties and matching bra. And Henry had on only his pants.

"Let me look at you," he said, stepping back from her.

He drew her arms out from her sides. "You are one sexy woman."

She shook her head. "I'm not of the same caliber as the women you usually date."

"No, you're not. You are sexier because you are real," he said. "Will you dance for me?"

She hesitated. She wanted to turn him on. She wanted to make him so hot that he couldn't wait to get inside of her.

"Yes," she said.

"Good. Stay here," he said. He left her standing in the middle of her sitting room, the light from the side table illuminating them in its soft glow. The scent of the coffee filled the air. He played with the remote until the song changed and a new tune started.

"'Let's Get It On'?" she said with a laugh.

"Yes, baby. Show me you feel like I feel."

She threw her head back and laughed. In this moment she felt so damned alive. Her hips moved unconsciously in time with the rhythm of the music, her gaze on Henry. He leaned back on the settee to watch her, and she felt her inhibitions slowly fall away until she was dancing toward him.

With her hands on the back of the settee, she leaned down to sing softly into his ear while moving her body over his.

"You have a sexy singing voice," he said.

"Do I?"

"Yes. Why didn't you tell me you could sing?"

She perched on his lap. "Because I'm not good like the singers you listen to all day."

"You're better," he said, "because you only sing for me."

His hands came up to her waist and caressed their way up her back. She stood up and took a step away from him, swirling out of his reach, only to realize he'd unfastened her bra. She let it slide down her arms and drop to the floor.

Suddenly, she felt his hands on her back open, stronger now, pulling her close until she was nestled in his arms. His body swayed with the rhythm of hers. His hands cupped her breasts. His hard-on nudged her buttocks, and she felt as if she was going to explode.

He put his mouth on the base of her neck and suckled gently while they danced to the music. She couldn't take much more. She felt achingly empty and tried to turn in his arms. But he held her in place with one big hand on her waist.

The music changed again. This time "Sexual Healing" played, and she couldn't help but shiver as his hands slid lower until his fingers were sliding between her skin and her panties.

She tried to turn and this time he let her. She pulled his head to hers, her mouth devouring his as passion overwhelmed her. She wanted him. She needed him. *Now.*

She walked them backward toward the couch and he followed her lead. She put her hands between them fumbling for his belt, but he stopped her. "Not yet."

"I need you, Henry."

"Soon, baby. But I want you to come first."

She shook her head, but Henry wasn't paying attention to her. He'd lowered his head and was kissing her breast. One hand stroked her and then she felt the warmth of his breath against her nipple.

She tunneled her fingers into his hair, holding him to her breast, needing him to continue sucking on her. Everything in her body reacted to the feel of him. It had been a long time since any man had made her feel the way he did.

"Henry." His name burst from her lips as his other hand slid back between her legs, pushing her panties down her thighs. She moved her legs until the wisp of material slid down to the floor.

Henry stroked her mons and her thighs, with touches that were everywhere, teasing her ceaselessly. Finally his forefinger brushed against her, and she almost screamed with the pleasure of it. But that touch was fleeting. He switched his mouth to her other breast. He rubbed her up and down and then swirled his finger in a light circle.

She did scream then, feeling the beginning of an orgasm ripping through her. She clenched her thighs together and dug her nails into his shoulders.

He lifted his head.

"I like the sound of you coming," he said. "Almost as sexy as you singing." She'd never seen anything more beautiful than this man in the flush of sexual need for her.

"No more waiting," she said.

"No more," he agreed. He lifted her in his arms and carried her down the hall to her bedroom, setting her gently down in the center of the bed. His clothes were tossed to the floor and he stood next to her completely naked.

She touched his erection, lingering at the tip where

a bit of moisture beaded. She swiped her finger over it and brought her finger to her mouth, licking it off.

He growled at the sight. Then he lowered himself until he covered her and they were pressed together, chest to breast, groin to groin. She wrapped her legs around his hips. His mouth ravaged hers. She shifted underneath him, and he rolled over onto his back, drawing her over him.

She'd never been on top. She wasn't sure what to do and felt so damned exposed, but when he leaned up and took one of her nipples in his mouth, she forgot everything except the sensations he stirred in her.

His mouth found hers. Their tongues tangled, and she felt overwhelmed as his hands roamed all over her body, his fingers rubbing and caressing every inch of her skin while he made love to her with his mouth.

She knelt with one leg on either side of his hips as his hands grabbed her waist. He wrapped his arms around her, and his mouth latched on to her nipple, suckling her strongly.

"Henry!"

Humid warmth pooled in the center of her body and she rocked against him, feeling him against her center. She wanted more. She needed him deep inside her. She needed it now.

This was nothing like the sexual encounters she usually had. It was more intense, more real, and she forced down the emotions that threatened to surface and focused only on the physical sensations. She wasn't ready to admit that this was anything more than a physical joining. She didn't want to start to care for Henry—not while she knew her secrets were still buried deep inside.

He was hot, hard and ready between their bodies.

She rocked against him, finding her own pleasure as he continued to lick and suck at her breasts. He held her in his strong hands, to control the movements of her hips.

Skimming his hands down her sides, he explored every inch of her skin. She felt raw and vulnerable and wanted to reach for him and turn the tables, but she couldn't. His hands and mouth were everywhere, making her crave more of his touch.

His mouth reached her mons at last and he rested for a moment, his eyes looking up at her. She wanted him so badly. Wanted to feel his mouth on her and his tongue and fingers inside her.

"Henry?"

"Hmm," he murmured, turning his head from side to side, caressing her with his entire face.

"Please…"

He moved back up over her body, stretching her arms over her head. She gripped the headboard, wrapping her fingers around the base of it. His strong, rough body brushed over hers in one big caress that brought every one of her senses to hyperawareness. She couldn't take this slow build to passion. She wrapped her legs around his waist and tried to impale herself on him but he pulled back.

He nibbled his way down the center of her body again, pressing her breasts against his face as he continued on his path straight back to her aching center.

She parted her legs, opening them widely for him, and he lowered his head, taking her in his mouth. First his warm breath caressed her and then his tongue. His fingers teased the opening of her body, circling but not entering her as his tongue tapped out a rhythm against her very center.

She gripped the headboard tighter and tighter as her hips rose and fell trying to force him to penetrate her, but still he held his touch only at the entrance of her body.

"Please, Henry. I need you. Now."

He caught her between his lips and sucked her into his mouth. At the same time he thrust his finger deep into her body. She screamed as her body spasmed. She rocked her hips against his finger and mouth as he kept up the pressure, not letting her come down from her orgasm, but building her up once again.

Henry moved slowly up and over Astrid. He was aching hard and needed a condom fast. She was languid as she moved against him, her legs tangling with his.

He'd drawn out this lovemaking, because he'd wanted to explore every inch of her passion, find out what it took to turn this woman on. He wanted to know her intimate secrets. And he refused to stop until he knew them all. Tonight was just the tip of the iceberg.

"I don't want to come without you again," Astrid said.

"Me, either. Are you on the Pill?" he asked.

"I won't get pregnant," she said.

"Good, because I don't have a condom," he said.

"You don't?"

"Why would I carry one around?" he asked her.

She just smiled up at him. "I guess you didn't plan this."

"Not at all," he said.

"You make me feel special," she said.

The words were honestly innocent as she wrapped her arms around him, rubbing her hands over his skin.

He loved the feel of her long cool fingers on him. When she found the sensitive area at the base of his spine, tracing her finger in a small circle, awareness spread through hers in waves, and a shudder went through his entire body.

He drew her hand away from his body and linked their fingers together, tasting her with long slow sweeps of his tongue against her neck and her collarbone. She smelled heavenly…sex and woman…his woman.

Was she his?

He lifted himself away from her, kneeling between her legs. She touched his thigh, the only part of his body she could reach.

Her fingers were cool against his hip. He needed her under him now. The teasing had gone on long enough— now he needed to be inside of her. To claim Astrid as his. Because whatever else happened between them, tonight she was his.

He tumbled her back on the bed. She held his shoulders as he slid up over her. He tested her body to make sure she was still ready for him. He held himself poised at her entrance. Felt her silky legs draw up along his and then fall open. Anticipation made the base of his spine tingle.

She shifted under him. Her shoulders rotated until the tips of her berry-hard nipples brushed against him.

He lowered himself over her, settling into place between her legs. She skimmed her gaze over his body, down to the place where they met.

He looked down at her but her eyes were shut. "Don't close your eyes," he said, wanting her to see this moment when she became his.

He lifted her hips and waited until their eyes met,

then slid into her body. She was a tight fit and he eased inch by inch until he was fully seated inside her. She wrapped her legs around his waist, her ankles resting at the small of his back.

She closed her eyes for a minute, her arms tightened around him. He couldn't breathe anyway as he started to move over her, found her mouth with his. She turned her head away from him, kissed his shoulders and his neck, scraped her nails down his back as he thrust slowly, building them both back toward the pinnacle.

He caught her face in his hand, tipped her head back until she was forced to look at him as he rode her. Her eyes widened and he felt something shift within him. He wanted to go so deep that the two of them would never be separated again.

She gasped his name as he increased his pace, feeling his own climax rushing toward him. He changed the angle of his penetration so that he would hit the G-spot inside her body.

Her mouth opened on a scream that was his name as her orgasm rolled through her body. He continued thrusting, driving himself deeper and deeper until he came in a rush, shouting her name.

He wrapped his arms around her, letting his body relax for a moment. He felt the strength in her arms as she hugged him, and he knew he couldn't let this be a mistake. Not just because of the work situation but because this woman meant more to him than he'd realized.

He got out of bed and went into her en suite bathroom. He had to search to find a flannel, then he wet it and brought it back to the bed where Astrid waited. He wiped her tenderly between her legs.

"Stay with me tonight?" she asked.

He couldn't deny her. He got into bed next to her and pulled her into his arms. Astrid was different than every other woman he'd dated, something he'd felt from the beginning, but in this moment he understood why.

He couldn't sleep as he held her. He knew that his life was complicated and he didn't know where Astrid fit into it. He stayed awake all night puzzling over what to do with this woman who was everything he'd ever wanted in a woman and nothing that he knew what to do with. But there were no easy answers where she was concerned.

When the sun started to rise, he rolled her over and under him, making love to her again. He left her dozing to shower and dress and when he came out of the bathroom she was no longer in her bed.

Astrid had wanted nothing more than to stay in bed and wait for Henry, and that scared her. She knew that it had been wrong to sleep with him without telling him all her secrets. Because he might start thinking that they could have a relationship that would be more than an affair…

And then what would she say? How would she casually bring up the fact that she couldn't have kids? That her one disastrous affair with Daniel had taken a bigger toll on her than she'd admitted?

"Astrid?"

"In here," she said from the kitchen. "I know you take your coffee black, but how do you like your eggs?"

Henry stood in the doorway freshly showered and dressed. Was she really going to fix him breakfast? She felt that she had to because otherwise she just seemed like a big coward for running away from him.

"I like them fried. But you don't have to fix me breakfast."

"Um…are you sure?"

"Yes," he said. "I'll take that coffee, though."

She poured him a cup of coffee. She couldn't sit across the table from him right now. There was too much on her mind. "I need to shower."

"Go ahead," he said. "Do you mind if I stay? I'll take you to breakfast when're done."

She nodded and left the room as quickly as possible. Standing in her own bathroom, she stared at her reflection in the mirror.

The problem with having a secret like hers was there was no outward sign that anything was wrong with her. Any man who saw her would assume she was a normal female with all the required working parts.

She shook her head. She didn't need to worry about that. Henry wasn't a family man—God, that was a lie. He might not have a wife and child of his own, but he was deeply committed to his mother and stepfather and half brothers.

She showered and quickly got dressed, thinking the sooner they got out of her flat the better.

"Do you mind working today?" Henry asked, as they left the building.

"Not at all." That would be a lifesaver, she thought. Hopefully it would bring an end to her thoughts and let her get back to normal footing with him.

"Great. Steph is in the studio and I think she needs some direction."

"I'd love to hear her tracks. I'm sure they are really good."

"She gets nervous in the studio. She likes having an audience and without one she kind of shuts down."

Henry drove them to the studios that Steph was using in East London. When they got there, everyone was bustling around, and Henry moved off to talk to Steph.

Astrid stood to the side, feeling as though she didn't fit in. She had worked in the music industry for years but she'd never sat in on a session with an artist. Daniel had said she'd just be in the way and now she realized she was. There wasn't anything for her to do but sit in the corner and sip her coffee.

Henry was in his element, though, and she saw now that he had a gift when it came to saying the right things. Before long Steph was singing, and the sounds were better than her live shows.

She wondered if Henry just intuitively knew what to say to all women. Were the things he'd said last night just lines? Had she fallen for a man who was willing to say whatever he had to to get results?

Fallen? Was she starting to care about Henry? She knew the answer was yes. She realized now that had happened the minute he'd kissed her at her flat the first night he'd taken her home.

The recording studio wasn't too crowded—the only people there were Steph's manager and her mother, who Astrid took a few minutes to chat with. In the control booth were Conan McNeil and Tomas Jimenez, the producer and the sound mixer for this project.

Tomas had been going through a rough patch lately, with his wife leaving him for another man. Unfortunately Tomas hadn't been leaving his problems at the door and Astrid heard the sound of raised voices and saw that Conan was arguing with Tomas.

Henry stepped over to get in the mix and Astrid followed, wanting to make sure things didn't get out of hand.

"If you are too drunk to operate a mixing board then you need to go home," she heard Henry say from across the room.

Astrid walked over to him. He was definitely mad and not afraid to show his temper. "Tomas needs a cab."

"I will call one for him," Astrid said.

Tomas glared at Henry. "You can't make me go home."

"You're right, I can't. But I *can* make sure you don't work until you clean up your act. Astrid, escort him out to the lobby."

She nodded and took Tomas by the arm, but he jerked away from her. His arms were swinging as he turned to confront Henry, and he hit her in the chest. The blow was solid and knocked her back against the wall where she hit her head.

"Ouch!"

Henry advanced on Tomas, his anger evident on his face.

"I'm sorry. I didn't mean to hit her," Tomas said, backing away.

"Out!" Henry pointed to the door and Tomas left without another word.

"Are you okay?" Henry asked, coming to her side.

"Fine. My head is a little sore, but I'm fine."

Henry hugged her close for a second but stepped away as soon as the door to the sound booth opened again and Duncan, one of Henry's producers, walked in.

As he went to talk to the man, she wondered if Henry was hiding his relationship with her. She hoped not.

She'd been Daniel's secret lover and that had ended horribly. She didn't want to make the same mistakes with Henry.

Chapter 8

Astrid stopped in the corner shop on her way to work for some headache tablets. All the late nights she'd been keeping with Henry were causing her to lose sleep. She smiled at Ahmed as she entered. He'd been running this shop since she moved here, and he always greeted her warmly.

"You are getting famous," Ahmed said. "Will you still shop here for much longer?"

She shook her head. "Stop being funny. I'm not famous and you are my favorite corner store."

She picked up a bottle of water, and as she went to the front to get her headache tablets, she saw on the cover of *Hello!* magazine a photo of her and Henry. She blanched at the image of the two of them on their first night working together when he had leaned in to kiss her.

"I…I'll take a copy of this."

She paid for her water and the magazine and walked out of the shop quickly. As she got on the aboveground commuter train, she felt that people were staring at her. She hated this. This feeling of being in the tabloids again. She'd been in them before—just a brief mention of the faceless girl—the latest tart to grace the bed of Mo Rollins's number-one producer. At least with the situation with Daniel and the Mo Rollins Group, her photo hadn't been in the papers.

She opened the magazine and saw that the photo was captioned simply: Latest bird to land in hot, hot, hot Devonshire bastard's love nest.

Ugh! That was horrible and made her sound like… like some sort of short-term affair for Henry. Which she might be. She had her secrets and presumably he had his.

But they'd also spent lots of time together, and she was coming to know him, the man behind the celebrity. He'd had dinner with her at Bethann and Percy's house, and she'd met his half brothers twice when they'd come to the office to celebrate the milestones that Henry was making with Everest Record Group.

Steph's first single release from their label was climbing the charts. She was in demand on all the talk shows in the U.K. and throughout Europe, and her performance on Graham Norton had caught the eye of an American concert promoter who wanted her to do a small tour of House of Blues venues in the States.

Henry had included her in everything with Steph, which made her feel part of the team. Things were going well professionally for both of them. But now, looking at this…

Her cell rang and she glanced down to see who was calling—Bethann.

"Hello, Bethann," she said as she answered the phone.

"Astrid, have you seen *Hello!*?"

"Just this morning. I don't—"

"Don't what? Know how to explain that you are his love bird? Do you want me to sue them?"

"No, Bethann. Thank you for the thought but I think it might be better for me to simply go with the flow here."

"Mum is not going to be happy."

Astrid doubted her mum would care either way. She suspected it was more her own friends that her sister cared about. "Bethann, am I embarrassing you?"

"Don't be ridiculous. I'm worried about you. How could you think otherwise?"

"Because the photo isn't that bad. And being with Henry means having pictures of myself in the mags sometimes." As she tried to reassure her sister, she re-alized what she was saying was true. If she was going to have a relationship with Henry, then this was going to be part of it.

That also meant she needed to be ready to tell Henry everything, and once she did that…well, then he'd have to decide if he still wanted to be with her. Because she knew that if she didn't tell him, the media would even-tually ferret out the truth.

"I've got to go, Bethann. We can talk later."

"Okay." Her sister sounded reluctant, but she gave in to the conversation's end. "Be careful. Love you."

"Love you, too."

Astrid hung up the phone and just sat there waiting

for her stop. She didn't know what she was going to say to Henry about all of this.

Her headache was back with a vengeance and she'd forgotten the tablets at the store. She shook her head. It was going to be one of those Mondays.

Henry's cell phone rang just as he finished working out at the gym. He glanced at the caller ID and saw that it was Edmond—Malcolm's solicitor. He debated half a second before answering the call.

"Devonshire," Henry said by way of greeting.

"It's Edmond. Do you have time to meet with me this morning?"

"I'm not sure. Why don't you give my assistant a call and she can set something up?"

"I'd like to speak to you away from the office. It's about the morality clause that Malcolm has established."

Henry wasn't too concerned about that. He hadn't done anything morally wrong and he knew it. "If you insist. There is a coffee shop here at my gym. I can meet you there in twenty minutes."

"I will see you then."

Henry showered and changed and then called his office.

"Everest Record Group, Henry Devonshire's office."

Just hearing Astrid's voice made him smile. He knew there was still so much of her that was clouded in mystery, but he was slowly getting to know her.

"It's Henry. I'm running late at the gym this morning. Is there anything pressing?"

"Well I spoke to Geoff. He and Steven want to meet here today for the weekly update meeting. I've pulled the financials and we are way ahead of last year's numbers. So that's good news for you."

"Yes, it is. I might beat them," Henry said.

"I'm sure you will."

"We will. And when we do, everyone on the team will be responsible for our success. Anything else?"

She paused and he heard the rustling of papers. "Well…there is a photo of you and me in *Hello!*."

"What are we doing?"

"Kissing. That night you dropped me off at home. The first day I worked for you."

"What can I say, I'm cheeky." He couldn't tell if she was upset by it or not. Was this what Edmond wanted to talk to him about? "Should I apologize?"

"No. Don't be silly. Paparazzi are a part of your life."

"But they aren't a part of yours," he said.

"No. But it's not so bad that I want to run away…yet."

"Yet? I'll have to make sure you don't change your mind."

"Am I that important to you?" she asked.

His phone beeped, indicating an incoming call, and he hesitated for a second. He couldn't tell Astrid that he was falling for her. That when he was with her he found a measure of peace that he hadn't experienced since he'd first stood on a rugby pitch and realized he was good at something on his own.

"I think you know the answer to that," he said, which he knew was no answer at all. "I have to go now. I've got another call."

"All right. Goodbye then."

He hung up, feeling like a jerk, but there was no stopping that. Astrid was complicating his life in numerous ways, and each day they spent together he wanted to extend into another one. But that was dangerous because he'd made a promise to himself to never depend on anyone. To be a part of the team but to keep himself safely insulated from actually getting too close.

Distracted, he clicked over to the other call without looking at the ID.

"Devonshire."

"Henry, it's mum. Why haven't you brought this girl you are seeing to meet us?"

Henry didn't normally bring women to meet his Mum and said as much to her.

"Well, she looks different that your normal type of woman, and I thought maybe she actually was different. Is she?"

"I don't know," he said, being honest with his mum and himself. "She's my assistant."

"Isn't that a conflict of interest?"

"No. Her job isn't threatened at all."

"Henry Devonshire, it's different for a man. Malcolm never said he'd stop producing my records when we broke things off—it was me. I couldn't stand to see him once we were no longer together."

"Mum, this is different."

"I'm sure you are telling yourself that. If you care at all for this girl then decide if she's different enough that you want her to meet your family. If she isn't, end it now so she can get on with her life."

His mum hung up and Henry stared at the phone. He hadn't thought of their affair in terms of how it would affect Astrid and her career. And from the beginning she'd said her career was important to her.

He left the locker room and went to the coffee shop to meet Edmond. When they'd spoken on the phone,

Edmond had mentioned that fact that he would rather discuss this in person than on the phone in the office where they might be interrupted.

Henry had assumed that meant the other man didn't want Astrid walking in on them as assistants sometimes could. They'd agreed on this coffee shop because it was in the building where Edmond had his office. The older man was already there and stood up to shake his hand.

"How's Malcolm doing?"

"Some days are better than others, Henry," Edmond said. "I'd be happy to check and see if he'd welcome a visit from you."

Henry shook his head. "I can't right now. I'm busy with making Everest Records the top performer at the Everest Group."

"You certainly are. Malcolm and I are impressed with the progress you've made. That is why I am here this morning. I would hate to see you lose the competition because of some woman."

Henry didn't like hearing Astrid referred to as *some woman*. "Astrid isn't just some girl I'm shagging."

"I'm glad to hear that, as I'm sure that Malcolm will be, too. Just be careful that nothing more risqué than this kiss ends up in the papers."

"Is Malcolm recovering?" Henry asked.

"He had his good days and his bad days," Edmond said. "I can't say more than that."

Henry nodded and checked his watch. "I have to go." They stood and the two men walked toward the door. "Does Malcolm ever regret not marrying?"

"I don't know, sir. I've never broached the subject with him."

Henry turned to go, but Edmond stopped him with a

hand on his arm. "I think he regrets that you and your brothers are strangers. That you don't know him or each other very well."

Henry nodded and walked away. He tried not to let any of that matter, but deep inside he was glad to hear that Malcolm had regrets. It made him seem more human.

When he entered his office, he saw that Astrid was on the phone. She looked up at him and smiled and he knew then that he had to choose just as his mum had said. Was he going to try for more permanency with her or should he let her go?

He'd invite her to a rugby match with his stepfather's team. Get the entire family—even those half brothers of his—involved and see how the day went.

There were a swarm of paps outside of Madejski Stadium as Henry and Astrid arrived. He parked his Aston Martin DB-5 and walked with a genial smile toward the stadium. He kept a hold on her hand and lead her through the crowd.

"Henry, who's your girl?"

"What are the details of Malcolm Devonshire's will?"

"Do you have any details on Lynn Grandings's health?"

"When will the other Devonshire heirs arrive?"

Henry waved and moved past the photographers and reporters who called questions to them. Astrid didn't really like the glare of the spotlight that followed Henry around.

Their working relationship continued to be strong the last three weeks and their nights…well, she blushed just thinking about them. With Henry she'd finally realized her sexual potential, she thought. He made love to her all the time and she'd come to find that she needed his touch as much as he needed hers.

"That wasn't too bad," Henry said. "I suppose they couldn't resist a chance to get a photo of Geoff, Steven and me all together."

"It would probably be worth a fortune if I sold it to *Hello!*. I brought my camera to try to get in on the action," she said.

"I bet," he said. "Would you do it? Sell a picture for the money?"

"No, I was teasing. I did bring my camera, though."

"Why?"

They had entered the stadium. "I thought my dad would snap a few photos. You said we'd get to meet the coach."

"And you will. Want to meet the team?"

"Of course. I've already met my favorite player," she said, leaning up to kiss him.

Henry wrapped an arm around her waist, deepening the kiss.

"Very nice," a droll female voice said.

Henry lifted his head and they turned to see a tall brunette. Whose full, pouty lips would put Angelina Jolie's to shame. Astrid had no idea who the woman was, but Henry obviously knew her. There was a tension between the two of them that even she could sense.

"Kaye," Henry said.

"Got a minute?"

"No, actually I don't. I'm hosting a group upstairs."

Astrid was a bit relieved that Henry didn't give in to her request. But a part of her hated the feeling of jealousy that rose in her. Henry and she didn't have that kind of relationship. Daniel had seen other women while he'd dated her. She's thought Henry was different.

"Kaye, this is Astrid Taylor, Astrid, this is Kaye Allen."

Kaye Allen was one of those supermodels Henry had dated. One of the women he'd told her she was sexier than. But standing next to Kaye, Astrid felt wanting.

"I'll head up and take care of the details," Astrid said.

"I'll come with you. Good day, Kaye."

Kaye nodded at them and Henry led the way farther into the stadium and up to the Royal Suite, which they had booked for today's match. Her parents wouldn't be the only guests, Henry's half brothers by Malcolm Devonshire would also be there, as well as XSU, who were providing an opening show before the match. It was their first professional gig.

Next week they'd be performing at the Everest Mega Store in London at a big event.

For the moment they were alone in the spacious suite with just one member of the catering staff. One long table had been set and several rounds of eight were spaced out.

"Sorry about that," Henry said.

"No problem. So that's Kaye Allen. She's very pretty."

"Yes she is. She's also very clingy."

Astrid wanted to ask more questions, but she'd been described the same way by Daniel at one time and she sensed the baggage hidden in that phrase. "Want to talk about it?"

"No, Astrid. I have no wish to discuss my ex-lover with you," Henry said.

She drew back at his sharp tone. "I was being nice. I don't want to talk about her, either."

It wasn't the first time she'd seen his temper. But it was the first time she'd seen it directed at her. He couldn't talk to her like that.

She walked to the window and stared down at the rugby pitch. The stadium started to fill with fans. Henry came up behind her and offered her a glass of champagne. He put his arm around her shoulder as she accepted the glass.

"I'm sorry. Kaye is…she's never accepted that things are over. And I never should have let my reaction to her upset you."

She turned to look at him. "It's okay."

"Cheers."

She clinked her glass against his.

She wanted to ask more questions, but knew better than to do that. Henry was careful to keep his secrets hidden, and Kaye seemed to be one of his. If she told him everything about Daniel, she'd have the right to ask him deeper questions. He kept his arm around her and chatted lightly about each player as they came on the field. Kaye's presence had changed the mood between them. Astrid knew he was trying to get them back to the mood they'd been in before running into that woman downstairs, but it was hard for her. For the first time she'd realized that Henry wasn't Mr. Congeniality, as he always appeared to be.

She wondered what else lurked beneath the surface he presented, realizing that no matter how well she thought she'd gotten to know him, he still had secrets that he hadn't shared with her.

"What are you thinking?" Henry asked.

She took a sip of her champagne. She needed to be on her A-game today and not mired in doubt about herself and her position with Henry. Even if she couldn't be the woman who'd keep him happy for the rest of his life. Because someday Henry would want a family and kids of his own, and that was one thing she couldn't give him. But today she needed to be that girl.

She smiled, but it felt forced even to her. "Just excited about the upcoming match."

Chapter 9

Henry couldn't relax as the afternoon match got started, though he enjoyed the company of Geoff and Steven. They'd each brought a date with them, and Henry, remembering the paps' question about Lynn, wondered what was going on with Steven's mum. This was the first time the three of them had appeared in public together.

Steven seemed in good spirits, though, and they talked at length about the plans to feature every new artist they signed in the stores—how they would have little live concerts there.

"Malcolm used to do that when he first opened the Mega Stores," Steven said. "But he got out of the habit in the nineties when he started focusing on his own pursuits instead of the company's. I think the three of us can bring the focus back to the core company values of satisfying our customers, caring about our community and creating synergy between our business units."

"I agree," Henry said.

"We're painting the side of the Airbus planes with the album art from Steph Cordo," Geoff said. "We've actually had a lot of positive comments due to that."

"Perfect," Henry said. He actually liked these men, his brothers. Over the past few months, they had found that they really had a lot in common. It was more than a business drive to succeed. It was something deeper, something he couldn't define.

Astrid glanced over at their table from where she was seated with the members of XSU. The room was like any other VIP room at an event. It was filled with sports stars, celebs and family. She was going to bring them over when he signaled her. And he was comfortable knowing she'd do what he needed her to.

She'd turned into a valuable asset to his work life. And he'd been very careful to keep their relationship private, though open. He didn't want Astrid to feel as though she was sneaking around with him.

And unlike Kaye Allen, whom they'd met earlier, Astrid didn't have any ghosts in her closet. Just a nice family and one ill-timed affair.

He nodded at Astrid, and a few minutes later the group got up and came over to their table. Angus, the lead singer, had met Steven before at the store and before long Henry had the conversation going around the table. He stepped away to see to his other guests. He wouldn't have thought being a record company executive was something he'd want to do, but it had been a challenge he enjoyed. And he was glad to have had it.

"It's going well," Astrid said. "I thought my mum

was going to die when you introduced her to Geoff. She thinks his mum is one classy lady."

Henry smiled at Astrid. She kept him real, he thought. It would be easy to look around and see himself as the architect for success at the Everest Group, and he was that, but he was also helping many people make connections that would help them to be happier.

Geoff's younger half sisters were dropping by an after party he was hosting at a local club in the hopes of meeting his mother. And hearing Steph Cordo perform. Her first single was climbing the charts.... There was more here than business. For the first time in his life, he felt connected to people in a good way.

It was odd, because he'd always basically been a loner, even though he'd surrounded himself with mates.

"I'm glad she enjoyed it. Spencer enjoyed his tour of the locker room?"

"Yes, he did. I took a dozen pictures of him in there."

Henry smiled. She had kept her digital camera out most of the time and after seeing that wall of photos in her flat, he knew that Astrid liked to document her life. She took photos of everyone and everything.

Henry watched Astrid take photos of everyone but him. He shouldn't have snapped at her the way he had. It was just that Kaye was one of those women from his past whom he would never have invited to this kind of event. An event where his family was present. And he hadn't wanted her to meet Astrid.

He didn't want Astrid sullied by anything from his past relationships. Okay, he thought, not going there today. He cornered her, but she turned to walk away again.

Taking her arm and drawing her close to him, he

turned his back to the room so no one could see their faces.

"I'm not mad anymore," he said.

"Good for you. I am."

"Astrid—"

"Don't, Henry. I'm sure you'll have some charming line about why I shouldn't stay mad at you, and I might buy it. But I'll know deep inside that you treated me like your assistant today, and I know that's what I am, but you invited me to this event as your date."

"I did. And I'm sorry, Astrid. I never wanted you to have to meet the women from my past. You are different to me."

"Am I?"

He nodded.

"How?"

"You are the first woman I've brought to meet my family," he said and then kissed her before she could ask him any more questions.

"Henry, come over here." Geoff was waving him over and he glanced down at Astrid.

"Are we okay now?"

"Yes," she said.

"Wait." She wrapped an arm around his waist, extended her arm and snapped a quick photo of the two of them. She wasn't a professional photographer, but her photos were usually very good.

"I want to get a picture of you and your brothers."

"To sell?" he asked with a wink.

"No," she said. "For you. You said you didn't have one."

He had mentioned that to her—though the media

had always linked them, they had never all been photographed together.

"The Devonshire heirs," Astrid said. "I'd like a photo."

The men were good-natured about it, and she snapped a photo of just the three of them. Then of them with the band. And as the afternoon progressed, Henry realized that he had the seeds of a life he didn't want to let go. He wanted to find a way to keep Astrid by his side. To keep these relationships with his brothers going and to continue to build the success he'd found at Everest Group. And he thought Astrid was the key to that.

They all watched the game as it heated up. There was a flat screen on the back wall, but most of the occupants of the suite preferred to watch the action on the field and not on the screen.

Josh and Lucas came up to the suite during a break in the game. Henry smiled at his two younger brothers as they walked into the room. Astrid snapped a picture of the boys and then went over to talk to them.

It was her first time meeting them, but soon she was laughing and chatting with the teenage boys as if she'd known them forever. It was something she did effortlessly. He realized she made everyone feel at ease. He'd seen it with Roger and others that came through their office. Something that he took advantage of at work.

"Henry, Mum wants you to bring Astrid down to the field after the game," Joshua said. He was the older of the two boys by only eighteen months.

"She does? Why?"

Lucas joined them. "Because she can't get up here to meet her until after she finished talking to the press with Dad."

Both of the boys looked a lot like Gordon except for
the eyes, which, like his, were the bright blue of their
mum's.

"Mum can meet her at the party later—when she
meets Geoff and Steven."

"She's not sure she wants to meet your other
brothers," Lucas said.

Henry nodded. The boys didn't have to say anything
else. He knew how his mum felt about Malcolm and the
proof of his affairs.

"I'll do what I can," Henry said.

"About what?" Astrid asked as she joined him.

"Mum wants to meet you," Joshua said.

"Then let's go," Astrid said, linking her arm through
those of his little brothers. "You stay here and keep your
party going. I'll be right back."

He watched her walk away and realized he was falling in love with Astrid.

"Hello, Astrid, I'm Tiffany Malone—Henry's
mother."

Tiffany Malone was everything that Astrid expected
her to be. She exuded a kind of larger-than-life presence, but Astrid felt some genuine kindness as Tiffany
hugged her close.

"Josh and Lucas have been telling me all about your
family. Your father is apparently an expert when it
comes to the history of this club," Tiffany said.

"Yes, he is," Astrid admitted. "He was beyond
thrilled to be here today."

Her parents had gone home early due to her father's
getting tired.

"Gordon? Come on over here and meet Astrid."

Gordon wore an open-collar shirt and sport coat over his khaki pants. There was a casual elegance to his style that Astrid saw reflected in a lot of the clothes that Henry wore.

He shook her hand and Henry drifted over to talk to the three of them. As Astrid stood there talking with Henry and his parents, she realized that she was seeing a very intimate glimpse into the private lives of these people.

Astrid was glad to finally be home after the long day they had. Henry had dropped her off first and then went to take his younger brothers home. He'd said he'd try to get back and she hoped he did. Today had been an interesting day.

She'd been worried when they had run into Kaye. She still didn't know the details of that relationship, but she was willing to let it be. After all, she didn't want to tell Henry about Daniel.

Though to be honest, she needed to. Daniel was nothing in her life now. Since she'd been with Henry, she'd come to feel that he was everything to her. Everything she wanted in a man and a lover. He'd pushed her expectations of what a relationship could be and made her realize that girlish fantasies had no place in her life anymore.

She washed her face and changed out of her party clothes into a French negligee that Henry had given her last week. She liked the way the soft silky material felt against her skin. But she also liked the fact that he'd purchased it for her.

He was always giving her little gifts, and she cherished each one of them because they meant that he thought of her during the day and whenever they were apart.

She poured herself a glass of wine to help her wind down after the day and plugged her digital camera into her laptop. A few moments later her photo program opened up and the pictures she'd taken during the day started flashing on the screen as they downloaded.

She smiled as she noted she got a few really good pictures of Henry. His earnestness as he talked to his half brothers came through and he was by turns, doting when he talked to his younger brothers and very confident as he talked to XSU.

He was everything to everyone, she thought. And to her he was quickly becoming the man she didn't want to live without.

Her phone rang and she glanced at the caller ID before answering. It was a blocked number, but she knew that Henry's number came up like that.

"Hello."

"Hey, baby. Are you still up?" Henry asked.

"I am. Are you coming back here?" she asked.

"I'd like to."

"Good. How long until you get here?" she asked. She'd almost asked him how long until he got *home*. But they didn't have a home together, which hadn't bothered her until this moment. Henry spent more nights at her place than she did at his, but he hadn't mentioned moving their relationship beyond this.

"Twenty minutes, maybe less."

"I enjoyed meeting your family today," she said, trying not to dwell on the fact that, despite her feelings for Henry, she was still probably just a casual affair. Her experience…her past relationships made her reluctant to push for more. What if she wanted their relationship to be more only to find he was content to let things ride?

She couldn't bear to have the dynamic of their relationship change too much. She needed Henry. Needed him to stay the man he was so she could stay the woman she was becoming. A woman who no longer felt shattered and less than other women. Henry made her believe she was worth being with—even if she couldn't get pregnant.

She felt as though finally she was maturing into the woman she'd be for the rest of her life.

"My brothers are in love with you," Henry said, interrupting her thoughts.

That surprised her. "Which ones?"

He laughed. "Joshua and Lucas. They talked about you from the moment we dropped you off until I left my mum's place."

"They are really cute kids. They'd surely cringe if they heard me call them that. But I like them," she said.

And she had. The teens were funny and smart. They didn't act like Henry was a celeb but treated him like their big brother.

"They are good kids. I'm proud to call them my brothers."

"What about Geoff and Steven? You seemed to be getting on well with them today."

She heard the signal of his blinkers in the background as he turned. "I did. It's always different with the three of us because we have so much between us but we are strangers…well, we were strangers. I'm starting to get to know them."

"Geoff is really reserved, isn't he?"

"Yes. But he lightens up the better he gets to know

you. Steven's pretty funny, which to be honest always surprises me," Henry said.

"I know. He is scarily smart. I overheard him talking to Percy about quantum physics."

"He is smart. I think that the three of us are a big reflection of the women who raised us."

"In what way?"

"Well, my own mother made sure all her sons cared about each other. We were all family—even Gordon and me."

"I'd agree with that. But there is a definite quality from Malcolm, as well. At least if the rumors about him are to be believed."

"What quality?"

"That charm. All three of you have an easy way about you when it comes to the opposite sex."

"Do we? Were you flirting with my brothers?" Henry asked.

Astrid smiled to herself. "No. There's only one Devonshire heir I'm interested in."

"That's what I like to hear. I'm parking the car and I'll be right up."

She disconnected the call and a minute later Henry was at her door. He took one look at the negligee she wore and lifted her in his arms and carried her back to the bedroom where he made love to her. Afterward, he held her in his arms and she rested her head on his chest right over his heart, hoping that this was where she'd spend the rest of her nights.

Chapter 10

Edmond showed up on Monday at the Everest Records office. Henry wasn't too pleased to see the other man, because Edmond to him always represented Malcolm's absence in his life.

"Is Malcolm okay?" he asked.

"Yes, he's fine. He has asked me to check up on you and your brothers face-to-face to see how things are progressing."

"Then you've seen the report I sent on the groups we've signed and our projections on how well they will sell."

"Yes, we received it. I hear you were at Madejski with your brothers this weekend."

Henry leaned back in his chair. What was the point of Edmond's visit? Was he here to warn him about Astrid again? He didn't want to be curt to the older man—

Henry was aware that Edmond was Malcolm's eyes and ears. Whatever he said to Edmond would make its way back to Malcolm.

"We did. I prefer you call Geoff and Steven the other heirs. We weren't raised as brothers."

"That always pained your father," Edmond said.

Henry shook his head. "How can you say that with a straight face? Malcolm barely knew we were alive."

"That's not true," Edmond said. "But you have your version of your life."

"Tell me one time…*one thing* that Malcolm did for me or Geoff or Steven."

Edmond stood up and walked over to the plate-glass windows looking down on the Thames. "He attended your rugby matches when you played with the London Irish."

"Bullshit," Henry said. "I think I would have known if he was there. The media would have gone crazy like they did when he attended Geoff's polo match."

"They were nuts about that, weren't they?" Edmond said. "We learned our lesson on that outing. After that Malcolm learned to be more circumspect when he attended functions for you boys. It wasn't easy for him. He's not a man given to that type of behavior."

Henry approached Edmond, laying a hand on the other man's forearm.

"Why are you here?"

"To check up on you. There was another photo in *Ok!* of you and that girl. Do you need our help in dealing with her?"

Henry shook his head. "I haven't needed you or Malcolm my entire life. Why would I need you now?"

"You might benefit from the experience he has."

Henry shook his head. "I know how to end relationships and this one with Astrid is fine."

Malcolm's advice might have been helpful when it came to business when he'd first started here, but he'd found his own way. Which Henry acknowledged was the way he preferred to work. He always had. He liked doing things his own way.

"I think Malcolm should stick to business in his communications with me. We are launching one of our artist's newest CD this afternoon at the Everest Mega Store. You might want to stop by there so you can see how I'm running things"

Edmond turned toward Henry. "Fine."

"I can't tell you how relieved I am," Henry said, then realized he was letting his own feelings of resentment toward Malcolm get the better of him. "I'd never deny a child of mine."

"Malcolm didn't either."

"We'll have to disagree on that. I'm glad you stopped by. If you need anything else, my assistant will take care of it for you."

Edmond nodded. "Good day, Henry."

"Good day."

Edmond left and Astrid came into his office. She closed the door behind her. She smiled at him. "Is everything okay? Isn't Edmond Malcolm's right-hand man?"

"He is. Everything's fine. Malcolm just sends Edmond out to check up on me—something he hasn't done since I was a kid."

Astrid walked behind his desk and leaned back

against it. He had sat back down in his executive chair so he turned to face her.

"There's a note in your voice," she said. He snagged her waist and drew her to his lap. "Why don't you like Edmond?"

His arms tightened around Astrid and he drew her close to just let her presence soothe those long-ago feelings of resentment Edmond always stirred up.

"Edmond is fine. I don't like that he is always standing in for Malcolm. *Gordon* is more of a father to me than Malcolm was, and I know that's the way that some men are. But every time I see Edmond, it just reminds me of all the times Malcolm wasn't there."

"I'm sorry," she said.

"It's okay," he said. "I know it sounds like I'm complaining, but I'm not. I always wished he'd just stay out of my life for good instead of dancing around on the fringes."

"Why didn't he?"

"Who knows," Henry said. If Edmond was right and Malcolm had attended his rugby matches, then there was more to the enigma of Malcolm Devonshire than Henry had previously suspected.

"Is everything on schedule for this afternoon?" he asked.

"Yes," she said, trying to stand up, but he held her close and claimed the kiss he'd been wanting since she walked into his office.

He was quickly realizing that having an affair with his assistant was very distracting. Astrid was temptation incarnate. No matter how many times he had her, no matter how often he felt her silky legs around his hips, he always wanted her again. He craved her.

He let his hand caress her body as he deepened their kiss.

"I want to lift you onto my desk and take your panties off," he whispered.

"Yes," she said, reaching for his belt, opening it and finding his erection—hot, hard and ready for her.

"Make love to me, Henry," she said.

And he did. Taking her on his desk and making her completely his. He knew that no matter what else he thought about Malcolm Devonshire, without his father he wouldn't have found Astrid, and that was something he didn't know if he could have lived without.

Henry's lovemaking was fierce and all-consuming as always, but afterward when they'd cleaned up, he pulled her into his arms. She knew they had work to do. There was a lot going on every day, but now he just held her and stroked her back.

She rested her head against his shoulder and felt the kind of closeness she'd never had with another person before. Any person. She looked up at Henry and realized it was long overdue for her to tell him about Daniel and everything that had happened.

"What are you thinking?"

"That you stopped asking me about my secrets. Does that mean you no longer want to know them?"

"Not at all. I just decided that when you are ready to talk to me about them you will." He kissed her tenderly. "I think it's time to get back to work."

She nodded and stood up to leave. But she felt as though he'd pushed her away. She wondered if she'd gotten too close to him. She hoped not. She didn't want to end up like Kaye Allen, clinging to a man who no longer wanted her.

* * *

Astrid moved through the crowded Everest Mega Store. It was situated in Leicester Square, the heart of the touristy area of London. The store was packed today and Rona, the manager of this store, was beyond giddy at the fact. She looked like a retro punker with her nose ring and the four-inch-wide stripe of pink down the center of her hair.

"Your girl is nervous. She's in the storage area pacing around. She even left her guitar in the cab."

"Did you get it back?"

"Yes."

"I'll go talk to her," Astrid said.

Astrid took the elevator up to the third floor and entered the storage area. Steph was indeed pacing around but she seemed fine. No nerves to speak of.

"Hello, Astrid."

"How's it going, Steph? Ready for today?"

"I think so," Steph said. "This is how I always get before I go on. So don't worry that I'm going to wig out on you."

"I'm not worried at all. Do you know who Mo Rollins is?"

"I haven't been living under a rock," she said with a quick grin.

"He would say you are in great company based on your nerves. He always says the great ones worry they will never match the sound in their head and that's why they are nervous before they go out and perform."

Steph smiled. "Dang it, Astrid. I hadn't even worried about that. I'm just nervous because BBC Radio One is here and they want to interview me when I'm done singing."

"Didn't the media coach get you ready for that?"

"Yes, but practicing at home is different than actually doing it. And I don't want to sound like some kind of muppet."

"You won't. You're smart and poised. And Henry would never have produced an album for you if you weren't."

Steph hugged her. "Thank you. My boyfriend is supposed to be coming today but he got stuck at work."

"How'd you meet?" Astrid asked. The more Steph talked the more she relaxed. And a relaxed artist would perform better.

"At university. We were both in elementary ed."

There was a rap on the door and one of the sound techs poked in his head. "We're ready for you in five minutes."

"Thanks." Steph went to fix her lipstick and the door opened. Astrid glanced over her shoulder to see Henry and Steven enter, talking quietly.

Henry winked at her, but didn't say anything as he went to talk to Steph. Astrid got a call on her cell from Rona that there was someone downstairs demanding to see Henry.

Astrid relayed the message. "I'll go see who it is and let you know if you are needed."

"Great. I'm switching my mobile to vibrate. Just send me a text, because I won't be able to hear a call. I don't like to be disturbed before a concert."

"Will do. Good luck, Steph," Astrid said as she walked to the door.

She stepped out onto the sales floor and saw that the Mega Store was impossibly busy today. Steven's business unit had to be making a fair profit. What would that mean for Henry?

She took the escalator down to the first floor where Rona waited. She pointed to the area near the registers. At first Astrid didn't recognize the woman, but as she got closer she realized it was Kaye—the woman from the rugby match.

"Hi. I'm Astrid Taylor, Mr. Devonshire's assistant. What can I do for you?"

Kaye gave her a scathing look. "Nothing. I need to talk to Henry."

Astrid tried to smile, but the other woman wasn't having any part of her friendliness.

"He won't have any free time today. If you give me your number, I'll have him call you tonight," Astrid said.

"He had my number," Kaye said.

"Fine. But if you give it to me then he won't have to search for it."

The other woman took a card from her handbag and handed it over. "It's urgent. I need to speak to him today."

"Very well. I will give him the message."

Kaye turned and walked away and Astrid watched the other woman go. She sent a text message to Henry informing him that Kaye was looking for him and giving him her number. She tried to shake off the negative feeling that meeting Kaye had produced in her. But it was hard.

She stood in the first floor crowd as Steph performed on the balcony area of the second floor. The acoustics in a retail shop weren't the best for a live performance, but the genuine quality of Steph's voice made up for that.

Astrid kept one ear on the music as she observed the people in the crowd. They really liked Steph's sound, and Astrid noted that as the performance wrapped up the queue to meet her grew. Her CD sales had been steadily high throughout the day.

Astrid went to the table where fans would be able to meet Steph and made sure everything was set up for her with bottles of water to drink, press photos to autograph. The digital photographer was there to take souvenir photos with any fan who wanted one.

Everything was perfect for the event and it cemented Astrid's belief that she and Henry were good at working together. But his reticence about the message from Kaye had her worried. Aside from the passion that was between them…what hold did she really have on him?

Henry left the mega store before Steph was finished performing. Kaye's message told him that this old girlfriend wasn't simply going to go away. And the underwear model had a bit of a temper, so if Henry didn't give her the attention she was demanding, he was afraid she'd do something to get his attention in another way.

Something that might involve Astrid. He didn't want that. He liked what he and Astrid had going. She brought a peace to his life he'd never found in another person.

Kaye answered her cell phone on the first ring. "It's about time you called me."

"What's up?" he asked her.

"I don't want to talk about this on the phone. Can you meet me?"

"Now?"

"Yes, now? This is urgent."

"Fine. Where are you?"

"There's a Café Europa around the corner from the Mega Store. Meet me there."

She hung up and Henry shoved his phone into his pocket.

"Everything okay?" Steven asked.

"No. I have to go take care of an urgent matter. Will you take care of Steph? Just get her down to Astrid and then she'll take over."

"I think I can handle that," Steven said in that wry way he had.

"I know you can. Thanks."

"No problem. Astrid is very efficient, isn't she? Do you think she'd like to work in retail?" Steven asked.

"No. She wouldn't like to work for anyone but me."

Steven laughed. "That's to the point."

"Indeed. But seriously she's interested in producing. I think she'll stay at the label for a long time."

"Good. I think she's a definite asset for the Everest Group."

Steven's comments demonstrated that the other man was thinking globally, thinking of the entire organization. And Henry realized that he didn't care quite so much about winning the chairmanship of the Everest Group. He liked running the record label. It suited him.

It was the first time in his life that he wasn't lusting after the next big thing. Was part of it to do with Astrid? Or had he simply found the place where he belonged?

That was an exhilarating thought. He walked out of the mega store and onto the street. There was the usual bevy of photographers, but none of them paid much attention to him as he walked away.

He found the coffee shop where Kaye waited at a table near the back.

"Hello, Henry."

He sat down next to her. "What is so urgent it couldn't wait?"

"I'm pregnant," she said.

Henry looked at her, trying to assess if she were lying. He was meticulous about birth control. Thanks to the circumstances of his own birth, he'd never wanted to have any kids without being committed to their mother.

"Are you sure?"

She gave him an exasperated look. "Of course I'm sure. Why wouldn't I be?"

"I have no idea. Look, sorry if I've offended you, I never expected to have this conversation. We were careful every time we were together," he said.

He sat back in his chair trying to see signs of her pregnancy in her body. She did seem a little fuller than she'd been before, but she wasn't thicker around the middle.

"How far along are you?" he asked.

"Four months."

Well, the timing was right for him to be the father. "What do you want from me?"

"I want you to support the child. I think it's the least you can do."

"Very well. Just have a paternity test and then we can move forward. I'll have my lawyers get to work on drawing up some kind of paperwork for this," Henry said, running his hand through his hair. This he didn't need, but he'd never deny a child of his own. He wasn't going to make the same mistakes Malcolm had.

"I don't see why we need a paternity test," Kaye said.

"Because I'm a wealthy man, Kaye, and I'm not going to simply take your word. If the baby is mine we will move forward on my terms," Henry said. "But I would never deny a child of mine, and I will be a father to this baby if it is indeed mine."

"On your terms? I don't think so. I don't take orders from you."

"When it comes to the baby, you will," Henry said. "Together we'll make the decisions for the child."

"Fine," she said. "I'll arrange for the test to be done as soon as I can. Will you stop dodging my phone calls?"

"Yes," he said.

Henry stood up to leave the café and walked back to the mega store with his mind in a mire of thoughts. *A child.*

He wasn't ready to be a father, he knew that. There was a reason why he'd been waiting to settle down. And there was only one woman he wanted to settle down with. Astrid.

How was she going to take the news that he might be a father?

"Henry?"

Astrid waited for him right inside the door of the retail store. There was a long queue still in front of Steph. This at least had been a huge success.

"Are you okay?"

"Yes. But we need to talk."

"Now?"

The retail store was jammed with industry journalists and other insiders he should talk to. Did he put business on hold for a personal discussion?

No, he thought. This situation with Steph was easier to handle than talking to Astrid right now.

"No, it can wait until later," he said.

Astrid looked up at him with questions in her eyes, and he had that feeling in his gut that he wasn't meant to have the life he'd been wanting with this woman. If Kaye was pregnant with his child, he couldn't be with Astrid.

Unlike his father, he would do the right thing.

Chapter 11

Astrid sat tensely across from Henry as he talked to the waiter. Their table on a lovely balcony overlooking London and the dinner that they'd planned to celebrate Steph's success and that of the record label had taken on a different feel. She also planned to come clean about Daniel and her inability to have kids.

Henry hadn't been himself when he came back into the store earlier. His entire behavior had been cold and a bit distant since Steven had told her that Henry had to go take care of an urgent matter.

And having had an affair at work before, she was afraid of what the future held for her. Not just here with Henry—though if this relationship ended it would be very painful—but also with the musicians she'd come to know.

Finally the waiter left and Henry turned his attention to her. "I think you'll like the food here."

"I doubt it," she said.

"Why not?"

"Because I'm nervous. What did Kaye want?"

Henry leaned back in his chair. "I'm not sure how to say this except to just say it straight out."

"Go ahead then," Astrid said. She clenched her hands tightly on her lap. Even when Daniel had broken up with her, she had never dreaded the words that might come from a lover's lips. That said it all, didn't it?

"Kaye is pregnant and she believes I am the father."

Shock made her speechless. He couldn't have said he was going to be a father. "I'm sorry."

"I…I don't know what to do. Of course I can't just walk away the way Malcolm did. I want to be more to my kid than a check once a month and gifts at birthdays and Christmases."

His words were a death knell to her. Henry was exactly what she expected him to be. When she'd told Daniel she was pregnant, he hadn't wanted any part of her life or her child's. When she'd lost that child, he'd fired her for attendance. And she'd walked away, feeling her faith in the goodness of men shaken. Somehow it wasn't surprising that Henry was the exact opposite.

"I can understand that. What are you thinking?" she asked.

"I've asked her to have a paternity test just to make sure the child is mine."

"Do you think there's a chance it might not be?"

Henry shrugged. "We were both dating other people as well as each other. So I'm not sure. I figure if Kaye came to me, she has to believe there's a good chance I'm the father."

"That makes sense. She wouldn't want to hit up her

ex-boyfriends indiscriminately," Astrid said. Hoping she didn't sound bitter or angry, she knew she was. She'd found the man she wanted to spend the rest of her life with and had been trying to figure out how to move their relationship to the next level and now…now she had no idea what was going to happen.

"If the child is mine, we're going to have to marry, she and I."

He kept talking after that, but to be honest she didn't hear another thing he said. Why was he going to marry Kaye?

But she knew why. Henry had told her how he'd felt when Malcolm had largely ignored him, and she knew he wouldn't want his own child to grow up feeling that Henry hadn't wanted him.

But what about them?

"I can see that this is important to you…and I admire the fact that you are doing the right thing by your child."

"Do you?" he asked. "You seem like you don't care, Astrid."

"What do you want me to do?" she asked, very aware that she was holding on to her emotions, just barely. She wanted to cry or yell at him that marrying anyone for a child was a dumb mistake. But she couldn't do that because it was very clear Henry wanted to make up for his father's mistakes.

"I want—hell, I don't know. I want to know that it matters to you—that I matter to you."

"You matter more than you can imagine, Henry, but I know that you aren't a man who changes his mind. If you have decided to marry Kaye, then that's what you'll do."

He nodded. The waiter brought their food and Astrid had a surreal moment as she realized that life went on. Even though it felt as if her world had just ended, it was still going on around her.

"I can't do this," she said, standing up.

"Do what? There's no need for you to leave," Henry said.

"Yes, there is. I can't just sit here pretending that nothing has changed when everything has. Listen, Henry, this has been nice, but I should never have let this develop into more than a working relationship."

"You didn't let anything happen. We did it together. There is no reason to walk away. Kaye hasn't determined anything. We can continue as we have been," Henry said.

She shook her head. Continue? Until what? "Think about what you just said. You plan to marry another woman *and* continue a relationship with me?"

Henry shook his head. "I sound like an idiot when I say that. But I don't want to give you up, Astrid."

"I can't do this," she said again. "I understand where you are coming from, but I can't live with a broken heart. I'm going to have to figure out what to do next."

Henry stood up, tossed some bills on the table and led her out of the restaurant. A part of her wanted him to make a big gesture, to say that he'd figure out a way to be involved in Kaye's child's life while still staying with her.

But she reminded herself as he pulled up to her building that she didn't believe in little-girl fantasies anymore. She was a real woman living a real life. And it seemed for her there was no happy ending.

* * *

Astrid left the restaurant and hailed a cab but when she got in, she didn't know where to tell him to go. Then she realized she needed her sister. Bethann was the absolute best at seeing through the crap and getting to the point. And as Henry's words kept repeating in her head and she felt the burn of tears at the back of her eyes she knew that she needed a shoulder to cry on.

"Where to, love?"

She gave the cabbie Bethann's address and sat back in the seat, unable to believe she had once again fallen for her boss. This time was so much worse. This time she knew she really loved Henry. An emotion that she'd tried to convince herself she felt for Daniel, but the words had always sounded hollow. Now she knew that with Henry it was the real deal.

How was she going to go on?

"Here you go, miss," the cabbie said.

She paid him and got out of the car. A light rain had started to fall as she stood on the street looking at her sister's townhouse. It was almost eleven, but she didn't hesitate as she walked up to the door and rang the bell.

The light came on over the door and a minute later she heard the key in the lock of the inner door.

"Who is it?" Percy asked.

"Astrid."

The door opened a minute later and Percy took one look at her face and sighed. "I'll get Bethann."

"Thank you," she said, following him into the sitting room.

He went up the stairs and less than a minute later Bethann came flying down the stairs. She wore a light blue nightgown with brown polka dots on it and her hair was in disarray, but the look on her face was fierce as she opened her arms and hugged Astrid.

"What happened? Do I need to get on the phone to his attorney and threaten him with some kind of lawsuit?" Bethann said.

Astrid shook her head. "No, Bethy, not that. He…"

She started crying as she tried to talk. She hated the way her voice deepened and the words just wouldn't come out. This was so not what she wanted from her life. She should have stayed firm in the vow she'd made to herself—no more men. That was what she'd said but somehow Henry Devonshire had managed to slip past her guard and into her heart.

"I don't know what to do."

"Tell me everything," Bethann said. She maneuvered them across the sitting room to the loveseat and drew Astrid down to sit next to her.

"His ex-girlfriend is pregnant and if the child is his, he is going to marry her."

"Oh, honey. I'm so sorry."

"I know. I understand why he's doing it—"

"I don't. I thought he was involved with you."

"He is," Astrid said. "But he won't give up a child of his. He doesn't want the child to grow up not knowing his father the way Henry did. I get that part of it. But the fact that he's going to marry her…."

"It is a noble thing to do," Bethann said. "Stupid but noble."

"He did say he'd like things to continue with me until he knew if he had to marry Kaye."

"Please tell me you said no."

"I'm not an idiot. Of course I did." Astrid felt tears

welling in her eyes again. "The really dumb thing is I love him and I don't know how I'm going to stop."

Bethann hugged her close and rocked her in her arms. "Stopping will be hard. You need something to concentrate on."

"Work. I am a career woman now," Astrid said.

"You were a career woman before," Bethann reminded her.

"But it's all I have now. I have to be focused on my job."

"Can you do it?"

Astrid thought about it long and hard. "I'm not sure but I have to try. I'm not about to lose another job because I fell in love with the wrong man."

Bethann agreed and then made up the sofa bed so that Astrid could spend the night there. After her sister went upstairs she heard the sound of her talking quietly to Percy and Astrid started to cry again, knowing that she wasn't going to have a man like that in her life. That she wasn't going to have Henry in her life anymore. And she knew she'd never be able to trust another man again. *Burn me once, shame on you*, she thought, *burn me twice, shame on me*. And she'd learned the hard way that love wasn't in the stars for her.

But work was. She was damned good at her career and if she played her cards right she'd be able to turn her job as Henry's assistant into one as a first-class producer. Nothing would keep her from achieving her goals…not now.

It took Henry about a day and a half to realize that letting Astrid walk out of his life was the biggest mistake he'd ever made. He couldn't imagine waking up next to Kaye every day. Even if he had his child there with them.

He knew that he was risking breaking the morality clause in Malcolm's damned agreement, but he didn't care. He simply couldn't marry Kaye to win a business deal. Business at the end of the day wasn't more important to him than family.

He dialed Kaye's number.

"It's Kaye."

"Hello, Kaye. I've been thinking a lot the past twenty-four hours about the baby and our possibly marrying."

"I've been thinking about it, too, Henry. I am so happy that you stepped up and did the right thing."

"I would never let a child of mine grow up without being a part of his or her life," Henry said. And those words were true. He had no doubts about being a father to Kaye's child.

That was one thing he'd realized about Malcolm and his mother's relationship—he didn't have to marry Kaye to still be the child's father. And unlike Malcolm he didn't see a personal life as an impediment to a successful life. In fact he thought that children would enhance his life and make it richer. His only doubts were of being a husband to the wrong woman.

"Great. I thought we could get married in Italy. I have a friend there who will lend us his villa. I think it will photograph nicely. I contacted a few friends at *Vogue*, and they have agreed to do a spread on us."

"No," Henry said. Finding the words to tell her he wouldn't marry her was harder than he expected.

"Well, fine. We can get married at your mum's place then. She has that fabulous country estate—"

"Kaye, stop. I'm not going to marry you."

"But you just said you wanted to be a father to my child."

"I do. I will. But I will not be doing it as your husband. We don't have to be married to raise a child."

"Henry, you *have* to marry me."

"No, Kaye, I don't."

"If you don't I'll make you regret it."

"Do your worst," he said and hung up the phone.

He wasn't too worried about Kaye. He'd called his solicitor and asked the man to draw up a paternity agreement and a visitation schedule.

He spent the rest of the night trying to think of a way to win Astrid back. He knew he'd hurt her and he was determined to make it up to her. The next day he was surprised to receive a call from Edmond.

"We need to talk," Edmond said.

"Sure. Is this about the fact that my unit is outperforming the others?" Henry asked. He'd seen the financials. He was clearly the winner in the competition that Malcolm had set up for them.

"No, it's about Kaye Allen and you. Have you seen the papers this morning?"

"Not yet. Why?"

"There's a photo of Kaye with a prominent baby bump and the caption 'The Devonshire Legacy Lives On. Another Devonshire Is Refusing to Marry His Baby-Muma.'"

Henry cursed. His phone rang and he glanced at the caller ID. "Can you hold?"

"I'd rather not."

"My mum's on the other line."

"I'll wait," Edmond said.

Henry answered the call.

"Hi, Mum."

"Don't hi me, Henry Devonshire. I've spent the last thirty years doing my best to make sure that the world saw you as Henry Devonshire and not simply Malcolm's love child and then you do something like get a woman pregnant and refuse to marry her."

"Mum, we're not even sure the child is mine."

"What? Why not?"

"We had an open relationship."

"Does Astrid know?"

"Mum, I told her everything. I had intended to marry Kaye but then realized I couldn't marry one woman when I wanted to share my life with another one."

There was silence on the line and then he heard her sigh. "Fine. But fix this and make it right."

"I will."

He hung up with his mum.

"Edmond?"

"I'm still here."

"Give me a few days to fix this. If I can't become CEO of the Everest Group, that's fine. But I'm not about to marry the wrong woman just to stave off gossip."

Again he hung up. He went downstairs and got the papers, reading them. Unfortunately Kaye's announcement had reawakened the frenzy that had started with the birth of him and his brothers.

Astrid wouldn't take his calls, and no matter what he did in his personal life he couldn't get it on track.

The results of the paternity test came back a week later, revealing that he wasn't the father of Kaye's child. Henry was relieved, but he'd screwed up his relationship with Astrid. No matter what he said to her, he couldn't fix that.

Since she wouldn't talk to him privately, he had an idea to do a public interview. He called a friend at BBC and arranged to do an interview about his biological father along with Steven and Geoff. The other men readily agreed because they were tired of seeing those old pictures of their mums showing up in the newspapers.

Henry hoped seeing the interview would make Astrid take his calls.

They all wanted a chance to put a new face on the scandal that the men's births had caused. The interview went well and his own mum met a producer who had heard about her game show and wanted to work with her. Tiffany Malone was over the moon. He was her golden boy once again, and he was happy to be back on good terms with his mum but he really longed to be back with Astrid.

He'd known from the beginning that he wanted her in his life. And that she was different from all the other women he'd dated, but he hadn't realized how much until they'd been apart. He missed so much of her.

Her keen smile, her sassy wit and her sexy body had won him over. He couldn't sleep at night because his arms felt empty without her.

Winning her back wasn't easy. After she continued not taking his calls, he'd tried to contact her family, but her parents were out of town. Bethann took one call from him only to curse him out.

He rubbed the back of his neck. A lesser man would give up, but Henry wasn't a quitter and he didn't intend to back down now.

The first copy of the XSU studio sessions were delivered to his office and he remembered the first night they'd heard the group play. That night had changed everything between them.

Astrid saved every message that Henry left on her answering machine. It would have been so nice if she could have instantly fallen out of love with him. Then she'd be able to really move on. Instead, each time she heard his voice she cried a little from missing him.

But she couldn't continue to be his mistress while he married another woman. Yet once she read in the newspapers that he wasn't going to marry Kaye and then when she'd learned he was going to appear on BBC One in an interview with Steven and Geoff…well, she couldn't resist the chance to see him.

Henry looked tired, she thought, as she watched the program. But he carried himself well in the interview as the reporter asked each of them questions about the scandal that had surrounded their births.

"Our mums all loved Malcolm Devonshire," Henry said. "He just loved the Everest Group more."

"Now each of us is running part of that company," Geoff added, "and we understand the difficulties of being in charge of a huge conglomerate and keeping up a personal life."

"And we can see why the media is so interested in us and our mothers. We've never really been together before this, but we hope that your curiosity about us is appeased," Steven said.

"Because we all have lives we'd like to get back to living outside of the spotlight," Henry concluded.

The rest of the interview focused on the three men, their mothers and how the boys had been raised. It was interesting to her and she saved it on her DVR so she could watch it again, which she did several times over the next few days.

Henry called again and told her voice mail that he wasn't the father of Kaye's baby and he needed to talk to her. And she wanted to talk to him, but now the fact that she'd never told him she couldn't have a child was at the forefront of her mind.

Having a child of his own was important to Henry and that was the one thing she couldn't give him.

Henry knew what to do.

It took him a few days to wrangle everyone into place, but on Friday night he drove to Woking with a framed photo of the two of them and an engagement ring in his pocket. He got there as everyone was getting home from work.

He had called the building manager and confirmed that Astrid was indeed at home, even though she refused to take his calls.

He also called Bethann, who was waiting for him when he arrived. He was surprised to see she wasn't carrying a pitchfork or accompanied by an angry mob.

"This better work," she said.

"No one wants that more than I do."

Success didn't matter without Astrid by his side. He needed her. They needed each other—together they were whole. And he wasn't going to back down.

XSU arrived twenty minutes later and Henry had the band set up. He just needed the confirmation that she was inside the flat itself. Bethann called up and Astrid did answer.

Now that he knew where she was, nothing could stop him from winning her back.

He remembered every big game he'd played and every big event in his life and how much he'd wanted to win. They all paled in comparison to what he wanted now. What he needed now.

Astrid.

"I'm going to go up and open her window so she can hear the band. Give me about ten minutes to talk to her."

Henry nodded. "Thank you, Bethann."

"You're welcome. Just make my sister happy for the rest of her life and we'll call it even."

"I intend to."

Bethann walked away, and a small crowd gathered as the band tuned up their instruments. Henry ignored them as his mum and stepdad arrived with his younger brothers.

"I'm glad you got here."

"Wouldn't miss it. I like Astrid. If you are going to ask her to marry you, we want to be a part of it."

He hugged his mum close, realizing how lucky he had been to have been born her son. Percy brought Astrid's parents. It had taken him a while to track them down and to tell them what had happened. He wanted Astrid to become his with the blessing of her family and his.

Finally he saw the window to Astrid's flat open, and he signaled the band, who started playing. He waited where he was until he saw Astrid's pretty blond head peek out the window. She looked down at him and covered her mouth with one hand.

Bethann appeared beside her, wrapping her arm around her sister's shoulder. When the band finished playing, Henry took the microphone from Angus but before he could speak Astrid did.

"Go home, Henry. This isn't going to do anything except make us both look ridiculous."

"That's not true. I'm here to set things right."

"How? There's no way you can do that."

"Not even if I tell you that I love you?"

Astrid wasn't sure she'd heard Henry properly. She knew he'd been trying to apologize since the day he'd told her he was going to marry another woman, but she'd steeled herself against those words. She knew that Henry was the one man on the earth that she loved with her entire heart and soul.

The pain he'd caused her had been deep, and she wasn't ready to forgive him. At first a part of her wanted him to suffer, but that hadn't made her feel any better. And then she'd been afraid to take his calls.

She'd watched the special on BBC just like everyone else. A part of her had felt a twinge of hope when he'd told the interviewer that he was involved with a special woman.

Now he was standing in the car park at her flat with the very band that had played the night they'd kissed. And he was looking up at her as if she mattered to him.

But she was afraid to believe in him. Afraid to get hurt again.

"You love me? What if—"

"Don't say anything else," Henry said. "Let me come up."

She noticed her parents and brother-in-law, Percy, were standing down there next to Henry. And Tiffany and Gordon and Joshua and Lucas were there, as well. He'd brought their families together.

"Okay," she said.

She looked around her familiar apartment with its open floor plan and IKEA furniture. She'd done her best to make this place into her home. There were pictures of her family on the wall and she felt safe here. It was the place she retreated to when she needed to escape from the world as she had when she'd miscarried.

This was where she'd been reborn. And she wasn't too sure she could do it again. There were only so many times she could recover from having her heart broken and she didn't want to have to do it again. Not with Henry.

She stepped back from the window. "I think he really loves me."

Bethann started laughing. "I think so, too, but only you can decide that. I'm going to go down and wait with Percy and Mum and Dad."

"Bethy?"

"Yes?"

"How did you know for sure about Percy?"

"He's the only man to make me feel alive. He's not perfect, but he's mine and when I look at him I know that he loves me even when I'm being a cow."

She hugged her sister as she left and thought about what Bethann had said. Love was more than just that grand illusion. It was about the quiet times when no one else watched.

Henry knocked on her door and she opened it for him. He handed her a wrapped present as he came inside. Through the open window she still heard the sound of XSU playing.

"You didn't have to bring a gift for me," she said.

"Yes, I did. I missed you every day," he said. He reached for her and drew her into his arms.

"This last week has been the longest of my life," Henry said. "I can't believe I was so stupid to think I could marry another woman when you own my heart."

She looked up at him and saw the truth in his eyes. Saw that he believed what he was saying. "I…I'm afraid to believe that you are really going to stay. So many times I've been left before."

"I know that. But I'm not like the other men you've loved before."

She shook her head. "I haven't loved any man before. Not like I love you."

"I love you, too, Astrid and I want to make a life with you. I want to get married and have children. I want us to continue to build our life together."

She wanted that, too, but Henry would have to know the truth. "I can't have children, Henry. I…I had an ectopic pregnancy and it was complicated. I lost the baby and my doctor warned that I…well, I can't have any kids."

Henry hugged her close. "As long as I have you I'm happy. You're the missing piece to this life I've made for myself. It didn't take me any time at all to realize that without you by my side nothing mattered."

He reached into his pocket and brought out a jewelers' box and got down on one knee in front of her. "Astrid Taylor, will you marry me?"

She looked down at him. At the man she'd had a crush on when she was teenage girl and the boss she'd thought was such a cutie and realized that the man he was, was so much more than that.

"Yes, Henry Devonshire, I will marry you."

He put the ring on her finger as he stood up and kissed her.

He went to the window and looked down at their family.

"She said yes."

They applauded and Astrid laughed, happy to have finally found the man she'd always searched for.

* * * * *

New York Times bestselling author **Elizabeth Bevarly** is the award-winning, nationally number one bestselling author of more than seventy novels and novellas. Her books have been translated into two dozen languages and published in three dozen countries. An honors graduate of the University of Louisville, she has called home places as diverse as San Juan, Puerto Rico, and Haddonfield, New Jersey, but now resides in her native Kentucky with her husband, her son and two neurotic cats (as if there were any other kind). Visit her online at elizabethbevarly.com.

Look for more books by Elizabeth Bevarly in Harlequin Desire—the ultimate destination for powerful, passionate romance! There are six new Harlequin Desire titles available every month. Check one out today!

THE TEMPTATION OF
RORY MONAHAN
Elizabeth Bevarly

For all the wonderful librarians who made the library a truly magical place for me when I was a kid. And for all the ones who keep it magic for me as an adult. Thank you all so much.

Chapter 1

Miriam Thornbury was testing a new Internet filter for the computers in the Marigold Free Public Library when she came across hotwetbabes.com.

She experienced a momentary exhilaration in her triumph at, once again, foiling a filter system—score one for the anticensorship campaign—but alas, her victory was short-lived. Because in that second moment she saw what, precisely, the Web site claimed as its content.

And she began to think that maybe, just maybe, censorship might have its uses.

Oh, dear, she thought further, alarmed. What was the world coming to when librarians began to advocate such a thing as censorship? What on earth was she thinking?

Of course Miriam knew librarians who did, in fact, support censorship. Well, maybe she didn't quite *know* any; not personally, at any rate. She was, after all, one of only two full-time librarians in all of Marigold, Indiana, and Douglas Amberson, the senior librarian, was as vehemently opposed to censorship as she was herself.

But she knew of colleagues like that out there in the world, few though they may be, fortunately. Librarians who thought they knew what was best for their patrons and therefore took it upon themselves to spare the poor, ignorant reading public the trouble of weeding through all the icky things in life, by doing the literary gardening—so to speak—themselves.

Worse, Miriam knew mayors like that. Mayors of towns like, oh, say…Marigold, Indiana, for example. Which was why she was sitting in her office at the library on a sunny July afternoon, trying to find an Internet filter that would effectively screen out things like, oh, say…hotwetbabes.com.

It was a task Miriam had undertaken with mixed feelings. Although she by no means approved of some sites on the Net, sites such as, oh, say…this one, she had a hard time submitting to anyone who deemed him—or herself so superior to the masses that he or she would presume to dictate what was suitable reading and viewing material for those masses. Anyone like, oh, say… Isabel Trent, Marigold's mayor.

Miriam glanced down at the computer screen again and bit back a wince. Hotwetbabes.com, however, did rather give one pause. All those half-naked, glistening female bodies right there on the Internet, for anyone to stumble across. That couldn't possibly be a good thing, could it? Especially since these particular half-naked, glistening female bodies were so inconsistent with what real women looked like, even wet.

Inescapably, Miriam glanced down at her own midsection, well hidden—and quite dry, thank you very much—beneath her standard librarian uniform of crisply ironed cotton blouse—in this case, white—over crisply ironed straight skirt—in this case, beige. Then, inevitably, she glanced back up at the screen. Not only was her midsection sadly lacking when compared to these women, but the rest of her suffered mightily, too.

Where the women on the computer screen had wildly billowing tresses—even wet, they billowed, she noted morosely—in hues of gold and copper and ebony, her own boring blond hair—dishwater, her mother had always called it—was clipped back at her nape with a simple barrette, performing no significant billowing to speak of. And instead of heavily lined, mascaraed eyes of exotic color, Miriam's were gray and completely unadorned.

No, the women on this particular Web site certainly were not what one might call usual, she thought with a sigh. Nor were they what one might call realistic. Of course, she reminded herself, the site *was* called hotwetbabes.com, so she supposed she shouldn't be surprised to find all those photos of, well, hot, wet babes. Still, she did wish *some*one would try to impose *some* measure of…of…of *accuracy* on existing Internet businesses.

There. That wasn't advocating censorship, was it? Who in his or her right mind would object to accuracy, after all? Accuracy was a very good thing. The world needed more accuracy. And in Miriam's opinion, it was high time the Internet became more accurate.

Yes, indeed.

She positioned the mouse to close the program with a convenient click—clearly this filter *wasn't* the one the Marigold Free Public Library would be using, if sites such as these found their way through—but her hand, and therefore the mouse, must have just missed the mark. Because she accidentally—and she was absolutely certain it was indeed an accident—clicked instead on an announcement. An announcement which read, of all things, *Visit our brother site! Hotwetbods. com!* And before she had a chance to correct her mistake—drat these fast new modems, anyway—a different screen opened up. And she suddenly found herself looking at—

Oh, my.

More half-naked, glistening bodies appeared on the screen, only this time they weren't female bodies. And this time they weren't naked from the waist up. Instead they were—

Oh, dear.

"Ah. Miss Thornbury, there you are."

Oh, no.

The only thing that could have possibly made Miriam's current state of abject embarrassment any more complete would have been to be discovered by a second party while she was gazing—however involuntarily—at hot, wet bods on the Internet. Even worse—which one might have thought would be impossible, all things considered—the second party in question was none other than Professor Rory Monahan, one of Marigold's most upright, forthright, do-right citizens.

And also one of Marigold's cutest citizens.

And one of the most eligible, too.

Not that Miriam was necessarily in the market for an eligible man. But she was only human, after all. And she did rather like cute ones. In fact, she rather liked Professor Rory Monahan. But everyone in Marigold— even a newcomer like Miriam—knew that Professor

Monahan was far too involved in his scholarly pursuits to ever show an interest in anything, or any*one,* else.

More was the pity. Because Miriam would have very much liked to pique his interest. Though, she had to admit, not while she was gazing at half-naked men on the Internet. It could, after all, only lead to trouble.

Guiltily, she shot up from her chair and positioned herself in front of the computer monitor, just as Professor Monahan strode through the door to her office. He looked even cuter than usual, she noted—and even more eligible, drat him—with his round, wire-rimmed glasses enhancing his pale-blue eyes, and his black hair tousled, as if he'd run restless fingers through it as he perused *The Encyclopaedia Britannica* with wild abandon. He was dressed in a pair of dark-brown, baggy trousers, a cream-colored dress shirt with sleeves rolled back over surprisingly muscular forearms—no doubt from carrying around all those heavy tomes, she thought—and a much too outdated, and not particularly attractive, necktie.

All in all, he looked adorably rumpled and delightfully disheveled. He was the kind of man a woman like her just wanted to take home with her at night and… and…and…

And *feed,* she realized with much annoyance. Because truly, that was what she wanted to do, every time she saw Rory Monahan. She wanted to take him home and *cook* for him, for heaven's sake, then present him with a homemade pie for dessert. And Miriam wasn't even a *good* cook. She was an even worse baker. Nevertheless, after she'd plied him with her dubious culinary creations, she wanted to linger over coffee with him, then take a walk through the neighborhood with him—hand in hand, of course—then pop microwave popcorn with him, and then watch a rented copy of an old romantic comedy like *The Thin Man* or something with him.

In fact, what Miriam wanted to do with Professor Monahan was so sweet and so quiet and so harmless, it scared the bejabbers out of her. The last thing she needed in her life was more sweetness, more quietness, more harmlessness. She was already the safest, most predictable, most boring woman on the planet.

If she was going to dally with a man, not that she had *any* intention of dallying with *any* man—even Rory Monahan, honest—then, she told herself, she should at least have the decency to seek out someone who was dangerous and thrilling and outrageous, someone who might, possibly, stir dangerous, thrilling, outrageous responses in her. Because she was truly beginning to worry that she wasn't capable of a single dangerous, thrilling, outrageous response.

Worse, her desire to pursue such sweet, quiet, harmless activities with Professor Monahan smacked much too much of domesticity, of settling down, of matrimony. Not that Miriam had anything against matrimony. *Au contraire.* She fully planned to marry and settle down and be domestic someday. Someday, she hoped, in the not too distant future.

But she wouldn't be settling down and being domestic with Rory Monahan, alas. Because Rory Monahan was, quite simply, already married—to his work as a history professor at the local community college and to his studies and to his research and to his quest for knowledge. When it came to women, he had the attention span of a slide rule. In the six months that Miriam had lived in Marigold, she had never once seen him out on a single date with a woman.

Then again, she herself hadn't been out on a single date with a man since she'd moved to Marigold, had she? And what was her excuse? She certainly had a longer attention span than a slide rule. And she had been asked out on a few occasions. She just hadn't accepted that was all. And she hadn't accepted, because she hadn't been interested in the men who'd asked her out. And she hadn't been interested in the men who'd asked her out because…because…because… She gazed at Professor Monahan and tried not to sigh with melodramatic yearning. Well, just *because*. That was why. And it was a perfectly good reason, too.

So there.

"Miss Thornbury," Professor Monahan said again now, taking a step forward.

Recalling what was on the screen behind her, Miriam shifted her position to the right a bit, to compensate for the angle at which he had placed his own bod. Uh, bod*y*, she hastily corrected herself.

"Yes, Professor Monahan? Can I help you?" she asked, innocently, she hoped. Because the thoughts suddenly parading through her head were anything *but* innocent. No, they were more of the hot, wet variety.

"I'm in a bit of a bind," he told her, "and I suspect that you're the only one who can help me out."

Well, that sounded kind of promising, Miriam thought. "Oh?" she asked.

He nodded. "I've looked high and low for volume fifteen of *Stegman's Guide to the Peloponnesian War,* but I can't locate it anywhere. And if there's one person who knows this library backward and forward…" He hesitated, arrowing his dark brows down in consternation—and looking quite adorable when he did so, Miriam couldn't help but notice. "Well, I suppose it would be Mr. Amberson, actually," he said. "But he's not here right now, and I know you're familiar with the system, too, and I was wondering if you could help me."

Well, she *could,* Miriam thought. It was, after all, her job. Not to mention it would offer her the opportunity to be close to Professor Monahan, and she could see if he smelled as wonderful today as he usually did, of that tantalizing mix of Ivory soap and Old Spice aftershave—he really was so adorable. But that would mean moving away from the computer monitor, and that would leave him looking at what she had just been looking at—namely, hot, wet bods—and that wouldn't be a good thing at all, would it?

So she did the only thing she could do. She pointed frantically toward the door behind him and shouted, "Oh, look! Isn't that the Artist Formerly Known as Prince?"

And when Professor Monahan spun around to see if it was, she hastily turned and, even more hastily, clicked the mouse to shrink the screen. Which left visible on the monitor nothing but the "Great Metaphysical Philosophers of the Eighteenth Century" wallpaper that she'd downloaded herself earlier that morning.

When she straightened again, it was to find that Professor Monahan was still craning his neck to gaze out the office door, toward the circulation desk. "I don't see any artist," he said. "Or any prince, for that matter." He turned back to face Miriam, his expression puzzled. "In fact, I don't recall any prince who *is* an artist. Not in this century, at any rate." He brightened. "Now, during the Renaissance, you had any number of—"

"Professor Monahan?" Miriam interjected lightly. She'd seen before how his scholarly tangents could go on for a long, long time, and she knew she had to nip this one in the bud, or else she'd never have time to complete all the work she had on her agenda today.

"Yes, Miss Thornbury?" he asked.

"Volume fifteen of *Stegman's Guide to the Peloponnesian War,* wasn't that what you wanted?"

He appeared bewildered again for a moment, as if he couldn't quite remember who or where he was. Then, suddenly, his expression cleared, and he smiled. "Why, yes. That's exactly what I was looking for. How did you know?"

She smiled back. "You just told me."

"Ah. I see. Well."

He blushed at his display of absentminded professorship, and Miriam's heart did a funny little flip-flop in her chest. Oh, he was just too adorable for words.

"Do you know where it is?" he asked.

"As a matter of fact, I do," she told him. "I guess it's true that great minds think alike. Because as providence would have it, I was reading it myself over lunch earlier." She turned again, this time hefting the fat, leatherbound book from her desk. Then she spun back around to stride toward him. "I always like learning about new things," she said as she went. "And I found the fifth chapter in particular to be quite interesting."

Professor Monahan grinned a bit shyly as he adjusted his glasses. "I know," he told her. "I've read it three or four times myself. It's quite outstanding. Thank you, Miss Thornbury," he added as he took the book from her.

Somehow, though, during the exchange—and Miriam had no idea how it happened, truly—their fingers became entangled, and as they vied for possession, the book went spilling to the floor. It landed on its back with a loud *thwack,* and both she and Professor Monahan stooped at the same time to pick it up. But as each of them reached for it—and Miriam had no idea how it happened, truly—their fingers wove awkwardly together again, and before she knew it, her hand was linked completely with his, and a dangerous, outrageous thrill was dashing through her body.

And all she could do was think that if this was the reaction she had to simply holding hands with the man, then what would happen to her if the two of them joined more intimately?

And then all she could do was blush—furiously. Because she glanced up to find that Professor Monahan's light-blue eyes seemed warmer somehow, and his cheeks were flushed with what *might* be embarrassment, but which could very well be something else entirely. His expression suggested that his own reaction to their light touch was none too sweet. Nor did it seem quiet. Nor did it seem harmless.

Oh, dear.

Immediately Miriam let go of both the book and Professor Monahan's hand, then she pushed herself quickly back to standing. She tucked behind her ear a stray strand of blond hair that had escaped her barrette and did everything she could to avoid his gaze. She realized quickly, though, that such an effort was unnecessary. Because no sooner had she stood than Professor Monahan bolted. Right through the office door, out to the circulation desk, with a *very* hasty, "Good day, Miss Thornbury, and thank you again," tossed over his shoulder.

And then Miriam was left feeling oddly dazed and disoriented, as if someone had just— What was the phrase they used in historical romances? She tried to remember. (Well, one couldn't exist on a steady diet of *Stegman's Guide to the Peloponnesian War,* could one?) Ah, yes. Now she recalled the phrase. She felt as if someone had just…tumbled her. Quite thoroughly, too. It was an odd sensation. But not altogether unpleasant.

No, not unpleasant at all.

She smiled what was almost certainly a wicked smile. She was almost certain of that, because she *felt* wicked at the moment. And speaking of wicked…

She remembered then that there was still a window open on the computer screen which she very much needed to close. She returned to her desk and had just brought the screen back up, when she was interrupted yet again in her effort to get rid of the, um, hot…wet… bods.

"Miriam, I need a word with you right away," Isabel Trent, Marigold's mayor, said as she entered.

Hastily Miriam spun back around, positioning herself in much the same way she had done earlier, when she'd been trying to spare Professor Monahan's tender sensibilities. Because Ms. Trent's tender sensibilities would go absolutely ballistic if the mayor saw what the town librarian had been inspecting prior to her arrival, even if the mayor was the one who was responsible for the town librarian's finding it in the first place.

"Yes, Ms. Trent? Can I help you?" Miriam asked innocently, feeling a wave of déjà vu.

"It's of utmost importance," the mayor told her.

Of course, *everything* was of utmost importance to Isabel Trent, Miriam thought with a sigh. Nevertheless she adopted her expression of utmost gravity as she replied, "Oh? I'm all ears."

Ms. Trent, too, wore a standard uniform for her job, Miriam had noted some time ago, a uniform of tightly buttoned, very conservative suits. Today's selection was dark blue in color—almost the same dark blue as her eyes—but it was as closely bound as all the others. Her spun-gold hair was closely bound, too, wound up in a terse knot at the back of her head. Huge, tortoiseshell glasses were perched on the bridge of her nose, giving the mayor the appearance of someone trying to hide from something. Like the world, for instance.

Honestly, Miriam thought, lifting a hand to her own dishwater—drat it—ponytail. Isabel Trent was an even blander-looking person than Miriam was herself. And that was saying something.

"It's about all those copies of *Metropolitan* magazine scattered about in Periodicals," the mayor said.

Miriam nodded. "Those are checked out and read very frequently. I apologize if there's a mess. I'll have someone tidy them right away."

Ms. Trent straightened to her full—and very militant—five feet four inches. "No, you'll have someone get *rid* of them right away."

Miriam's dishwater-blond eyebrows—drat them—shot up beneath her dishwater-blond—drat them, too—bangs. "I beg your pardon?" she asked.

"I said you'll get rid of them," the mayor echoed. "Completely. Cancel the library's subscription."

"But…but why?" Miriam asked. "As I said, *Metropolitan* is one of the library's most popular periodicals."

"Yes, well, it's also one of the library's most unacceptable periodicals."

"Unacceptable? In what way?"

"Don't tell me you haven't noticed some of those headlines that appear on the cover of the magazine," the mayor stated in a cool, clipped tone.

"Well, no, I haven't," Miriam said honestly. "I don't read *Metropolitan* myself." She braved a halfhearted smile. "I'm not much of a *Metro* Girl, I'm afraid."

"Well, I should hope not," Ms. Trent said. "That magazine is about nothing but sex, sex, sex."

Which went a long way toward explaining why Miriam never read it, she thought, and why she wasn't much of a *Metro* Girl. Sex, sex, sex wasn't exactly a big part of her life, life, life. Or *any* part of her life, for that matter. Not her real life, anyway. As for her fantasy life, well…

There *were* those occasional daydreams in which she indulged, daydreams about herself and Professor Rory Monahan, even though his preference for the reference section of the library far outweighed his interest in the librarian herself. In fact, the reference section of the library also played a significant role in Miriam's daydreams, come to think of it. More significantly, the tables in the reference section played into her daydreams. Because it was on one of those tables in the reference section that she and Professor Monahan were invariably engaged in—

Oh, dear. She was doing it again. Or, rather, fantasizing it again. *Doing it,* after all, didn't actually show up on her agenda anywhere—more was the pity. Why schedule something that wasn't going to happen?

"And on top of all that…" she heard Ms. Trent say, clearly concluding what had been a long diatribe against the mass media that Miriam had thankfully missed because she'd been too busy daydreaming about—oh, never mind. "…those women who appear on the cover of *Metropolitan* are, quite simply—" Instead of voicing a word to illustrate her feelings, the mayor made quite the sour face. "Suffice it to say," she then continued, "that *Metropolitan* is completely inappropriate reading material for our library. As are these other magazines that I want you to remove from the periodical section."

The mayor strode forward, pausing within arm's length of Miriam, and extended a handwritten list, which Miriam accepted in silence—mainly because she was so surprised by the gesture that she didn't know what to say. She was even more surprised when she glanced down at the list to find that some of the other journals and magazines that Ms. Trent deemed inappropriate for the library patrons were, like *Metropolitan,* wildly popular with the library patrons.

Evidently mistaking Miriam's stunned silence for complete agreement, the mayor hurried on to her next point. "There are some novels in the browsing section that I'd like to see removed, as well," she said. "*Love's Burning Ecstasy,* for instance…" Her voice trailed off, but its tone held enough chilly disapproval to generate a new Ice Age.

"But *Love's Burning Ecstasy*…" Miriam began.

"Don't tell me *it's* popular with the library patrons," Ms. Trent said, clearly incredulous.

"Well, no," Miriam conceded reluctantly. *Not with*

the library patrons, necessarily, she added silently to herself. But Miriam had enjoyed it immensely. Several times, in fact.

"I want it gone," Ms. Trent concluded simply. "Along with these others."

She extended another list toward Miriam, who took it automatically, still having no idea what to say with regard to this blatant attack of censorship.

"And I want to make a more thorough inspection of the British literature section, too," the mayor continued. "It was purely by chance that I stumbled upon *this*." She held up a slender, bound tome as if it were exhibit A and continued, "I'm shocked to find something entitled *The Rape of the Lock* in our facility. I don't think it's at all appropriate. Do you, Miriam?"

For a moment all Miriam was able to manage in response to the mayor's question was a series of quick, incoherent—and none too polite—expulsions of air. But she quickly recovered enough to say, "*The Rape of the Lock* is a virtuoso piece of writing, Ms. Trent, arguably Alexander Pope's crowning achievement."

The mayor gaped at her. "A man named *Pope* wrote that piece of trash?" she gasped. "I can hardly believe it."

This time Miriam was the one to gape. "Piece of *trash?*" she sputtered. "It's one of the poet's most luminous performances!"

She took a giant step forward to snatch the book from the mayor's hand and to read her a few verses, because clearly Ms. Trent had not taken the time to do that herself. Otherwise she would have realized the work was a social satire of completely inoffensive—and quite riotous—humor. Unfortunately, Miriam never achieved her goal, because she had barely completed her giant step when Ms. Trent's face went white, and the book slipped right out of her fingers.

"Good heavens, Miriam," the mayor cried in a hoarse whisper. "*What* is *that?*"

Miriam squeezed her eyes shut tight when she remembered what had been displayed on her computer screen when Isabel Trent entered her office. Unable to quite help herself, however—the mayor was such a... such a...such a *prude*—Miriam pretended not to be affected by the scene herself. Feigning bland indifference to the subject matter of hotwetbods.com, she glanced swiftly, once, over her shoulder, then back at Ms. Trent.

"Actually, seeing as how there are considerably more than one displayed there, I believe the correct phrasing of your question should be, '*What* are *those?*' And really I'm rather surprised you have to ask, Ms. Trent. But if you must know, the correct term for them is peni—"

"*Shhhh!*" The mayor shushed her before Miriam could fully pronounce the word. "Don't say it." She narrowed her eyes. "And don't mock me, either, Miriam. You haven't been working for the Marigold Free Public Library very long. You are by no means inexpendable."

Miriam narrowed her eyes right back at the mayor, but said nothing in response. It was true that her job wasn't exactly secure. She'd only moved to Marigold six months ago, specifically to accept the position. Douglas Amberson was senior librarian, even though Miriam was assigned the most hours and completed the most work. And although there was an unspoken agreement between her and Douglas that when he retired next spring, she would move directly into his position, Douglas and Miriam were, unfortunately, the only two people in Marigold who knew about that agreement. And the mayor of Marigold had the authority to accept or reject Douglas's recommendation for his replacement, when that time arose.

So, for now, Miriam remained silent and waited to see what Isabel Trent was going to object to next.

"I see our latest attempt at finding an effective Internet filter has failed. Again," the mayor said.

"This one won't meet with your approval, no," Miriam agreed. "But truly, Ms. Trent, I don't think it's necessary for us to use filters in the library. It is a form of censorship, you know."

Ms. Trent gave her an icy glare. "And your point would be?"

"That since the computers in the children's and young adults' sections aren't hooked up to the Internet," Miriam said, "then a filter isn't necessary. The people who use the Internet at the library are adults, Ms. Trent. They don't need policing."

"Of course they need policing," the mayor immediately countered.

"Why?"

Ms. Trent waved awkwardly at the sight on Miriam's computer screen, but at no time did she steer her gaze in that direction. "So that they don't find themselves looking at something like *that*."

Miriam sighed. "Ms. Trent, it's none of our business if they find themselves looking at something like that," she said softly.

"It is if they're using computers purchased with the taxpayers' dollars."

Miriam wasn't sure how to reply to that, mainly because she knew Isabel Trent had already made up her mind that the Marigold Free Public Library *would* be using a filter system, and there would be no reasoning or arguing with her on that score. And, truth be told, having viewed the contents of hotwetbabes- and -bods. com, Miriam was hard-pressed to launch much of a defense, anyway.

"At any rate," she finally conceded, "this particular filter isn't effective in the way you demand that it be effective."

Isabel Trent lifted her chin a fraction. "Well then, try the next one on the list."

Miriam inhaled a deep breath and expelled it slowly. "Whatever you say, Ms. Trent."

In one swift, graceful gesture, the mayor scooped up the book she had dropped on the floor and tossed it onto Miriam's desk. Then, averting her gaze, she felt around awkwardly until she found the button to switch off the computer monitor. Miriam bit her lip to prevent herself from pointing out that, in her effort to avoid seeing all those male members on the monitor, Ms. Trent brushed her fingers inadvertently over quite a few of them in her pursuit of the power button.

After finally succeeding in switching the monitor off, the mayor spun back around. "I'm going to start inspecting the children's section this weekend," she said starchily. "I'll make a list of everything I want removed from there."

Once again, Miriam gaped. "But that's—"

"Don't argue with me, Miriam," the mayor interrupted. "I have the approval of the majority of members on the board of aldermen behind me on this. I want this library to be a facility where families can feel comfortable."

Miriam chose her words carefully. "Families have felt comfortable in this facility for more than a hundred years, Ms. Trent. The Marigold Free Public Library can take care of itself. And so can all the Marigoldians who use it. They don't need someone else telling them what they are and are not allowed access to."

She might as well have been talking to a brick wall, because the mayor offered no indication that she'd heard a word of Miriam's admonishment. "Keep looking for an effective filter," Ms. Trent said. "And get rid of those magazines on the list I gave you. Today. When I come back this weekend, I want to see that this library reflects the decency and family values of all who use it."

And without awaiting a reply, the mayor of Marigold, Indiana, spun on her heel and exited the office. Miriam watched her go with a sinking heart. It wasn't the decency and family values of the library patrons that Isabel Trent wanted reflected here, she thought. No, what Isabel Trent wanted the library to reflect was the decency and family values of Isabel Trent. Period.

Miriam decided to take the matter up with Douglas when he returned from his vacation the following week, but for now she had no choice but to do as the mayor had instructed. She glanced down at the list of periodicals she still held in her hands and shook her head with much disappointment. It appeared her afternoon was going to be quite full now, what with all the censoring and blacklisting she had to do.

My, my, my, she thought. A librarian's work was never done. With a sigh of defeat Miriam went to work.

Chapter 2

Rory Monahan was, as usual, far too absorbed in his work to notice that the library was closing—until he was plunged into almost total darkness. He sighed as he glanced up at the extinguished lights overhead and waited for his vision to adjust. Then he carefully inserted an index card to mark his place in the heavy tome he'd opened on the table before him, and flipped it closed. Damn. Just when he'd found exactly what he'd been looking for, too.

But Rory didn't mind leaving his work where it lay. It would be here waiting for him tomorrow afternoon when he returned, as he invariably would. He was confident that no one would come along and reshelve all the work and trouble he'd gone to tonight, because the table at which he sat was, unofficially, Professor Monahan's domain. Everyone who worked in the Marigold Free

Public Library, from Mr. Amberson, the head librarian, right down to Gladys Dorfman, who cleaned up after hours, knew not to touch a thing on this particular table.

After settling his wire-rimmed glasses back on the bridge of his nose, Rory launched himself momentarily into a full-body stretch. Upon completing it, he shoved a restless hand through his black hair, noting, without much surprise, that he was long overdue for a trim. He made a halfhearted—and only partly successful—effort to straighten the knot in his tie but didn't bother rolling the cuffs of his shirt back down to his wrists. He collected his tweed jacket—which was really much too warm for July, but Rory couldn't imagine going anywhere without it—then scooped up his notes and filed them meticulously in his leather satchel. Then he neatly stacked, in volume order, all the reference books he'd used that evening, and he rose to make his way out.

He was confident that whichever librarian was on duty, either Mr. Amberson or Miss Thornbury—though, for some reason, he was thinking Miss Thornbury was working today, but he couldn't remember now just *how* he knew that—would be waiting for him by the main exit, just as he or she was always inevitably waiting for Rory by the main exit when they were closing the library. Whichever librarian it was would greet him warmly, ask him how his research was going, accompany him through the front door and lock up behind them.

It was, after all, a routine. And routine was a very good thing, as far as Rory Monahan was concerned. Routine was exactly the way he liked things. Well planned. Predictable. Secure. Safe. Life, to his way of thinking, was good.

It got even better when he saw that it was indeed Miss Thornbury waiting by the doors this particular evening, and Rory recalled then why he had known it would be her. They'd had an interlude of sorts in her office that afternoon, hadn't they? The details of that interlude escaped him now, swamped as they had been over the last several hours by great, hulking chunks of *Stegman's Guide to the Peloponnesian War.* But for some reason, he recalled the interlude with a feeling of fondness. In fact, for some reason, he recalled it with a warm flutter of something rather intense skipping through his midsection, a warm flutter of something that felt very much like…desire?

Oh, surely not.

Ah, well. No matter, Rory thought. All that mattered was that his mind had retained the important things, the details he'd garnered and analyzed and recorded from numerous volumes of *Stegman's.*

As he drew nearer Miss Thornbury, though, those details began to fade a bit, and something warm and easy and indolent wound through him. Involuntarily, Rory smiled. She always had that effect on him for some reason, every time he saw her. He had no idea why. But invariably, when he encountered her, something that had previously felt off-kilter seemed to shift right into place.

Not that Rory felt as if anything in his life was currently off-kilter. On the contrary, everything was going surprisingly well. But Miss Thornbury had a way about her, a way of making a person feel…right. Steady. Complete. And somehow, whenever he saw that it was Miss Thornbury standing there waiting for him at night, the discovery was infinitely more appealing to Rory than finding Mr. Amberson there instead.

Not that he didn't like Mr. Amberson. On the contrary, Mr. Amberson had been one of Rory's idols since he was a child. The man knew virtually *everything*. What few things the elder librarian wasn't entirely sure about, he knew exactly where in the library to look, to discover the answers. And because Rory had always craved knowledge above all else, even as a child, Douglas Amberson had always seemed something of a god to him. Rory had admired and respected the older man that much—certainly above everyone else in Marigold.

Which, he supposed, meant that he should see Miss Thornbury as something of a god*dess*. Because she, too, was well read, well educated, well spoken, well everything. She, too, was utterly familiar with the library and knew exactly where to find anything, even having worked there for such a short time. He admired and respected her as much as he did Mr. Amberson. For some reason, though, her distinction as *goddess* carried a significantly different connotation than Mr. Amberson's status as *god*. Yes, Miss Thornbury was every bit as smart as Mr. Amberson, but for some reason the feelings she roused in him went well beyond admiration and respect. Rory just wasn't quite able to identify exactly what those "beyond" feelings were.

Furthermore, for some reason when he thought of Miss Thornbury as a goddess, it always evoked a mental image of her wearing some flowing, gossamer—really almost translucent—gown, the kind that dropped off one shoulder and dipped low over lush breasts, draping seductively against an elegant waist, with the side slit high enough so that one firm, naked, creamy thigh was exposed, and—

Ahem.

Where was he?

Oh, yes. The translucent, goddesslike garment. Rory *never* envisioned Mr. Amberson in something like that when he thought about him as a god. It was something of a paradox, really.

Tonight, however, Miss Thornbury's translucent garment was nowhere to be seen, something about which, Rory discovered, he had mixed feelings. Still, her smart white blouse and straight beige skirt were practical and not unattractive, even if there was nothing even remotely goddesslike about the attire. Coupled with the dark blond hair caught at her nape and the deep-gray eyes unadorned with cosmetics, she was by no means a remarkable-looking woman. But her mouth was rather good, he noted, not for the first time, wide and full and lush, and the sight of it now roused deep inside him something hot and wanton and demanding and—

Ahem.

Where was he?

Oh, yes. He was leaving the library to go home. Alone. Where there wouldn't be anyone with a full, lush mouth, dressed as a goddess, waiting for him.

"Good evening, Professor Monahan," Miss Thornbury greeted him warmly at his approach.

"Hello, Miss Thornbury," he replied, as was his custom.

"How's the research going?"

"Very well, thank you."

As was likewise the custom, they chitchatted as they passed through the main entrance—evidently she'd forgotten the details of their earlier interlude, too, because she made no reference to it at all as they spoke—and then she locked the doors behind them. As was not customary, however, she juggled a large, unwieldy box under one arm as she performed her nightly routine. Rory was about to offer her some assistance when the box pitched forward, dumping its entire contents onto the walkway just outside the entrance. An assortment of glossy magazines fanned out between the two of them, and immediately he stooped to help her pick them up.

"I didn't realize you were such a fan of *Metropolitan,*" he said when he noted what the majority of the magazines was.

Somehow, Miss Thornbury just didn't seem the *Metro* Girl type, even with the translucent gown thing going. On the contrary, the models depicted on the covers of *Metropolitan* were much more scantily dressed than even his goddess-vision of Miss Thornbury, and they wore cosmetics that had evidently been applied with trowels and other such garden implements. But even at that, not a single one of them had a mouth that was as lush and as ripe and as erotic and as hot and as—

Ahem.

Where was he?

Oh, yes. None of them had a mouth that could compare with Miss Thornbury's.

She expelled an exasperated sound as she, too, dropped to her knees to join him in gathering up the scattered periodicals. "I'm not such a fan of *Metropolitan,*" she said, sounding a bit breathless for some reason, though what that reason might be, Rory could scarcely imagine. "But our illustrious mayor," she continued, "has decided these are inappropriate for the library, and she's ordered them removed."

Rory nodded, finding the revelation not at all surprising. "I did get the impression upon meeting Ms. Trent that she was something of a...of a...a, um..."

"A prude?" Miss Thornbury offered helpfully—and not a little acerbically.

Rory smiled. "Well, yes, I suppose that would be a suitable enough word for her."

"Mmm," the librarian murmured. "I can think of a few others for her, as well. Ultraconservative. Right winger. Dictator. Fascist."

Rory chuckled. He'd never seen Miss Thornbury so passionate about something. And now that he did see her so passionate...

Well, he hastily decided that it might be best not to dwell upon it.

"I think Ms. Trent is just trying to make a good impression on the community," he said instead. "She is, after all, Marigold's first woman mayor. And she's also the youngest mayor we've ever had. And she did run on the family-values platform."

"I don't think it has anything to do with making a good impression, or even family values," Miss Thornbury said. "I think it has to do with her being completely terrified of her own sexuality."

Miss Thornbury reached forward for a magazine at the same time Rory laid his own hand on it, and in the ensuing volleying for possession, their fingers somehow tangled together. That scant physical contact, coupled with hearing the word *sexuality* emanating from Miss Thornbury's luscious lips, made something go tight and hot and urgent inside Rory. And suddenly he remembered very well the details of their earlier interlude. He remembered, because that same tight, hot, urgent sensation had shot through him then, too, the moment his hand had touched hers.

Good God, he thought as the sensation shook him for a second time. What on earth *was* that?

He glanced up at the same time Miss Thornbury did, only to find her blushing. And somehow he knew—he just *knew*—it was because she had experienced a similar reaction herself. How very, very odd.

And how very, very interesting.

"I am so sorry I said that," she apologized, her cheeks going even pinker. He couldn't help but note, however, that she did nothing to untangle their fingers. "I spoke out of turn," she added quickly, huskily. "I never should have said such a thing about Ms. Trent. I don't know what I was thinking."

Well, clearly, Rory thought, she'd been thinking about sexuality. The mayor's, if not her own. Though how one could think about someone else's sexuality without at least giving one's own some little consideration was beyond him. Not that he himself spent any gratuitous amount of time thinking about anyone's sexuality, he quickly reminded himself, but on those few occasions when he did, he could never think about someone else's sexuality without allowing his own a quick run. Which meant that at the moment he was pondering not just the mayor's sexuality but his own sexuality, too, and also, since she was the one who brought it up in the first place—if one could pardon the incredibly tacky pun—Miss Thornbury's sexuality, as well.

And that brought him right back to the translucent goddess gown again, only this time it was infinitely more translucent than it had ever been before, and it was dropping far too seductively off one shoulder, and it was dipping dangerously low over her lush breasts, and as for that one firm, naked, creamy thigh, well—

Ahem.

Where was he?

Oh, yes. Miss Thornbury's sexuality. *No!* His own sexuality. *No, not that, either!* The mayor's sexuality. Ah, yes. That was something he could think about safely. Essentially because Isabel Trent, as far as Rory was concerned, anyway, had no sexuality to speak of. And still Miss Thornbury had not freed her hand from his, and somehow Rory found himself reluctant to perform the task himself.

"I…I…I…" Miss Thornbury stammered. But she seemed not to know what else to add, so she clamped her mouth shut tight.

Which was a shame, Rory thought, because in doing so, she ruined the sensual line of those full, ripe, rosy lips, lips that just begged for a man to dip his head to hers and cover her mouth with his and taste her deeply, wantonly, demandingly—

And good *God,* where was his head this evening?

Quickly Rory released her hand and surrendered the magazine to her—but not before he caught a headline that screamed, Love Your Man Orally TONIGHT! which just brought back that translucent-gown thing yet again and, worse, the ripe, luscious-mouth thing again, both with much more troubling explicitness than ever before.

"I really must be going," he said suddenly, rocketing to his feet. "I have to get home and prepare an oral sex—I mean an oral sexam, uh…oral *exam*—for my students tomorrow."

And before Rory could further humiliate himself, he spun on his heel and fled.

Miriam carefully sipped her hot Sleepytime tea, snuggled more deeply into the cool, cotton pillows she had stacked between her and her headboard, listened to the soothing strains of Mozart that drifted from the stereo…and squirmed a bit on the mattress as she read about loving her man orally TONIGHT! Honestly. The things they printed in magazines these days. She'd seen college girls reading *Metropolitan* magazine and hadn't thought a thing about it. Now…

Well, now Miriam was thinking that the girls growing up in Marigold today knew a lot more about things than she'd known as a girl growing up in Indianapolis. So much for big-city sophistication.

She sipped her tea again and closed the magazine—after finishing the article, of course, because librarians never left an article unfinished—then she arced her gaze over the other issues of *Metropolitan* that were scattered about her bed. She hadn't known what else to do with all the magazines she'd confiscated that afternoon, except bring them home with her. Naturally, she hadn't wanted to discard them, because she was sure that eventually she—or else Douglas Amberson—would be able to talk Isabel Trent out of her misguided notion that the Marigold Free Public Library needed policing. And then Miriam could return the issues of *Metropolitan* to their rightful place in periodicals, along with the issues of the half dozen other magazines she'd been required to remove.

For now, though, all of those magazines would be living here at her apartment with her. And since she was a librarian with a love for the written word, Miriam was naturally drawn to the magazines. Especially the issues of *Metropolitan,* though she was absolutely certain that the *only* reason for that was because of the bright colors and simple composition the covers seemed to uniformly present, and *not* because of all those scandalous headlines with the proliferation of capital letters and exclamation points. At any rate she had found herself sifting through the magazines and had eventually started to read them.

Which was how she came to be in her current position, encircled by the glossy journals on her bed. Now scantily clad, heavily made-up women gazed back at her with much boredom, their images surrounded by headlines that screamed instructions like, JUST DO IT—in Every Room in the House! and Find His Erogenous Zones—and Help Him find YOURS! and Call of the Siren—BE the Devil with the Blue Dress On!

Miriam shook her head in bemusement. Did women truly read these articles? she wondered. Did they genuinely find them helpful? Did they honestly put their "tips" to good use? Because she herself couldn't imagine the magazine actually offering any information that the normal, average—i.e. *not* a nymphomaniac—woman might be able to actually apply to her normal, average—i.e. *not* oversexed—everyday life.

Miriam set her tea on her nightstand and was about to collect the assortment and return them to the box in which she'd originally placed them, when her gaze lit on one headline in particular.

Awaken Your Inner Temptress! it shouted at her. And below it, in smaller letters, You Know You Want to!

Hmm, thought Miriam.

And in the same issue: Go from Invisible to Irresistible in Just Seven Seductive Steps!

And somehow Miriam found herself reaching for the issue in question, telling herself, *Well, it won't hurt to look, now, will it?*

She flipped to the Inner Temptress article first, and read all about how she was suppressing a very natural part of her psyche by refusing to admit that she could turn any man of her acquaintance into putty with her bare hands—all she had to do was uncover the secrets of what those bare hands could do. And as she read further, she discovered that her bare hands, the very ordinary-looking ones with the short, clipped nails, the ones that sorted efficiently through the card catalogue everyday, the ones that capably sliced fresh, nutritious vegetables for her regular evening repast, could also, very easily...

Oh, my.

Oh, my goodness, *no.* They couldn't do *that.* Could they? Well, *perhaps* they could, she finally conceded as she read a bit further. Maybe if she *did* awaken her Inner Temptress.

Miriam blushed furiously when she realized the avenue down which her thoughts had traveled. Oh, no, her bare hands could *not* do that, either, she told herself sternly. They couldn't even do it if they had on gloves. Which, when one considered such a scenario, actually added a rather naughty dimension to the potential, all things considered, especially if they were latex gloves, and—

No, she insisted more firmly. She was *not* going to indulge in such...such...such *wanton* behavior, Inner Temptress or no Inner Temptress. Miriam Thornbury simply was not that kind of girl. The very idea. Honestly.

So what else did the article have to say…?

As she continued with her reading, Miriam also learned that she wasn't putting her store of repartee to effective use at all. No, where she had always been under the impression that good repartee was generally used more for, oh, say…conversation, she now discovered that it was widely used, particularly in Europe, as a tool for sexual enticement. She'd had no idea, truly. How she had lived her life for twenty-eight years without such knowledge was beyond her.

Reading further, she also learned how one's very wardrobe could be used as a weapon of seduction. This actually came as no surprise, because Miriam did, after all, receive the Victoria's Secret catalogue, even if the only thing she had ever ordered from it were those wonderful flowing, white Victorian nightgowns that took up only two pages of the publication. She had at least *looked* at the rest of the catalogue. And she'd been reasonably certain that most of those other undergarments were *not* worn for the sake of comfort and functionality. Mainly because they looked in no way comfortable or functional, what with all their squeezing and lifting and expanding of a woman's—

Well. At any rate the undergarments weren't what one might call *practical*. Which meant they were worn for some other purpose than to be, well, practical. And it didn't take a genius to realize what that purpose was. *S-E-X*. 'Nuff said.

Still, it had never occurred to Miriam that she *herself* might don one of those sexy fashions. One of the cute little black ones, say. Made of that delicious-looking, see-through lace. With those brief, naughty demi-cups. And garters. Oh, yes. According to *Metropolitan* magazine, one must wear garters if one was to proceed successfully with awakening one's Inner Temptress. And now that Miriam *did* think about donning such… accoutrements…

She blushed furiously, that's what she did.

How on earth could she even *think* of such a thing? Miriam Thornbury was not the black-lace, demicup, garter-belt type. No, ma'am. Flowing, white, ankle-length, embroidered cotton was much more her style. Still, she might make some headway in the repartee department, she told herself. She'd always been very good at repartee. She'd just never tried to use it for… temptation. Now that she did give some thought to the possibility of doing so…

She blushed furiously *again*.

Absolutely not. There was no way she would be able to walk up to Professor Rory Monahan at the library and say something like, "Hello, Rory. Is that volume fifteen of *Stegman's Guide to the Peloponnesian War* you have in your pocket, or are you just happy to see me?"

Oh, no, no, no, no, no. That would never do.

She sighed fitfully as she tossed the magazine back onto the bed. Clearly, her Inner Temptress was sleeping quite soundly. Clearly, her Inner Temptress was out like a light. Clearly, her Inner Temptress was buried much too deep inside to ever show her face in Marigold, Indiana. It was ridiculous to even think about becoming such a thing. She was practical, pragmatic Miriam Thornbury. Capable, competent Miriam Thornbury. Staid, sensible Miriam Thornbury.

Drab, dull Miriam Thornbury, she concluded morosely. No wonder Rory Monahan scarcely paid her any heed.

Ah, well, she thought further. Even if she was a devil with a blue dress on, Rory Monahan still probably wouldn't pay her any heed. He was a man on a quest. A quest for Knowledge with a capital *K*. Not even a devil with a blue dress on would have a hope of swaying him from his chosen course. Not unless that devil with a blue dress on was holding volume fifteen of *Stegman's Guide to the Peloponnesian War,* or some such thing.

Hmmm, Miriam thought again, brightening.

Just how badly did she want Rory Monahan to notice her? she asked herself. And immediately she had her answer. Pretty badly. After all, she'd spent virtually the last six months wanting him to notice her. She'd spent virtually the last six months *wanting* him, period.

For six months she'd been walking into the Marigold Free Public Library in her usual fashion, to find the good professor sitting at his usual table in the reference section, performing his usual research in his usual manner. And she'd always melted in her usual fashion at how his blue eyes twinkled in their usual way, and how his mouth crooked up in his usual shy smile, and how his fingers threaded through his jet hair in his usual gesture of utter preoccupation. And she always responded to him in her usual way—by becoming very hot and very confused and very flustered.

And she'd spent the last six months, too, doing things and thinking about things that no self-respecting librarian should ever do or think about. Not in a public facility like a library, anyway. Because Miriam had spent the last six months *fantasizing* about Rory Monahan. Naturally, she'd also spent the last six months trying to reassure herself that the *only* reason she fantasized about him was because…because… Well, because…

Hmmm. Actually, now that she thought more about it, she wasn't sure why she'd been fantasizing about him. Suddenly, though, now that she thought more about it, she realized that she very much wanted to find out.

Because suddenly, after reading all those articles in *Metropolitan* magazine, Miriam found herself armed with new knowledge. And she began to wonder if maybe all this new knowledge—whether she applied it the way *Metro* suggested or not—might just have some use. Although Professor Monahan had always been pleasant to her, had even gone so far as to smile warmly at her on occasion, he'd never shown any indication that he reciprocated her, um, interest. In fact, he'd never shown any indication that he reciprocated anything about her. Except, of course, for volume fifteen of *Stegman's Guide to the Peloponnesian War.*

Knowledge, she reiterated to herself. That was all Rory Monahan wanted from life. Knowledge, knowledge and more knowledge. And as much as Miriam admired knowledge in a person…

She sighed fitfully. She'd like to show Rory Monahan knowledge. Boy howdy, would she. And as she thought more about it, she began to think that maybe, just maybe, there might not be any harm in putting her own newly acquired knowledge to good use.

Not *all* of it, necessarily, she hastily qualified when she remembered the gist of some of those articles. Not even a lot of it, really. But some of it, perhaps. A little. Surely there had been one or two things in that Inner Temptress article, for example, that might prove useful.

Provided, of course, she could use them without completely humiliating herself.

Because if Miriam did manage to use one or two of *Metro*'s suggestions to capture even a tiny bit of Professor Monahan's attention, then she might just be able to garner a bit more of his attention all by herself. And if she did that, then she might very well win a nice prize for her efforts. She might very well win Professor Rory Monahan.

As prizes went, that was a pretty good one, as far as Miriam was concerned.

Now, where to begin? she wondered. Hadn't there been another article of interest in that Inner Temptress issue? Something about going from invisible to irresistible in seven seductive steps? Not that Miriam would use all seven steps—heavens, no. She didn't want to overwhelm the good professor, did she? Not yet, anyway. But surely one or two of those steps might be helpful, she thought. She hoped.

Reaching for the issue in question, she settled back against the pillows again to read.

Chapter 3

Rory was quite vexed. He was utterly certain he had left volume fifteen of *Stegman's Guide to the Peloponnesian War* sitting right here on his table in the reference section the night before, when he'd left the library at closing time. Yes, indeed, he was positive he had done so. Because he recalled very clearly stacking volumes twelve through eighteen in numerical order, and not one of them had been missing. Now, however, fifteen was gone.

It was quite the mystery, to be sure. No one—absolutely *no one*—at the Marigold Free Public Library had *ever* had the audacity to remove a reference book from his table. Everyone knew his research was far too important to him for anyone to ever interfere with it. Yet at some point between closing last night—he glanced down at his watch to discover that it was nearly 3:00 p.m.—and roughly 2:52 p.m. today, someone had used stealth and heaven only knew what other means to confiscate his book.

All right, all right, so it wasn't *his* book, per se, Rory admitted reluctantly. Technically it belonged to the library. The transgression was no less severe as a result.

Let's see now, he thought further. Who could possibly be the culprit? Gladys Dorfman, the custodian? It was entirely possible. Not only was she here alone at the library during the dark hours of the night, able to commit, unobserved, whatever mayhem she might want to commit, but she'd also been a student in one of Rory's morning classes last spring and had shown an inordinate amount of interest in the Peloponnese.

It could be significant.

Mr. Amberson? Rory pondered further. Possible, but unlikely. Although Mr. Amberson had keys to the library and lived alone—a condition that would make an alibi difficult to either prove or disprove-the elder librarian's preferred area of history lay decidedly further west and a good two millennia ahead, most notably in the New World at the time of its colonization.

Besides, Rory vaguely recalled, Mr. Amberson hadn't been working the night before, and he doubted the man would make a special effort to come to the library for that particular volume, unless it was an emergency, which, Rory had to admit, was also entirely possible. He himself had experienced such crises of research from time to time, and they were by no means pleasant. They could conceivably drive a man to commit an act which, under normal circumstances, he would never consider committing.

Still, Rory doubted Mr. Amberson would have had reason to be in the library last night. No, it had been

Miss Thornbury who had worked the previous evening, Miss Thornbury who had closed the li—

Miss Thornbury, Rory thought with a snap of his fingers. Of course. She must be the culprit. Not only had he caught her red-handed with volume fifteen of the *Stegman's* yesterday afternoon in her office, but she was a relative newcomer to Marigold, having lived here only… Well, Rory wasn't sure how long she had lived here, but it wasn't very long.

At least, he was fairly certain it hadn't been very long. Although he remembered—surprisingly well, actually—the day she had started working at the library, he couldn't quite pinpoint when, exactly, that day had occurred. It had been snowing, though. He did recall that much. Because she had just come in from outside when he first made her acquaintance, and her nose had been touched adorably with red, and her eyes had glistened against the cold, and her mouth had been so full and so red and so luscious, not that that had necessarily been caused by the elements, but Rory had noticed it, and…and…and…

Where was he?

Oh, yes. The missing volume of *Stegman's.* At any rate, there was a very good chance that Miss Thornbury didn't even know about the unofficial don't-touch-Professor-Monahan's-table rule that everyone else in town held sacred.

Of course, that didn't excuse her violation, Rory told himself. Ignorance was never an excuse. And he was confident that Miss Thornbury herself would agree with him on that score. He was going to have to make clear to her that his research was of utmost importance in and to the community at large. He owed it to her. And once he explained the situation, he was certain she would never commit such an egregious error in judgment again. He was also certain that she would thank him for setting her straight.

Sufficiently convinced now of the nobility of his errand, Rory went in search of Miss Thornbury, and, consequently, volume fifteen of the *Stegman's*. But he didn't have to search far. Because he located her almost immediately, standing on a ladder, two stacks away from his table in the reference section, where she was in the process of shelving—

Good heavens, it was volume fifteen of the *Stegman's!* Rory realized triumphantly. He'd caught her red-handed *again!* He prepared himself for battle, hiked up his dark gray trousers, pushed back the rolled cuffs of his white dress shirt, straightened the skewed knot in his plaid—but it was a tasteful plaid, truly—necktie, and raked both hands through his shaggy black hair. Then, after settling his glasses intently on the bridge of his nose, he bravely entered the fray. Or, at the very least, he bravely entered the stacks. And he didn't stop entering until he stood at the foot of the ladder upon which Miss Thornbury had perched herself.

As he halted before her, though, Rory, well…halted. Because he vaguely realized that she was standing on a rung at such a height as to put her thigh directly at his eye level. And, less vaguely, he realized that there was a side slit in her straight, black skirt. It was conservative enough to be acceptable for a librarian's wardrobe, but open just now—thanks to her position on the ladder—in such a way as to make a professor of history take notice. And somehow, this particular professor of history found the sight of Miss Thornbury's leg to be strangely…arousing?

Oh, surely not.

Rory shook off the sensation and forced his gaze higher, toward her face. But his gaze got held up at her torso, because on top of her slim skirt with the intriguing, though conservative, side slit, Miss Thornbury was wearing a rather snug, rather red, knit top. A snug, red top that had no sleeves, he noted further, offering him just the merest glimpse of a bare shoulder, a glimpse that he'd never had before, a glimpse that was strangely…arousing?

Oh, surely not.

Rory steered his gaze away from the glimpse of shoulder, intent now on finding Miss Thornbury's face, only to have his attention get held up elsewhere on her torso, this time on the elegant swell of her breast, which pushed against the taut fabric of her sweater in such a way as to make the vision strangely…arousing?

Oh, surely—

It was then that a burst of recollection shot the memory of his previous night's encounter with Miss Thornbury to the very forefront of his brain. They had been outside, in front of the library, Rory remembered, and something had kept making him envision her in that goddess getup that he caught himself thinking about her wearing every now and then. But not very often, truly. Only once, or maybe twice, a week. Three times *at most,* honestly. Like when he happened to see her, oh… Rory didn't know. Perched on a ladder, for instance. Like now.

Uh-oh…

And last night, he hurriedly rushed on, dispelling

the realization, they'd been holding hands for some reason, too, hadn't they? But why…? Oh, yes. Now he remembered. For a purely innocent reason. He'd been helping her gather up an assortment of periodicals that she'd dropped on the ground. What had they been…? Oh, yes. Now he remembered. *Metropolitan* magazine, which he'd thought an odd choice for her. Especially when he pondered what some of those headlines had contained. Hadn't there been one, in particular, that had caught his attention? Something about loving one's man orally to—

Oh, yes. Now he remembered. Now he remembered very, *very* well. *Too* well. He remembered how Miss Thornbury's mouth had been so full and luscious. And he remembered wondering if her other body parts would be as full and luscious as her mouth. And he remembered wondering—well into the night, in fact—how it would be to have her mouth, not to mention her other body parts, being full and luscious alongside his own body parts. Preferably while they were both alone. And horizontal. And naked.

Uh-oh, indeed…

"Miss Thornbury," he called out quickly, hoping to distract himself enough that the memories—not to mention the sudden discomfort in his lower regions—might disappear. And he called her name out quietly, too, of course—he was in the library, after all, and didn't want to disturb anyone.

However, it wasn't, evidently, quiet to Miss Thornbury. Because when he uttered her name, she gasped in surprise and started visibly, then immediately lost her balance on the ladder. As she began to fall backward, Rory instinctively stepped forward, extending his arms before himself in an effort to steady her. But to no avail. Because she fell from the ladder, at an angle which, upon impact, created enough propulsion to send them both stumbling back. And then, before Rory could say *Stegman's Guide to the Peloponnesian War,* he had landed hard on his fanny, and Miss Thornbury had fallen quite literally into his lap.

For a moment neither of them seemed to know what had hit them, and neither reacted in any way. Rory sat with Miss Thornbury seated across his thighs, and having the weight of her body pressing against that particular part of him was a surprisingly appealing sensation. And that sensation, coupled with the memories he had just been entertaining—not to mention her slim skirt and snug top—left him feeling more than a little dazed.

He glanced down to see if they both still had all their parts in place, only to discover that he could see one of her parts still in place quite clearly. Probably more clearly than was actually prudent or, at the very least, socially acceptable. Because, at some point during their tumble, Miss Thornbury's slim skirt had ridden up on one side, and now the slit that before had offered only a hint of the leg beneath, suddenly offered a view that went way, *way* beyond the hint phase.

And Rory saw that his goddess-vision of Miss Thornbury's creamy thigh simply had not done justice to the reality of Miss Thornbury's creamy thigh, that the silky skin beneath her skirt was as smooth as satin and as flawless as a sheet of glass, and as warm and welcoming as a summer afternoon. And then he wondered hazily how he could possibly know that her thigh was smooth and warm, and to his astonishment—nay, to his utter *horror*—he realized he could know that because he had his hand placed firmly on that smooth, warm thigh, his fingers curling into her bare flesh as if they had every right to be there.

Immediately Rory snatched back his hand, mumbling an incoherent apology for having placed it where it was to begin with. For a scant, delirious second, Miss Thornbury gazed back at him with lambent—yes, *lambent* was most definitely the word he was looking for— eyes, and for one brief, dizzying moment, he thought she was going to ask him to put his hand right back where it was, if he pleased. And Rory realized then, with much amazement, that it would have pleased him, very much, to do that very thing. He even felt his fingers begin to curl slightly and creep forward again, as if they'd already decided to take matters—or, at the very least, Miss Thornbury's thigh—into their own hands.

Or something like that.

But before his fingers could complete their journey, Miss Thornbury, in a jumble of movement, scurried off Rory's lap, pushed herself up to standing and struggled to return her slim skirt and that snug, red top back to their original positions. Which, quite frankly, did nothing to dissuade Rory's fingers from wanting to pursue their original quest to find her thigh, because the skirt and top were considerably more…more…*snug,* and more…more…*red,* than the clothing Miss Thornbury normally wore to work.

And her hair, Rory noted further. There was something different about it today, too. She wasn't wearing it the way she usually wore it. At least, he didn't think she'd ever worn it down loose that way before now. Because he'd never realized before now how long it was, how it could cascade over both her shoulders, curling softly into perfect, elegant *U*s right above her breasts. Nor had he realized how silvery highlights shimmered so abundantly amid the silky mass. Nor had he ever had the urge to reach out and clutch a fistful of her hair in his hand and lift it to his nose to see what it smelled like, and then rake the long tresses back and forth over his mouth and then…and then…and then…

And *good heavens,* what had come over him today? Rory wondered. He'd all but forgotten about…about… What was it he had been about to do? Why was it he had gone searching for Miss Thornbury? Surely it couldn't have been to ponder her hair. Could it? Oh, surely not. Still, he couldn't quite remember now *why* he had been seeking her out. In fact, he couldn't remember much of anything.

He shook his head fiercely, once, as if trying to dislodge some unpleasant thought, but he hadn't had any unpleasant thoughts today, only thoughts about Miss Thornbury and Miss Thornbury's thigh and Miss Thornbury's hair and Miss Thornbury's mouth and—

No, wait a minute. He hadn't thought much about Miss Thornbury's mouth today, had he? But now that he *did* think about her mouth, now that he turned his attention to that part of her forthwith, he realized her full, ripe, luscious lips were even fuller, riper and more luscious than they usually were—he knew that, because he *had* noticed her mouth on several other occasions— and also much more…red…than they usually were. And suddenly his fingers began to curl again, because his fingers—and, all right, the rest of him, too—suddenly wanted very badly to go to that mouth and…

Rory growled under his breath, squeezed his eyes shut tight, fisted his hands resolutely at his sides and began reciting dates of great historical significance, to pull his mind back to where it belonged. *The Magna Carta was signed in 1215,* he thought. *The Protestant Reformation began in 1517. The U.S. Bill of Rights was ratified in 1791. The Emancipation Proclamation was made in 1862. Miss Thornbury's mouth was fuller and riper and redder and more luscious than usual in 2001.*

Damn, he thought further, opening his eyes. He'd almost made it.

"Miss Thornbury," he said softly, driving his gaze to some point over her shoulder—anywhere but her ripe, red mouth. Or her lambent gray eyes. Or her silky, silvery hair. Or her creamy, warm thigh.

Good God, man. Get a hold of yourself.

"Are you all right?" he asked further, still focusing on the books behind Miss Thornbury, instead of Miss Thornbury herself.

"Um, yes, I believe so," she replied a bit breathlessly.

And there was something about her being a bit breathless, and something about the fact that Rory had been responsible for her breathlessness—even if it had only been because he had knocked her off of a ladder—that made his own breathing skip a few necessary stages.

"I apologize if I…caught you off guard," he added. Still, it was only fair, he thought further to himself. Because she had caught him off guard, too.

"That's all right," she said, her voice still sounding low and husky. "No harm done."

Oh, that was what she thought.

"Was there something you wanted, Professor Monahan?" she asked further.

Oh, he really wished she hadn't phrased her question quite that way. Because Rory suddenly realized, too well, that there was indeed something he wanted. Something he wanted very badly. And he wanted it specifically from Miss Thornbury. And it was something he hadn't had for a long, long time, from any woman. Something that suddenly seemed of utmost importance, something which, if he didn't get it very, very soon, might just make him spontaneously combust.

And no, it *wasn't* volume fifteen of *Stegman's Guide to the Peloponnesian War,* either.

"I, uh," Rory began eloquently. "That is, um... What I meant to say was... Ah..."

As he stammered and stumbled over his words, Miss Thornbury bent to retrieve the book that had fallen on the floor between them when they'd taken their tumble. But, polite woman that she was, she didn't stop looking at Rory as she completed the action. And, automatically, Rory allowed his gaze to follow her movements. And as she bent down, he accidentally—truly, he did *not* do it intentionally—found himself...well, um, looking down her snug, red top, which wasn't so snug that it didn't fall open a bit at the low neckline, to reveal the pearly swells of her breasts encased in—

Good heavens.

He was shocked and scandalized to see that Miss Thornbury was wearing—even Rory's mental voice dropped to a lower volume as he realized it—*pink, lacy underthings.*

He'd had no idea.

Not that he spent an inordinate amount of time thinking about what Miss Thornbury might be wearing under her clothing—well, not *too* inordinate an amount of time, not until today, anyway, because it was usually that goddess thing he had in his thoughts where she was concerned—but somehow, now that he did think about it, she simply did not seem like the pink-lacy-underthing type. No, she'd always seemed more like the white-unadorned-cotton-underthing type. Functional. Practical. No frills. To the point. At least she had seemed that type before. Before he'd seen her in the slim skirt and snug top and red lipstick. Now, however—

And why was Rory standing here speculating about a woman's underthings in the first place? What was the matter with him? He had infinitely more important things to be pondering. If he could only remember what those more important things were...

He lifted a hand to his forehead, rubbing fiercely at an excruciating ache that erupted out of nowhere. And he wondered if it might not be possible for him to simply turn on his heel and exit the library, then reenter and start all over again. Maybe then Miss Thornbury would be wearing her usual type of clothing, and her hair would be in its usual ponytail, and Rory's pulse would return to its usual steady rate.

Because with her looking so unusual today—and with him feeling so unusual today—Rory got the distinct impression that he was going to be preoccupied with thoughts of Miss Thornbury, and her mouth and her thighs and her underthings, for quite some time to come. Certainly for the rest of the afternoon. Maybe even for the rest of the day. And Rory couldn't afford to be preoccupied by anything other than his studies, for any length of time. Least of all by a woman.

Because he *had* been preoccupied by a woman once before, many years ago. In fact, he'd been so preoccupied by her he'd nearly married her. He'd been that far gone in his preoccupation. Of course, that woman had been nothing like Miss Thornbury. Miss Thornbury was practical and pragmatic, and capable and competent, and staid and sensible. At least, she had been before the slim-skirt, snug-top, red-lipstick episode. Rory's fiancée had been anything but practical or capable or sensible. No, Rosalind had been, well...

In hindsight Rory supposed the best way to describe Rosalind was well formed, but empty-headed. Not that she had been stupid—well, not *too* stupid, though she'd never been able to remember the date of the Battle of Hastings, which had always annoyed him to no end, because it had been the PIN number for their bank account—but she rarely thought of anyone but herself. In fact, so self-involved had Rosalind been, that she'd dumped Rory without a second thought the moment something she'd perceived to be better came along. Worse, she hadn't bothered to tell Rory she had dumped him until she'd married the something better, three months later.

Of course, had Rory been more observant, he probably would have noticed long before that three months was up that Rosalind had, well, dropped off the face of the planet. There had been signs, after all, which he'd recognized once he'd received her telegram informing him that she wouldn't be returning. There had been the fact that her clothes had disappeared from their closet, something he hadn't noticed until he received her telegram. And he'd been forced to acknowledge then, too, that what he had thought was her coming to bed late and rising for work early every morning had in fact been her, well, not being there at all.

But that was beside the point.

The point was that Rory couldn't afford to get that preoccupied by someone again. Because it would only serve to disrupt his wonderfully routine existence. Rosalind's departure had disrupted his routine for weeks—once he'd realized that she had, in fact, departed. And he didn't want to suffer such a disruption again.

He simply was not the kind of man who could invest heavily in a relationship. He was too interested in other things. He felt no lack in his life, romantically speaking, and it wouldn't be fair to get involved with a woman who would expect him to do things like pay attention to her from time to time. Rory was perfectly content on his own. Or, at least, he had been. Until a few minutes ago.

Besides, he didn't need a woman in his life, he told himself. Who did? What purpose could a woman possibly serve in his life that wasn't already being met?

When Miss Thornbury straightened, Rory's gaze fell on the plump swell of her breasts again, then dropped to the knee revealed by the side slit in her skirt once more. And way, way, *way* deep down inside him, very close to what felt like his libido, something stirred to life that hadn't been stirred for quite a long time.

All right, all right, he conceded. Perhaps there was a purpose Miss Thornbury might meet in his life that wasn't already being met. Was it really such an important purpose? And was it worth sacrificing his peace of mind?

That something close to his supposed libido stirred again, jumping and dancing this time as if it had been touched by a live wire. All right, so maybe it *was* an important purpose, he conceded. And maybe his peace of mind right now was moot. Because it wasn't his mind that was responding to Miss Thornbury. No, it was something infinitely more primitive and intrinsic and uncontrollable. It was that essence inside him which made him a man, something from which he absolutely could not separate himself, even if he'd wanted to.

She was very attractive, he thought as he studied her more thoroughly. And her hair did look to be very soft. And her eyes were quite lovely. And her mouth… Well, best not to ponder that one again. Best not to ponder any of the rest of her again, he told himself. Somehow, though, he didn't think he'd be able to heed his own advice.

"Actually, Miss Thornbury," he said, "I can't remember now what it was that I wanted."

And he hoped God would not strike him down for uttering so blatant a lie. Because he knew very well what he wanted. He wanted Miss Thornbury. There was no way, however, that he was going to tell her—or anybody else—about that. Because it wouldn't last. Of that, he was certain. The moment he remembered whatever it was he had intended to do… The minute he began studying and researching whatever it was that he was supposed to be studying and researching… The second he remembered that… He sighed inwardly. Then he would forget all about Miss Thornbury. And her hair. And her thigh. And her mouth.

"I apologize again for startling you," he added.

She smiled, and that something inside him that had stirred to life began to quiver and hum like a finely strung wire. "Think nothing of it," she told him, clasping the heavy book possessively to her breasts.

The book, Rory thought vaguely as he watched her complete the gesture. There was something about that book… That was what he had wanted to ask her about initially, wasn't it? Volume fifteen of the *Stegman's?* Yes, of course. Now he remembered. Miss Thornbury had been about to shelve it. And now she had it clasped to her breasts. Clasped affectionately to her full, ripe—

Oh, he was never going to be able to look at *Stegman's Guide to the Peloponnesian War* the same way again.

"Is that volume fifteen?" he asked softly, dipping his head toward the book in question.

She glanced down at it, then back up at Rory. "Why, yes. As a matter of fact, it is. I was reading it on my lunch hour again and was about to put it back where it belongs."

"Actually, Miss Thornbury, where it currently belongs is on my table."

She offered him a faintly puzzled expression. "Your table?" she asked.

He nodded again, more resolutely this time. "You see, I was using it last night for my research, and I placed it with the other volumes I'd consulted, on my table, because I knew I would need it again today. I'm sure that's where you found it in the first place."

She seemed to give his remark thorough consideration. "Yes, I did find it on a table, now that you mention it," she said, "but I didn't realize you were using it."

"Well, now you do," he replied mildly.

He told himself to remind her that the table from which she'd taken the *Stegman's* was Professor Rory Monahan's table, and to reiterate how essential it was that she never, ever touch a single volume of any book she might find there. He told himself to stress most forcefully how important his research was, and how it was imperative that he have a place where he might be able to pursue that research unhampered.

Unfortunately, Miss Thornbury chose that moment to extend the book toward him, and when she did, the faint scent of lavender seemed to come at him from out of nowhere, and Rory could no more form words in that moment than he could have changed lead into gold.

So he only took the book from her and tried not to notice how warm it was from being pressed against her, or how rosy and plump the upper swells of her breasts were where she had held it. Somehow, he managed to mumble his thanks under his breath. And then, without a further word, he spun on his heel to return to his desk. To his studies. To his research.

He told himself he was *not* fleeing in terror from an attractive woman. And he assured himself that there was *nothing* more important than the work that he needed—and intended—to pursue that afternoon.

Nothing.

However, Rory very much feared that for the rest of the afternoon he would be able to think of little other than Miss Thornbury's…assets. And suddenly the word *research* took on an entirely new meaning.

Chapter 4

Well, that had gone *very* well, Miriam thought as she watched and marveled at Professor Monahan's speedy retreat. Very well indeed. She'd had no idea about the power one could wield with no more than a slim skirt, a snug top and a tube of really red lipstick. Had she realized how easy it was to turn the tables on a man, she might have tried to do it a long time ago.

Then again, there hadn't been many men in her life upon whom Miriam had actually wanted to turn the tables. Oh, certainly there had been the occasional romantic interest—one or two of them had even become somewhat serious over time. But eventually, all of those romantic interests had fizzled out and wandered off. And in the long run Miriam had been left feeling surprisingly unhurt by the failure of any of them. Really, she supposed she'd just never felt for any of those men the kind of...well, whatever it was she found herself feeling for Rory Monahan.

And just what precisely *was* she feeling for Rory Monahan, anyway? she asked herself. Before today she had thought she was just more or less infatuated with him. She had thought she was experiencing a crush on him, albeit a rather substantial one. Though, granted, she had hoped she might broaden that infatuation, that crush, into something more, for both of them.

After the interlude they'd just shared, however, she was beginning to think that her feelings for the good professor already went much, much deeper than simple infatuation or a mere crush. Recalling the way he had looked upon her just moments ago, with such heat and such fire building in his eyes... Remembering the way he had clenched his fingers tighter on the bare flesh of her thigh...

Well, something equally fiery and hot had sparked to life inside of Miriam. Something very significant. Something totally unrecognizable. Something she'd never come close to feeling before.

And she very much suspected that it was her Inner Temptress awakening.

Goodness, she thought. *Metropolitan* magazine was right. Where Professor Monahan was concerned, she had indeed gone from invisible to...well, something *visible,* she told herself, if not irresistible. And she had done it in fewer than "seven seductive steps." Because she'd only used two seductive steps so far—the one about opting for brighter, snugger clothing, and the one about donning really red lipstick. And look at the results she had already achieved. At this rate it might not even be necessary for her to go as far as seductive step number seven, which involved—

Well. Miriam would just as soon not ponder what seductive step number seven involved right now. Not here, in a public place. A public place that was supported by the tax dollars of hardworking citizens.

Instead she pondered the amazing results she had already achieved with regard to her…temptressing…of Rory Monahan. Because she had definitely become visible to him, she thought with much satisfaction. He had definitely seen her. He'd also felt her, she recalled as a rush of heat raced through her. And the article had said nothing about going from invisible to malleable, in *any* number of steps, so that was *really* an accomplishment.

And she congratulated herself, too, for using her own ingenuity to supplement seductive steps number one and two. After all, she had been the one to theorize that if a woman wanted to draw a man's attention, then she must have something that the man in question wanted. And what could Rory Monahan possibly want more than volume fifteen of *Stegman's Guide to the Peloponnesian War,* hmm?

Well, if things worked out the way she hoped, Miriam thought, there would indeed be something that Rory Monahan wanted more than volume fifteen of the *Stegman's.* He would want *all* the volumes of Miss Miriam Thornbury, along with all assorted indices, appendices, tables and charts.

She smiled as she began rehearsing in her head how she would go about applying seductive step number three with regard to her temptressing of Professor Monahan. That particular step involved repartee, so she knew she would have to do some practicing before she actually put the step into motion. And truly, there was no reason why she had to rush into repartee today. She had already made herself visible to Rory Monahan this afternoon. If she used repartee now, it might very well be too much for him. She didn't want to overwhelm the poor man, after all.

Plus, she needed to prepare *herself,* in case the results of that foray ended up being as successful as her results today had been. Should Rory decide he wanted to…oh, grip her thigh—or some other part of her—again, Miriam wanted to be ready for it.

My, my, my, she thought with a smile—and a nervous stomach. She had never been much of a magazine reader in the past, but suddenly she couldn't wait to get home to see what words of wisdom *Metropolitan* had to impart to her today.

Miriam gave Rory Monahan as little time as possible to recover before she launched into the next phase of her plan. And it wound up being a very good next phase, too, one she should have thought of undertaking a long time ago, and as much more than just a next phase. Because two days after Miriam had awakened her Inner Temptress, she read in the Marigold *Messenger* that the final section of summer adult extended education classes would be starting at the Marigold Community College. And one of those extended education classes just so happened to be an intensive five-week session taught by Professor Rory Monahan, a session called "Introduction to Classical Civilizations II."

Miriam could not believe her good fortune upon reading the announcement. Not only could she enroll herself in a class that Rory Monahan would be teaching, but she'd always wanted to learn more about classical civilizations, anyway. It was a definite win-win situation. She stopped by the community college on her way to work that very afternoon to register for the class that, very conveniently, began the following Monday night. Then she rearranged her workload at the library so that Lucy Chin, one of the assistant librarians, could cover some of her hours.

Intensive, Miriam reiterated to herself now, as she strode toward the classroom where her session would be meeting. That was what the course description had called Professor Monahan's class. *Intensive.* Oh, yes. She hoped it would be very intensive indeed.

She ducked into a nearby ladies' room before entering the classroom to drag a brush through her hair and reapply some of the really red lipstick that had worked so successfully on the good professor the week before. She also ran a hand over the snug, sapphire-blue Capri pants she'd purchased over the weekend to compensate for her wardrobe's current—and profound—lack of perky, peppy, fun fashions, which was what *Metropolitan* magazine assured her she must wear. Miriam contemplated her sleeveless, sapphire-blue blouse, too, as she studied her reflection in the mirror, and, very daringly, decided to unfasten the top button before heading off to class.

My, but she was audacious. She hoped Professor Monahan wasn't *too* awfully overcome by her taunting behavior. Or, rather, by the taunting behavior of her Inner Temptress. Because that was who was behind the unbuttoning, Miriam told herself. Normally Miriam would never do such a bold thing. Her Inner Temptress, however, had no such qualms.

Only as Miriam was turning away from the mirror did she begin to have second thoughts about what she was doing. Did she really want to come across as such a…such a…such a taunting temptress? Especially since that wasn't her natural state at all? What if she did finally manage to snag Rory's attention, and more, only to realize that he had fallen for her Inner Temptress, instead of her Real Self?

It was entirely possible that such a scenario might occur, she thought. After all, he'd never paid her much heed before the day she'd awakened her Inner Temptress. Oh, certainly he had always greeted her politely when he encountered her at the library, and he had always paused long enough to make small talk with her. He had also usually, and very chivalrously, walked her to her car on those evenings when the two of them left the library together alone.

But that had probably just been because his car was invariably parked close to hers, she told herself now. Or simply because he was a gentleman who would perform the same service for any solitary woman. It wasn't necessarily because he was interested in Miriam specifically.

Though she was confident that he did like her. At least, he liked her when he gave her some thought, she amended with a heavy sigh. Unfortunately, he didn't seem to give Miriam Thornbury much thought once she was out of his direct line of vision. He had certainly seemed to like her Inner Temptress much better. Certainly he had noticed her Inner Temptress more.

Then again, Miriam argued to herself, it was *her* Inner Temptress, wasn't it? Therefore, it must be a part of *her*. Somehow. Somewhere. Some way. Right?

Right?

Ignoring, for now, the sick feeling that was squishing around in the pit of her stomach, she squared her shoulders and lifted her chin and hoped that she appeared more confident than she actually felt. Then, throwing caution to the wind, and her hair back over her shoulders, Miriam reached up to unfasten a *second* button on her blouse.

Well, what could she say? she asked herself. Her Inner Temptress made her do it.

Rory had just completed his first time line on the chalkboard when he turned to face the students in his intensive, five-week "Introduction to Classical Civilizations II" session. He didn't normally teach night classes during the summer—that was time he liked to reserve for his research—especially the classes in the adult extended-education program. But the regularly scheduled professor had, at the beginning of the summer, been presented with an opportunity to spend a full three weeks at the end of July studying Hippodamus of Miletus—in Piraeus, no less. How on earth could Rory have refused to fill in for her, by teaching her class, so that she could take advantage of such an amazingly fortuitous circumstance? Provided, of course, she shared all of her notes and photographs with him upon her return.

Now as Rory spun around to face his class, he realized it might not be such a bad thing to teach this session. It was one of his favorites in spite of its lack of in-depth analysis, and nothing brought him greater joy than imparting the fascinating details of Classical life to people who were unfamiliar with those details.

Teaching, Rory thought, was almost as gratifying

and fulfilling as learning was, and he always looked forward to both. Especially when the faces gazing back at him from the classroom were so rapt and eager and focused…

And luscious and tempting and ripe and red and…

And good God, was that Miss Thornbury and her ripe, red, tempting, luscious mouth sitting there in the very front row? With her calves showing? And two buttons of her blouse unfastened? Was it?

Oooh, it was going to be a long five-week session, Rory suddenly thought. And intensive, too. Very intensive indeed.

He sighed as he tossed the stub of chalk into the tray behind himself, then pushed away from the blackboard to take his place behind the dais he'd set on the table between him and his class. Not that a dais was going to do him any good with Miss Thornbury looking like… like…like *that.*

He gripped the dais fiercely, anyway, cleared his throat and said, "Good evening, class. I'm Professor Rory Monahan, and this is 'Introduction to Classical Civilizations II.' I hope you've all come to the right place."

One person, Rory noted, stood and gathered her things together, having evidently realized she was indeed in the wrong place. But it wasn't Miss Thornbury. And that, Rory discovered, was a development about which he had mixed feelings. On one hand, it would make his going infinitely smoother if he didn't have to be distracted by Miss Thornbury's mouth—or, rather, by Miss Thornbury, he hastily corrected himself—seated there in the center of the front row. On the other hand, an oddly pleasant sensation spiraled through him

at seeing Miss Thornbury's mouth—or, rather, Miss
Thornbury, he hastily corrected himself—seated there
in the center of the front row.

What to do, what to do…

Well, what could he do? Rory thought. He must teach
the class, as he normally would teach it. He couldn't exactly ask one student to leave because she was too ripe
and luscious and tempting, could he? No, that would be
frightfully impolite. Not to mention it would open up the
community college to a sexual harassment lawsuit the
likes of which Marigold, Indiana, had never seen. And
Rory didn't want to harass Miss Thornbury sexually.
No, what he had planned for Miss Thornbury, sexually
speaking, was in no way harassing. Fun, by all means.
But not harassing.

And good heavens, where was his mind tonight?
Certainly not on anything classical—that was clearly
evident. He had *no* plans for Miss Thornbury, Rory reminded himself, sexual or otherwise. She was far too
distracting. Among other things. He'd never be able to
focus on his studies and his research if he began plan-
ning things with her.

Then again, would that necessarily be such a bad
thing? he asked himself.

He was utterly shocked by the question when it unrolled in his head. Of *course* it would be a bad thing to
be unable to focus on his studies and research. Why, the
very idea. Rory's studies and research were *every*thing
to him. Life without the quest for knowledge would
be…would be…

Well, it would be meaningless. What other reason was
there to exist, if not to seek and gain more knowledge?

Inescapably his gaze wandered back to Miss Thornbury, over her shins, her calves, her arms, her two un-fastened buttons and, inevitably, her mouth. And he began to think that there might be one or two things besides the quest for knowledge that would give his life meaning, and make it more enjoyable.

Nevertheless, he cautioned himself, he wasn't the sort of man who could make the kind of commitment to a relationship that a woman like Miss Thornbury would demand and deserve. It wouldn't be fair to promote a liaison with her, because regardless of how…incandescent…such a liaison might be, in the long run Rory would need more than just a ripe mouth and tempting calves. He would need knowledge. That would override any potential relationship that might develop between him and the luscious librarian. And that, Rory thought, simply would not be fair to Miss Thornbury.

He cleared his throat again, and tried to proceed in his usual fashion once more. "I'm Professor Monahan," he began again on behalf of his eight remaining students. "And in this particular session, we'll be covering the period between 735 B.C.—we'll begin with the Messenian wars between Sparta and Messenia—and 554 A.D., with Emperor Justinian's attempts to reclaim the Roman Empire from the Byzantines. Yes, it's a lot to cover, and very exciting stuff to boot," he said with a smile, "but if we all work very hard, pay attention and complete our assigned reading, we shall all be better people for it by the end of the term. Now then. Let's get started."

Rory plunged immediately into his lecture—they only had three hours, two nights a week, after all, and much to cover—losing himself completely in the lesson. Whenever he glanced up to gauge how his students were faring, his gaze inevitably fell first on Miss Thornbury, who, invariably, seemed to be wholly absorbed in every word he uttered. That wasn't necessarily true of some of his other pupils, though, which was why, Rory was certain, his gaze fell more and more often on Miss Thornbury, and less and less often on her classmates.

At 7:25, exactly eighty-five minutes into class, Rory told his students to take a ten-minute break. "But only ten minutes," he admonished them carefully. "We shall reconvene at 7:35 and continue with the lesson. Hurry back. As I said, we have much to cover over the next five weeks."

All but one of his students abided by his instructions—some more quickly than others, he couldn't help noting—filing out of the classroom to see to whatever needs they might have. Miss Thornbury, however, apparently didn't have any needs. Or, at least, she seemed not to have any needs outside the classroom. Because she remained seated exactly where she had been sitting for the last hour and a half. And she continued to look every bit as delectable as she had been looking for the last hour and a half. And Rory found that he was in no way immune to her appeal. Nor, God help him, could he think of any way to tactfully escape.

"So," he said suddenly, surprising them both, if the jerk to Miss Thornbury's entire body was any indication of her reaction. "I'm puzzled to find you in class, Miss Thornbury. Your name wasn't on my original class list. I just now noticed it was penciled in at the end."

"I only enrolled on Friday," she replied. "They told me in admissions it wasn't too late."

"No, no, of course not," he assured her. "After all, it's never too late for knowledge."

Oh, hell, had he actually just said that? Rory groaned inwardly. To an attractive woman? An attractive woman whose calves were exposed, and whose blouse had two—count them, *two*—buttons unfastened? He fought off a cringe.

However, Miss Thornbury didn't seem to be put off by his inane comment, because she smiled at him in response. "No, you're absolutely right, Professor Monahan," she agreed. "It's never too late for...*knowledge.*"

For some reason Rory couldn't comprehend, she dropped her voice a bit on that last word, fairly purring it the way a cat would. In fact, she was speaking in a voice that bore no resemblance whatsoever to her usual voice. It was huskier somehow, lower, more throaty.

"Miss Thornbury, do you have a cold?" he asked.

Her eyes widened in something akin to panic. What an odd reaction, he thought.

"No," she replied, still in that same, rather hoarse, voice. "Um, why do you ask?"

He pointed to his own neck. "You sound like you have a frog in your throat."

If he didn't know better, he'd swear he had just said something to embarrass her, because her cheeks were suddenly tinted with red. But he couldn't imagine why she might be embarrassed. Then another thought struck him. He hoped she wasn't running a fever, as well as having a sore throat.

"I'm fine," she told him softly, her voice sounding much more normal now.

But her cheeks were still red, and Rory had to battle the urge to place his open palms against them. Just to see if she was indeed feeling feverish, he hastily qualified. Not for any reason other than that. It was a simple concern for her health, that was all.

"Well, that's good," he said, still not quite convinced.

He was disconcerted by the intensity of her gaze, too. She had her attention fully fixed on his face, as if she were preparing to ask him something very, very important. Rory waited to hear what that question might be.

And waited. And waited. And waited.

For, truly, a full minute must have passed with Miss Thornbury doing nothing but stare at him, as if she were trying to unravel a particularly troublesome riddle. Finally, though, she opened her mouth to speak. But what emerged was really the oddest thing.

"Professor Monahan," she said. "Do you mind if I call you Rory?"

He arched his brows in frank surprise. Really, the request was unprecedented. Had she asked him such a thing in her capacity as librarian, it might not have been quite so unexpected—though, even then, he would have been surprised. But in her capacity as his student, it was really rather unusual.

"I mean, we are colleagues of a sort, aren't we?" she asked further. "We both work in jobs that contribute to the education of people."

Rory opened his mouth to respond, but found that he honestly had no idea what to say.

"And we're contemporaries of a sort, too, yes?" she asked. "I mean, how old are you?"

This time Rory gaped slightly in response. He'd never been asked such a personal question, point-blank this way, by anyone outside his family. Although, now that he thought about it, he'd never been asked such a question by his family, either. Of course, he reminded himself, they all already knew how old he was, so asking him something like that would have been unnecessary, not to mention silly. Still, coming from Miss Thornbury, it was a peculiar request.

He suddenly wondered if she had been drinking. That would explain her hoarseness, and even the blush on her cheeks. Nevertheless, she didn't seem intoxicated....

"I—I—I'm thirty-two," he heard himself reply. Though he didn't recall making a conscious decision to do so.

She smiled, a smile that was quite dazzling. "There, you see," she said. "I'm twenty-eight. We're practically the same age."

"Yes, well, that's true, but I—I—I—"

"And we do seem to share all kinds of interests in common, don't we?" she hurried on. "Not the least of which is Classical Civilizations."

"I—I—I suppose, but I—I—I—"

"So it only makes sense that I should call you Rory."

"I—I—I—"

"And you should call me Miriam."

Oh, now wait just a minute, Rory wanted to say. Instead, what he heard come out of his mouth was, "I—I—I suppose it would be all right."

"Especially now that I'm one of your... *students,*" she added, her voice once again pitching to that strangely husky timbre as she uttered—nay, *purred*—that final word.

How very, very curious, Rory thought. Perhaps she *had* been drinking.

"And I've always wanted to *learn* more about...what you have to *teach,*" she continued in that same husky, peculiar, emphatic tone. Then, even more huskily, even more peculiarly, even more emphatically, she added, *"Rory."*

"I—I—I see," he managed to reply. Somehow.

My, but it suddenly seemed warm in the classroom. Was the custodial staff turning the air conditioner off at night now, to conserve energy and save money? he wondered. With a quick twist of his head, he shook the observation off quite literally.

"Well then," he said. "You've, um, you've come to the right place, haven't you?" Just to be polite, he concluded, "Miriam."

"Oh, I do hope so," she said with a smile.

A smile that was even more puzzling than what she had been saying, a smile that Rory could only liken to… wicked? Oh, surely not. She just wasn't feeling well, obviously, in spite of her assurances to the contrary.

Or perhaps she really had been drinking.

He was about to say something else—though, truly, he knew not what—when a pair of his students ambled back into the classroom, having concluded their break. Within moments, a few others joined them, until, at precisely the time Rory had indicated, everyone was back in his or her designated seat, ready for the last half of class.

He breathed a sigh of relief to see it. For several moments there, his wonderfully steady, predictable existence had felt a bit…skewed. As if the Earth had somehow tilted, just the tiniest bit, on its axis. Now, though, with everyone seated back in their earlier places and prepared for his lecture, he felt as if everything had reverted back to normal again.

Until, involuntarily, he turned his attention to Miss

Thornbury again. Or, rather, he corrected himself, to…Miriam. Because…Miriam…still sat at rapt attention, her hands folded daintily on her desktop, her legs crossed, her calves exposed, her two buttons unbuttoned, her mouth luscious. And the moment Rory's attention lit on her, damned if the Earth didn't do that tilting thing all over again. In fact, damned if the Earth didn't threaten to go spinning right out of its orbit.

He sighed heavily. It was going to be a long—and intensive—five weeks.

Well, seductive step number three—repartee— hadn't gone well at all, had it?

Miriam drew her conclusion with a sigh of defeat as she watched Rory Monahan erase the elaborate time line he'd drawn on the chalkboard behind himself, and as the rest of her classmates paraded by her and out the door. He'd barely noticed her during class, she thought. Only when she'd remained behind for the break to deliberately waylay his attention had he spared her little more than a glance.

Still, the evening hadn't been a total waste, she tried to reassure herself. Because Professor Monahan's—or, rather, she corrected herself, *Rory's*—lecture had been utterly fascinating. The man was amazing. His store of knowledge was, she was certain, limitless. And so casual about it he was, too. Why, he'd pulled dates and locales and names from thin air, facts with which Miriam hadn't even had a nodding acquaintance. Had she not already found him thoroughly attractive, she would be half-gone on him now.

In fact, she realized with some trepidation as she gathered together her own things, she *was* half-gone on him now. She had been half-gone on him for nearly six months, since the first day she had laid eyes on him at the library. And she feared it would take very little to make her fully gone. The problem was, of course, that once she *was* fully gone, she would be there by herself. Because Rory Monahan certainly wasn't going anywhere with her.

Ah, well, at least she'd managed to convince him to address her by her first name, she consoled herself. That was something, wasn't it? She still grew warm at the recollection of how he had voiced it, too. Miriam. She'd never considered her name to be a particularly beautiful one. No, she had always thought it too sedate. Too plain. Too functional. Much like the woman upon whom it had been bestowed. But when Rory said it, *Miriam* became the stuff of legends.

It had been rather exhilarating, really. And it was just too bad that hearing him say her name was evidently going to be the high point of their relationship.

She rose from her desk to make her way out of the classroom just as Rory stepped around the table upon which he had placed his dais. As a result, their bodies collided, her right shoulder connecting with his left arm, and the action jostled her just enough to send her book and notebook flying to the floor. Immediately she bent to retrieve them, but when she did, her oversize straw purse fell from her opposite shoulder and likewise dropped to the floor. In doing so, it spilled much of its contents, including a six-month old issue of *Metropolitan* magazine that cried, in big red letters, How to Seduce a Man—and Keep Him Coming Back for More!

Naturally, Rory, being a gentleman, fell to his knees beside Miriam in an effort to help her collect her things, lightly offering the observation that they just *had* to stop meeting like this. And naturally, Rory, being a searcher of knowledge, reached first for the written word. And naturally, closest to him was the issue of *Metropolitan*. and, naturally, he read the headlines upon it.

When he realized what they said, though, and what sort of knowledge he held in his hands, he blushed, hastily stuffing the magazine back into her bag. Then he scooped up her book and notebook and handed those to her, as well. Miriam was left to chase after an errant pen, a runaway roll of breath mints, a purse-size atomizer of Chanel No. 5, and her much-celebrated tube of really red lipstick.

Oh, what a girly-girl she had become, Miriam thought as she stuffed all her feminine accessories back into her bag, alongside the copy of *Metropolitan*. Really, until today, all she'd ever carried in her purse were her wallet, her sunglasses, a package of tissues, and, it went without saying, a good book—usually one of the classics, but sometimes it was a well-thumbed paperback from the browsing collection with words like *temptation, seduction* and *irresistible* in the title. Much like *Metropolitan* magazine, she couldn't help but think. And now, suddenly, thanks to *Metropolitan* magazine, Miriam had discovered that she had needs she'd never realized she had before.

She was fast becoming, she suddenly realized—oh, dear—a *Metro* Girl.

Good heavens, she thought. How could this be happening? Although she'd been reading the magazine and taking the articles to heart, she hadn't actually intended to become one of…*them*. One of the sultry, sexy, sleepy-eyed temptresses who appeared on the front cover. Of course, all of those temptresses, she reminded herself, had considerably more tools of temptation to work with than Miriam had herself. Still…

"This seems to be becoming a habit with us," Rory said as he straightened, extending her book and notebook toward her.

Grateful for his remark, because it scattered her troubling thoughts, Miriam took her belongings from him and slid those, too, into her big purse. "Yes, it does, doesn't it?" she replied.

Replied inanely, she couldn't help thinking. Too bad she'd used up all of her repartee during the class break. Not that her repartee then had been particularly stellar, she amended when she recalled the dubious results of her earlier conversational endeavors. Nevertheless, she could really use some repartee now, regardless of its questionable quality.

But words truly did escape her. Because Rory Monahan was standing right next to her, close enough to touch, close enough for her to turn him around and drape her arms over his shoulders, close enough for her to thread her fingers through his dark hair, close enough for her to push herself up on tiptoe just the slightest little bit and touch her mouth to his, and—

Well, he was just standing very close, that was all, she thought with some shakiness. Much too close for her peace of mind. Among other things.

"Once again, your choice of reading material surprises me, Miss—I mean, Miriam," he said, smiling.

But his smile seemed a bit nervous somehow, she noted, and she couldn't help wondering if maybe he, too, was just now realizing how very close the two of them were standing.

"Well, I don't know why you should find it surprising, Prof—I mean, Rory. This may come as a surprise to you, but librarians do, on average, rather enjoy reading. A variety of things, as a matter of fact."

"Oh, of course," he readily conceded. "I didn't mean... I mean, I wasn't trying to... That is, I hope you don't think me..." He sighed heavily. "Oh, never mind. Can I walk you to your car?" he added, seemingly impulsively. His expression, she noted, suggested that he was as surprised by the sudden offer as she was. Even so, he dipped his head toward the door as he continued, "Everyone else seems to have deserted us."

So they had, Miriam realized when she trained her gaze in that direction. "Thank you," she said. "I'd appreciate it. I had to park farther away than I normally would."

Not that Marigold, Indiana, was in any way dangerous, she knew. Even a newcomer like her could easily see that the place was as safe and secure as a Disney film. Still, she thought further, every now and then, those Disney films had surprisingly heinous villains, didn't they? So it was doubtless best not to let oneself get complacent.

Besides, Miriam really did want to spend as much time with Rory as she could. And he really was staying very close to her. And he really did look and smell so nice.

The night sky outside was black and clear and limitless, the near-full moon spilling silver light over the couple as they walked toward Miriam's car. She strove to find some kind of light, meaningless conversation that might make the stilted silence of the quick trip less awkward, but truly, all that was going through her mind at the moment was how nice it felt to be walking with Rory, even if it wasn't hand in hand, and how warm his body seemed to be next to hers, and how very much she wanted to touch him, and how wouldn't it be so wonderful if he just leaned right over and kissed her.

And then, too soon, they were standing beside her car, and Rory was waiting politely for her to unlock it and climb inside and drive away, out of his life, at least until he encountered her in the library the following afternoon. And it hit Miriam then that if she wanted Rory Monahan to ever become anything more to her than her teacher or an escort to her car, she was going to have to do something drastic—something even more drastic than enrolling in Classical Civilizations II.

Oh, what the heck? she asked herself. She might as well just skip right over seductive step number four and proceed onward, to seductive step number five: making the first move.

After unlocking and opening her car door, she tossed her purse and books over the driver's seat, into the passenger seat, to make room. Then, her hands freed, her stomach churning with nervousness, she spun back around. She gripped the car door fiercely with one hand, then lifted the other to push back—seductively, she hoped—a stray length of her hair.

And then, before she lost her nerve, "Rory," she said, "would you like to have dinner with me tomorrow night?"

Her question seemed to hit him the same way a two-by-four upside the head would. For a moment he only gazed at her blankly, as if he didn't understand the language she was speaking. Then, abruptly, he shook his head once, as if to clear it.

"I—I—I beg your pardon?"

"Dinner," she repeated. "Tomorrow night. With me." Maybe by keeping the sentences short, she thought, they would gel more quickly in his—admittedly crowded with knowledge—brain.

For another long moment he only gazed at her face— or, more specifically, she noted, at her mouth—without replying one way or the other. Miriam held her breath, preparing herself for his rejection of her offer, and waited to see what he would say.

And waited, and waited, and waited…

Chapter 5

No matter how many times or how many ways he re-played the previous evening's events in his head, Rory still couldn't quite figure out how he had come to agree to have dinner with Miriam Thornbury. He only remem-bered that one minute he had been walking beside her, enjoying the comfortable silence that had settled over them and the tantalizing fragrance of her that seemed both familiar and exotic, and then in the next minute he had been gazing down into her clear gray eyes, noting how they reflected her smile as well as her mouth did, and marveling again at the lusciousness of that mouth.

And *then,* in the *next* minute that mouth had opened and formed some words, mesmerizing Rory with their subtle movement and soft sound. And although he could vaguely remember eventually replying in the affirma-tive to Miriam's request, he couldn't remember precisely *why* he had replied in the affirmative. Because he had been promising himself for days that he would stay as far away from her as possible.

It would, he was certain, remain one of history's greatest unsolved mysteries.

In spite of his confusion, though, he now stood poised to rap his—rather damp, he realized—fist lightly on Miss—on *Miriam's* front door. His other—rather damp, he realized further—hand clutched a cellophane box that contained a pink corsage. Truly. A corsage. A pink corsage, at that. He couldn't recall ever buying such a thing for a woman, not even for his date to the senior prom in high school.

His date that night had been... Oh, let him think for a moment... The girl's name was right there on the tip of his tongue...Daphne. That was it. Or perhaps Danielle. Or maybe Denise. Anyway, he'd taken Daphne/Danielle/Denise Somebody to his senior prom—after she had asked him to—and although he did recall her wearing a wrist corsage, he was reasonably sure that the girl had purchased it, and donned it, on her own.

It wasn't that he was thoughtless, Rory hastened to reassure himself. It was just that he was... Well, he supposed he *was* thoughtless, when he got right down to it. About things other than his studies and his research, anyway. But it wasn't an intentional sort of thoughtlessness. It was a negligent sort of thoughtlessness. Rory's brain, for all its vast store of knowledge, was a simple organ. He just didn't think about things he didn't care about. Ergo, thoughts of corsages didn't normally make appearances in his crowded cranium.

Tonight, however, he had honestly had the foresight to stop by a florist on the corner near his apartment building and ask the proprietress what would be appropriate for a first date. Even though the phrase *first date* had suggested that there would be a *second* date, and perhaps even *more* dates, to follow it, and that was something Rory really didn't want to get into right now. Which was why, when the phrase *first date* had initially unrolled in his head, he had shoved it back to the furthest recesses of his mind and focused on orchids instead.

Orchids, he marveled now. Never in his life had he thought of orchids, until this night. Somehow, though, the moment he had beheld one of the splendid, extraordinary, intoxicatingly fragrant flowers, he had known it would be perfect for Miriam. He just hoped she didn't misinterpret the gesture. He hoped she wouldn't think he'd done it out of something like thoughtfulness. Because, truly, he was only doing it to be polite. If she misconstrued his gesture to be a thoughtful one, then it would only lead to trouble.

He knocked on her front door with a trio of deft, confident raps before he even realized he had intended to complete the action, and within moments he heard a soft shuffle of sound from the other side. Instinctively he lifted his free hand again, this time to straighten the knot in his tie and smooth out any wrinkles that might be lingering in the fabric of his best navy-blue suit. He hoped his attire was appropriate, as he had no idea where Miriam was taking him tonight. Which, in itself, signified a host of oddities.

First, that he was allowing a woman to call the shots, an idea at which Rory would have thought his masculinity, however unmacho it was, would balk—but it did not.

Besides, he had compensated by insisting that *he* would pick *her* up in *his* car, and not the other way around.

Second, that he was allowing himself to be led into the unknown, something he normally would never do, because he always insisted on very detailed advance knowledge about any outing—but this time he had not.

And third, that whatever their outing involved, it almost certainly did not include the quest for knowledge or the performance of research, and he couldn't remember the last time he had engaged in any activity that didn't include those things, at least in part—and tonight, he didn't care.

It was proving to be a most educational experience all the way around.

The realization had just unwound in his head when the door to Miriam's apartment opened completely, and he saw her standing on the other side. And, oh, what a sight she was. She'd left her hair loose again, and it fell in a silky, dark blond cascade over one shoulder. One *bare* shoulder. At least, Rory assumed it was bare. Because the one he could see, the one that didn't have silky hair cascading over it, was bare, and it only made sense to conclude that such would be the case with the other one, as well. Miriam Thornbury was nothing if not symmetrical.

And her shoulders were bare, he noticed further, because her dress had evidently run out of the silvery, satiny fabric from which it was made not far above her breasts. Not that Rory minded, really. He just noticed, that was all.

And there *was* a good bit of the dress above her breasts, because it nearly met with the necklace she wore, a silvery wisp of filigree that matched the earrings dangling from her ears. And the garment dipped well below her knees, too, at least on the right side, because her stance provided him with a very nice view of her leg extending from another one of those intriguing slits on the left side, a slit much like the one that had intrigued him in the library that day, except that this one wasn't nearly as conservative as that one had been.

Or something like that.

My, but his thoughts were run-on this evening, Rory mused. What could possibly be the cause of that? Normally his thoughts were very well ordered and to the point. Then again, normally his thoughts focused entirely on historical data. Normally his thoughts didn't include things like legs and side slits and silky hair and silvery dresses. His thoughts had sometimes included the goddess-gown thing, of course, he conceded, but even that reflection had generally tended to be well structured. Probably because he rehearsed it so frequently.

At any rate, Miriam's attire tonight indicated to Rory that he had, in fact, dressed appropriately by donning his best navy-blue suit. However, he couldn't think of a single place in Marigold where *her* attire would be appropriate.

"You look, ah…lovely," he said with profound understatement after greeting her.

She smiled, her cheeks pinking with the gesture. "Thank you," she said shyly.

Shyly, he marveled. In that dress. Amazing. "Here," he said, extending the cellophane box of orchid toward her. "This is, um, for you."

She blushed even more as she took the corsage from

him, and something inside Rory hummed to life at seeing it. A blush, he marveled. In that dress. Amazing.

"Thank you," she said softly. She glanced up demurely and asked, in that same soft voice, "Would you help me put it on?"

Rory swallowed hard. Well. He hadn't anticipated this at all. When he'd purchased the corsage, it hadn't occurred to him that she might want help donning it. It hadn't occurred to him that he might be required to... touch her. All in all, though, touching Miriam Thornbury didn't seem like such a bad deal.

"Of course," he said.

He reclaimed the cellophane box from her, deftly flipped it open, and carefully removed the fragile blossom from within. After handing the box back to Miriam, he lifted her hand and, very slowly, nearly hypnotically, slipped the elastic band over her fingers and hand, settling the flower resolutely on the back of her wrist. Immediately she lifted the delicate bloom to her nose, closing her eyes as she inhaled deeply its sweet aroma. Rory, too, could discern the fragrance from where he stood, a powerful, exotic scent that seemed, somehow, wholly appropriate for her.

"So...where are we going to be dining?" he asked.

"I thought we could drive into Bloomington," she told him as she held her hand before her, gently fingering the fine petals of the orchid.

Something about the gesture captured Rory's complete attention, making his heart race frantically in his chest as he noted the way she so gingerly traced each thin vein in each delicate petal. For one long moment he only watched the slow, precise, mesmerizing motion of that finger, his body temperature rising with each meticulous revolution it made.

Then the gist of her comment hit him square in the brain, and he arched his eyebrows in surprise. "Bloomington?" he repeated. "But that's a half hour's drive, at least."

"More like forty-five minutes," Miriam corrected him as she returned her attention to his face. "But it's a beautiful drive," she added. "And it will give us a chance to chat."

Chat? Rory echoed to himself. She wanted to *chat* with him? In that dress?

"I—I—I…" he began.

"And there's the most wonderful restaurant in Bloomington called Winona's," she continued blithely, oblivious to his distress. "It only opened a few months ago, and it's very popular. And I don't mind telling you that I had to pull some pretty big strings with the owner to secure reservations for us this evening on such short notice. Usually one has to call weeks in advance to get a table at Winona's."

"I—I—I—"

"Fortunately, the owner happens to be my sister, Winona, so it worked out very well. She frequently does me favors like this, because she still feels guilty for beheading my Malibu Barbie when we were young."

"I—I—I—"

"Not that it was an intentional beheading," Miriam rushed on, still apparently unmindful of Rory's state. "No, it was most definitely an accident. Winona had no idea Barbie's head would explode that way when she attached a missile to her back and sent her rocketing down the clothesline."

"I—I—I—"

"It was an experiment Winona was performing for her physics class—all very scientific, I assure you. She's ten years older than me, you see. Which, now that I think about it, makes one assume she would have known better than to attach a missile to Barbie's back and send her rocketing down the clothesline." Miriam shrugged, a gesture that did wonderful things to her dress, Rory couldn't help noting. "But there you have it just the same," she concluded. "Well then. Are you ready to go?"

"I—I—I—" he stammered again, still preoccupied with the comings and goings of her dress.

"We're driving in your car, yes?" she asked. "You did sound so insistent about that, after all."

"I—I—I—"

"Well then," she said again. "Let's be off, shall we? Our reservation is for seven, and it's just past six now. Thank you for being on time, by the way. It's always so gratifying when a person is punctual."

"I—I—I—"

Rory realized then that it would probably be best for him to just keep his mouth shut for the next several minutes—or, more accurately, for the next forty-five minutes—because, clearly, Miriam Thornbury could run rings around him in the chat department. Still, there was something about her loquacity that gave him the impression she herself was more than a little nervous about the evening ahead.

Hmmm…

"Drive," he said. "My car. Yes. Let's."

Oh, well done, Rory, he congratulated himself. Women were always impressed when a man was as articulate as a famous literary character. Unfortunately, in Rory's current state, the literary character in question would be Frankenstein's monster.

He bit back a growl. "I'm ready when you are," he said.

Though, truly, where Miriam Thornbury was concerned, he was coming to suspect that he would *never* be ready.

Winona's, Rory noted upon entering the establishment, was a very busy place, and he could see why Miriam had been forced to take advantage of her sister's decades-old guilt in order to ensure a table for the two of them. Winona's was also, he noted further, a very *nice* place. The decor resembled a turn-of-the-century luxury hotel, very elegant, very opulent, very abundant.

He was immediately reminded of the set for that movie that had been so popular a few years ago.... What was the name of it again? His ex-fiancée, Rosalind, had dragged him to see the film, oh...ten or twelve times, at least. Some blond prettyboy had appeared in the starring role.... What was the actor's name again? *Titanic,* that was it. Not the blond prettyboy, of course. The movie Rory remembered because of the film's historical significance.

At any rate, the set for *Titanic* was what the restaurant reminded him of. But even he could see that the beauty and splendor of the place wasn't the focal point of the decor. No, the focal point of the decor would have to have been the antique-looking telephones, one of which was perched at the center of each of the tables. They must be the focal point, he reasoned, otherwise, they wouldn't have been perched there.

Miriam must have noticed where his attention was directed as their hostess—whose outfit and hairstyle likewise resembled something from *Titanic*—seated them. Because she immediately told him, "The telephones are very popular here at Winona's. Those, along with the food, which is quite excellent, are what keep bringing people back."

"Yes, but why are they sitting on the tables that way?" Rory asked.

Miriam smiled. "So that people can call each other from the tables. It was Winona's idea. The telephones have made for a very successful gimmick to bring people into the restaurant." Her smile broadened. "And they've been rather effective matchmaking tools, as well."

"Matchmaking tools?" Rory repeated, not liking the sound of that *at all*.

Miriam nodded. "Winona told me she's hosting a wedding reception at the restaurant next month for a couple who met here on opening night, via the telephones on the table. There's a number above us," she added, pointing upward.

Rory turned his attention in that direction, only to discover that the two of them were indeed numbered with an ornately scrolled sign—sixteen, to be precise. And, sure enough, as he arced his gaze around the rest of the room, he saw that every other table had a similar sign, complete with number, floating above it, as well.

"Are you telling me," he said, gazing back at Miriam, "that I can pick up this telephone, dial one of those numbers, and the phone on the corresponding table will ring?"

She nodded again. Then, as if cued to do so, the telephone on their own table rang with a delicate whir. They glanced at each other in surprise, but Miriam was the one who answered the phone.

"Hello?" she said into the receiver. Then she chuckled. "It's Winona," she told Rory. "She's up at the hostess stand."

Rory turned toward the door where they had entered and saw a startlingly beautiful woman speaking into a telephone there. She had pale-blond hair and pale eyes, as well, though he couldn't quite discern the color from this distance. She did, however, most definitely resemble Miriam, though he could see that she was a bit older. Her attire was in keeping with the rest of the restaurant's mood, right down to her Gibson Girl hairstyle.

"Yes, the table is perfect," Miriam said into the receiver. "Thank you again for making room for us. It was very nice of you. No, honestly, Winona, I'm not mad about that anymore. Really. Yes, I know Malibu Barbie was my favorite, but all good things must come to an end. No, please don't beat yourself up over it anymore. I grew as a person thanks to the loss. I did. Really. Yes, I did, too. Oh, Winona…"

The woman at the hostess stand looked gravely distressed now, and Rory couldn't help wondering why she didn't hang up the phone and approach the table to address her sister in person. Perhaps she felt too guilty. Evidently, these childhood traumas ran deeper for some people than others, he mused.

Then again, Rory himself recalled his own tragic loss of Sir Stuart, the Silver Knight of the Noble Knights, when he was seven. After all, all thirty-three pieces of armor had disappeared with Sir Stuart. Not to mention the twenty Medieval scale weapons. It had been heartbreaking. But, as Miriam had just told her sister, he, too, had grown as a person for having dealt with his grief afterward.

After a few more minutes of reassurance from Miriam, her sister, Winona, began to look appeased. Then the hostess signaled for her employer's attention, so the sisters broke off the conversation, and each hung up her phone.

"Your sister seems very devoted to you," Rory observed as Miriam completed the action.

She nodded gravely. "I'm beginning to think that Winona was more traumatized by the Barbie beheading than I was." She brightened, smiling again, and Rory was, quite simply, dazzled. "Still, it did get us a nice table, didn't it?" she asked.

He was about to agree with her when his gaze lit on a man who was seated by himself at another one of the tables behind her. What on earth was his brother Connor doing here? Rory wondered. Instinctively, he picked up the phone and dialed the number 27, which was what was hanging over Connor's head.

"Who are you calling?" Miriam asked.

"I just saw someone I… Hello, Connor?" Rory said when his brother picked up at his end…or, rather, at his table.

"Who's this?" came Connor's gruff reply.

"It's Rory, your big brother," he told his sibling, "and don't you dare use that tone of voice with me, young man. What are you doing here in Bloomington all by yourself? Does Mom know you're out? Alone?"

Connor began to gaze frantically around the room until his eyes lit on Rory, wherein they narrowed menacingly. "I can talk to you any way I want to, Rory," he said tersely. "And I can go anywhere I want to, anytime I want to, and it doesn't matter if I'm alone or not. I'm twenty-eight years old, in case you've forgotten. You're not my keeper."

"What are you *doing* here?" Rory asked again, side-stepping, for now, the fact that he was going to give his little brother a good talking to the next time he saw him back in Marigold. How dare Connor use that tone of voice with him?

"I'm *working*," Connor said, fairly hissing the words. "Now hang up the phone and don't call me again."

"Working?" Rory repeated. "You're a police detective. And a brand-new one, at that. Why would you be working here?"

"Shhh," his brother cautioned him. "Will you pipe down? Don't say another word about me to *any*one. And hang up the damned phone, will you?"

Connor immediately followed his own instructions, slamming his receiver back down in place. Rory gazed in silence at his receiver for a moment, then, feeling more than a little puzzled, replaced it.

"Your brother is here?" Miriam asked. She began looking around the room. "Where is he? I'd love to meet him. I want you to meet Winona, too, before we leave."

Rory shook his head lightly. "Well, I *thought* it was my brother," he said. "He certainly didn't sound like himself, though. Perhaps I was wrong."

She shrugged her—deliciously bare—shoulders, and a thrill of something warm and dangerous shot through Rory. "They say everyone has a double in the world," she remarked. "Maybe it's just someone who looks like your brother."

"Actually, Connor does have a double in the world,"

Rory said. "His twin brother, Cullen. But that didn't sound like Cullen, either."

Because it wasn't Cullen, Rory told himself. It was Connor. Still, he'd respect his brother's wishes—or, rather, his brother's edict—and not divulge his identity. The nature of Connor's work as a detective—however new he was at the job—often called for such discretion. Nevertheless, Rory couldn't help wondering what his brother, a Marigold, Indiana, police detective, would be doing working here in Bloomington.

Oh, yes. He would definitely be having a talk with Connor the next time he saw him at home.

Chapter 6

Miriam still couldn't believe she was sitting in a four-star restaurant, in a town forty-five minutes away from her home, with Rory Monahan. She couldn't believe she'd had the nerve to ask him out in the first place, and she couldn't believe she'd had the audacity to suggest a restaurant this far away. Most of all, though, she couldn't believe she'd donned the dress she had for the occasion, regardless of how insistent *Metropolitan* magazine had been about her attire.

But she had followed the magazine's instructions to the letter tonight. Because tonight, one way or another, she was determined to capture Rory's interest. And keep it.

She couldn't believe she'd managed to keep her wits about her this long, either—not to mention keep up reasonably intelligent chitchat, not to mention keep from flinging a coat on over her dress—as they'd made the long drive together alone.

Although, considering the heightened state of her nerves, Miriam supposed she should be grateful that she'd been able to *stop* talking long enough to catch a few breaths along the way. Otherwise, she might have passed out from oxygen deprivation. And it would have been frightfully embarrassing to have had to make the bulk of the trip with her head lolling awkwardly against her shoulder and—horror of horrors—drooling.

But she was here with Rory now—fully conscious and drool-free—and her nerves did seem to be settling down. A little. Of course, when she noted again just how yummy he looked in his navy-blue suit, how the color made his eyes seem even bluer and more expressive than usual behind his wire-rimmed glasses, how it brought out blue-black highlights in his hair...

She bit back an involuntary sigh. Even Winona was impressed, she thought. Because Miriam had seen the look in her sister's eyes when she and Rory had first entered the restaurant, and Winona most definitely approved. Now Miriam just hoped she could carry off the rest of the evening as well as she had so far.

Their server had come and gone and returned with a bottle of white wine, which Rory had selected from the extensive wine list, assuring Miriam that she would enjoy it and that it would go beautifully with the pecan-encrusted chicken dish that she had ordered. Honestly, though, she could be drinking lighter fluid as an accompaniment to a rubber chicken, and as long as Rory Monahan was her dinner partner, the meal would taste like ambrosia.

Nevertheless, she thought, after an experimental sip

of the pale yellow wine, it was a very choice good. Clearly, his store of knowledge did indeed extend to things other than historical facts. Somehow she was relieved to discover that.

And somehow, before she could stop herself, she found herself wondering, as a warm rush of anticipation washed through her, that she couldn't wait to find out what else, *precisely,* he was knowledgeable about. Perhaps, she thought further, if she was very, very lucky, then later in the evening she might possibly find out.

Oh, my, she immediately thought, shocked by the new avenue down which her thoughts had just turned. Where on earth had *that* idea come from? She hoped her Inner Temptress wasn't awakening. She had hoped her Inner Temptress needed her beauty sleep. That could only lead to trouble. Because Miriam was quite certain she could handle Rory perfectly well tonight *without* her Inner Temptress's interference.

Oh, boy, could she handle Rory tonight. And she couldn't *wait* to do it.

Hush, Miriam told the Temptress inside her. *Go back to sleep. Ro-o-ock-a-bye, Temp-tress, in the tree to-o-ops...*

Lovely, Miriam thought. This was just lovely. It was going to be all she could do now to restrain the little vixen for the next few hours. Surprisingly, though, she did manage to keep her Inner Temptress unconscious for the duration of their meal. In fact, she and Rory dined quite companionably for the next hour or so, their conversation never once straying into dangerous waters.

More was the pity, Miriam couldn't help thinking, in spite of her efforts to keep her Inner Temptress at bay. Though, once or twice, she couldn't help but think that her and Rory's gazes did connect in a way that might be construed as, oh, perilous, perhaps.

A girl could dream, couldn't she?

And a girl could not only dream, Miriam realized some time later, but a girl might actually realize those dreams, too. Because after bidding goodbye to Winona—with their compliments to the chef, of course—Miriam and Rory spent another hour strolling through the neighborhood where the restaurant was located. It was a charming little historic area in Bloomington, filled with tiny boutiques and antique and curio shops, canopied by mature trees and lined by old brick town houses and wrought-iron railings and cobbled sidewalks.

And at one point, as she and Rory strode side by side under the twilit sky, their hands and arms occasionally bumping, it occurred to Miriam that she was indeed realizing one of her dreams where Rory Monahan was concerned. Not that she had taken him *home* and fed him, as she often thought about doing, but she had taken him *out* and fed him—even if he *had* insisted, quite vehemently, on paying for that meal himself. And now they were walking—almost hand in hand—through the neighborhood, even if it wasn't her *own* neighborhood. And she discovered, not much to her surprise, that the reality of the dream was even better than the dream itself.

And then she wondered if maybe some other dreams might turn to reality soon.

"It's lovely here," Rory observed at one point. "Although I've been to Bloomington on several occasions, I've never seen much of the town." Hastily, he added, "Outside the IU library, of course."

Miriam nodded. *Of course,* she thought. "This part of Bloomington is a lot like Marigold," she said. "Winona and I grew up in Indianapolis, but we both attended IU and fell in love with the place. She decided to stay here after she graduated, oh…fifteen years ago, I guess. In fact, I lived with her while I attended college. Winona just loves it here. Almost," Miriam added, glancing over at Rory now, "as much as I love Marigold."

"But you haven't lived in Marigold very long, have you?" he asked.

"Six months," she told him. "Before that I worked and lived in Indianapolis."

"You've been in Marigold that long?" he asked, seeming surprised by the information. "Funny, but it doesn't seem as if any time at all has passed since you came to town."

She smiled as she asked, "You noticed when I came to town?"

He colored faintly and glanced away. "Yes, well… I, um, I couldn't tell you the exact date of course, but, ah, actually… Yes," he finally confessed. "I noticed when you came to town." He continued to gaze straight ahead when he finished his admission, as if he would be uncomfortable under her scrutiny. "It was snowing that first day I saw you in the library, and you hadn't yet shed your coat when I came down to the circulation desk looking for Mr. Amberson."

Suddenly he stopped walking and then, surprisingly, turned his body to face her. Miriam, too, halted beside him and likewise turned to face him. Her breath caught in her chest as she studied him, because he had fixed his gaze on hers, his blue eyes piercing and intense. She watched, stunned, as he began to lift a hand toward her hair, but when he realized what he was doing, he must have reconsidered, because he hastily dropped it back to his side. Nevertheless he continued to hold her gaze steady as he spoke.

Very softly he said, "Snow had melted in your hair, and it looked like little fairy crystals scattered about your head. And I thought your eyes were the most unusual shade of gray. And they seemed to be filled with intelligence and kindness and gentleness. I couldn't help but notice you."

His confession set off little detonations of heat throughout Miriam's midsection. She realized suddenly that she was still holding her breath, so, slowly she released it and slowly she filled her lungs again. But she had no idea what to say to him now. Not unless she told him the truth. Which, ultimately, was precisely what she decided to do.

"I, um, I noticed you, too," she said. "That first day at the library, I mean." But she couldn't think of a single thing to add to the statement.

Rory continued to gaze at her for a moment, as if he were mesmerized by something in her eyes. Then his gaze fell to her mouth, and he swallowed visibly. He parted his lips, presumably to say something in reply to her own confession, but not a word emerged to identify his thoughts. Instead he leaned forward and, after only one small, eloquent hesitation, covered her mouth lightly with his. He kissed her gently, tenderly, very nearly chastely. And then, a breathless moment later, he withdrew.

When he pulled back, Miriam realized her eyes were closed and her heart was racing and the entire world was spinning out of control. Then she opened her eyes again to find that Rory was watching her, smiling softly, and...blushing.

He said nothing to explain his action, simply turned forward to stare straight ahead again. And then he started walking, very slowly, and all Miriam could do was follow. Amazingly, in spite of her muzzy-headedness, her steps never faltered. She scrambled for something to say, then worried that speaking might somehow spoil the magic of the moment. Rory seemed to share her sentiments, because he, too, remained silent.

Miriam, optimist that she was, decided to take it as a good sign. She'd left him speechless, after all. That had to be good, didn't it?

Eventually they both found their voices again, even found the wherewithal to make chitchat as they completed their evening constitutional, making a full circle back to Winona's parking lot and Rory's car. For some reason Miriam found herself both looking forward to and dreading the ride back to Marigold. Although the trip guaranteed they would have a little more time together alone, she wasn't sure what awaited them at the end of it. Tonight had been full of uncommon revelations and unexpected surprises, but she feared the enchantment would end once they returned home.

Worse, she worried that by tomorrow Rory would have forgotten everything he'd said and done—everything *she'd* said and done—tonight. Or, worse still, she would awaken in her bed in the morning, only to discover the whole evening had been nothing but a dream.

But dreams came true sometimes, she reminded herself. One of her fondest had come true tonight, only moments ago. Rory Monahan had kissed her. Of his own free will. And although it hadn't been the kind of passionate embrace she often found herself fantasizing about, it had certainly been very pleasant and very promising.

And the evening wasn't even over yet, she reminded herself. They still had the long drive home....

They were almost exactly midway between Bloomington and Marigold—traveling on a deserted two-lane state road that was infrequently used after work hours during the week—when a loud gust of sound alerted them to the fact that there was something terribly wrong with Rory's car.

Well, the loud, gust of sound alerted them to that, along with the way the car suddenly jolted and jerked and slipped and swerved and then nearly ran right off the road. That, Miriam concluded as the car fishtailed dangerously and its tires squealed ominously, was most definitely a key clue that something was amiss.

"Damn," Rory muttered, once he had the vehicle under control again and crawling to a stop on the narrow shoulder of the road. "I do believe I have a flat tire. Again."

"This happens to you often?" Miriam asked, her heart still pounding, thanks to the rush of adrenaline that had shot through her during the momentary vehicular commotion.

"No, not often," Rory told her. "But I had another flat tire not long ago. About, oh… Let me think… Well, I forget now. I'm not sure exactly how long ago it was, but it wasn't very long ago. Certainly it was long enough to give me time to buy a new tire and stop driving on the spare."

Miriam breathed a silent sigh of relief. "Well, thank goodness for that," she said.

He glanced over at her, and even in the dim, bluish light that emanated from the car's dashboard, she could see that his expression was…sheepish? *Oh, dear.*

"I, um, I said it was long enough to *give me time* to buy a new tire and stop driving on the spare," he repeated. "I, ah, I didn't say that was what I had actually done."

"Oh, dear," Miriam said aloud this time.

"Because what's lying in the spare compartment right now, is I'm afraid," Rory said, "my old tire."

"Oh, dear," she said again.

"My old tire with a whopping great hole in it."

"Oh. Oh, dear."

"I rather forgot to buy a new one."

"Oh. Dear." With a good, swift, mental kick, Miriam roused herself off that riff, and tried to look on the bright side. "Well, then," she said. "We'll just call Triple-A. You *are* a member of Triple-A, aren't you?"

Rory hesitated a moment, then slowly shook his head. "I've always meant to join, but I, um… I keep forgetting."

"Not to worry," she reassured him. "I've been a member since I first got my driver's license. They're wonderfully efficient and should be here in no time at all. Do you mind if I use your cell phone?"

Again Rory looked worried. "Well, of course I wouldn't mind you using my cell phone," he said. "If, that is, I had a cell phone for you to use."

She gazed at him blankly. "You haven't a cell phone?"

He shook his head again. "I've always meant to get

one. They do seem like they'd be so convenient. Especially in circumstances such as these. But I just—" he shrugged again "—I keep forgetting to get around to it."

This time Miriam wasn't quite so reassuring. Because although she *did* normally carry a cell phone, tonight, her tiny little handbag—the one *Metropolitan* magazine had promised her she absolutely must have to carry off this particular dress with any amount of success—was far too small for necessities like cell phones. Oh, there was room enough for necessities like identification, lipstick, hanky, money, *Triple-A card,* breath mints and um…a condom, she recalled with a blush— well, she *was* a *Metro* Girl now, wasn't she, and *Metro* insisted that she *always* carry one, just in case, didn't it?—but no room for anything as practical and important as a cell phone.

Not that Miriam had any desire to diminish the importance of fresh breath, mind you. Or of safe sex, either. But at the moment if she'd had a choice between good oral hygiene, sexual preparedness or a link to the outside world on a dark, isolated, potentially dangerous stretch of road, she was fairly certain she would opt for the last. Especially since it was looking like the sexual preparedness wasn't going to be an issue with Rory Monahan for quite some time.

"Well then," she said again, striving for an optimistic tone, even as her optimistic attitude bit the dust. "I guess we'll just have to make the best of a bad situation, won't we? Surely some Good Samaritan will come by and render aid soon, if you turn on the emergency flashers. Besides," she added with an—albeit forced— smile, "it could be worse, you know."

"Could it?" Rory asked wearily, sounding nowhere near convinced of that.

She nodded. "Oh, yes. It could definitely be worse. It could be raining."

And then, as if cued by her remark, a rumble of thunder sounded overhead.

"Oh, dear," Miriam said—yet again—when she heard the inauspicious echo.

"Then again…" Rory muttered at the same time.

And as if by speaking as one, they'd uttered a magical incantation, the dark skies opened up above them, dumping what sounded like buckets of water over the midsize sedan. Rain sheeted the windows and windshield, completely obscuring the view—what little view there had been, anyway, considering the fact that it had been pitch-dark on the road when they'd been forced to stop.

For long moments neither Rory nor Miriam said a word, only sat there waiting to see if maybe, just maybe, this was nothing but a bad dream. Then, just when it seemed as if those long moments—not to mention the rain—might go on interminably, Rory had to go and ruin it.

"Well, it could still be worse," he commented. "It could be hailing."

"Oh, don't say it, Rory," Miriam cautioned him, "because if you do—"

Sure enough, before she could even complete the admonition, she heard a rattling *nick-nick-nick* from somewhere beyond the sheets of rain. After a moment the *nick-nick-nick* was followed by a louder and more threatening *thump-thump-thump* that beat relentlessly against the hood and roof of the car with much maliciousness. The rain abated for a moment, just long enough for Miriam to see marble-size bits of ice pinging—nay, bulleting—off the hood of the car, then the downpour seemed to triple in severity, blocking her view with a watery curtain again.

She sighed in defeat. "Usually," she said softly, "the arrival of hail heralds a dip in the temperature." And even as she uttered the comment, little goose bumps erupted on her arms. Without consulting Rory, she reached for the car's air conditioner and switched it off, then crossed her arms over her midsection in a completely useless effort to ward off the chill.

"Here," he said as he noted her actions, struggling to remove his jacket.

He turned off the car's ignition completely, then flicked on the emergency flashers—not that Miriam thought for a moment that anyone would be able to see the blinking lights through this downpour. Not that she thought there would be anyone out there *to* see them in this downpour. After all, who in his or her right mind would be out driving on a night like this, unless they were returning home after a truly lovely interlude with someone about whom they cared very deeply?

"It looks as if we're going to be stuck here for a while," Rory added. "And I'm afraid to run the engine any longer, even the heater, in case we need the battery for something later. You just never know. But this should keep you warm," he told her, generously extending his jacket toward her, holding it the same way a gentleman would hold a lady's wrap for her.

"How gallant," she couldn't keep herself from saying as she smiled and took the garment from him.

And when she did, Rory blushed. Even though Miriam couldn't see his face very clearly, now that the car's interior lights had been extinguished, she still somehow sensed intuitively that he was indeed blushing. And realizing that only endeared him to her that much more.

Honestly, she thought. One would think she was in love with the man. Which of course wasn't true at all. What Miriam felt for Rory, she was sure, was simply an intense attraction and a powerful longing and a soul-deep need. That was all. Certainly she wasn't denying the possibility that love might occur later in their relationship. But first, she told herself, they must *have* a relationship. She wasn't in love with him. Not yet. Heavens, no.

"This deplorable weather shouldn't last long," he said as she awkwardly thrust her arms through his suit jacket and wrapped it snugly around herself. "These summer storms seldom do. We can wait it out."

Although she knew what he said about summer storms was normally true, Miriam was also certain that Rory had just jinxed it completely the moment he'd spoken the observation aloud. Now it was doubtless going to rain for another forty days and forty nights.

Drat, she thought. They were going to be stranded out here, on this dark, deserted strip of highway, with nothing to keep them warm, all night long, all alone. Immediately upon forming the realization, though, Miriam suddenly brightened. Because now they were going to be stranded out here, on this dark, deserted strip of highway, with nothing to keep them warm, all night long, all alone.

Well, well, well. Maybe this date wasn't going to end up being so disastrous after all. If nothing else, the two of them would now have an opportunity to talk, and perhaps an opportunity to get to know each other better. And maybe, if she was very lucky, they'd even have an opportunity to get to know each other intimately.

Oh, dear, Miriam thought as that last idea unrolled in her head. Her Inner Temptress must be awakening again. And right on time, too, she couldn't help remarking. Sleep all day, and then wake up to carouse all night. That was her Inner Temptress, all right. The little minx.

Miriam snuggled more comfortably into the jacket she had wrapped around herself, inhaling deeply the familiar scents of Rory Monahan and enjoying the warmth of his body that still clung to the inside of the garment. She smiled. Wearing Rory's jacket was almost as nice as being touched by Rory himself, she thought. Then he reached across her for something, and, in the darkness, his arm brushed lightly over her breasts.

And she realized as a thrill of electric heat shot through her that wearing Rory's jacket was absolutely *nothing* like being touched by Rory himself.

"I'm sorry," he immediately apologized as he jerked his arm back again. "I was reaching for the glove compartment. I think there's a flashlight in there."

"That's all right," Miriam said genuinely, if a little breathlessly. "No harm done."

All right, so that last part of her statement hadn't been quite as genuinely offered as the first part. Although it certainly had been all right for Rory to touch her, he'd actually just done plenty of harm—to her thoughts, to her well-being, to her sense of propriety and to her libido.

"Perhaps you could look for the flashlight," he suggested. "You're in a better position to find it than I am, anyway."

Obediently she felt around the dashboard until she located the knob to open the glove compartment. And when she reached inside, she wasn't surprised to discover how tidy and well organized were the contents. It took her no time at all to find the flashlight. But when she withdrew it and switched it on, no light flashed forth. She shook it gently, hoping to rouse some scant illumination, but to no avail.

"I think the batteries must be dead," she said.

She heard Rory's frustrated sigh part the darkness between them. "They are," he told her. "I recall now that they ran out while I was changing my last flat tire. I meant to put new ones in, but—" he shrugged apologetically "—I forgot."

"Oh, Rory," Miriam said as she replaced the flashlight and closed the glove compartment. In spite of their difficult situation, she couldn't quite halt the smile that curled her lips. "You need someone to look after you."

She felt him stiffen in the seat beside her. "I beg to differ," he said curtly. "I've been looking after myself for my entire adult life."

"Have you?" she asked, still smiling.

"Of course I have."

"Well, I do apologize then," Miriam told him. "And I do stand corrected."

Now that her eyes were adjusting better to the darkness, she could distinguish his features fairly well, and she saw him relax some. But there was no way she would ever believe that Rory Monahan looked after himself. Not with any degree of success, anyway.

"Well, then," she continued after a moment, "as you said, we may be stuck here for a good while. What on *earth* shall we do to pass the time? What could there *possibly* be available to two people—two consenting adults, I might add—who are stranded alone together on a dark and stormy night, with absolutely no hope of discovery for hours and hours and *hours* on end?" She leaned toward him a little and cooed softly, "Hmmm, Rory? What would *you* suggest we do?"

Chapter 7

At no time had Miriam intended for her questions to be in any way suggestive. Somehow, though, even as she was uttering them, she realized they sounded exactly that. Not just suggestive, but... *sexually* suggestive. How on earth had that happened?

Probably, she thought, it was because the voice in which she had uttered the questions hadn't been her own voice at all. No, the voice that had spoken just then had most definitely belonged to her Inner Temptress, no two ways about it. Because the voice had been very low and very throaty and very, well, tempting.

Rory must have noticed that, too, because he turned to face Miriam fully and said, with much surprise lacing his own voice, "I—I—I— What did you say?"

She opened her mouth to make amends, not to mention an explanation, for having created such an awkward situation—presumably by making a light jest, somehow, of what she had just said. But she realized fairly quickly that, what with her Inner Temptress being awake and all—drat the little firebrand—she wasn't about to be corralled anytime soon. No, in fact, Miriam's Inner Temptress—little vixen that she was—made matters even worse.

Because what came out of Miriam's mouth, instead of being a hasty, jesting explanation for her previous, dubious, suggestion, actually wound up being a throatily—and temptingly—offered, "Oh, come on, Rory. Surely, an educated man like you can think of *some*thing for two consenting adults to do that would pass the time in an…interesting…fashion."

Heavens, had she actually said that? Miriam marveled. Well, of course, she could argue that no, she *hadn't* actually said that, that her Inner Temptress—the little tigress—had been the one behind it. But Miriam had been forced to conclude some time ago—shortly after awakening her Inner Temptress, as a matter of fact—that she alone was responsible for the little rabble-rouser. Ergo, the little rabble-rouser was a part of her makeup, and no amount of denying that would change anything. So when her Inner Temptress spoke, Miriam had no choice but to listen. And to take responsibility.

And she would have to take the initiative, too, she thought further, if she didn't want to completely humiliate herself now by backing down and apologizing profusely for her Inner Temptress's questionable behavior and shrinking back into her seat like a docile little lamb. Then again, taking the initiative with Rory Monahan wasn't such a bad prospect, she decided. Because maybe if she took the initiative, then he might take something else. Like liberties, for example. That might be fun.

After all, he had kissed her not long ago, she reminded herself as a warm, wanton little curl of anticipation unwound inside her. Granted, it had been a nice, simple, harmless kiss, but it didn't take much effort to turn a nice, simple, harmless kiss into a seething, passionate, relentless embrace. Not according to *Metropolitan* magazine, anyway. All Miriam had to do was give her Inner Temptress free rein.

So, without allowing herself time to think about what she was doing, Miriam surrendered herself to her Inner Temptress. And immediately after doing so, she found herself lifting a hand toward Rory's face and threading her fingers through his hair.

Oh, my, what a vamp that Inner Temptress was.

Then, very softly and very seductively, Miriam heard herself telling him, "Do you realize how incredibly handsome you look this evening? Honestly, Rory, Winona would never forgive me for saying this, but all through dinner, all I could do was think about how our meal couldn't possibly be any more delicious than you must be."

He gaped hugely at her, but Miriam couldn't quite blame him. She felt like gaping hugely at herself. Goodness. She must have taken those articles in *Metropolitan* magazine closer to heart than she realized.

Finally, and not a little nervously, Rory said, "Miss… I mean…Miriam…I—I—I think maybe, perhaps, possibly you may have had a little, small amount, tiny bit too much to drink tonight."

"I only had two glasses of wine," she reminded him, weaving her fingers through his hair again. And as she did, she couldn't help noticing that, for all his verbal objecting, Rory had done nothing to remove her hand.

"Yes, but those two glasses were more than three-fourths full," he pointed out. "Which actually goes against the proper pouring procedure for any fine dining establishment."

"Winona is a generous hostess," Miriam said, twining one dark lock of his hair around her index finger. She pushed her body to the edge of her seat, as close to Rory as she could, and still he did nothing to physically dissuade her physical advances.

"Yes, well, if she gets any more generous," he said, "she may just compromise her profits and drive herself right out of business. Not to mention compromise the virtue of her patrons."

"Is that what I'm doing?" Miriam asked innocently as she leaned further over, to push herself closer to him still. She lifted her other hand to join the first, threading those fingers, too, through his hair, and she marveled at the satiny softness of the dark tresses as she sifted them through her fingers. "Am I compromising myself?" she asked further, hopefully.

Rory's discomfort seemed to compound, but he still made no move to halt her brazen actions. "Oh, I never meant to suggest that you're compromising yourself," he told her. "It's the wine that's compromising you. I'm sure of it."

She waited one telling moment, then said huskily, "I'd rather it be you compromising me."

To punctuate the statement, she reached for his glasses and gently removed them, then set them on the dashboard, her eyes never leaving his. Then she pushed herself to the very edge of her seat and dipped her head to his, nuzzling his nose softly with her own.

Her heart rate quickened as she performed the gesture, her body temperature rocketing into triple digits, she was certain. He smelled spicy and well-scrubbed and manly, an intoxicating combination that dizzied her, dazzled her, dazed her. The storm blustering outside the car was nothing in comparison to the one that was suddenly raging inside her. Miriam had no idea where it had come from, and she was astonished by its utter potency, but there it was all the same. She felt Rory's heat surrounding her, wrapping her, enclosing her completely. And she wanted him. Badly. More than she had ever wanted anything before in her life.

"Miss Thornbury," he began to protest. Though she couldn't help thinking his objection sounded more than a little halfhearted. "I—I—I—"

"Miriam," she immediately corrected him. "Call me Miriam."

"Miriam," he repeated obediently. "I—I—I—"

"I like the way you say my name," she interrupted him. For good measure, she added, "Rory. In fact," she continued, still in that low, husky voice that she couldn't help thinking sounded much more convincing now than it had before, "I like you, period. I like you very much."

As Miriam urged her body closer to his, Rory couldn't, for the life of him, figure out what had come over her. Or him, for that matter, because he certainly wasn't doing what he should to put a stop to her advances. Odder still was the fact that he didn't *want* to put a stop to her advances. In fact, he felt like making a few advances of his own. He was just too startled at the moment to know where to begin.

In spite of his suggestion that Miriam had had too much to drink, he didn't think wine was what had generated her current actions. Not only had they each only had two glasses, as she'd said, but they'd topped them off with coffee over dessert. Then they'd fairly well walked off what scant inebriation may have remained while exploring the neighborhood around the restaurant.

All right, so when he had kissed her, there may have been some kind of intoxication involved, he conceded, but even that, he was sure, hadn't come from a bottle of wine. Where it *had* come from, Rory couldn't quite say at the moment, but he and Miriam both had been as sober as the proverbial judges by the time they'd returned to his car. Until a few moments ago, she'd seemed fine.

And then, suddenly, a few moments ago…

Well, Rory still couldn't figure out exactly where or when things had begun to go awry. One minute they'd been settling in to await the end of the storm, and the next minute…the next minute…

Well, the next minute another sort of storm entirely had begun to brew.

Because suddenly Miriam had been sitting close enough for Rory to fill his lungs with the faint scent of lavender that clung to her, close enough for him to feel her nearness, her heat, her desire. And she'd begun to run her fingers through his hair, and nuzzle his nose with hers, and all of it had just been so overwhelming, all of it had simply felt much too good to ask her to stop any of it, not that he wanted her to stop any of it, even if he knew it would definitely be a good idea to ask her to stop it, but asking her to stop it might make

her stop it, and he didn't want her to stop it because…
because…because…

Where was he?

Oh, yes. Miriam's nearness. And her scent. And her
heat. And her touch.

It was all coming back to him now.

And it was no less confusing now than it had been
a few moments ago, when it all began. Even more confusing, though, was his own reaction. Because instead
of pushing Miriam away, which Rory assured himself
any self-respecting gentleman would do when faced
with an amorous—and surely inebriated, right?—escort, he found himself wanting to lean right back into
her and thread his fingers through her hair, and wind
one or two tresses around his hand to bring her closer
still, close enough for him to cover her lips with his and
kiss her more deeply.

And suddenly Rory realized that that was exactly
what he was doing. His hands, half-filled with her silky
hair, were cupping her jaw, and he was tilting her head
slightly to one side so that he could press his mouth
more intimately against hers. And never in his life had
he tasted anything as sweet as she.

Forget about the wine, he thought vaguely. Miriam
Thornbury was infinitely more intoxicating.

His eager return of her kiss was, evidently, all the
encouragement she needed. Because the moment Rory
conceded even that scant surrender to her, she looped
her arm around his neck and crowded her body even
closer to his. He felt the soft crush of her breasts against
his chest, felt her palm open wide over his shoulder before gripping it with much possession. And in that moment all Rory knew was that he wanted—needed—to

be closer to her. Even though the two of them were already as close as two individuals could be in the narrow confines of an automobile.

So, ignoring those close confines, he hauled her from her seat into his lap as he deepened the kiss, reaching awkwardly to the side of his seat to release the lever that would glide it back as far as it would go. Then he skimmed the tip of his tongue along the plump curve of her lower lip and moved one hand from her jaw to her neck, strumming his fingertips lightly over the slender column before dipping them into the elegant hollow at its base.

Miriam murmured something incoherent—but incredibly arousing—against his mouth, and Rory moved his fingers sideways, tucking them beneath the opening of his jacket, to trace them along the graceful line of her collarbone. Back and forth, back and forth, back and forth he drew his hand, her skin growing hotter and hotter beneath his touch, her breathing growing more and more rapid, more and more ragged, with each pass he made.

The soft fabric of her dress skimmed along his wrist as he completed each movement, creating a surprisingly erotic friction. Without even thinking about what he was doing, Rory moved his hand down over that soft fabric, so that he might explore more of it. Once there, though, he realized that what lay beneath the dress was infinitely more interesting than the garment itself. Because his hand was suddenly cupped over one full, soft breast, a breast that fit perfectly in his earnest grasp.

Without thinking, acting purely on instinct, he reached for the top of the dress and urged the fabric lower, until, much to his delighted amazement, that soft, perfect globe lay bared to him. Miriam gasped in surprise when he placed his palm over her warm, naked breast, and he took advantage of her reaction by thrusting his tongue into her mouth and tasting her more deeply still. She melted into him with a sigh, and even as he located the tantalizing, and quite aroused, peak of her breast beneath the pad of his thumb, he told himself he should remove his hand immediately, that he shouldn't be taking such liberties with Miriam, because she was far too nice a girl.

Really, though, removing his hand was the last thing Rory wanted to do. So he hesitated, rolling the tight bud beneath his thumb again. Miriam arched her body toward him, pushing that part of herself more completely into his possession, and that was when all thoughts of stopping anything fled his brain completely. Instead he flexed his fingers tighter, and he rotated his palm so that he could grasp her yielding flesh more flagrantly. In response she curled her fingers over his biceps and squeezed hard.

And in a very rough, very aroused voice she said, "Oh, *Rory.* Oh, *please…*"

And then, before he realized what was happening— and although he truly didn't know which one of them released the lever this time—the driver's seat was reclining at a 180-degree angle, with Rory flat on his back and Miriam flat on top of him. Their legs got tangled beneath the steering column, so he adjusted their bodies as well as he could until they lay slantways, though still awkwardly, with their legs in the passenger seat. The press of Miriam's body along his then was…oh. Simply too delicious. And she in no way discouraged their position, either, because she fairly crawled on top of him once the seat was fully back, her body touching his now from chest to knee.

For a moment all Rory could do was gaze up at her face, noting the way her breathing was as ragged as his was, and how she seemed to be gazing back at him with a hunger that only mirrored his own. Her hair cascaded down over them, creating a silky privacy curtain—not that either of them seemed to be particularly concerned with privacy at the moment—and he wrapped a great fistful of it around one hand before cupping that hand over her nape. Then he urged her head lower, down to his own, and kissed her once again. Thoroughly. Completely. Utterly.

This time, though, Miriam was the one to seize control of the kiss, parting Rory's lips with her tongue and plunging inside, to taste him as deeply as he'd ever been tasted before. He looped his other arm around her waist, opening his hand at the small of her back, urging his fingers lower, over the soft swell of her derriere. Miriam gasped at the liberty, and when she did, Rory reclaimed the kiss as his own. This time he was the one to taste her, cupping his free hand now over the crown of her head to facilitate his penetrating exploration.

She uttered a wild little sound at the contact, opening one hand over his chest before moving it down over his rib cage and his torso, to his hip and back up again. He felt her fingers skimming along the length of his belt, back and forth, back and forth, back and forth, in much the same way he had caressed her collarbone only moments before. And, just as he had done moments before, she dipped her fingers lower, then lower still, until she, too, had claimed with her hand an intimate part of his anatomy.

Rory sprang to life at her touch, his member swelling and stretching against his suddenly too-tight trousers. He curved his fingers more resolutely over her bottom and pushed her hard against himself, bringing her pelvis into more intimate contact with his own as he arched his body upward to meet her. She cried out at the contact, pushing her upper body away from his, far enough to move her hand to his belt buckle. And then, almost ferociously, she began to tug the length of leather free.

As she wrestled with his belt, Rory dipped his head a bit and captured her breast again with his mouth, tantalizing the taut nipple with the tip of his tongue. Her fingers faltered in their quest for a moment, then, when he drew her more fully into his mouth, sucking her hard, she moaned, a long lusty sound, and went studiously back to work. As she loosed the length of leather from its buckle and began to unfasten his pants, Rory pushed the fabric of her dress up over her thighs, her hips, her fanny. And he was shocked—truly, shocked—to discover that, beneath her dress, Miriam was wearing skimpy little panties over an even skimpier little garter belt to hold up her stockings.

Oh, Miss Thornbury, he thought as he dipped his fingers beneath the silky panties to cup his palm over the sweet curve of her bare bottom beneath. *The things I never knew about you...*

Her fingers fell to the zipper of his trousers then, and she clumsily tugged it down as their bodies continued to bump each other in the restricted boundaries of the car. Before Rory could say a word—not that he necessarily had any idea what to say at that moment—she, too, tucked her fingers inside the garment, curling them intimately over his hard shaft. Rory closed his eyes at the sharpness of the sensation that shot through him. Really, it had been much too long since he'd indulged in this sort of thing. And something about indulging in it with Miriam just made the whole experience…

Oh, God, he thought as she squeezed him briefly in her hand. *Extraordinary.* That was what the experience was. That was what the woman was, too, he couldn't help thinking further. Extraordinary.

And then he couldn't think at all, because Miriam moved her hand upward, curving her palm over the ripe head of his shaft, rolling it beneath the heel of her hand before steering her fingers lower again. The hand he had placed on her derriere dipped lower, too, scooting her panties along with it. Miriam must have known what he had in mind, because she arched her bottom higher, so that he could move the garment down over her hips and thighs. Then she lowered herself again, bending one knee this time, in a silent bid for Rory to remove her panties completely.

And although he couldn't quite manage that, thanks to their restricted position, he did manage to free one of her legs, thereby granting him enough access to… Well. Thereby granting him enough access, he thought dazedly. His hands skimmed upward again, over the backs of her knees and thighs, to crease the elegant cleft in her firm bottom with one long finger.

"Ohhh…*Rory,*" she said again. But her voice was thicker now, and the words were slower than they had been before.

By now, she had opened his trousers and urged down the waistband of his briefs in front, far enough to free him completely. She wrapped her fingers possessively around him, claiming him manually again and again, trailing her fingers up along his heavy length, circling the firm head before moving oh, so leisurely back down again, until he was nearly insensate with wanting her.

Oh, things really had gone much, *much* too far, he thought. If they didn't stop this *immediately,* they were going to...

"Make love to me, Rory."

Too late.

The realization occurred to him vaguely, through a red haze of very urgent desire. And although his rational, thinking mind told him he absolutely must cease and desist *now,* his irrational, unthinking mind—which he would have sworn was not nearly as powerful as it currently seemed to be—insisted he follow her instructions to the letter. Rory was about to do exactly that when his thinking mind interceded again, this time with a very good argument as to why he must put a stop to things *now.*

"I don't have any..." he began roughly. "I mean, I'm not prepared for... That is, I haven't a, um..."

"Check my purse," she told him breathlessly.

"I—I—I beg your pardon?" he replied.

And vaguely it occurred to him that he would be begging for something soon if she didn't stop doing that thing she was doing with her hand.

He knew he must sound like the most inane human being on the planet, begging her pardon—of all things—at the moment, but truly, Rory had no idea what else to say. How could she have possibly known? he wondered. Not just what he'd been talking about when he was making absolutely no sense, but that there would even be a need tonight for that thing he was making no sense about?

Right now, he thought further, dizzily, was probably not the time to ask her.

Before he could say another word, anyway, Miriam shifted her body slightly on his and reached back toward the seat she had vacated—or, rather, the seat he had helped her vacate by pulling her off it and onto his lap himself—what seemed now like hours ago. And he watched with astonishment as she opened her purse and withdrew a small plastic packet from within. He watched with even more astonishment as she hastily tore the packet open and withdrew the prize from inside, holding it aloft as if it were a trophy.

And then she said something *so* astonishing as to be nearly unbelievable: "I'll help you put it on."

"I—I—I beg your pardon?" Rory stammered again before he could stop himself.

"Oh, it's all right," she assured him. "I've been doing some reading."

As if that would explain all of this, Rory thought. Reading. Honestly. He hated to think what.

But before he could ask, Miriam nestled her body atop his again, and, as she had just promised him she would do, she, um…helped him with it. In fact, she took matters completely into her own hands. So to speak. And no sooner had she completed her task than Rory surged to life again—not that he'd ever really fallen much—his member disagreeing quite vehemently now with his brain, insisting that what she was proposing was a very good idea indeed.

"Now then. Where were we?" she asked.

Immediately, though, she answered her own question, by positioning herself in exactly the same place she had been before. Now if Rory could only remember what she had been saying to him at the time...

"Make love to me, Rory."

Oh, yes. It was all coming back to him now.

"Please," she added, her voice low and husky and tempting...and, well, demanding.

"Are you sure this is what you want?" he asked breathlessly, still feeling hazy and flustered. "This is all happening so quickly," he pointed out.

"Is it?" she asked him. "Funny, but it feels to me as if it's taken forever."

For some reason Rory didn't disagree with her. He only repeated, "Are you sure, Miriam?"

"I've never wanted anything more than I want you right now," she said.

And something in her voice assured him that that was true. In spite of her utter certainty about her avowal, though, Rory could tell she was as confused and surprised by this new development as he was. Then again, he supposed it shouldn't come as a surprise. He had been dreaming about her for months now—nearly since her arrival in Marigold—and in his dreams, the goddess gown had, on occasion, disappeared.

And there had been that odd, sexually charged interlude in the library only days before, where she had fallen, quite literally, into his lap. And there had been those moments in the classroom when the two of them had seemed to connect on a level that went far beyond the scholarly. And there was that kiss that he had stolen from her—and which she had so freely given—earlier this evening. Even though that kiss had seemed relatively harmless at the time, Rory's intentions behind it, he knew now, had been anything but.

He wanted Miriam. Only now did he realize that he had wanted her for a very long time. Never had anyone so…so…so *distracted* him the way she did. Why, there had been times over the past six months when he hadn't even been able to concentrate on his studies, because Miriam Thornbury had walked by his table at the library, scattering every thought he had except the ones involving her.

So maybe he shouldn't be surprised at all, he told himself now as he dropped his hands to her waist again and covered her mouth with his. Maybe he should have seen this coming a long, long time ago…

And then he stopped thinking about what he should or should not have seen, what he should or should not have known, what he should or should not be doing. He bunched her dress in his hands again and shoved the garment back over her hips, then urged her body up a bit, so that he could position himself beneath her. Then he lowered her again and settled his straining shaft at the entrance to the innermost heart of her.

There was one taut moment when he wondered if they were both having second thoughts, then Miriam grasped him in her hand and moved him toward herself. She lowered her body to his, and began to draw him inside herself, encasing him in her damp heat.

She felt… Oh. So fine. So sweet. So perfect. So right. Rory didn't think he had ever welcomed a sensation as eagerly as he did this one. They both sighed their satisfaction as, slowly, he parted her, opened her, entered her, going deeper and deeper, taking longer and longer, until he was buried inside her totally. For a moment they only lay still, allowing their bodies to grow accustomed to the newness of their joining. Then Rory pushed his hips upward, once, thrusting himself deeper still.

Miriam cried out at the extent of his penetration, and for one frantic moment he feared he was hurting her. Then she lifted her hips up a bit, allowing him to glide slowly out of her, before lowering herself over him again. Rory closed his eyes, held tight to her hips and let her set the pace. And the pace she set was slow at first, almost leisurely, a steady, repetitive parry and thrust that nearly turned him inside out.

Gradually, though, her rhythm increased, quickened, deepened. Again and again she covered and released him, pulling him in and out, further with each motion. Rory cupped both hands over her bare bottom and pushed her harder, thrusting his own hips up to meet her. He felt a hot coil beginning to compress inside him, pulling tighter and tighter with every movement they made, until it finally exploded in a white-hot rush of relentless response. Miriam cried out her own climax at the same time, then her body went limp atop his, and, vaguely, Rory wondered if the two of them would ever be the same.

He buried his face in the fragrant curve where her neck met her shoulder and pressed an urgent kiss to the heated flesh he encountered there. He was about to tell her something very, very important, wondering just how he should phrase the complicated sentiment that was spiraling frantically through him, when a trio of—very loud—raps rattled the driver's side window.

Chapter 8

Between the rapid raging of his heartbeat and the dizziness ricocheting around in his brain, Rory somehow realized that it had stopped hailing outside and that the rain had lessened to a mere pitter-pat against the roof of the car and the windshield. He also noticed that every single window his car possessed was fogged up enough to make the glass completely opaque.

And then he noticed that someone was rapping against the driver's side window again.

Miriam must have noticed that, too, because as quickly and as feverishly as the two of them had come together in the darkness, they now sprang apart. She retreated to her seat and began to hastily rearrange her clothes, while Rory fumbled to remove and discard that convenient sexual accessory that was suddenly anything but convenient.

After a long, awkward moment—wherein another

trio of raps, louder this time, came at the driver's side window—he had managed to rearrange himself well enough to suit, his shirttail spilling over the waistband of his pants to hide the fact that they were unfastened. Miriam, he noticed, had managed to get her dress back down over her hips and held his jacket closed tightly over her torso.

Gingerly he lifted his arm and used his shirtsleeve to wipe away enough of the fog on the window to reveal a dark figure standing on the other side. A dark figure who was cast briefly into red light, then blue light, then red again, then blue again. Rory could only see the figure from the chest down, but he could tell it was a man wearing a raincoat, a raincoat that appeared to be part of some kind of uniform.

Coupled with the red-and-blue-light business, Rory, scholar that he was, deduced that the figure was, most likely, a policeman.

And for one brief, delirious moment, he wondered if the policeman had come to arrest him, because the activity in which he'd just engaged with Miriam must certainly be illegal. His response to her, after all, had felt more than a little illicit. Then he remembered that he and Miriam, in addition to being consenting adults— oh, boy, had they been consenting—were also stranded on a deserted stretch of road with a flat tire and the emergency flashers were turned on.

Of course, Rory thought further, inevitably, the emergency flashers weren't the only things that had been turned on over the last who-knew-how-many minutes....

Hastily he thumbed the button on the steering column to turn the flashers off. Then shook his head once fiercely, in an effort to dislodge the confusing, confounding conflagration of thoughts that were parading through his head. Then he snatched his glasses from the dashboard and settled them on the bridge of his nose, and somehow found the presence of mind to roll down the car window. The moment the glass began to descend, the police officer tilted his body to the side a bit, to gaze into the car's interior.

"Is, um, is there a problem, officer?" Rory asked. Funny, though, how his voice bore absolutely no resemblance whatsoever to its usual, even timbre.

"You tell me," the policeman said. "You're the one parked here on the shoulder of the road with your emergency flashers turned on."

Among other things, Rory couldn't help thinking. "Ah, yes," he said. "We, um, we were driving home, you see, when we suffered a flat tire, and with the weather being so severe and all…"

He left the explanation unfinished. Not so much because he knew the policeman would be able to infer the rest of the story himself, but because Rory suddenly felt too fatigued to go on. As if he were completely physically spent. As if every cell in his body had just breathed a collective sigh of release and then decided to lie back and light up a cigarette.

It was the strangest sensation. He'd never experienced anything like it before. And he and Miriam hadn't even done what they had done in the most ideal setting. They'd just made love in his car, for heaven's sake. He hadn't even done that when he was a teenager. Probably because he'd never had sex when he was a teenager, he couldn't help thinking, but still.

And if he felt this spent after a quick interlude in his

car—fiery and intense though that interlude might have been—then how would he fare with Miriam in a more intimately friendly situation? Like a bed, for example. Where they wouldn't be confined by a steering column or bucket seats? Where they wouldn't be interrupted by a police officer and could prolong their encounter for hours and hours and hours on end?

Good heavens, Rory thought. He might never be able to speak coherently or get around under his own speed again.

"Need any help changing the tire?" the policeman asked, rousing Rory from his troubling thoughts.

He started to shake his head, then remembered that he did, in fact, need some help—at least to alert someone who could bring them a new tire. "Actually, the spare tire I have is useless," he told the policeman. Then he gestured toward Miriam. "But my, um…my, uh… my…"

He turned his full attention to Miriam and found her sitting in the passenger seat staring straight ahead, clutching his jacket fiercely around herself and saying not a word. Her cheeks were flushed, her hair was a mess, and her chest still rose and fell with her rapid respiration. She looked, Rory thought, like a woman who had just been thoroughly tumbled. Which, of course— all modesty aside, he thought modestly—was precisely what she was. And he wondered just how he should classify her to the police officer who was waiting for his reply.

Just what was Miriam now? he wondered. Well, let's see now. She was his…his…his…

His *friend,* he told himself. That was what Miriam was. Wasn't she? That was what he had considered her to be before. Before she'd lain prone atop him with her breast in his mouth and her bottom fitted lovingly into his palm. Before she'd taken him into her body and glided herself along his length, over and over and over and…

Okay, so perhaps *friend* wasn't quite an appropriate term for her anymore. Because Rory had never done any of those things with any of his other friends.

Companion? he wondered. But no, that didn't seem like a fitting label for her, either. It conjured up an image of one of them being old and frail and infirm, and as they'd just realized, that wasn't the case with either of them at all.

Escort, too, seemed like an inappropriate designation for her, because it was too impersonal, too formal. And with Miriam wearing the dress that she was wearing—not to mention looking as if she'd just been thoroughly tumbled—a man of the law might very well misinterpret the word *escort* to be something that went way beyond inappropriate.

Significant other? Rory wondered further. Oh, absolutely not, he immediately told himself. That indicated that the two of them had the kind of relationship he wasn't about to enter into again. Well, probably not, anyway, he amended reluctantly for some reason.

Lover? he asked himself. Although that was technically true after what had just happened—in the connotative sense, at least—Rory was uncomfortable applying that tag to her, as well. For one thing, it offered the policeman insight into their relationship that Rory had scarcely had time to consider himself. For another thing… Well, for another thing, he wasn't sure just how much *love* actually entered into things.

So then what, exactly, he asked himself again, *was* Miriam to him now?

"My, um…" he began again, still gazing at her as he tried to find the right word to give the police officer. "My, uh… My, ah…"

"Your wife?" the policeman offered helpfully.

"Oh, God, *no,*" Rory replied vehemently, jerking his head back around to look at the police officer. "She's not my *wife.*"

"Oh, it's like that, is it?" the policeman asked with a knowing nod.

Rory arrowed his eyebrows down in confusion. "Like what?" he asked, genuinely puzzled.

The policeman shrugged carelessly. "You're out with your girlfriend instead of your wife," he said blandly. "You get a flat, you get home late, you get in big trouble… Hey, I know how it is. I got two ex-wives. And two ex-girlfriends."

"No, no, no," Rory said quickly, adamantly. "Absolutely *not.* She's not my *girlfriend,* either." Because that word, too, seemed utterly inadequate in describing what Miriam was to him. She was much more to Rory than a girlfriend. She was…she was… Hmmm…

He tried again to pinpoint her role in his life, aloud this time, for the policeman's sake. "She's my… She's my…my…"

"I'm his librarian," Miriam said softly from the other side of the car. "That's all I am."

And even though that, technically, was true, somehow Rory knew he was going to have a lot of trouble thinking about Miriam Thornbury as only that in the future.

The police officer dipped his head lower, looking

past Rory this time, deeper into the car's interior, at the woman seated beside him. And Rory could tell by the expression on the other man's face that there was no way—*no way*—he would ever believe that all Miriam Thornbury was to Rory was his librarian.

Which was just as well, Rory supposed. Because that wasn't all she felt like to him anymore, either.

"Yeah, well, whatever," the policeman said as he straightened again. "So do you need a hand changing the tire or not?"

Rory backpedaled to where they had been before in their conversation. "As I was saying, my, um, my librarian, is a member of Triple-A, but we don't have access to a telephone at the moment, so—"

"You don't have a cell phone?" the policeman asked. "But they're so convenient. Especially in circumstances like these."

Rory bit back a growl. "Yes, well, I'll take it under advisement," he said. "In the meantime, if you could be so good as to place a call to Triple-A for us, telling them we'll need a new tire in addition to help changing it, we'd very much appreciate it." He forced a smile and hoped it didn't look as phony as it felt. "And then," he told the policeman, "you could…carry on."

Oh, Rory really wished he'd come up with a better phrase than that one to use. Because he knew right away that the policeman was going to respond with—

"And, hey, then you two could carry on, too."

Somehow Rory managed to refrain from indulging in a knee-slapping guffaw and a riotously offered *Oh, hardy-har-har-har.*

"I'll just go back to my car and make the call for you," the policeman said as he turned and strode away.

"I'll get the emergency number off my own card. I'm
a member, too, of course. You shouldn't have to wait
long. Just to be on the safe side, though, I'll hang around
until the wrecker shows up. Wouldn't want you and
your… librarian…getting home *overdue*," he added
with a wink. "Wives hate that."

"But I'm not—" Rory began. But he halted when
he saw that the police officer was out of earshot. And
as grateful as he was for the other man's departure, he
realized with a silent, heavy sigh that now that the policeman was gone, Rory was once again all alone with
Miriam. And he had no idea what to say to her.

Except maybe for "I apologize for my abominable
behavior a few minutes ago."

She nodded halfheartedly but said nothing.

"It really was unforgivable," he added.

"Yes," she concurred quietly. "It was."

He was surprised to hear her agree with him so
readily. Although his behavior *had* been unforgivably
careless—and at the risk of sounding like a tantrum-
throwing child—Miriam had started it. Not that that
gave Rory an excuse to go along with her so willingly—
after all, if she jumped off a bridge, would he jump,
too?—but he didn't think he should be forced to shoulder the bulk of the responsibility for what had happened. She was the one who'd purred out such intimate
suggestions about consenting adults in the first place.
Just because he hadn't done anything to stop what had
happened—and just because he had enjoyed it so immensely—that didn't let her off the hook.

In spite of his mental pep talk, however, he said,
"Truly, Miriam. I am sorry for what I did."

She lifted her shoulders and let them drop, a small

shrug that seemed in no way careless. "It's all right," she told him softly. "It's not like you said anything that was untrue. And I am your librarian, after all."

He opened his mouth to say more, then realized how badly she had misunderstood him. She thought he was apologizing for something totally different from what he was actually apologizing for—though he wasn't entirely sure what she thought he *was* apologizing for. In any case, her response suggested that she *wasn't* upset by their sexual encounter, which was what Rory had actually been apologizing for.

"No, Miriam," he said gently, "I meant I'm sorry for…for…for pouncing on you the way I did." He dropped his voice to a softer pitch as he spoke, even though there was no one to overhear him. "For taking advantage of you the way I did. Sexually, I mean."

She glanced over at him, her expression puzzled. "You didn't pounce on me," she said. Then, very matter-of-fact, she added, "I pounced on you."

"Well, perhaps so," he conceded, guarding his surprise that she would so freely admit her part in what had happened. "But I did nothing to stop you. I went right along with it."

"And you're apologizing for that?"

"Of course I am."

She gaped at him in disbelief for a moment. Then, "Oh," she said in a very small voice. "I see."

"Well, don't you think I should apologize?" he asked. After all, he thought, she certainly deserved better than a quick tumble in his car. She deserved satin sheets and candlelight and soft music and a man who took his time with her, loving every luscious inch of her body. Several times over, in fact.

"Are you sorry it happened?" she countered.

"Of course I'm sorry," he told her again.

Their first time together should have been much nicer than what the two of them had just had, he thought. Though, mind you, what the two of them had just had had been very nice. Oh, yes. Very nice indeed.

"Oh. I see," Miriam repeated in that same small voice.

"Well, aren't *you* sorry it happened?" he asked.

She inhaled a deep breath and released it slowly. "I wasn't before," she told him. "But I suppose I am now."

Well, then, he thought triumphantly. Somehow, though, his triumph felt in no way victorious.

Miriam said nothing more in response—not that anything more seemed necessary—so Rory, too, remained silent. In a few moments the police officer returned to say that a wrecker was on the way to the scene with a new tire, and should be there shortly. And less than twenty—totally silent—minutes after that, the tumble of yellow lights in the darkness heralded its arrival.

The police officer left after a knowing smile and a casually offered, "Good luck to you both," and then Rory and Miriam stood outside the car—in silence— as the mechanic deftly changed the tire, and recorded her AAA information, and said good-night.

And then, in what seemed like no time at all, Rory and Miriam were sitting alone—and silent—in his car once again.

"Well, I suppose it would be best to get home," he finally said as he turned the key in the ignition.

She nodded slowly, but said nothing.

"Unless you'd like to stop somewhere for coffee," he added, surprised to hear himself make the offer.

He was even more surprised to realize how much he wanted her to take him up on it. They really did need to talk, he thought. Then again, maybe now wasn't the time. There was a definite awkwardness in the air. Perhaps once they both had time to reflect upon what had happened, they would be better able to figure out what was going on.

"No," Miriam told him. "That's all right. Thank you." But the words were flat, mechanical, emotionless. She didn't sound at all the way she usually did.

Still feeling as if he should say *some*thing—but having no idea what that something might be—Rory reluctantly guided the car back onto the road, and they continued on their way back to Marigold. In silence. Somehow, though, he didn't quite feel as if they were going home. Because somehow he suspected that when they got there, nothing was going to be the same.

And when he pulled up to her apartment building a little while later, and turned off the engine to accompany her to the door, only to have her tell him in a very soft, very wounded voice, that it wouldn't be necessary… As he watched her walk slowly and wearily up the walkway to her front door and enter her building alone… When he recalled how wilted and crushed had been the corsage still affixed to her wrist…

Well. Then Rory was sure nothing was going to be the same.

When Miriam unlocked the front doors to the library the morning following what was to have been a momentous date with Rory Monahan, she felt none of the usual zest or élan she normally experienced when she arrived at work. And not just because it was raining, either, although the rain did rather hamper her mood, because it only served to remind her what had happened the night before with Rory.

Oh, God, she thought as she entered the library with one explicit image after another replaying itself in her muddled brain. Her stomach pitched with a mix of anxiety and desire with each recollection. What *had* happened the night before with Rory? she wondered. In spite of her efforts to tempt him last night, at *no* time had Miriam intended for things to go as far as they had gone. *Metropolitan* magazine may have talked her into carrying a condom around, but not once had she honestly thought she would ever have cause to use the silly thing. Not until after she and Rory had gotten to know each other *much* better.

Then again, she told herself, she knew him as well as she knew anyone. Better than she knew most people, actually. At least, she knew all the things about him that were important. And she knew that the feelings she had for him were anything but casual.

But she still couldn't believe she and Rory had actually made love last night, in his car, no less, like two hormonally unstable teenagers. She still couldn't imagine what had come over her to make her lose control the way she had. As much as she wished she could blame her Inner Temptress, Miriam knew that she alone was responsible for her behavior. Even if her behavior had been completely alien to her.

She simply had not been able to help herself. The moment Rory had kissed her so deeply, when he'd covered her bare breast with his hand… Something had exploded inside of her, unlike anything she'd ever felt before. She'd just been so overcome with wanting him, with needing him. She'd assumed that whatever it was that was building between them, it was unique, and it was special, and it was eternal. She had been so sure that he must feel the same thing for her that she felt for him. She had been so certain that he must...that he must...

She sighed deeply. That he must...love her the way she loved him. There was no way she could have stopped what had happened the night before with Rory. Because it had felt so natural, so perfect, so right.

But it wasn't what had *happened* the night before with Rory that caused her to feel so melancholy today, she knew. No, the reason she felt so melancholy today was because of what she had *learned* after what had happened the night before with Rory. Because she had learned that he didn't want her. Not the way she wanted him to want her, at any rate. Not the way she wanted him. She only wished now that she had learned it before things had gone too far.

Oh, certainly he had *wanted* her last night. In exactly the way *Metropolitan* magazine made clear that a man *should* want a woman. Why, what she and Rory had experienced together was exactly the stuff that *Metropolitan* headlines were made of: Roadside Attractions Your Mother Never Told You About! Or Finding His Gearshift When He Goes into Overdrive! Or Make-Out Blowouts: What to Do When the Tire's Flat, but He's Not!

Oh, yes, Miriam thought wryly, sadly. She would have to write a letter to the editor immediately and suggest that the next issue of *Metropolitan* magazine be the car-and-driver issue. She herself could be a major contributor.

So, yes Rory had *wanted* her last night, but only in a sexual sense. Not that it would normally bother Miriam to have him wanting her sexually—not in the least. Provided he wanted her in other, less tangible ways, as well.

Oh, God, no. She's not my wife.

Absolutely not. She's not my girlfriend, *either*.

But he didn't want her in other, less tangible ways, she thought as the echo of his unmistakable aversion reverberated in her brain. Judging by the way Rory had spoken the night before, the prospect of having a wife, or even a girlfriend, was about as appealing as finding a dead slug in his dinner salad—after he had added a liberal amount of salt.

Only now did Miriam realize—too late—the difference between *tempting* a man and having him *fall in love* with her. Because she realized now that what she had really wanted all along—what this whole, silly *Metro* Girl fiasco was supposed to have achieved—was for Rory to fall in love with her. And although he certainly had been tempted and had certainly wanted her, loving her evidently wasn't part of the bargain. Not to his way of thinking, anyway.

And just what was *Metropolitan* magazine going to do about that, hmmm? Miriam wondered as she strode behind the circulation desk and began flicking the rows of switches that would illuminate the first-floor lights. Because no matter how furiously she had searched the night before, sifting through the box of magazines that still occupied her bedroom, there hadn't been a single headline on a single issue that had mentioned the word *love*.

As she entered her office and struggled out of her raincoat, she realized she had fallen into the same trap that so many women fall into—equating sex with love and love with sex, and completely forgetting about the fact that the presence of one didn't necessarily include the presence of the other.

Au contraire.

People could certainly have sex without love, she reminded herself, as evidenced by Rory's reaction to her the night before. And people could have love without sex, too, as witnessed by her own reaction to Rory.

Because she did love him. She admitted that to herself freely now. She had loved him for months, probably since her arrival in Marigold. Certainly long before she had experienced sex with him. And she knew she would continue to love him for some time to come. Perhaps for all time to come. And she would feel that love despite her plans to *not* have sex with him again. Because there was no point to pursue such a thing when he so readily dismissed the idea of having her for his wife or his girlfriend.

Miriam was an intelligent woman, after all. She knew better than to have sex with a man who didn't love her. She just wished she had been smart enough to identify that lack of love before she had gone too far.

She sighed heavily again as she tossed her damp raincoat onto the hook affixed to the back of her office door. Would that she had been smart enough not to fall in love with Rory in the first place, too, she couldn't help thinking further.

Inescapably her mind wandered backward then, to that single, sweet kiss the two of them had shared while walking through the neighborhood near Winona's after dinner. Miriam still wasn't sure what that had been all about. Rory had taken the initiative for that one, but his initiative had been so innocent, so solicitous, so tentative then. How had they gone from a simple, chaste kiss during their promenade, to a raging conflagration of need only an hour or so later?

Miriam feared she had a response to that, but it wasn't one she cared much for. While walking with Rory, she had been Miriam Thornbury, librarian. Later, in his car, she had been a Temptress. And where Miriam the librarian might have stood a chance with Rory, had she just let things move forward at their own pace, Miriam the temptress had gone and ruined everything by jumping the gun. Among other things.

And now here she stood, Miriam the librarian again, dressed once more in her standard attire of straight gray skirt and pale-pink blouse, her hair caught at her nape with her standard tortoiseshell barrette. And where was Rory? she wondered. Probably at home sleeping, dreaming about the temptress who had seduced him the night before.

Damn *Metropolitan* magazine anyway, Miriam thought. Someone should put a warning label on the publication.

So bleak was her mood by now that if Mayor Isabel Trent had come striding into her office at that moment and asked her to hold a public book-burning in the town square for *Metropolitan* magazine, Miriam could very well have seen fit to bring the marshmallows.

"Oh, wonderful, Miriam, you're here early. I knew you would be. You're so dependable."

As if conjured by her thoughts, Mayor Isabel Trent did, in fact, come striding into Miriam's office at that moment. But she carried neither *Metropolitan* magazine nor gasoline can nor propane torch, so although

Miriam's hopes of igniting the publication were dashed, she at least had hopes that she might have a reasonable conversation with the mayor for a change.

At least, she had hopes of that until Mayor Trent told her, quite adamantly, "Miriam, I want you to dance for me."

Miriam tried very hard to keep her eyes from bugging out of her head—that was such a frightfully impolite thing to do—but wasn't sure she was able to manage it as she replied, as courteously as she could, *"Huh?"*

"Oh, nothing difficult, I assure you," Ms. Trent said with a negligent wave of one hand. "Just a little foxtrot. Maybe a waltz or two. Surely you took lessons when you were a girl. You have that look about you."

Miriam tried to maintain her courtesy as she repeated, a bit less impulsively this time, "Huh?"

"All right, if the waltz is too challenging, then perhaps it would be all right if you stuck to a simple box step," Ms. Trent told her magnanimously. "But I do want you to dance for me."

This time Miriam made no bones about it. Quite forcefully now, she demanded, "Huh?"

Ms. Trent seemed to finally notice her discomfort, and she must have realized how strangely she was articulating whatever it was she wanted to articulate. Because she laughed lightly and lifted a hand to nervously twist the top button of the charcoal blazer that topped her straight, charcoal skirt.

"Well, I suppose that sounded rather odd, didn't it? I should offer you a little more by way of an explanation, shouldn't I?" she asked.

Miriam nodded enthusiastically. "That would be most helpful, Ms. Trent, yes."

"The local Kiwanis Club is holding its annual fund-raiser this weekend, at Tony Palermo's Stardust Ball-room," the mayor said. "They do this every year, which, of course, you couldn't possibly know, because you're a relative newcomer to Marigold. But everyone in town looks forward to it, and everyone comes, and the Kiwanis always need extra dancers, because Tony Palermo never has enough for this sort of function. And this year there's a shortage, because Tiffany Parmentier broke her ankle, and Debbie Sherman is on her honeymoon, and Shannon Epstein just had twins. So you're up, Miriam."

Miriam's head was fairly spinning with the wealth of information—little of it coherent—that was buzzing around in her brain. "I...huh?"

"We Marigoldians always chip in when a helping hand is needed," Ms. Trent admonished her. "I myself have offered to trip the light fantastic in Debbie's place." She sniffed a bit haughtily. "I would *never* ask one of my constituents to do something that I wouldn't do myself."

Of course not, Miriam thought. Which was why she had no trouble asking the local librarian to ban books. She fixed her gaze levelly on the mayor's. "I'm afraid I don't understand, Ms. Trent. Just what kind of fund-raiser is this, anyway?"

"I told you. It's the Kiwanis Club's annual 'Trip the Light Fantastic Night' at Tony Palermo's Stardust Ball-room. The money raised goes to their scholarship fund. It's the social event of the summer. And it usually earns enough to send several students off to IU in the fall."

"But...dancers?" Miriam asked.

"Well, that's what tripping the light fantastic is all about, isn't it? Ballroom dancing?"

"I suppose, but...why me?"

Mayor Trent smiled warmly. Miriam recognized it as her "family values" smile. "Well, it's always nice to have attractive young men and women present at this event, to dance with the elderly widows and widowers."

"Um, why can't the elderly widows and widowers dance with each other?" Miriam asked.

Isabel Trent gazed at her blankly. "Because they'd rather dance with attractive young men and women, that's why."

"Oh."

"It costs fifty dollars per person to attend, and that doesn't include refreshments," the mayor added, as if that explained everything.

And, Miriam supposed, in a way, it did. Even with the family-values thing going. "But this is such short notice," she protested. "I'm not sure I can take the night off. I was going to have my car worked on this weekend. I don't have anything to wear."

Let's see now, she thought further. Were there any other lame excuses she'd forgotten about?

Not that it mattered, because Isabel Trent clearly wasn't buying any of the lame excuses she'd already offered. "Find the time," the mayor decreed. "You can have the car worked on another time. And Lola Chacha, Tony Palermo's top dance instructor—which, of course, isn't her real name, but it's appropriate nonetheless—has plenty of ballroom-type dresses she'll be glad to loan out for the occasion. She's already told me she has one for me that's perfect.

"So that settles it," the mayor concluded with a satisfied smile. "I'll see you Saturday night at Tony Palermo's. Wear comfortable shoes. I'm sure you'll be dancing all night."

And without even awaiting a reply, Isabel Trent swept from the office, doubtless off to recruit another unsuspecting dancer.

Miriam shook her head ruefully and wondered if she should call the mayor back, to tell Ms. Trent that for generations the entire Thornbury family had been notorious for having two left feet, and none of them could dance to save his or her life.

Oh, well, Miriam thought further. She'd only be dancing with elderly widowers. And they probably wouldn't even notice or care how many feet she had, or of what variety. She tried not to feel too morose when she realized that Rory Monahan fell into that category, too.

Then again, Rory Monahan wouldn't be at the dance, she reminded herself. Because in spite of Mayor Trent's assurance that the fund-raiser would be the event of the summer and that everyone in Marigold looked forward to it, Miriam knew that one citizen, at least, wouldn't be in attendance. Because while she was tripping the light fantastic with a retiree in a borrowed ball gown—Miriam, of course, would be the one in the ball gown and not the retiree…she hoped—Rory Monahan, scholar, would doubtless be sitting at his usual table in the library, carousing openly with volume fifteen of *Stegman's Guide to the Peloponnesian War.*

And somehow Miriam couldn't help thinking that he would be having a much better time than she. Because Rory, at least, would be with the one he loved.

Chapter 9

Rory entered his classroom on Wednesday night for the second session of his evening Classical Civilizations II class, feeling nervous and anxious and totally unprepared. Not that he felt this way because of his lecture, mind you. No, he knew his history backward and forward and inside and out. But—and this was a *most* remarkable development—history was the last thing on his mind tonight. Because all Rory had been able to think about all day was Miriam Thornbury.

Surprise, surprise.

When he'd awoken that morning—from a very restless sleep—he'd been convinced that he had only dreamed the episode of the night before. There was no way, he had told himself, that he and Miriam Thornbury could have possibly made love in his car. Not just because of the limitations of the physical logistics involved, but because they were both rational, intelligent, thinking adults, far above being controlled by their basic, instinctive, irrational natures.

Yes, surely, he had told himself all morning long, he had only dreamed about the smoothness of Miriam's soft skin and the sweetness of her silky hair and the luscious taste of her breast in his mouth and the exquisite sensation of himself inside her. Only a dream, he had repeated to himself over and over again. Only a dream. Only a dream. Only a frantic, hot, erotic dream.

Then he had gone out to his car to drive to work, and had discovered a bit of champagne-colored silk sticking out from beneath the passenger seat. And when he had tugged on that bit of silk and discovered it to be a complete pair of panties, he had realized that what he had thought was a frantic, hot, erotic dream had actually been frantic, hot, erotic reality.

He *had* made love to Miriam Thornbury. In his car. On a dark stretch of highway. As if he'd had no more control over himself and his body than a sixteen-year-old boy would have. Then again, that was precisely how Miriam made him feel—like a rank adolescent, in love for the first time.

Wait a minute, he told his scrambled brain now as he settled his briefcase on the dais at the front of the empty classroom. *Hold on. Back up. Repeat.*

In love for the first time… In love… Love…

Love?

Could that possibly be what lay at the crux of his current preoccupation with Miriam? Because, truly, no one had ever distracted Rory to the point where he didn't think about his studies or his research. To the point where he didn't even *want* to think about his studies or his research. Come to think of it, his distraction with Miriam didn't feel anything like his distraction with Rosalind had felt. It didn't even feel like his *preoccupation* with Rosalind had felt. In fact, it didn't feel like preoccupation at all. What it felt like went way, way beyond preoccupation. What it felt like was…was…was…

Well. He very much suspected that this was, in fact, what it felt like to be in love with someone. Because suddenly the only thing Rory wanted in life was to be with Miriam.

What a startling development, he thought. But, surprisingly, it wasn't at all unpleasant.

Then again, maybe that wasn't surprising at all. Because for some time now, Rory's thoughts—and fantasies—about Miriam had been fast usurping his intellectual pursuits. And even Rosalind, although certainly distracting, hadn't invaded his thoughts or his life to the extent that he had disregarded his intellectual pursuits. Neglected them, yes. He had indeed neglected his studies when he'd been involved with Rosalind. But he hadn't forgotten about them entirely. He hadn't even assigned them to second place. That was the place Rosalind had held. Which, he supposed, was why she had left him. Not that he could blame her.

Since last night, however, Rory hadn't given his lessons or his research a second thought. Hell, he hadn't given them a *first* thought. Because the only thing he'd been able to think about was Miriam. The only thing he had *wanted* to think about was Miriam. In fact, thoughts of Miriam made thoughts of everything else pale. Even thoughts about his studies. Even thoughts about his research. Even thoughts about history. Even thoughts about the Peloponnesian War.

Good heavens. He *was* in love with her, he realized suddenly. That could be the only explanation for why he felt the way he did. Because although he was as excited as usual to be coming to class tonight, although he was anticipating the sharing of information with as much pleasure as he always did...

It wasn't teaching and learning that captivated him so at the moment. No, it was the prospect of seeing Miriam again. The thought of seeing *her* again excited him. And he anticipated with pleasure the opportunity to share information with *her.* Though, if he were honest, it wasn't information about classical civilizations that he wanted to share with her. It was information of a much more intimate nature.

His heart began to race wildly in his chest when he finally realized what was going on. Rory Monahan. In love. Who would have ever suspected such a thing? Certainly not Rory Monahan.

Well. He supposed now that he *really* should have called her today. This was something, after all, he was going to want to tell her about.

And he had actually thought about calling her earlier that morning, after he'd discovered her panties in his car and realized he hadn't, in fact, been dreaming about what had happened between the two of them the night before. But he'd been so stunned by the realization that he quite frankly hadn't known what to say to her.

Hello, Miriam? Did you know you left your panties in my car last night? Yes, I had a nice time, too. We'll have to do it again very soon.

No, somehow that just didn't seem quite right.

What Rory needed to say to Miriam, he needed to say in person. But he hadn't wanted to interrupt her at her work, at the library. And he'd wanted to have some time to prepare. And he'd known he would be seeing her tonight, in his class. So he'd assumed, or at least hoped, that afterward the two of them might go someplace—someplace quiet and private and conducive to intimate discussion—and talk about what had happened. About what it all might mean. About how they were going to approach the future.

Because Rory very much wanted a future with Miriam. A future that involved infinitely more than research and knowledge and intellectual pursuits. He could only hope she felt the same way.

He inhaled a deep breath to steady his heart rate, but the moment he exhaled, his pulse began to beat erratically again. It quickened even more when he heard the classroom door creak open, and he jerked his head in that direction, hoping with all his might, and all his heart, that the person who strode through would be Miriam.

But the person who entered wasn't she. Nor was the next person who entered the classroom. Nor was she the third or the fourth or the fifth. And fifteen minutes later, even after Rory had done something completely unprecedented—holding off starting his lecture until the rest of the class arrived—there was still no sign of Miriam.

And he told himself this couldn't possibly be a good development.

Where was she? he wondered as his students began to grow restless—as if they could be any more restless than he was himself. Certainly Miriam might feel a little awkward about things, just as Rory did himself. But he had thought she would still come to class tonight, if for no other reason than that *she* wanted to talk to *him* afterward, too.

Why hadn't she come? he wondered again. Unless, he thought morosely, after what had happened, she simply didn't want to see him again.

Could that be possible? he asked himself. Although she had seemed as enthusiastic and overwhelmed as he had been last night, perhaps her reasons for being so didn't mirror his own. Where Rory's heart had been engaged with his behavior—even if he hadn't realized it at the time—maybe Miriam had only been driven by her physical needs. And now that those needs had been met—at least he hoped he'd met them—then perhaps her interest in him was waning.

Still, he couldn't see that being the case. Miriam Thornbury didn't seem like the kind of woman who could divorce her physical needs from her emotional ones. Not needs like the ones they'd shared the night before, anyway.

No, Rory was certain—well, fairly certain—that Miriam had feelings for him, too. He just wished he knew the depth of those feelings. What if, having made love with him now, in a situation that had been anything but ideal, she was having second thoughts? he wondered. What if she thought him a heel because he had taken advantage of her on a dark, deserted strip of road? Granted, she had told him she thought *she* was the one who'd taken advantage, but still. What if, now that she'd experienced the next level of emotion with Rory—the most intimate level of emotion—she'd decided she didn't want any part of it?

In other words, what if he'd disappointed her last

night? What if she didn't like him, didn't want him, anymore?

Oh, he definitely needed to talk to her, he told himself. Tonight. After class, this very evening, he would stop by her apartment for a chat. He had to know where he stood with her. And he needed for her to know where she stood with him. He only hoped they both stood in the same place. Or at least on the same level. He didn't think he could stand it if Miriam told him she didn't want to see him anymore.

And not just because the library was his favorite place on earth, either. No, it was because Miriam was his favorite librarian on earth. Among other things.

With a heavy heart and a total lack of enthusiasm, Rory began his lecture. But there was none of the joy in teaching that he usually felt, none of the contentment that came with sharing his thoughts and observations about classical culture. History held no appeal. Nor did anything else. Because Miriam wasn't here to share it with him.

And somehow that just didn't feel right at all.

Unfortunately, when Rory went to Miriam's apartment that evening, she wasn't home. At least, she didn't answer her door. Not any of the ten times he knocked upon it. Which was odd, because he knew she wasn't working, either. She would have had to arrange for the night off so that she could attend his class. And she would have made that arrangement *before* they had gone out to dinner, *before* the two of them had made love. So it was unlikely she was at the library.

In spite of that, after scribbling a quick note telling Miriam he had stopped by to say hello— Well, what

was he supposed to have said? That he had stopped
by because he was obsessed with thoughts about her?
What, and scare her even more?—and slipping it beneath her front door, Rory checked the Marigold Free
Public Library, too. But she wasn't there, either, not
much to his surprise. And the assistant librarian confirmed that. So Rory wrote her another note, saying
he had stopped by to see her— Well, it wasn't like he
could write *I love you, I want you, I need you, come
back to me please, sweet Miriam,* and then hand it over
to a stranger, was it?—and then he left.

And he felt strangely bereft as he exited the library
to return home. Honestly. It almost felt as if Miriam
had dropped off the face of the planet. If she wasn't in
class and she wasn't at work and she wasn't at home,
where else could she be? And how was he supposed to
talk to her if he couldn't find her? And what if it was
her intent to avoid him forever?

No, he decided. She couldn't do that. He knew where
to find her, knew she would be at the library tomorrow, just as he would be himself. And the library was
a quiet place, a peaceful place, a place full of potential
and possibility. Granted, one wasn't supposed to talk
in a library, but he was sure the librarian would make
an exception in this case.

At least, he thought the following afternoon, the librarian would make an exception if he could *find* her.
But once again Miriam was nowhere to be found. Although she was indeed working—one of the students
manning the circulation desk had confirmed that for
Rory—she was never where she was supposed to be.
Her office was empty, she was nowhere in the stacks,

and volume fifteen of *Stegman's Guide to the Peloponnesian War* was right on his table, where he had left it.

Funnily enough, though—or maybe it wasn't so funny, at all—Rory had no desire to peruse the *Stegman's* today. No, what he wanted to peruse today—and, more than likely, every day for the rest of his life—was Miriam Thornbury. Evidently, however, Miriam had no such desire to peruse *him*.

Fine, he thought sullenly as he left the library again. If she didn't want to see him or talk to him, he couldn't very well force her, could he? Maybe she just needed some time, he told himself. Time to make sense of what had happened between them. Time to adjust to what he hoped were some newfound feelings for him. Time to decide how they should proceed.

Soon, he promised himself. Soon she would come around. Surely she would. He only hoped that when she did she would still want Rory Monahan. Because he was beginning to suspect that there would never come a time when Rory Monahan wouldn't be wanting her.

By Saturday night Rory still hadn't seen hide nor hair of Miriam, much to his discontent. And he couldn't remember agreeing to attend the local Kiwanis Club's fund-raiser at Tony Palermo's Stardust Ballroom with his brother Connor, either. But Connor had assured him most adamantly that afternoon that Rory had, indeed, agreed to go, if for no other reason than to help Connor further his romantic pursuit of one Miss Erica Heywood.

Though, as Rory stood now at the fringe of the crowded dance floor, eyeing the swirling, twirling, gaily dressed dancers with much wariness, he couldn't imagine how he might be helpful in Connor's romantic pursuit. In fact, at the moment Rory couldn't even remember who Miss Erica Heywood was or why Connor was romantically pursuing her in the first place.

Well, he'd formed one or two *ideas* why Connor was pursuing her…especially after Rory had received his first glimpse of Miss Erica Heywood shortly after entering Tony Palermo's Stardust Ballroom earlier that evening. Because Miss Erica Heywood was… Well, she was quite stunning, actually, Rory had thought when he'd seen her. If one went for statuesque redheads with full breasts and hips, that was. And, he recalled, that was generally the type of woman that Connor went for.

Somehow, though, Miss Erica Heywood wasn't what Rory himself considered an ideal woman. No, to his way of thinking, the ideal woman wasn't quite so showy. In fact, to his way of thinking, the ideal woman wasn't statuesque or redheaded or even full in breast and hip. No, to his way of thinking, the ideal woman had dark-ish-blond hair and storm-gray eyes and a slender build and a mouth that just begged to be nibbled and a goddess outfit that was cut down to and up to *there,* and—

Oh, not again, he thought. Honestly, for an educated man he was certainly having some flights of fancy lately. Then again, seeing as how he was able to ponder little other than Miriam, he supposed he should be happy he could think at all. Because thoughts of Miriam only bewitched, bothered and bewildered him. Mostly because he still had no idea what was going on between them or what the future held in that regard— if anything at all.

In spite of the notes he'd left at both her apartment and the library, she hadn't contacted him once. And although he'd made another foray to the library in an effort to find her, she had eluded him again. He was beginning to think she really did want nothing to do with him. And that was the most heinous thought of all.

So he quickly stopped thinking and brought himself back to the matter at hand…and promptly realized that he couldn't remember, exactly, just what the matter at hand was. Something to do with dancing, obviously, considering his current location was Tony Palermo's Stardust Ballroom. But what precisely to do with dancing, Rory couldn't remember.

Now, the *history* of Tony Palermo's Stardust Ballroom, Rory knew quite well. It had been a Marigold fixture since 1937, and, from all accounts, had changed not one iota in the last six-plus decades. It was even still owned by Tony Palermo, though the current Tony Palermo was a junior version of the original owner, Tony, Sr. Oh, there had been a scare in the late seventies, when it was said that Tony, Jr., intended to turn the place into a discotheque, but that, thankfully, had ended up being nothing more than a particularly nasty rumor. And with the resurgence of swing music during the nineties, Tony Palermo's Stardust Ballroom was seeing new life. There were even a couple of members of the current in-house band who were the offspring of members from the original swing ensemble who had performed there in the thirties and forties.

And although Rory also knew all about how the local Kiwanis Club held their annual ballroom dancing fundraiser here at Tony Palermo's every summer and how, each year, virtually the entire adult population of Marigold turned out for it, this was, surprisingly, Rory's first encounter with the event. Because until tonight it had never once occurred to him to attend.

It wasn't that he had anything against fund-raisers or swing music or ballrooms—or the local Kiwanis, for that matter. He just usually forgot that the event took place. He'd only remembered it this year because Connor had shown up at his front door just as Rory was sitting down to dinner and had reminded him of the promise Rory still couldn't recall making.

But even that wasn't the real reason Rory had come. No, Rory had come because *everyone* in Marigold generally turned out for this event. Including, he hoped, Miriam Thornbury.

At any rate, the two brothers were here now, and Rory was dressed in his very best navy-blue suit again, along with his very best tie—an inoffensive burgundy silk he couldn't recall purchasing himself—and his very best shoes—black tasseled loafers of Italian design, though he couldn't recall the precise manufacturer without removing one and reading the instep.

All in all, he felt very dapper indeed, and he rather wished he'd had the foresight to bring along an escort. Which of course, he would have, had he been able to locate Miriam. She would have been infinitely more fun than his brother was. Although, technically, since Connor was the one who had dragged him here, Rory supposed that he himself was the one who was actually playing the role of escort. And since Connor had abandoned him the moment he'd seen Miss Erica Heywood standing on the other side of the room, Rory further supposed that he himself was playing the role of wallflower now.

Of course, Rory thought further still, had he had the

foresight to bring along an escort—even Miriam—it might have posed a slight problem. And not just because both of them would have been playing the role of escort, something that rather skewed the workings of the universe in a way, even if Rory wasn't sure, exactly, what way it might skew the universe.

Or something like that.

But worse than any skewing, if Rory had brought along an escort—even Miriam—that escort would, no doubt, have wanted, even expected, to dance. Tony Palermo's Stardust Ballroom was, after all, a ballroom, just as its moniker indicated. And Rory, quite simply, didn't know how to dance. Worse than that, he had two left feet. Even if he knew enough steps to fake it, he'd probably get them all mixed up and make a fool of himself.

Ergo, he thought now, it was a good thing he hadn't brought along an escort. Even if he was feeling rather like a wallflower at the moment.

He really should have brought a book with him.

No sooner had the thought formed in his head than something even better than a book—imagine that— materialized in the crowd, in the form of the local librarian. And *not* Mr. Amberson, either. But Miriam Thornbury herself.

At least, Rory *thought* it was Miriam. Though he began to wonder as the woman spun around and disappeared into the crowd again. Because she had been dancing with an elderly gentleman who was at least three times her age and a good six inches shorter than she. And judging by the way the man was hobbling about, either he was terribly infirm, or else Miriam was an even worse dancer than Rory was. And having had just a glimpse of the woman's attire, he grew even more doubtful. Because he was fairly certain he'd never seen Miriam dressed in a ball gown before. Certainly not a ball gown like that one.

Then he remembered what she had looked like the last time he'd seen her—like a silver cloud bursting with good tidings. And he remembered what she had smelled like—like a garden full of ripe purple lavender. Better still, he remembered what she had *felt* like the last time he'd seen her—soft and warm and sensuous.

He really should have tried harder to get in touch with her, he told himself again. And when he hadn't been able to locate her physically, he should at least have tried to call her. And although he *had* intended to call her—had, in fact, picked up the telephone to do so on a number of occasions over the last few days— something had always stopped him. Not just because he wanted so badly to speak to her in person. And not just because she had so clearly been trying to avoid him. But because he couldn't stop thinking about how awkwardly their last evening together had ended. And because he still honestly wasn't sure if she even *wanted* him to call her.

Still, he really should have called her, Rory told himself again.

And he really should have eaten something for dinner, too, he thought further. Connor had purchased a handful of drink tickets at the door and had stuffed half of them into Rory's pocket before abandoning him, so Rory had taken advantage by having a couple of glasses of a surprisingly nice red, thinking he would feel better if he had something on his stomach. And the wine *had* felt good on his stomach. It felt even better zinging through the rest of his body, as it was now.

Hmm...

Yes, it probably would be best to have something to eat, he told himself. By then Miriam should be finished dancing—or whatever—with the elderly gentleman who currently had her attention, and then maybe Rory could draw her aside for a little conversation.

Naturally, though, the band struck up an even livelier, even louder, number just then, assuring Rory there would be little opportunity for conversation—not as long as he and Miriam remained inside. The crowd on the dance floor shifted along with the music, and he caught another glimpse of the woman he'd been certain was Miriam. Yes, that was most definitely her, he told himself. And before the night was through, he *would* talk to her. Among other things.

Not sure when he even chose to move forward, Rory suddenly found himself approaching the place on the floor where he'd last spotted her. He halted again, though, when she disappeared, feeling profoundly disappointed by her disappearance. He spent several minutes more trying to locate her among the throngs of people on the dance floor, then finally gave up in frustration.

But when he turned to make his way back to the wall, where a wallflower should be, he found himself gazing instead at a vision—for truly, a vision was what Miriam was—in blue.

"Rory?" she said softly.

"Miriam," he replied, just as softly.

She gazed at him gravely, appearing in no way happy to see him. In spite of that, though, she took a step toward him. And when she did, a side slit in her dress parted, revealing a length of slender, creamy leg from ankle to thigh. And oh, what memories that glimpse of leg roused inside him.

Somehow he managed to pull his gaze away from her thigh and return his attention to her face. And, oh, what a face, he thought. What a lovely, splendid, beautiful face. How had he resisted her for so many months? he wondered. She was even more breathtaking than had been Miss...Miss— Oh, whatever the name of Connor's romantic pursuit was. At the moment Rory couldn't have cared less about *her*. Not when Miriam was looking like...like...like...

Well. Like a devil with a blue dress on. That was what she looked like.

And it had most definitely been Miriam whom he had seen earlier in the evening dancing—or whatever—with the elderly, either-infirm-or-in-pain gentleman. But strangely, where from a distance he had identified her fairly well, up close he scarcely recognized her.

Her dark blond hair was wound up the back of her head in an elegant twist and held in place by what appeared to be two chopsticks. Except that the chopsticks were decorated with bright blue enamel paint, something that led Rory to conclude that they were, in fact, *supposed* to be stuck there in her hair, and weren't the result of some practical joke a friend had played over dim sum earlier in the evening. Her gray eyes were shaded by a silvery-white tint, making them appear larger somehow and more compelling. Her cheekbones, which he had admired on a number of occasions, seemed more prominent tonight, thanks to the presence of a darker color that shadowed them. And her mouth...

Oh, good God, her *mouth*. That mouth that had

caused Rory *so much* preoccupation over the past six months was, once again, as plump and as glistening and as tempting as a ripe, red raspberry. And all he could do was wonder if those full, damp lips tasted as sweet and as luscious as they looked—as sweet and as luscious as he recalled them tasting only a few nights before.

He squeezed his eyes shut tight, hoping that this vision of Miriam Thornbury, this…this…this devil with a blue dress on…might disappear in a puff of lavender-scented smoke. Because although he had assured himself he could have a rational discussion with her about what had happened the last time they were together, seeing her this way now, Rory was confident that *rational* was the last thing he could hope to be, and *discussion* was the last activity in which he wanted to engage.

Alas, however, when he opened his eyes again, he saw that she was still there, still luscious, still a devil with a blue dress on. She also seemed to be standing closer to him than she had been a moment ago. And she appeared to be preparing to move closer still.

"What brings you to the fund-raiser?" she asked innocently. Innocently. In that dress. Imagine. And, just as he had suspected she would do, she took a step toward him.

"I—I—I," he stammered. Immediately, he closed his mouth again, fearful that he would ridicule himself even more than he already had, especially when she completed *another* step toward him.

"Rory?" she asked as she approached.

"I—I—I came with my brother," he managed to get out. "Connor."

She nodded, seeming relieved for some reason. "I see. I thought maybe you'd come with a date."

A date? he repeated to himself. Why on earth would he have come with a date? Why, the only date he'd had in the past two years had been with Miriam, so how could he possibly be here with anyone other than—

Then again, he was here with her now, wasn't he?

"Actually, I'm glad to see you here, Miriam, be-cause—" he began.

But before he could finish, he and Miriam were joined by a third person, another woman dressed in at-tire similar to Miriam's, except that her dress was, im-possibly, even *more* revealing than Miriam's was, and screaming-red in color to boot. Even more shocking than either of those two observations, however, was the one Rory made when he gazed at the woman's—rather overly made-up—face.

"Mayor Trent?" he asked, aghast. How could she be dressed like that? he marveled. She'd run on the Fam-ily Values platform.

She blushed at Rory's unmistakable astonishment—at least he thought she was blushing; it was hard to tell for sure under all those cosmetics—but said nothing to comment. Instead, she turned her attention to Miriam.

"I've been looking for you all night," she said in a clipped tone. "I wanted to apologize for the dress."

"Oh, but it looks lovely on you, Ms. Trent," Miriam assured the other woman, sounding utterly sincere.

And although Rory was inclined to agree that Isabel Trent did indeed look more fetching than usual, *lovely* wasn't the adjective that came to mind when he con-sidered the mayor's red, revealing dress again. No, in keeping with the rock 'n' roll metaphors—which Rory normally wouldn't do, except that Miriam *was* such a devil with a blue dress on—Isabel Trent, he supposed, rather resembled a hunka hunka burnin' love. Yes, that analogy, he thought, would be very appropriate.

"No, I'm apologizing for *your* dress," Mayor Trent said, her voice a fair hiss, even with the music blaring. "There can be no apologizing for mine," she added, clearly distressed.

Why on earth she would be apologizing for Miriam's dress, though, Rory couldn't imagine. There was absolutely no need to apologize for something so goddesslike, after all. Well, goddesslike save the glittering sapphire sequins and the sweep of marabou that trimmed the bottom.

Miriam, however, seemed to share the Mayor's anguish, however, because she, too, glanced down at her garment rather apologetically. "Yes, well, Miss Chacha's idea of a ball gown and my own idea of a ball gown were a tad at odds, but…" She shrugged philosophically, a gesture, Rory couldn't help noting, that did wonderful things to her dress. "She insisted this was the best she could do."

Mayor Trent nodded. "Yes, well, her idea of appropriate attire and my idea of appropriate attire were likewise at odds. But it's too late to do anything about it now. I just wish I hadn't taken her up on her offer to do my makeup, as well." She sighed heavily as she considered Miriam's face. "I see she did yours, too."

"I'm afraid so, yes," said Miriam.

Honestly, Rory thought, he couldn't imagine what the two women were objecting to. Although he'd never really been the kind of man who liked heavily made-up women, he had to admit that there was something rather, oh…appealing…about how Miriam and the mayor looked. Why, they rather resembled the models on that popular women's magazine, he thought further. What was the name of it again? Something about city living, wasn't it? *Urbanite? Metropolis? Municipality?* Something like that. It would come to him eventually.

"At any rate, when I saw you out there dancing and realized what you had on, I felt I should apologize to you," the mayor was telling Miriam again, "since this was my idea in the first place. If I'd had any idea Miss Chacha would be dressing us up as...as...as..." She made a sour face. "Well, I'd rather not say what I feel as if I'm dressed as right now," she finally concluded. "But had I known I'd end up this way..."

"Just remember that it's for the scholarship fund," Miriam told her. "It's for the children, Ms. Trent."

The mayor didn't look much appeased by the reminder, Rory noted. But she did still look rather fetching.

Suddenly, however, when something over Rory's shoulder caught her attention, her expression changed to one of utter panic. "Omigosh," Ms. Trent said, ducking quickly behind him. "No one told me Cullen Monahan was going to be here tonight."

"Cullen?" Rory echoed.

He glanced at the entrance and, sure enough, saw that his younger brother, Connor's twin, had indeed arrived. But why that should make Isabel Trent panic, Rory had no idea. After all, Cullen worked for the mayor. He was, in essence, her right-hand man. Why would she be concerned to find him here at the fundraiser? Especially since, in his capacity as a public servant, Cullen *always* attended functions such as these.

"I thought he was going to be out of town," the mayor

said, still hiding behind Rory. "If Cullen asks, tell him you haven't seen me."

Rory gaped in disbelief. A woman who'd been voted into office on the Family Values platform, encouraging her constituents to tell a falsehood? Dishonesty in a politician? Now *that* was a shocking development.

"Ms. Trent, I'm afraid I can't do—" Rory began.

But before he could say another word, Isabel Trent spun on her heels and fled, disappearing onto the crowded dance floor like so much stray marabou. And all Rory could do was shake his head in wonder at what could possibly be going on with the mayor and his brother.

The music kicked up again, another lively tune, just as Cullen joined them and might potentially offer an explanation. He, too, was wearing his best suit, Rory noted. Plus, his black hair was combed expertly—perhaps even recently cut—and his blue eyes reflected something akin to…anticipation? How interesting.

Really, Rory thought, Cullen looked much better than he usually did. As if he were trying to impress someone. In a word: Hmmm…

Naturally, after greeting them with "Hey, Rory. Hi, Miss Thornbury," the first question out of Cullen's mouth was, "Have either of you seen the mayor? I overheard her saying she was going to be here tonight. And I really need to talk to her about something."

Rory opened his mouth to respond, even got so far as to say, "Actually, she just…" when Miriam circled firm fingers around his wrist and began to tug him away.

"Hello, Mr. Monahan," she said to Cullen as she dragged Rory off. "I'm sorry, but we can't chat right now. Rory promised me this dance, and I intend to collect."

Dance? Rory repeated to himself. *Dance?* With her? In that dress? She must be out of her mind.

"But…" he began.

And again, he was forced to halt midsentence, because Miriam began to jerk on his arm more forcefully, propelling him out toward the dance floor, whether he liked it or not. And Rory couldn't say another word, because he had to pay very close attention to where he was going, otherwise he would have gone barreling right into her, sending them both toppling to the floor. Which, upon further reflection, he decided, might not be such a bad thing.

Then again, he asked himself, why topple to the floor in a place where the two of them would be surrounded by onlookers, not to mention an entire swing band on the stage? No, no, no, he told himself. *Much* better to topple later, when the two of them were alone, and the swing band was on the stereo.

Fortunately for Rory—where the dancing part was concerned, at any rate—there were far too many people on the floor for him and Miriam to have any room to move about, so his horrific lack of knowledge, dance-wise, would no doubt be left undiscovered. *Un*fortunately for Rory, however—where *other* parts were concerned, at any rate—there were far too many people on the floor for him and Miriam to have any room to move about, so the moment they came to a stop near the center of the crowd, their two bodies were immediately squashed together. Close together. And as the squashing occurred, inevitably he recalled how the two of them had been squashed the last time they'd been together.

Oh, yes. It was all coming back to him now.

And suddenly the last thing Rory wanted to do was dance. So he told his partner, a little breathlessly, he couldn't help noting, "Really, Miriam, I'm not much of a dancer."

To his surprise she replied, just as breathlessly, he couldn't help noting, "Oh. Good."

He arched his eyebrows in surprise. "Why is that good? I thought you wanted to dance."

She shook her head. "Oh, no," she told him. "In fact, *dancing* is the last thing I want to do with you."

Chapter 10

Oh, dear, Miriam thought as soon as she uttered the statement. She probably should have phrased her last remark a little differently. Because, judging by the expression of utter shock etched on Rory's face, there was a good chance he might have mistaken her intent.

Oh, she *knew* she should have just stayed away from him tonight, she told herself. But when she'd left the dance floor after ending her wrestling match with ninety-five-year-old Leonard Federman, whose hands, at least, hadn't quite made it out of puberty, and had seen Rory standing at the edge of the crowd, she hadn't been able to resist him. She'd felt as if someone had pulled taut an invisible thread that was attached to her, winding it tighter and tighter, pulling her closer and closer, until she stood within a few feet of Rory. And once she was that close to him, well… She could no more have pulled herself away than she could have pushed the moon out of the Earth's orbit.

She should have known it would be futile to try to keep avoiding him. Marigold was a small town. They were bound to run into each other sooner or later. Especially since her place of employment was, in effect, his home away from home. Still, she hadn't known what to say or how to act around him. The notes he'd left her had been so casual, so impersonal. And he hadn't once tried to call her on the phone. Although he'd made clear his desire to talk to her, to see her, she had feared he would only tell her that what had happened between the two of them had been a mistake, one he couldn't risk repeating.

He had, after all, regretted making love to her immediately after it had happened. Why would he want to repeat it?

She wished she hadn't pulled him onto the dance floor, because being this close to him again was a such a sweet torture. But she'd felt it was essential to get him away from Cullen, because Rory had been about to tell his brother exactly where Isabel Trent was.

And there was no way Miriam was going to let him do that, because Isabel Trent had obviously been uncomfortable with the idea of Cullen seeing her dressed the way she was—not that Miriam could blame the other woman for a moment, because Miriam wasn't any too comfortable herself being dressed like a…like a… Well. Like a devil with a blue dress on. Even if *Metropolitan* magazine assured her that men went for such a thing, because Miriam had vowed days ago that she would never, ever, be a temptress—inner *or* outer—

again. The sooner she could remove this ridiculous get-up, the better.

At any rate, in spite of her frequent disagreements with the mayor, Miriam didn't want to see Isabel Trent put on the spot with Cullen Monahan the way Rory had been about to put her on the spot. Not when Isabel was a kindred spirit. Not when Isabel was clearly suffering from the same affliction Miriam herself was suffering from these days.

Because Miriam had seen the look on the mayor's face when Cullen Monahan had entered the Stardust Ballroom. And it had been a look with which Miriam was very well acquainted—after all, it was the same look she saw on her own face every time she glanced in the mirror. Because Isabel's expression had been the expression of a woman who wanted a man—a special man. A special man who didn't want her in return.

Oh, my, Miriam thought. Mayor Trent had a major thing for the man who was her former campaign manager and current assistant—Cullen Monahan. And Cullen Monahan evidently didn't have a clue.

Goodness, she thought further. What was wrong with the Monahan men, that they couldn't see the most obvious things in the world? Really, for being so popular and so prominent in the community, the Monahan boys had a lot to learn about life. And love. And women.

In spite of having just told Rory that she didn't want to dance with him, Miriam did nothing to stop the swaying of their bodies. Not just because she was too preoccupied by thoughts of other things, but because, thanks to the overpopulation of the dance floor, she had no choice but to keep moving. People were crowded around them, and everyone seemed to be moving in perfect time with the music.

Well, *most* of the people were moving in perfect time, she thought when someone bumped into her from behind, thrusting her forward, more resolutely into Rory's embrace. She tried her best to extricate herself from the awkward situation, then realized that Rory was doing absolutely nothing to help her disengage. For a man who had so recently made clear his reluctance to embrace any woman—in more than a physical sense, anyway— it was an interesting response. Then again, she thought, the embrace *was* awfully physical...

Then again...again she thought further, perhaps Rory hadn't pushed her away simply because there was no place to push her. Because in spite of the physicality of their current clinch, she still remembered, too well, how utterly he had assured the police officer the other night that Miriam was neither his wife nor his girlfriend, thereby ensuring that he didn't entertain any thoughts— or any enthusiasm—of having her assume either role.

This in spite of the fact that Miriam had assigned the role of boyfriend—and even husband—a time or two to Rory, if only in her dreams. This in spite of the fact that, despite his assurances to the police officer, Rory had done nothing that night to halt the passion that had erupted suddenly between the two of them. This in spite of the fact that he had, on the contrary, pulled Miriam closer and kissed her just as deeply as she had kissed him, something that rather negated the whole premise of wanting neither a girlfriend nor a wife, she thought.

Or maybe it didn't negate that, she further pondered. Maybe it only served to illustrate what Rory *did* want in his life—a sex partner.

Men had physical needs, after all, Miriam reminded herself. Then again, women had physical needs, too, something to which she herself could attest. *Oh, my,* could she attest to that. And maybe that was all that had been on Rory's mind that night when he had denounced the girlfriend/wife idea—his physical needs and perhaps even her own. That was why he had so eagerly embraced her physically while mentally and emotionally repelling the idea of her involvement with him in any other capacity. He had wanted to assuage a physical need. And he may have thought that was all she wanted, too.

And perhaps that was exactly what was on his mind tonight, as well—their physical needs. Perhaps that was why he was embracing her physically again right now. After all, she was dressed as such a temptress. And if he *was* only thinking about their physical needs at the moment, then there was a very good chance he would once again repel her mentally and emotionally later.

Then again, Miriam's physical needs *had* been on her mind that night, too. And they were on her mind tonight, as well. *Oh, my,* were they on her mind tonight, she thought as she splayed her hands open over Rory's chest and felt the firm expanse of muscle beneath. And now that she thought more about it, seeing to one's physical needs, even if it meant neglecting one's emotional needs, might not necessarily be such a terrible thing....

She sighed heavily her frustration, and she reminded herself of what she had been telling herself for the past few days—that she should get over Rory Monahan and put him out of her mind and move on to live her life. Unfortunately for her, though, her mind—and, evidently, several other parts of her body—simply refused to give him up. Probably because the thought of living her life didn't seem like much fun without Rory in it.

"Um, at the risk of pestering you, Miriam…" Rory began, his voice sounding soft in spite of the fact that he had raised it to compensate for the blaring music.

"Oh, by all means, feel free to pester me," she told him. "In fact, pester away. Please."

Good heavens, Miriam, she told herself, *don't beg.*

She took a moment to berate herself for her weakness where Rory Monahan was concerned. Honestly, she thought. Had she no pride left at all?

Well, actually, Miriam, if you must *know…*

Then again, it did feel so good to be back in his arms, even if only temporarily. There was nothing wrong with enjoying this momentary reunion, was there? She wouldn't let things go too far. Certainly not as far as they had gone the other night. No matter how badly she might want them to.

When she realized he still hadn't pestered her, she said, "If there's something you want to know, Rory, do please ask. At the risk of pestering me…?" she echoed, encouraging him to finish.

He hesitated a moment, gazing at her face as if he might gauge the answer to his question there, without having to ask it aloud. Finally, though, "If you don't want to dance with me," he told her, "then…why are you dancing with me?"

"Oh, that," she said.

"Yes, that," he concurred.

"That's not pestering," she told him, hedging.

"No?"

"Of course not. It's a perfectly good question."

He waited for her to respond to it, and when she only

remained silent—mainly because she couldn't come up with a perfectly good answer to go along with his perfectly good question—he said, "Then why don't you answer it?"

"Answer what?" she asked, still stalling. Stalling lamely, too, she couldn't help thinking.

He inhaled a deep breath and released it slowly, his eyes never leaving hers. "Why are we dancing?" he asked succinctly.

"Um, because the music is so nice?" she replied.

He nodded, but she didn't think he bought her phony sincerity.

"Yes, well, just so you know," he continued, "I can't dance to save my life. You're risking very serious injury to your feet if you continue."

"I think you're doing very well," she told him. With real sincerity this time, too.

"Yes, well," he said again, "when the people are packed together like sardines, it isn't hard to keep time with the music. It's when the music ends and the people begin to separate that things will become a bit troublesome."

Oh, truer words were never spoken, Miriam thought.

But instead of ending, the music grew more raucous, even as Rory spoke his observation aloud. And when it did this time, someone bumped into him from behind, launching his body forward into Miriam's with enough force to make her stumble backward. Where before Rory had settled his hands loosely on her hips, now he circled an arm around her waist and placed a hand at the small of her back to steady her. Normally this would have been a perfectly legitimate reaction, a perfectly innocent touch.

But Miriam wasn't dressed normally, was she? No, she was wearing a Lola Chacha original, which meant that her gown—in addition to boasting sequins and marabou and a side slit that could potentially be considered criminal—dipped as low, both in front and in back, as it possibly could without risk of having the wearer arrested. As long as the lights were low enough that the police couldn't see her, anyway.

Which meant that Rory's hand, when it landed on the small of her back, landed not on her gown, but on *the small of her back*. The *naked* small of her back. And having even that slight skin-to-skin contact with him sent Miriam's temperature skyrocketing.

Automatically her own hold on him—she had settled her hands innocently on his chest—contracted, something that caused her fingers to curve intimately, even possessively, into his firm flesh. Before she could right herself or him—not that she necessarily *wanted* to right herself or him, really, not with his hand on her naked back that way—the person who had jostled Rory from behind jostled him again. This time, when his body was shoved forward, Miriam pushed her hands higher, to his shoulders, which she then found herself gripping for dear life.

She told herself her reaction was simply a result of having responded instinctively, unmindful of the fact that there was little chance she would fall, thanks to the density of the crowd surrounding them. It *hadn't* been because she just wanted to get a better hold of Rory. It *hadn't* been because she wanted to take advantage of even this small moment to touch him one last time.

Really. That hadn't been the reason. She'd just over-reacted a bit, that was all.

Rory's reaction, though, seemed to come from something other than a simple instinctive response. Because there was something very deliberate, not to mention very arousing, about the way he had placed one hand on the—quite naked—small of her back and had cupped the other hand over her—equally naked—shoulder blade.

Oh, yes, his movements were very deliberate, Miriam thought as both of those hands on her back then began to dip lower—considerably lower than was actually necessary for keeping her righted. And she knew that those hands *were* dipping lower, not just because she felt the soft glide of his fingertips along the heated, sensitized flesh of her back, but also because she felt his fingertips come to a halt curving over the upper swells of her derriere.

"I'm okay, Rory," she told him a little breathlessly. "You don't have to…to…to…"

"To what?" he asked. And although his voice was all innocence and curiosity, the expression on his face was anything but.

Miriam told herself his cheeks were only flushed because he was embarrassed to have been discovered touching her the way he was touching her—even though he did nothing to remove his hands. And she told herself his lips were only parted that way because the air was close, and it was hard to breathe—even though he didn't seem to be lacking for breath. And she told herself his eyes were only darkening and fairly glazing over because the throng of people surrounding them created a heat that was nearly overwhelming—even though the heat enveloping them didn't seem to be generated by a throng of people at all.

And she told herself that her own response to him— the flush she felt warming her own cheeks, the shallowness of her own breathing, the heat coursing through her own body—was simply a result of the crowd, too.

Unfortunately she didn't come close to believing any of the things she told herself.

The music slowed then, and segued into something by Gershwin, though Miriam was too befuddled at the moment to identify just what the song was. Surprisingly, a number of people left the dance floor then, presumably because they needed more of a rest than a simple slow tune. She waited for Rory to release her and lead her off the floor, as well, but he did neither. Instead he pulled her closer—something she would have sworn was impossible to do—and tucked her head beneath his chin and circled her waist loosely with both arms.

Immediately she was surrounded by the scent of him, a mixture of Old Spice, damp cotton and hot man. The combination was intoxicating, narcotic. And all Miriam could do was relax against him, feeling as if it were the most natural place on the earth for her to be. Their torsos bumped together, their legs brushed against each other, and she didn't think she'd ever experienced a more exquisite sensation than feeling as if she were tangled up with Rory Monahan.

Unable to help herself, but calling herself a fool just the same, she looped one arm around his neck, wove the fingers of the other through his hair and let him guide her body back and forth, back and forth, back… and…forth…

And then she heard him say, very softly, "We need to talk, you and I."

The lights had gone low by now, canopying the entire room with darkness, and something about that must have emboldened Rory. Because the hands that he had linked around her waist suddenly began to wander, skimming lightly over her bare flesh again. His fingers drifted up her spine, then back down. Then they ventured up again, over her rib cage this time, and down the other side once more. And with every soft skim of his fingertips over her back, Miriam's heart rate quickened, her uncertainties multiplied and her confusion compounded.

"Talk?" she echoed. "A-a-about what?"

He hesitated only a moment before saying, "Us."

"Oh."

But instead of launching into whatever he wanted to say about *us,* Rory told her, "This is a, um, a, uh…a rather amazing gown." His voice was a mere murmur near her ear. "What little there is of it, I mean."

"Ah. Yes. Well. It isn't mine," Miriam told him, a delicious shiver of excitement spiraling through her at the way he voiced the comment, and the way his fingers began to make slow spirals over her sensitive skin. "Normally I never… I mean, I'm not usually so… This isn't the sort of thing I customarily…" But she gave up trying to explain, when she was unable to finish any of the anxious thoughts crowding into her brain.

"No, neither do I," Rory told her, agreeing with her all the same.

Somehow he had made sense of her mental meanderings, Miriam realized. And for some reason that didn't surprise her at all.

"I just, um…" she began again. "I mean, I was trying to… It was all because of…"

"Yes, I understand completely," he told her.

And again somehow she knew that he did.

"But you wear it well, Miriam," he said, his voice a velvet caress against her ear, her neck, her throat. "Because you look…" He inhaled deeply, then released the breath slowly, as if he wanted to illustrate the rest of his statement, which happened to be, "You look… breathtaking. In fact," he added further, his voice still sounding a little uneven, "you smell breathtaking. And you *feel* breathtaking." Once again, he sighed deeply. "You *are* breathtaking," he told her. "I don't know why I didn't realize that a long time ago."

Well, obviously, Miriam thought morosely, it was because she hadn't, until recently, been a devil with a blue dress on. An Outer Temptress, so to speak. That was why Rory was responding to her now when he hadn't noticed her before. Not for any other reason than that.

She realized then the folly of her situation—Rory would never want her for who she *really* was—and tried to pull away. But the hand that had returned to the small of her back dipped lower again, to the upper swell of her bottom, pulling her into the cradle of his pelvis. She bit back a groan when she felt how hard and ready he was for her. Or, at least how hard and ready he was for her Inner Temptress.

"We need to talk," he said again. "About us."

She shook her head. "There is no us."

She couldn't be sure in the darkness, but she thought his expression changed then, from one of hopefulness to one of discouragement. "What do you mean?" he asked. "Of course there's an us. There's been an us ever since we…"

She shook her head again, more vehemently this time. "No, there's no us," she insisted. "There's Rory

Monahan, and there's my Inner Temptress. Miriam Thornbury doesn't fit into the picture at all."

Now his expression changed again, to one of total confusion. "Inner Temptress?" he echoed. "What are you talking about? Not that I don't find you tempting," he quickly assured her, sweeping his hands slowly over her bare back again.

And all she could think was, *Oh, Rory.*

"It isn't *me* you find tempting," she told him. "It's my Inner Temptress."

He smiled, albeit in a puzzled way. "I still don't understand. If there's someone inside of you who's tempting me, Miriam, then it's *you* tempting me."

As much as she wished she could believe that, Miriam shook her head. "No," she told him. "It isn't me tempting you. It's a fictional creation of *Metropolitan* magazine."

"Now I'm hopelessly confused," he said. "What would a magazine have to do with my feelings for you?"

"It's a long story." She sighed heavily and avoided his gaze. "But when I removed all those issues of *Metropolitan* magazine from the library that Mayor Trent wanted removed, I took them home and I started reading them, and there were a few articles that—" And then the gist of his question struck her, and Miriam narrowed her eyes at him. "You have feelings for me?" she asked.

He chuckled. "Well, of course I have feelings for you. Miriam," he said. "I love you."

She gaped at him for a moment, feeling, for one scant second, like the happiest woman on the face of the Earth. Then suddenly she sobered. Because she realized what Rory said didn't apply to her. "No, you don't love me," she told him softly. "You love my Inner Temptress."

He uttered a sound that very much resembled a growl of frustration. "Miriam," he said. "What. Are. You. Talking. About."

As quickly as she could, she tried to explain. She revealed to Rory the crush she had had on him for six months, then described how the magazine articles led her to create what she'd thought was a foolproof plan to lure him and tempt him and make him her own. She told him of her delight that the venture had been such a success, until she realized that he had fallen, not for the person she really was, but for the fictional temptress she had fashioned from a series of magazine articles. She reiterated that he couldn't possibly be in love with Miriam Thornbury the librarian. Because he had fallen in love with Miriam Thornbury the temptress instead.

"So you see," she said, "if you're in love, it's not with me. It's with a…with a…a…" She, too, uttered a dissatisfied snarl. "A devil with a blue dress on," she fairly spat. "It isn't with the woman who's fallen in love with you."

For one long moment Rory only gazed at her in silence, his expression now offering her not a clue as to what he might be feeling or thinking. Then, very softly, he began to laugh. A laugh of utter delight, of total freedom, of uninhibited joy. And when he did, Miriam thought he looked…he looked…

Well. He looked breathtaking. She couldn't help but sigh as she watched him.

And she also couldn't help asking, "What's so funny?"

"You," he said as he pulled her closer. "My sweet

Miriam. My erudite librarian. My keen student. My ardent paramour. My bewitching temptress. For you are all of those things, my darling. And then some."

At his softly uttered words, Miriam began to feel a bit breathless again. And a bit dizzy. And a bit contemplative. And then she began to feel very, *very* happy. Because suddenly she began to see that Rory was right. She didn't have to be just one thing. She wasn't just Miriam the librarian. And she wasn't just Miriam the temptress, either. She was many things to many people. Many things to Rory. Just as he was many things to her. And always would be.

All along Miriam had told herself she had to take responsibility for her Inner Temptress's behavior, because her Inner Temptress, for all her alien qualities, was a product of Miriam herself. So if she was so insistent she be responsible for the little vixen's behavior, then why couldn't she reap the little minx's rewards, too?

Rory *must* love all of her, Miriam told herself. No matter who or what she was, because that was the nature of love. Just as she loved all of him, no matter who or what *he* was.

Oh, my, she thought. It was all so clear to her now. Honestly. For an educated woman—not to mention a successful temptress—Miriam truly did have a lot to learn. And she couldn't wait to have Rory teach her. Mostly because she had one or two lessons for him, as well.

Rory must have sensed her train of thoughts, because he lowered his head to hers, pressing his forehead gently against her own. "So you can see that you are many things to me, Miriam," he said, reiterating his earlier statement. "And I can only hope that there's one more thing you'll become."

"What's that?" she asked, still feeling breathless and dizzy and contemplative and happy.

"My loving wife," he told her. "Will you be that, too?"

"Oh, *Rory...*"

Instead of finishing her answer verbally, Miriam thrust herself up on tiptoe and pressed her mouth to his. Again and again she kissed him, more deeply and possessively with every passing second. Rory responded with much enthusiasm, roping his arms around her waist now and slanting his head to the side to facilitate their embrace.

Vaguely Miriam heard the sound of music and of laughter and of applause. And when she pulled away, she found that the entire population of the Stardust Ballroom—nay, the entire population of Marigold, Indiana—were witness to what was, quite possibly, the most shameless public display of affection ever perpetrated in town. Even Mayor Trent, Miriam couldn't help but notice, was smiling and clapping. Miriam smiled, too. Because right behind the mayor was Cullen Monahan, looking quite flummoxed.

Maybe there was hope for the Monahan clan yet, Miriam thought with a grin.

Then, after bestowing another quick kiss on Rory's lips, she moved her mouth to his ear and whispered, "Let's get out of here."

He nodded eagerly. "I have my car."

She smiled. "Oh, good. I hope you parked it in a secluded area."

Amazingly, not only did Miriam and Rory make it to his car without succumbing to their passion—well, without succumbing *too* much to their passion—but they also made it back to Rory's apartment before succumbing to their passion. Well, no more than some soul-deep kissing at a stoplight. And copping a few feels at a stop sign. And then, once, pulling over to the side of the road in a delirious effort to remove Miriam's panties, only to reconsider and finally—*finally*—make their way to Rory's place.

But once they were at Rory's place all bets were off. And all clothes were off, too, in no time flat. Before Miriam realized what was happening, the two of them were standing completely naked in Rory's bedroom, and he freed her hair and filled his hands with it. Not that it had taken any more than a couple of quick tugs on the chopsticks in her hair—or on the gown she was almost wearing—for Miriam to find herself in that state, though Rory's clothing had presented a bit of a challenge because he'd had on considerably more than she. Not to mention he wouldn't quit kissing her and tasting her the whole time she was trying to undress him.

And even when she'd finished undressing him, he still kept on kissing her and tasting her—not that she minded at all, because she was doing some kissing and tasting of her own by then and remembering all over again just how delicious Rory Monahan was.

And then she stopped remembering anything, because he slowly began to walk her toward his bed, his hands skimming lightly over every exposed inch of her. And of course it went without saying that every inch of her was indeed exposed. Little by little he urged her backward, onto the mattress, then followed her down and covered her body with his.

Oh, this was *so* much better than a car, Miriam

thought as he stretched out alongside and atop her. Because now Rory's naked skin was pressed against her own naked skin, from shoulder to toe, and there was nothing—absolutely *nothing*—to inhibit them. Not that either of them seemed to feel particularly inhibited at the moment. On the contrary...

Miriam wound her fingers in Rory's hair as he dragged a line of openmouthed kisses along her neck, her throat, her shoulder, her collarbone. And as she tightened those fingers, gasping, he ducked his head lower, drawing her erect nipple into his mouth to suck hard on her tender flesh. But even that didn't seem to be his final destination, because he moved his kisses lower again, to the underside of her breast, along her rib cage, over her flat belly, into her navel. And then lower still, to her hips, her pelvis, the sensitive insides of her thighs.

So senseless was she with wanting him by the time he began to move his head upward again that Miriam didn't realize his final destination until she felt his mouth upon that most sensitive part of herself. She gasped again at the initial contact, then expelled her breath in a rush of exhilaration and sucked it in again, harder this time. Oh, no one had ever— Oh, she'd never felt anything like— Oh, it was simply too— Oh—

Oh!

Again and again Rory tasted her, teased her, taunted her, until it seemed as if he would never satisfy his hunger for her. Finally, he gripped her hips hard in each hand and lifted her to his mouth, for one final, furious onslaught that very nearly shattered her. Then, as if he couldn't tolerate their separation any longer than she, he climbed back up onto the mattress beside her.

Without a further word he propped his upper body on his elbows, folding one on each side of her head. Then he settled himself between her legs and pushed himself toward her, his hard shaft coming to rest between the damp folds of her flesh without penetrating her. Miriam, barely coherent now, looped her arms around his neck, and met his gaze intently.

"Now," she told him. "Make love to me now."

His breathing was ragged, and his eyes were dark with wanting. But he told her, "I don't have anything. Any protection, I mean. In spite of wanting to talk to you and tell you how I felt tonight, I honestly hadn't anticipated this happening again yet."

"And I'm not a *Metro* Girl anymore," Miriam told him. "Not primarily. So I don't have a condom in my purse this time. Not that I had any more, anyway. Just the one."

In spite of his overwrought state, he chuckled. "Someone sold you one condom?" he asked.

She shook her head. "It was a party favor."

He arched his eyebrows in surprise. "You went to a party where they passed out condoms?" He twisted a stray lock of her hair around his finger. "My, but you are a temptress, aren't you?"

"Actually, it was a bridal shower," she told him.

This time he gaped at her. "Promise me, Miriam, that at your bridal shower, you'll only pass out petit fours or some such thing."

She smiled. "I'm not sure what we'll be passing out at my bridal shower. Depends on who's in charge that day. Whether it's Miriam Librarian or Miriam Temptress or Miriam Hostess, for that matter."

"Right now, at this moment," he said, "I'm hoping you're Miriam Overcome-with-Desire."

"Oh, yes," she assured him, cupping his warm jaw in her hand. "I am that."

"But without a condom…"

"I might become Miriam Mommy," she finished for him.

"Yes," he told her, resigned.

"And you might become Rory Daddy," she added.

"Yes."

"And would that be so terrible?" she asked him.

He shook his head. "No. Not at all."

"Then maybe we should just hope for the best," she suggested.

He grinned. "Maybe we should."

And as Rory entered her, slowly, deeply, thoroughly, Miriam thought that hoping for the best certainly brought the best. Because there was no other word to describe what Rory was.

She closed her eyes as he penetrated her more deeply now, burying himself inside her as far as he would go. For a moment they only lay there, motionless, allowing their bodies to become reacquainted. Then Rory withdrew some, with an exquisite slowness and carefulness that made Miriam writhe with wanting him. Instinctively she shot her hips upward, to reclaim him, and he responded by thrusting himself down toward her again.

This time, there was no retreating, no withdrawing, only a steady plundering of her body with his. She wrapped her legs snugly around his waist, her arms around his shoulders, claiming him more completely, until the rhythm of their coupling generated an incandescent reaction. And somewhere amid the conflagration, Miriam and Rory melted into each other, physically, emotionally, intellectually, spiritually. And as, little by little, they quieted and calmed, she knew they would never, ever part.

For long moments they only lay entwined, their bodies and hearts and souls and minds still joined. Then, very softly Rory said, "As much as I look forward to making love to you in the proper surroundings for all time to come, I think I'll always look back on that first time in my car with very fond memories."

Miriam pushed her hair back from her forehead and gazed intently into Rory's eyes. Then she smiled. "Me, too. As awkward as it was at the time, it was also...unforgettable."

He nodded. "One of these days we'll have to do it again, just for old-time's sake. But we'll use the back seat instead, for logistical reasons."

"And one of these days," she added, "we'll have to make love on one of the tables in the reference section at the library, too." She laughed at his scandalized expression, then added, "And I know just which table to use, too, *Stegman's* or no."

"Why, Miriam," Rory said mischievously. "You've been holding out on me."

"Never again," she assured him. "From now on, no matter what's on my mind—and no matter which one of me is thinking it—you'll be the first to know. And guess what I'm thinking about right now."

He smiled wickedly. "I'm not sure exactly what—yet—you're thinking about, but I'll wager good money I know which one of you is thinking it." He maneuvered their bodies so that they had switched positions, with Miriam lying atop him now. Then he looped an arm around her neck and pulled her down to him for another kiss. "Come here, you little temptress you...."

Epilogue

There was no better time for a wedding, Rory thought, than springtime. Not that he and Miriam intended to wait that long to get married—heavens, no. But having watched his brother Connor plan his springtime nuptials for the last several weeks, Rory was more certain than ever that he and his wife-to-be had made the right decision to marry *now*. Before there was time to argue over whether the bridesmaids would wear pink or peach, before there was time to worry about whether to serve chicken or beef at the reception, before there was time to be concerned if the ushers should wear black or charcoal-gray.

Before Miriam Thornbury got away.

Not that Rory feared she would leave him, but he was an intelligent man, after all, and he knew better than to leave anything to chance. Besides, he was so preoccupied by thoughts of marrying Miriam these days that he scarcely ever got any work done. Not that he minded. Oddly enough, having his head filled with thoughts of her was infinitely more satisfying than thoughts of…

Oh, whatever those things were that his head used to be filled with. He could barely remember now.

In spite of November's arrival, the weather was surprisingly mild, one of those gifts of a day that the Midwest sometimes received from the weather gods before winter moved in for the duration. Therefore, the garden behind the Marigold Free Public Library was the perfect place to be wed. He and Miriam had planned to hold the ceremony indoors, amid the books and authors they both loved so well, but being outside now, surrounded by the *people* they loved instead, made the ceremony all the more wonderful.

And so many people had come: His sister, Tess, rosy and round with child, along with her husband, Will. His brother Sean and Sean's fiancée, Autumn. Connor and his intended. And of course Cullen was there, too, staying very close to the mayor, who, Rory and Miriam both had been surprised to find, had RSVPed in the affirmative after the wedding invitations went out.

Everyone seemed to be coupling up, Rory thought. His sister, Tess, had started a summer-long tradition for the Monahans when she and Will had become an item last June. Because Sean and Autumn had begun dating shortly after that. Then Rory and Miriam had hooked up. Connor hadn't been long after them, and if Cullen's reaction to the mayor was any indication, then, by Christmas, he, too, would be among the recently engaged or married.

It was just too bad that Rory's oldest brother, Finn,

showed no sign of ever joining himself to a woman. Not that Rory was surprised, mind you. Finn, he was certain, would never give up the torch he carried for Violet Demarest, even if Violet would, if she was smart, never show her face in Marigold again. Poor woman.

"That's our cue."

The words pulled Rory from his reverie, and he turned his attention very willingly to Miriam.

"All set?" he asked her, already knowing the answer.

And, just as he had known she would, she smiled and nodded quite enthusiastically. "Oh, yes," she told him. "I've been waiting for this for a long time. Longer even than you."

He narrowed his eyes at her playfully. "I'm not so sure about that," he said. Because he had realized some time ago that, deep down, he had wanted Miriam from the first day he had lain eyes on her. It had just taken him a while to realize that. His brain, after all, had been so cluttered with nonessential information, and he'd had to make room by storing up thoughts and images and memories of her.

He bent his arm at the elbow in a silent bid that she should take it, and Miriam did so eagerly. Her dress was a flowing, snowy gown with a full skirt and long train. It scooped low over her breasts, and in spite of its lack of a side slit, Rory thought she looked very goddess-like in it. Especially with the wreath of tiny pearls that circled her head, and the length of translucent veil that cascaded down to the edge of her gown's train.

"You look beautiful," he told her. He smiled as he added, "Very tempting."

She smiled back. "And you," she replied, "must have

been doing some reading behind my back. Because you look like the very devil with a black tuxedo on."

He grinned. "Yes, well, I do confess that I have picked up an issue of *Metropolitan* or two. It's amazing what a man can learn about a woman reading that publication."

"Oh?" Miriam said with interest. "Like what?"

"Well, there was that one headline that said Help Him Find Your G-Spot—Then Go After His! that I found very intriguing. Not to mention educational."

"Mmm," she said. "I must have missed that article."

"That's all right," he told her. "I took notes."

"I can't wait for you to teach me what you learned."

"Oh, Miss Thornbury," Rory said with a wicked smile. "The things we'll learn together."

"Oh, my," she responded with an equally wicked smile. "You are a devil, aren't you?"

"And you, my dear, are such a temptress."

"Then I think we shall both be very happy together."

Rory smiled again as he led her toward the garden. Oh, yes. He was more than certain of that.

* * * * *

We hope you enjoyed reading this
special collection from Harlequin® books.

If you liked reading these stories, then you
will love **Harlequin® Desire** books.

You want to leave behind the everyday.
Harlequin Desire stories feature sexy,
romantic heroes who have it all: wealth, status,
incredible good looks…everything but the
right woman. Add some secrets, maybe a
scandal, and start turning pages!

Enjoy six *new* stories from
Harlequin Desire every month.

Available wherever books and
ebooks are sold.

#2353 HER FORBIDDEN COWBOY
Moonlight Beach Bachelors • by Charlene Sands
When his late wife's younger sister needs a place to heal after being jilted at the altar, country-and-western star Zane Williams offers comfort at his beachfront mansion. But when he takes her in his arms, they enter forbidden territory...

#2354 HIS LOST AND FOUND FAMILY
Texas Cattleman's Club: After the Storm
by Sarah M. Anderson
Tracking down his estranged wife to their hometown hospital, entrepreneur Jake Holt discovers she's lost her memory—and had his baby. Will their renewed love stand the test when she remembers what drove them apart?

#2355 THE BLACKSTONE HEIR
Billionaires and Babies • by Dani Wade
Mill owner Jacob Blackstone is all business; bartender KC Gatlin goes with the flow. But her baby secret is about to shake things up as these two very different people come together for their child's future...and their own.

#2356 THIRTY DAYS TO WIN HIS WIFE
Brides and Belles • by Andrea Laurence
Thinking twice after a reckless Vegas elopement, two best friends find their divorce plans derailed by a surprise pregnancy. Will a relationship trial run prove they might be perfect partners, after all?

#2357 THE TEXAN'S ROYAL M.D.
Duchess Diaries • by Merline Lovelace
When a sexy doctor from a royal bloodline saves the nephew of a Texas billionaire, she loses her heart in the process. But secrets from her past may keep her from the man she loves...

#2358 TERMS OF A TEXAS MARRIAGE
by Lauren Canan
The fine print of a hundred-year-old land lease will dictate Shea Hardin's fate: she must marry a bully or lose it all. But what happens when she falls for her fake husband...hard?

HDCNM0115

Jake had spent the past four years pointedly not caring about what his family was doing. They'd wanted him to put the family above his wife. Nothing had been more important to him than Skye.

He was not staying in Royal long. Just enough to get Skye back on her feet and figure out where they stood.

Just then, the baby made a little hiccup-sigh noise that pulled at his heartstrings.

Jake's brother picked the baby up so smoothly that Jake was jealous.

"Grace, honey—this is your daddy," Keaton said as he rubbed her back. Then, to Jake, he added, "You ready?"

Not really—but Jake wasn't going to admit that to Keaton. He tried to cradle his arms in the right way. Then Keaton laid the baby in them.

The world seemed to tilt off its axis as Jake looked down into his daughter's eyes. They were a pale blue—

just like her mother's. Up close now, he could see that Grace had wispy hairs on her head that were so white and fine they were almost see-through.

She didn't start bawling, which he took as a good sign. Instead, she waved her tiny hands around, so of course he had to offer her one of his fingers. When she latched on to it, he felt lost and yet *not* lost at the same time.

He was responsible for this little girl from this moment until the day he drew his last breath. The weight of it hit him so hard that if he hadn't already been sitting, his knees would have buckled.

This was his daughter. He and Skye had created this little person.

God, he wished Skye was here with him. That things between them had been different. That he'd been different.

But he couldn't change the past, not when his present—and his future—was gripping his little finger with surprising strength.

Don't miss what happens next in
HIS LOST AND FOUND FAMILY
by Sarah M. Anderson!

Available February 2015,
wherever Harlequin® Desire books and ebooks are sold.

JUST CAN'T GET ENOUGH?

Join our social communities
and talk to us online.

You will have access to the latest
news on upcoming titles and special
promotions, but most importantly,
you can talk to other fans about your
favorite Harlequin reads.

Harlequin.com/Community

 Facebook.com/HarlequinBooks

 Twitter.com/HarlequinBooks

 Pinterest.com/HarlequinBooks

Love the Harlequin book you just read?

Your opinion matters.

Review this book on your favorite
book site, review site, blog or your own
social media properties and share
your opinion with other readers!

Be sure to connect with us at:
Harlequin.com/Newsletters
Facebook.com/HarlequinBooks
Twitter.com/HarlequinBooks